"Fans of Suzanne Woods Fisher will love this story of three sisters coming together on a rugged Maine island to refurbish a camp. Even as their tumultuous lives create havoc, romance blooms between one of the sisters and a handsome lumberjack/teacher. Readers will enjoy watching the island and camp take shape even as the sisters' own lives undergo a renovation of the everlasting kind. *On a Summer Tide* is an enduring tale of love and restoration."

Denise Hunter, bestselling author of *On Magnolia Lane*

"Suzanne Woods Fisher may be best known for her Amish stories, but this contemporary romance is a charmer. *On a Summer Tide* is filled with memorable characters, gorgeous Maine scenery, and plenty of family drama. I can't wait to visit Three Sisters Island again!"

Irene Hannon, bestselling author of the beloved Hope Harbor series

On a Summer Tide

Novels by Suzanne Woods Fisher

LANCASTER COUNTY SECRETS

The Choice
The Waiting
The Search

SEASONS OF STONEY RIDGE

The Keeper
The Haven
The Lesson

THE INN AT EAGLE HILL

The Letters
The Calling
The Revealing

THE BISHOP'S FAMILY

The Imposter
The Quieting
The Devoted

THE DEACON'S FAMILY

Mending Fences

THREE SISTERS ISLAND

On a Summer Tide

On a Summer Tide

SUZANNE WOODS FISHER

Revell

a division of Baker Publishing Group
Grand Rapids, Michigan

© 2019 by Suzanne Woods Fisher

Published by Revell
a division of Baker Publishing Group
PO Box 6287, Grand Rapids, MI 49516-6287
www.revellbooks.com

Printed in the United States of America

Library of Congress Cataloging-in-Publication Data
Names: Fisher, Suzanne Woods, author.
Title: On a summer tide / Suzanne Woods Fisher.
Description: Grand Rapids, MI : Revell, a division of Baker Publishing Group,
    [2019] | Series: Three Sisters Island ; 1
Identifiers: LCCN 2018049153 | ISBN 9780800734985 (pbk.)
Classification: LCC PS3606.I78 O5 2019 | DDC 813/.6—dc23
LC record available at https://lccn.loc.gov/2018049153

ISBN 978-0-8007-3628-6 (casebound)

Published in association with Joyce Hart of the Hartline Literary Agency, LLC.

21 22 23 24 25 26 27   12 11 10 9 8 7 6

Cast of Characters

Paul Grayson (age 59)—retired sports announcer, father of Cam, Maddie, Blaine, grandfather of Cooper

Camden Grayson (age 28)—VP of a renewable energy start-up company, eldest daughter of Paul, adoptive mother of Cooper

Madison Grayson (age 24)—working on getting certified as a Marriage & Family Therapist, middle daughter of Paul

Blaine Grayson (age 19)—college student who can't decide on a major, youngest daughter of Paul

Cooper Grayson (age 7½)—third grader, son of Cam

Tre (age 25)—Maddie's longtime boyfriend

Artie (age 20)—college friend of Blaine

Peg Legg (won't reveal her age)—runs the Lunch Counter and General Store on Three Sisters Island

Seth Walker (age 28)—schoolteacher on Three Sisters Island

Baxtor Phinney (55-ish)—self-appointed mayor of Three Sisters Island, even though it is too small for a mayor

Porter and Peter Phinney (in their twenties)—sons of Baxtor Phinney

Captain Ed (ageless)—runs the Never Late Ferry between Mount Desert and Three Sisters Island

One

CAMDEN GRAYSON TOOK THE TURN into her dad's driveway a little fast. She was never late to anything—except when it came to family events. Like this one. She threw the car into park, grabbed the key, and instead of jumping out, she leaned back against the headrest, squeezed her eyes shut, and took in a deep breath. *Just one minute. Give me just one minute of peace.*

Instead, her cell phone chirped a text. She groaned, then glanced at it.

Blaine
WHERE ARE YOU?

Her sister always texted in full caps, her version of acceptable shouting.

Cam blew out an angry breath as she pushed open the car door. From the yard across the street came the happy shrieks of children playing and a dog barking, but she focused on her dad's front door, the landscaping, the new trim on the windows, anything but that house across the street. Three years later and she still couldn't bring herself to look at it, with its floodgate of pain.

The front door was unlocked. She hurried inside to the living room, where her dad and sisters were waiting. "Sorry! I know I'm late, and I can't stay long. I left Cooper with my neighbor."

Dad disspelled her frenetic arrival with a friendly wave. "Not a problem," he said in his scratchy voice. "I haven't gotten started yet."

Cam exchanged a puzzled look with Maddie, then they both turned to Blaine. Their youngest sister's chin was tucked to her chest as she texted rapidly on her phone with both thumbs. Typical Blaine. *Was I like that when I was nineteen?* No, Cam decided. She had no time to be.

A week ago, Dad had asked all three girls to come to the house on Sunday afternoon. He gave no explanation, only that he'd tell them everything then. As Cam sat down on the edge of the sofa, she glanced at her dad, wondering what to expect. He seemed more rested than he had on her last visit home—was it in January?—his face wasn't as lined or careworn. In fact, she realized, he wasn't bad looking for a man of his age, fit and trim, with graying hair.

"Girls, I have an announcement."

Cam leaned forward, bracing herself for serious news. Her dad had seen one specialist after the other, trying to get his voice back in working order. Over Christmas, he'd had a severe case of laryngitis and his vocal cords had never recovered. His normal speaking voice wasn't much more than a hoarse whisper. Maddie had already given them a list of dreaded possibilities: nodules, tumors, cancer.

"Blaine, put away your phone. On silent, please."

They all watched and waited as she finished her text, sent it, and put her phone in her purse.

Dad's eyebrows lifted as he inhaled a deep breath and let it out. "I sold the house."

Cam, Maddie, and Blaine looked at each other, then back at their father. That was the last thing Cam had expected. This house? Their childhood home, filled with sentiment. And stuff. And memories of Mom.

He wasn't finished. "And . . . I bought an island."

Cam exchanged panicked looks with Maddie and Blaine.

No. He didn't. Dad sat there beaming.

He did.

"Dad," Maddie said, "do you think you had a seizure? Or maybe a stroke?"

"Not to my knowledge."

"Hold it," Blaine said, now fully attentive. "You did *what*?"

"I bought an island. A little one. Part of one, actually. Not the whole thing. It's off the coast of Maine."

"You bought an island," Cam said in a flat tone.

"I did."

Blaine grinned. "He's pulling our leg." She laughed. "Just one? Why not a bunch of islands? I think there's over three thousand off the coast of Maine."

"Just one. It's the place where your mother and I met as camp counselors, back in the day. Camp Kicking Moose."

He wasn't kidding. Cam glanced at Blaine and watched her smile fade. "Why, Dad? Why?"

"Because it's time for a change."

Maddie's mouth dropped open in an O. "I knew it." She looked at her sisters and covered her face with her hands. "Dad is dying."

"Whoa! Not dying! Not even close."

Cam squeezed her hands together, trying to stay calm. "Dad, what did the specialist say? What's wrong with your voice?"

"He had nothing new to say. Just like all the others. There's nothing he could figure out and nothing he could do to help. I promise. That's all." He slapped his hands on his knees. "But it was a fortuitous meeting. That specialist was the very one who told me about this island. The village—and that's a pretty nice word for it, more like a hodgepodge of buildings, plus the campground—well, the village is nearly bankrupt."

Blaine peered at him. "Were you under anesthesia when this doctor sold you the island? That might be grounds for malpractice."

11

"I was fully cognizant when I bought the island. And just to be clear, I bought the island from the camp owners, not from the doctor, who had no personal interest in the island. It only came up in conversation because I recognized a picture in his office. He went to camp there as a kid. When he told me it was up for sale, I couldn't resist calling the owners to find out more. When I heard the price they were asking, I snatched it up." He snapped his fingers. "Bargain-basement price."

Maddie gave a woeful shake of her head. "This is all about turning sixty, isn't it? You missed your midlife crisis in your forties, so you're having it now."

Cam wanted to scream. Her sister Maddie had just completed graduate work for a master's degree in marriage and family therapy, and although she had never been married nor had children, she considered herself adept at diagnosing others.

Oblivious, Maddie carried on. "It's a textbook case. Human beings can't miss stages of development. They'll circle back until it's dealt with." She paused, as if watching the effect of her words on everyone.

Dad's hands were clasped together on his lap. Cam saw them tighten involuntarily with Maddie's assessment. "I'm only fifty-nine. And no, this is not a delayed midlife crisis. This is something your mother and I had always wanted to do. Planned to do. Until . . ."

Mom died.

Blaine lifted her palms in disbelief. "You and Mom wanted to own an island? That's news to me."

"The camp part, that we had talked about. You know how much we loved that camp. Everybody loves summer camp."

"Not me," Blaine said. "I hated it."

No surprise there. Blaine hated everything.

Maddie looked at each one of them. "I think we should talk about Mom. We never do. You all pretend like it was a blip on the radar. Like it was no big deal. And now look what's happened."

Cam actually flinched. Maddie was wrong. It *was* a big deal, but talking wasn't going to help.

Maddie steepled her fingers together. "So then, Dad, this is some kind of unfulfilled obligation for Mom. A fulfillment issue."

Dad wagged a finger in the air. "Not an issue, Maddie. No issues here."

Acting all counselor-y, Maddie leaned forward and looked gravely at each one of them. "Talking about it, just saying a few words, is often enough to help."

Oh boy. Here we go. Cam checked her watch. Cooper had warned her not to be late. Ever since he'd received a wristwatch for his seventh birthday, he'd become a taskmaster of time. "For now, let's stay focused on Dad's crisis."

"Not a crisis," Dad said.

Cam carried on. "So let's review the facts. You bought an island to run a summer camp."

He clapped his hands. "Yes! I want to breathe new life into this island."

"Delusional," Maddie said, resting her cheek in her hand. "Or perhaps premature dementia."

"Facts. Let's stay with the facts. Dad, you're a smart fellow. You've always drilled due diligence into us. So, what is the reason this island is bankrupt?"

"Thank you, Cam, for your vote of confidence."

"Confidence?" He sat there looking pleased as punch with himself. Did he not understand how serious this was? "I'm not giving you a vote of confidence, Dad. I'm right there with Maddie. I'm worried you're losing it."

Dad frowned. "Not losing anything." He tapped his forehead. "It's all still here. As for why this island needs our help. It has a declining population. All the young people have left for greener pastures."

"There might be a good reason for that." Cam tried to keep her voice calm and reasonable.

"Yes, but that's going to change."

"How?"

"I have big plans for this island. Big plans. And girls, you're part of this project."

All three girls jumped out of their seats, interrupting each other with objections. "No way!" "Not a chance." "I'm not moving to a deserted island!"

"Girls, calm down! Calm down and sit down."

Slowly, they eased back into their chairs, eyeing him suspiciously.

"I told you that I have big plans. Good plans. This will be a great thing for each one of you, I promise. All good."

Cam folded her arms across her chest. "You can't expect us to uproot our lives to help you run a summer camp."

"Hold on. I understand that. You've each got your own interests. Cam, you've got your career on track."

"More than just on track, Dad. Did you not read that *Wall Street Journal* article I forwarded you? Everyone wants our technology. You can't believe the buyout offers the CEO is getting." She lifted a finger in the air. "Not to worry! Evan's promised everyone the company won't be sold. He says he can't be bought."

Dad shifted in his seat. "And Maddie is trying to find an internship."

Maddie nodded vigorously. "Lots of options brewing."

"Anything nailed down yet?" Cam said.

"Not quite yet." Maddie stiffened her back at Cam's question. "Close, though. And of course there's Tre to consider."

As if on cue, everyone groaned. "You're still with Tre?" Blaine said.

Maddie frowned. "Of course we're still together. What's wrong with Tre?"

"Oh, where to start?" Blaine said. "Maybe . . . his name."

"There's nothing wrong with his name. Thompson Robinson Smith the Third. I think it's dignified."

"When I first met him," Blaine said, "I figured Tre was a nickname for a guy who regretted getting stuck with three last names. But oh no! It's for the Third."

This time Dad reined in the conversation from departing farther down a bunny trail. "Blaine, you've got a college major to settle on."

"Narrowing it down, Dad."

"To what?"

"Art history or women's studies. Maybe ornithology."

That stopped the conversation, right there. Dad sighed. His voice was fading to a whisper. "What happened to majoring in business? A good, solid foundation."

Cam let out a hoot. "That was eight majors ago. Maybe ten."

Blaine scowled at her, then turned to their father. "I've crossed off a business major from the list. I can't support capitalism."

Dad's eyebrows shot up. "You can't *support* capitalism? But you'll let me pay for your college tuition, room and board?"

Cam raised a hand. "Let's hold that conversation for another day. I have to pick up Cooper soon and you know how he gets when I'm late."

"About Cooper," Maddie said. "Cam, we need to talk."

"Nope. Nope." She waved her hand impatiently. "Nothing to talk about." She turned her attention to Dad before Maddie could launch more psychobabble. "Your point is an excellent one. We all have our own lives. We can't drop everything and rush to this island. This is your venture. Not ours."

"Unless you *are* dying," Maddie said, brow furrowed with concern.

"Not dying! I just want to make an offer to each one of you that might entice you to move to the island."

"Entice away," Blaine said. "I'm all ears."

Dad pointed at her. "You, young lady, will have to graduate from college before any incentives are offered."

Blaine's mouth dropped. "So I'm exempt from this . . . this . . . venture?"

"Partially. For now."

"Like always! I'm never treated like an adult!"

Cam patted Blaine on her shoulder. "That's because you're not one."

"Fine," Blaine mumbled, sulky. She picked up her purse and stood. "Then can I leave?"

"No," Dad said. "I want you all to be a part of this story."

Blaine let out a moan and collapsed against the sofa like a rag doll. Everyone ignored her.

"The island needs some new businesses. Cam, that's where you come in with business plans."

"Nope. Not happening."

"And Maddie, I'm sure the island church is desperate for a counselor. You can get your hours in to get certified."

Maddie hesitated, just long enough for Cam to look at her with suspicion. "What about all those brewing opportunities?"

Dad kept going. "Blaine, here's where you come in. Short term, that is. Come summer, I want your help running the camp."

"Can't."

"Why not?"

"I don't like kids."

Dad let that pass. "And here's the best part. Because I own the island—well, actually, 51 percent of the island—I get to call it what I want."

Now everyone's curiosity was piqued. Blaine tipped her head. "What's wrong with the name it has?"

"Too hard to pronounce, so most don't bother. Its official name is Niswi Nummissis."

"Dad!" Blaine said. "You can't march in, throw your money around, and steal the heritage of an island. That's such typical white male entitlement. Everyone will despise you."

"I've thought of that, Blaine," Dad said in a rasp. His voice was grinding down so that all three girls had to lean forward to hear him. "But I'm keeping the meaning of the name, just translating it to English. Part of its new beginning."

"So wrong," Blaine said sadly. "So, so wrong."

"Aren't you even interested in knowing what it means?" He had a smile on his face like a cat that swallowed the canary.

Maddie took the bait. "What does it mean?"

"Niswi Nummissis is Algonquian for Three Sisters." His grin spread from ear to ear. "I'm calling it Three Sisters Island." Then, scarcely audible now, he said, "Because someday, my dear daughters, it'll all be yours."

The three sisters exchanged a look. They rarely agreed on anything, but on this topic, they shared the same thought. At the exact same moment, in such perfect unison it seemed they had rehearsed it, they shouted, "Count me out!"

That went well, Paul Grayson thought cheerily to himself as he watched his three daughters drive off. Better than expected, anyway. He sat in his too-quiet home and sipped some tea with honey. Fifteen minutes of talking was about all he could muster. His voice was scoured down to a scratch.

Aside from his weary voice, he felt pretty darn good. In fact, he hadn't felt this interested in the future since long before his wife, Corinna, had passed away. It was terrifying, what he was doing, and that might be why it felt so right. It was good to feel alive again.

Maddie thought he was having a delayed midlife crisis, but what she didn't realize was that *this*—retiring and doing something entirely out of the box—was what he and Corinna had dreamed of doing their entire lives. She also didn't realize that he was doing it much later than he should have. He'd always thought they'd have plenty of time for this, for being together. But he'd discovered the hard way that time ran out.

This loss of his normal speaking voice, as frustrating as it was, had brought him a gift. Ironic for a man who spent his life on radio as a sports announcer. The spoken word had always come easily for him. He'd been blessed with a memorable voice, a deep baritone that emerged in adolescence and quickly gained him a foothold with the popular crowd in high school. Sounding like somebody's father, he would call in to the school's attendance office to excuse one friend or another from classes. The school receptionist never caught on. Paul was a very popular guy.

During college, he worked summers at Camp Kicking Moose. Part of his job was to make announcements over the loud speaker. During his last summer there, a cute college girl named Corinna Kent came on kitchen staff, and by summer's end, Paul knew she was the one for him. Years later, Corinna told him that she'd fallen in love with his voice, booming out the day's activities in that rich deep baritone, before she ever laid eyes on him.

That voice got him his first job out of college as a radio sports announcer, working for minor league baseball teams. One job led to another, then to the majors, and suddenly he was at the point where he needed an agent to negotiate his annual contracts. In a way, he stumbled into a successful career. And in the same way, he stumbled right out of it. He was now a radio man without a voice. Not much of one, anyway.

He'd loved his career, much too much. He was on the road more than he was home. Corinna half teased that he loved radio more than he loved her and the girls. It wasn't true, but radio came in a close second. Today, the way Cam's eyes lit up as she told him about her company, it reminded him of himself. Cam had always been the daughter most like him. Focused, driven, competitive. It worried him in a vague way.

Why was that?

Maybe it was because when a career ended, like his did—like they all do, sooner or later—and you'd given up so much for it, what were you left with?

He looked around the living room. An empty, quiet house.

These last few months, losing his voice . . . it was kind of a silent life he'd been forced to live. The funny thing was that he was seeing and hearing much more than he ever had.

Cam was now a single mother, juggling a demanding career with a needy little boy. Maddie, a middle child in every way, seemed to be heading toward something serious with that Tre guy—another worry hovered overhead, though it too was vague and nameless. And Blaine, his youngest? She was all over the place, easily influenced by everyone except her father and sisters.

Sisters.

That's what worried him the most. The wedges that divided his daughters. The girls were growing increasingly distant from each other. From him too. He had thought Cooper's arrival would draw them all together. Maddie, the one who made efforts to keep the sisters together, had even declared a family mantra: raising Cooper would take a village . . . and they would all be his village.

It worked for a while, but the girls rarely spent time with each other. When they were together, they spent more time on their phones than talking to each other. One day he overheard them in the kitchen arguing about which one of them should stay home at Christmas to mind Dad—*mind Dad*, like he was a family dog—and it stunned him. They'd rather be with their friends than at home or with each other.

Corinna had been the glue that held them together. Without her, they were fast becoming strangers. A family of strangers. Yes, his children were alienated.

It was time for a radical change. For him, for his daughters. When he heard that Camp Kicking Moose was up for sale, the idea seized hold of him, wouldn't let him go.

Funny, the things one remembered. All these years later, the memory of that sleepy little island was still fresh. He could practically smell the sun-warmed pine trees, the salt spray of the ocean as it hit the rocks. Every view was a picture postcard of pine trees and seawater.

Maybe, just maybe, Camp Kicking Moose could bring them together. On an impulse, he had offered a ridiculously low amount to the previous owners. Embarrassingly low. To his shock, the owners accepted without a counter, as long as he bought it *as is*. What could be so bad about that? Suddenly it was his. He had bought an island off the coast of Maine.

Terrifying. Crazy. *Thrilling.*

Two

CAM NOTICED BLAINE'S NAME LIGHT UP on her phone, but she let the call slip over to voice mail. She couldn't handle her sister's crisis right now, whatever this one happened to be. She had too much to absorb. Her boss, Evan Snowden, had just told her he needed her to get to London, pronto, to fix some problems over there. *London.*

Her heart was racing and her mind was spinning, processing everything Evan had told her. Wow. She blew out a puff of air. She felt a wash of excitement, joy, adventure. Stunned. She was floored. This was the single most thrilling moment of her twenty-eight years.

When Evan had asked her if there'd be any problem if she left as soon as possible, Cam had tried to play it cool. She had to practically sit on her hands to keep herself from jumping out of her chair to dance around the office, shouting, "I'll go! I'll go!"

Her smartphone lit up again and she barely glanced at it, expecting it to be Blaine, but this time it said Westbrook Private School. Her carefree feeling of joy deflated like a popped balloon. She braced herself as she answered with a cautious hello.

"Cam, this is Ada Voxer."

The principal. Cam cringed. "Is anything wrong?" Of course. Of course there was.

"We've got a situation here at the school with Cooper."

"What does that mean . . . a situation?"

"During lunch, he slipped into his classroom and tied string around all the desk chair legs, including the teacher's desk. It looks like a giant spiderweb in there."

Cam hit her forehead with the palm of her hand. Not the string thing again! Why did Cooper do this kind of thing? She had no idea. "I'm sorry, Mrs. Voxer. I'll talk to him."

"Have you followed up on any suggestions we've made? Have you seen a child psychologist?" Her tone was almost accusatory.

"Yes, yes, I have." She tried not to sound defensive. "He wanted to put Cooper on anti-anxiety meds and I don't want to start that stuff. He's just a little boy." When the pause on the other end of the line went too long, she started rambling. "Really, he's fine! You know Cooper. He's very . . . conscientious, that's all. As for his interest in string . . . well, don't you wonder if that was how Benjamin Franklin got started with his kite experiment?"

Silence. Bad time to make a joke.

"Cam, Cooper's behavior is not typical of most boys."

Cam didn't know how to respond to that kind of remark. So Cooper wasn't typical. Was that such a bad thing? Average was overrated.

"What about my other suggestions? Therapy, counseling?"

"We started it once, but he didn't like it. I don't blame him. The therapist was a little odd."

"I meant for you."

"Me?" It came out a full octave higher.

"Cam, how you handle Cooper's issues is key."

Issues? What issues? He was a little boy! "I'm doing the best I can. I may have been a little slack now and then, but things can get, you know . . . hectic."

A deep sigh from Mrs. Voxer. "There's going to be a meeting next week. It's very possible that Cooper will not be able to continue here."

Cam gasped. "Mrs. Voxer, you can't kick him out! Not in March! There's only a few more months to go. That's just not reasonable."

"It's not something we want to do, but we aren't convinced we are able to provide for his needs. There's the well-being of other students to consider. Cooper's behavior is . . . alarming."

Alarming? It was just a ball of string. String! Good grief. Mrs. Voxer could be as much of a fearmonger as Maddie. Cam heard another deep sigh on the other end of the receiver. She knew what *that* meant. Conversation over.

"I'll keep you apprised of the outcome of the meeting." On that gloomy note, Mrs. Voxer ended the call.

As Cam put down her phone, her thoughts remained on Cooper. No way. There was no way the school could vote Cooper out. Ridiculous! No possible way.

He was such a sweet little boy. Smart, too. If only his teachers understood his giftedness. Maybe he did need a change of schools. Maybe there was a better place out there for him—smaller classes, a greater emphasis on academics, to help him get over this weird fascination with string. Right? She rubbed her forehead. Right.

Maybe this timing was fortuitous. Next week was spring break for Cooper. He could stay with her dad while she went to London. Today was the day Dad was moving to the island—such a ridiculous undertaking!—and she'd been wanting to see what he'd gotten scammed into, anyway. Cooper would be excited to be with his grandfather, wherever he happened to be. Whenever Cooper was with her dad, he didn't seem to miss Cam so much.

The morning had started like a typical day, oatmeal for breakfast and packing lunch and rushing out the door. A few hours later . . . she was ironing out details for an international trip. Her first. Wow. London.

Life . . . it was *amazing.*

23

Blaine closed the door to the administration building and crossed the grass quad, stunned. In the last weeks, life had thrown her one curveball after another. Her father quit his job, sold her childhood family home lock, stock, and barrel, to move Down East to a forsaken and bankrupt island, all with the ridiculous notion of fixing it. Crazy! And then he informed all three daughters of an incentive plan to persuade them to move to the island with him. Even crazier!

But now there was this . . .

An hour ago, Blaine had received an email from her advisor to inform her of a problem with spring quarter's class registration. She'd rushed from the library to the advisor's office, worried about her class schedule for next quarter. She'd spent hours choosing just the right classes, just the subjects she wanted to study, with just the right professors. Such careful plotting! What could have gone wrong? She racked her brain for possible problems, but what the advisor eventually explained to her was the last thing she could've considered.

"None of these classes are building blocks to a vocation or a major, Blaine, and you're even starting to repeat classes."

"Yes, but with different professors."

"The goal of a junior college is to prepare students for the next step. You've dabbled in classes from every department, but there's no common denominator. You've got to start moving forward. It's time. It's more than time. You've been here two years and you're basically still a freshman. A very well-educated freshman, but a first year nonetheless."

"I've been trying to find a major!" Blaine sputtered in defense. "I just need to take a class or two first, before I stake my degree on it. Once I decide on that, then everything else will fall in place and I'll be able to figure out where to transfer. What's wrong with that?"

The advisor had only sighed, deep and weary, in a way that reminded Blaine of her father's sighs. "Because it would take you ten years to graduate."

"With all due respect, if my tuition is getting paid on time, why would the college care how long it takes? I mean, it's making money off me."

The advisor stared at her for so long that Blaine started to squirm. "Off of *you*? I'm going to pretend you didn't say that. I'm going to forget that you just disregarded your father's hard work and good intentions to provide for your education. To help you reach your potential. I'm going to ignore that profoundly selfish and immature remark."

Blaine lowered her eyes and bit her lip. Well, sure. Put *that* way, it did seem a tiny bit immature.

"Look, Blaine. In all good conscience, we can't let this continue. As much as we appreciate your curiosity about all things in life, it would be irresponsible of the college to not make sure you reach the finish line."

Finish line. As if an education was a race!

"I think it's time for you to leave."

Blaine got to her feet. "I'll get back to class."

"You misunderstand me. I meant the time has come for you to leave the college."

Blaine slid back into her chair, stunned. She didn't know what to say, and that didn't happen very often.

"Finish up finals this week, and then go home."

Home? She had no home! Her father had just sold it and left the state. "And do what?"

"Think through what you want to do with your life."

"You're kicking me out?" She felt her heart start to race. "Can you do that?"

"Blaine, you're an excellent student. You've racked up an impressive amount of classes. You just can't seem to move forward. There's really nothing left at this junior college for you."

Blaine spent the next hour trying to call both sisters, but they never picked up. Finally, she gave up and started to pack up her dorm room. The advisor's words kept circling through her head: There was nothing left at this junior college for her.

There was really nothing left for Blaine, period.

⁓

Paul waited in his packed-tight truck for the Never Late Ferry to arrive to deliver him to Three Sisters Island. There was no schedule, so it was never late. But it was. He'd been waiting over an hour, and if he squinted, he thought he could see it docked across the harbor.

He'd never been any good at waiting. Today, he could barely contain his excitement to get onto the island and discover what the camp looked like after so many years. He remembered it as pristine, idyllic. A young man drove up on a moped and parked behind Paul's truck. He got off his moped and strode over. The fellow, a big guy, looked like a contemporary version of Paul Bunyan, complete with plaid flannel shirt. "Seth Walker," he said as he thrust out his hand.

"Paul Grayson," he said in his scratchy voice. As he shook the lumberjack's big hand, he felt like a 99-pound weakling.

Seth's head jerked up. "The Paul Grayson who bought the island out from under us?"

"Under you?"

"Not me, actually. From the locals. I've only been here a couple of years so I'm not considered a local yet. That would take a couple of generations."

"Hold it. The locals were trying to buy it?"

"They tried, a little halfheartedly, but they couldn't raise enough money. There's only so much Peg's bake sales can do."

"Well, I bought Camp Kicking Moose and most of the island came with it."

Seth nodded thoughtfully. "You'll probably get a cool reception from most locals, but I'm glad to meet you. In fact, as long as we're waiting, there's a few things I need to go over with you."

He pointed to his throat. "Unless your throat is too sore? Sounds like a nasty case of laryngitis."

"Getting over it. I'm okay if you do most of the talking." Paul tented his eyes to peer across the harbor. "How long until the ferry arrives?"

"Hard to tell. Captain Ed is out checking his lobster trap."

Captain Ed? Paul remembered him from his Camp Kicking Moose days. "He must be old."

"Really old."

"Still quirky?"

"Very. In a good way." Seth leaned against Paul's truck. "You know that the Never Late Ferry is passenger only, right?"

"What? How do cars get across?"

"Two ways. Captain Ed can run a flat-bottomed barge back and forth, if the tide is high enough." He rubbed his fingers together with a grin. "And the price is right enough. It's not cheap. Most everyone just drives back and forth at low tide. There's a bar that's built up over the last few decades. It's underwater now, but it's a sight to see."

Paul let out a sigh. He needed to expect changes, he supposed.

"Or you could get a moped, like I did. Captain Ed lets me take it on the ferry." Seth crossed his arms against his chest. "So about the island school."

"School? What about it?"

"You might not know this, but there are one- or two-room schoolhouses dotted through the coastal islands. They're public, taxpayer funded. There's one on that island." He pointed across the water.

"Three Sisters. That's what the name means in English, and that's what I'm calling it. It came with the deal of buying 51 percent of the island."

Seth blew a puff of air out. "Oh wow. That's not going to help your popularity with the locals."

"Give me some time. I'll prove you wrong. It's a sign of new life on this island."

Seth shrugged. "Don't say I didn't warn you. Anyway, the school has only nine students enrolled. By late August, you'll need twelve to get a state-funded teacher." He jabbed his thumb at his chest. "That'd be me."

"Or what?"

"Or those kids will have to be sent over to Mount Desert for schooling."

Paul tented his eyes again, squinting at the ferry sitting idle. "On that? They may never get there. Or back again."

Seth laughed. "Low tide is always an option. Makes for a long day for the kids."

"Well, sounds like there's a solid plan if there's not enough students by fall."

"That's not all. You're responsible for the maintenance and upkeep of the school, since it's on private property." He pointed to Paul. "Yours."

Paul pressed a hand on his chest. "Mine?" It came out as a squeak.

"The school happens to sit on the old camp land. It used to have a building in town, but it burned down about ten years ago. The camp owners loaned the village the old carriage house to use."

"What kind of shape is the school building in?"

Seth shrugged. "Like everything else on the island. Run-down."

"Run-down, as in needing a fresh coat of paint?"

"For sure. New paint would be first on my list. Definitely for the manor and carriage houses." He gave Paul a cautious sideways glance. "Don't you agree?"

"I haven't seen the camp in years."

Seth's eyebrows lifted. "Don't tell me you bought it without seeing it." When Paul didn't respond, he swallowed a laugh, then cleared his throat. "Well, yes, it needs new paint. Hopefully a new color. And the school needs a new roof before next winter hits."

Oh. Paul let out a sigh. School. It never occurred to him that he would be responsible for a school building. He vaguely remembered an old carriage house that the camp used to store things, and he wondered if that was the same building. If so, it was old then. What would it be like now? But if there were no school, there would be no young families to entice to the island. And that would mean a continued decline in population.

"You might have bitten off more than you can chew."

"No, no," Paul said, too quickly. "I know what I'm doing. Just give me a little time before you make a judgment."

Seth lifted his palms in the air. "No judgment here. I'm from New Jersey, so everyone is suspicious of me."

"What brought you up here?"

"Opportunity Maine. Have you heard of it? It's a government program offered to help graduates pay off rather substantial school loans. It took a while to get used to Maine, but it's growing on me. The people might seem a little chilly at first, but they'll look out for you, all the same." He shielded his eyes and peered past Paul. "Look. There he is. He must have seen your truck at the dock. He's bringing the barge over."

The gray barge was on its way toward them. Paul could see Captain Ed at the helm, and he smiled. Now this . . . it was one sight that hadn't changed at all. Captain Ed's chin wore the same white shoehorn beard, on his head was the same yellow fisherman's hat. A quintessential Mainer. Paul felt the years roll off. He was nineteen again, heading to camp for the summer.

A white Volvo sedan pulled up behind Seth's moped and out jumped Maddie. "Dad!"

"Maddie, what're you doing here?"

"I've given it a lot of thought and realized that I'm proud of you for what you're doing. You're making a fresh start, and trying to help people, and it's really wonderful, Dad. It really is. So I decided I should help. That you shouldn't be trying this alone. I thought I'd check out that church job you mentioned. You know, get my hours certified here this summer."

Paul was stunned speechless and it wasn't because his voice

was giving out, which it was. When the pause went on too long, Maddie tipped her head. "The church. The counseling internship. It's still open, right? I'm not too late?"

Paul sent a cursory glance in Seth's direction and noticed the confusion on his face. Captain Ed blasted the horn as the barge backed up to the ramp. "Ah! Look at that. Perfect timing."

Maddie gasped. "I have to find my phone. I need to take pictures to send to Cam and Blaine. They've been calling and calling, but I didn't pick up because I didn't want to get distracted while I drove. You know how that slogan goes: Alert Today. Alive Tomorrow." She ducked her head back into the car to hunt for her phone.

Seth scratched his head. "Paul, which church job are you thinking of? There are only two churches on the island. The Unitarian church has a building but no members. Then there's a little church plant that has members but no building."

Maddie popped her head out of her car, eyes wide. "What's that about the church?"

"Later. We'll talk later," Paul whispered, pointing to his throat. This voice-impaired situation wasn't entirely without benefits.

Three

HEADING NORTH ON I-95 with Blaine's red Prius trailing behind her powder blue Volkswagen, Cam explained the situation to Cooper in great detail: they were going to an island for spring vacation, and he would stay with Grandpa and Maddie and Blaine while she went on a business trip. There were some questions he asked that she couldn't answer: Why did Grandpa sell his home? Why did he buy an island? Why was Aunt Blaine kicked out of college? Why was Aunt Maddie going to stay with Grandpa when she should be job hunting? If only she knew.

She steeled herself for Cooper's next question. There was always a next question with that boy, and you could never predict what it would be. She tried I Spy games and that kept him occupied for a while. She glanced at the dashboard clock and pressed on the gas pedal. Late. She wanted to get to the island before it was dark.

Finally, Cooper's questions slowed down. He nodded off and she relaxed. Sort of. She had a lot of thinking to do. What if her boss was sending her to London as a preliminary meet and greet to an international position? This trip might be a test, to see how she performed in an international setting. Evan had hinted about such a possibility. It would be a dream come true to be transferred overseas.

But there was Cooper to think of. She glanced in the rearview mirror. He was sound asleep, his chin was tucked to his chest, and the little blond rooster tail on the top of his head was sticking straight up. Her heart melted. Taking him so far away from her dad and sisters . . . that couldn't be good for him, could it? She could hear Maddie's voice in her head, pointing out all the reasons a separation from family would create lifelong trauma for Cooper. And yet, Cam countered back in her head, what an enriching experience it could be for him to live overseas too.

Ridiculous. She was ridiculous to even think about it. She was being sent to London to solve a profitability problem. That's all. Evan wanted better figures for third-quarter reporting. It was the kind of work she did all the time. She'd be back in a week's time.

But . . . as long as she was in London, if she could snag a few free hours, she might check out some schooling options for Cooper. From that grim and resolute tone in Mrs. Voxer's voice, it sounded like he'd need one soon.

Appalled did not even come close to the feeling Maddie had about Three Sisters Island. She knew she'd made a terrible mistake when the barge passed a handful of fishing boats bobbing in the harbor and approached the landing dock. Above the dock was a big sign: Welcome to Boon Dock.

One small block, she gathered, could be considered Main Street. Grass grew in the middle of the road. Bordering each side of the weedy street were ramshackled, paint-blistered buildings. They looked to be vacant; most of the windows and doors were shuttered up for off-season. A small steepled church, once handsome, sat at the far end of the street, facing the harbor. It, too, was in dire need of painting. Her father drove slowly up the road before he eased to a stop. Maddie pulled over and parked next to him. She clicked off the motor. Silence enveloped her, broken only by the waves hitting the pilings under Boon Dock. Through the windshield, she noticed a huge bald eagle perched on the top of a telephone pole. It watched her unnervingly, its fierce golden eyes bright.

Her father got out of his car and stood in the middle of the street, hands on his hips, turning in a circle, a look on his face like a kid encountering his first candy store.

Maddie rolled her window down and in flew two huge mosquitoes. "Dad, are you sure we're in the right place?"

He grinned. "Absolutely."

Maddie felt a spike of panic. Her father should be tested immediately for dementia. And on the heels of that thought came a swirl of emotions over how she had left things with Tre. A few days ago, he'd surprised her with plans for their future, and she didn't like surprises. She panicked and packed up. Ran away. She'd run away to *this*. "Look around, Dad. There's only a couple of stores open."

"Well, it is off-season." A laugh burst out of him and he pointed to one. Captain Hook's Bait and Tackle. "Pretty clever, huh?"

Pretty corny. Next to the bait shop was a sporting goods shop called Baggett and Taggett. Maddie squeezed her eyes shut. Was it too late to try to get her apartment back? She could get a job bagging groceries. Or waitressing at night? That could give her time during the day to keep hunting for a counseling internship.

"There. A diner that looks open. The Lunch Counter. Let's go introduce ourselves." Dad started toward it, stopped, pivoted, and waved her to join him.

There was a handwritten sign taped on the window of the diner: "Let's wander where the Wi-Fi is weak." A horrible thought sank in. Maddie pulled out her phone and held it up above her head, hoping some invisible passing satellite could make a connection. Nothing. "Dad, don't tell me there's no Wi-Fi here!"

He squinted. "Not yet. Eventually."

This was worse than she thought.

"Now, now, Maddie, we just arrived. Give it a chance." Dad

kept marching on, so she hurried to keep up. As he opened the door to the diner, a bell tinkled overhead. A short, round woman was mixing something in a big bowl. She looked up, surprised to see them, and her face lit up with happiness. "Well, I'll be. Folks from far away."

"Not so far," Maddie said. "Just Boston."

"Honey, if you're not born here, you're from far away. Come on in. Don't be shy. We don't get many tourists around here at this time of year."

"We're not tourists," Dad said.

Her face fell. "Oh shoot. Are you lost?"

"Not lost," Dad said. "But found! In fact, we're locals. As of five minutes ago."

"Year-rounders?" She clapped her hands with joy, and it felt like someone turned the dimmer switch up. "No kidding? Well, then, welcome to Paradise!"

Dad grinned. "Now, that's just the kind of welcome I'd imagined."

"I'm Peg. And let me get you something for that sore throat. I've got just the thing." She came out from behind the counter to head down an aisle, on the search for something. "Found it! Fennel-honey lozengers. Captain Ed says they always do the trick when his throat gets sore after preaching. I try telling him to cut his preaching time in half and that would cure him, but—" she popped her head up over the shelves and rolled her eyes—"that'll be the day."

"No need for the lozenges. Just a gruff voice. I'm Paul Grayson."

Peg's smile faded. "The Paul Grayson who bought Camp Kicking Moose?"

"The very one."

Her entire demeanor changed as she returned to her spot behind the counter. She slapped the lozenge package on the countertop. "I heard you're changing the island name."

"Yes. To Three Sisters Island." He rubbed his chin. "How in the world did you hear about the name change?"

"News travels around here like water heading downhill," Peg said. "Three Sisters is the English version of the name."

Peg tipped her head and narrowed her eyes. "You're putting me on."

"He's not," Maddie said. "I confirmed it."

"Well, I'll be. Would you believe that I never did know what Niswi Nummisis meant? No two people ever pronounced it the same way. Even natives." She warmed up as she looked at Maddie. "So, hon, what's your name?"

"I'm Maddie." She pointed her thumb at her father. "He's my dad."

Peg grinned. "Well, Maddie honey, it's a pleasure to meet you."

Maddie hadn't been called "honey" by anyone in years. She liked it. She liked Peg. Her short auburn hair was held back in two pig-tails, with a red polka-dotted knotted headband wrapped around her head. It was a hairstyle that would seem silly on most grown women, but not on Peg. It gave her a certain panache, like a signature statement. Maddie gazed around the diner. It was a curious place—a long lunch counter on one side. The other half of the space held long aisles chock-full of all kinds of unusual sundries. Shampoo, first-aid kits, skin care products, aspirins and toothpastes, boxes of greeting cards, Scotch tape and duct tape, feminine products for women, batteries in all shapes and sizes.

Peg noticed. "Yup, it's a sundries shop too. Little bit of every-thing. That's the island way. Most of us hobble together jobs to make ends meet."

Dad grinned. "So, then, you flip burgers and serve them with a side of pencils?"

Peg gave him the Look. Wise woman. Maddie liked her even more.

She ignored Dad and turned to Maddie. "What can I get you, hon? Coffee? Scones should be out of the oven in a few minutes."

"Thank you, Mrs. . . ."

"Legg. But just call me Peg."

He leaned over the counter to peer at her legs. "Just checking to see if you live up to your name."

Oof. Dad's lame jokes! They were terrible at best, mortifying when others weren't used to them. Cam, Blaine, and Maddie had a policy of discouraging his joke telling.

Peg's face turned to stone. "Locals know not to mess with me."

Now it was Dad's turn for his smile to fade. "Uh, sorry."

Peg burst out with a laugh. "Just tweaking you. My ex-husband had promised himself he'd marry the first girl he met named Peg. That was me."

"A low bar."

Peg's eyebrows shot up to her red headband.

"Dad!"

"Not you! I don't mean you're a low bar! I just meant that your husband had a low bar. For matrimonial choices."

"We'd better go," Maddie said quickly. This was going from bad to worse. Five minutes on this island and her dad had already insulted their first new friend. Coupled with his scratchy voice, he seemed weird, even to Maddie, who was accustomed to him.

"Hold on!" Peg took a baking sheet of scones out of the oven. "Can't leave without trying one of my scones. Do you like ginger? Hope so. There's crystallized ginger in them." She grabbed a spatula and scooped two big scones in a to-go bag. She handed the bag to Maddie. "Are you pretty well outfitted?"

Maddie looked down at her T-shirt and jeans. "I try my best. My sister Cam is the one with the fashion sense."

"Not fashion, hon. I meant outfitted for the outdoors. In case you have an encounter with the wild."

"Wild what?" Maddie said uneasily.

"Moose, coyotes, bears."

"Bears? Here? On an island?"

"There's been a mother sow and two cubs spotted. We think she came over the bar from Mount Desert." She pointed to a can of bear repellant. "Not a bad idea to have that on hand." Then she reached over to take a bottle of insect repellant off a shelf. "And then there's this. A must-have to fend off the state bird. At all times, until the first hard freeze in September."

"Wait. What? What is the state bird?"

"Mosquitoes."

"And the first freeze hits in September?" September! Maddie grabbed the can of bear spray, then another, and took three bottles of mosquito repellant. She topped it off with a water bottle. Arms full, she turned to Peg. "Wait a minute. Are you trying to scare us off? Because I promise I'll make sure Dad stops with his jokes."

Dad huffed. "What's wrong with my jokes?"

"What jokes?" Peg said, smiling, and Maddie was smitten with her. "Not trying to scare you *off*. But I don't mind scaring you. At least a little. It's pretty remote out here. You don't want to do anything foolish."

Maddie tipped her head. "Foolish, like . . ."

"Like getting caught near the water during high tide —it comes in hard and fast on a rocky island. A twelve-foot tide too. Then there's foolishness like hiking alone. Not bringing a compass with you, no drinking water. Not letting others know where you've gone or when you'll be back. Happens every year. Someone gets himself into trouble. Then the valiant rescuers"—she thumped her chest—"and that's us, the locals, because this island's too small to have a fire station so they have to come from Mount Desert—we locals have to risk life and limb to save the sorry butts of tourists. Happens every single year. Some dumb city slicker thinks he's smarter than Mother Nature. Well, let me tell you a solid-gold fact, Mother Nature always has the last laugh."

Maddie was dumbstruck.

"Remember last summer, Peg?" The guy on the ferry emerged from the shadows of the back of the store with a guitar in one hand. "A New Yorker took a nap in a bed of poison ivy."

Peg burst out with a short laugh. "Poor guy! Talk about self-inflicted misery."

The guy stopped at the door and turned around, eyes resting on Maddie. "Don't let Peg frighten you. If you use your head, you'll be fine."

"Says a six-foot-two lumberjack with boulders for shoulders." Peg returned the guy's wave as he left the store.

Maddie watched the guy from the ferry cross the street—he did resemble a lumberjack. He was dressed in a flannel shirt, faded jeans, and leather construction boots. But the guitar threw her off. More likely, she would've expected an ax in his hand. "Who's he?"

"That's Seth Walker. He's the schoolteacher, if you could call less than a dozen kids a school. And he does a bunch of everything else to make ends meet, just like most of us around here."

Maddie opened her mouth to ask a question, but the electricity suddenly went off and the room grew dim. Dimmer. It was already poorly lit, with only one bald lightbulb hanging from the ceiling.

"Shoot," Peg said, looking up at the darkened lightbulb.

"Breaker?" Dad said. "I can fix it."

"Not such an easy fix," Peg said. "The whole town loses power at some point each day."

Maddie looked at her. "Why?"

Peg shrugged. "Island living, hon. Every blessed thing gets imported, even electricity." She pointed a finger at Dad. "Fix *that*, and you'll make some lifelong friends on this island. Starting with me." She put her hands on her hips. "So, Paul Grayson, why in the world did you buy the island out from under us?"

"I didn't mean to take anything from you. I was only trying to buy Camp Kicking Moose and a goodly portion of the island got thrown in."

Peg lifted an eyebrow. "Well, then, I guess it's pretty timely that Seth's been working so hard to find a preacher to fill that empty church." She clapped her hands again, almost like a pleased child. "Because, honey, after you see the condition that camp is in, you are going to need the Almighty's help!"

Wait. What? "Dad, I thought you said the camp was turnkey."

Dad pointed to his throat and gave her a helpless shrug. Maddie scowled at him. Amazing how his voice seemed to give out at just the right moments.

Next to a cash register—not a computer, just a big fat old machine with a cash drawer attached—Peg leaned her hands on the counter. "Look, you two. Here's the skinny. You might get the cold shoulder for a while, seeing as how you swooped in and nabbed our island, but don't let folks chase you off. Everyone on this island, we all got each other's back. There aren't many of us year-rounders, so we stick together. You need anything, and I mean anything, you just sing out."

"Wi-Fi?" Maddie said meekly.

Peg laughed. "Oh honey! You're going to fit right in here. Locals love a gal with a sense of humor."

But Maddie wasn't making a joke. "Is there any cell phone service on the island?"

"I've heard," Peg said knowingly, "that if you stand in just the right spot down near Boon Dock, you might be able to pick up a signal."

No internet, dubious phone service. Maddie felt she was losing her last touch with the known world.

Stopping in Bar Harbor for gas, Cam wandered through the downtown for a while before heading back onto Route 3. When she spotted a small ice cream shop, she pulled over. Blaine parked beside her and opened her car door. "Are we finally going to eat? I'm starving again."

Now that was Blaine for you. Cam and Maddie always had to watch their weight carefully. They were both petite, like their mom, where there was no hiding an extra five or ten pounds. Blaine got the Grayson genes: tall, lean, lanky, with an annoying hummingbird-like metabolism. And her hair! That gorgeous hair really irked Cam and Maddie. Blaine's long blonde hair was stick straight and always looked like she'd just combed it. She never combed it! Cam's hair needed expensive upkeep every six weeks to ensure it was looking its best, sharp and professional. Maddie fared a little better with curly ash-blonde hair. Too thick, she complained, as if there could be such a thing.

All those thoughts ran through Cam's head as she helped Cooper out of his straitjacket car seat. Maddie had picked it out for his seventh birthday after extensive research. Cam had assumed that a seven-year-old could finally get sprung from a child's car seat, but no! Maddie had provided plenty of evidence to prove that theory wrong.

"Let's get an ice cream cone," she told Cooper.

They headed inside and she ordered a cone for Cooper, a small dish of frozen yogurt for herself, and—of course—a banana split for Blaine. She handed Cooper his cone and glanced at her cell phone to check the time. The other two orders came and they took a seat.

"We'll make this quick and get back on the road. I want to get to Dad's island before dark."

"Dad's island." Blaine clapped her hands around her cheeks. "Sounds so weird to say that. What has he gotten himself into?"

"We'll find out soon enough," Cam said with a shrug. "Have you heard anything from Maddie? Radio silence is not typical of her."

"Not a peep."

Cooper's head shot up. "Mom, do you think something's happened to Maddie and Grandpa?"

Shoot! Cam thought he was absorbed in licking his chocolate ice cream cone and not listening to them. She wiped a drip off his chin with her napkin. "They're fine. They're busy unpacking, is all." She changed the subject before Cooper could start fabricating possibilities of accidents. "Blaine, who was that fellow standing by your car back at the dorm?"

"Artie Lotosky. He helped me pack my car."

"Boyfriend?"

"Friend."

"He acted like you were his girlfriend."

"Just a friend."

"So he's not-your-boyfriend."

"Correct. End of discussion."

Hmm. Artie Lotosky sure looked like he wanted to be Blaine's boyfriend.

"Why couldn't Dad have bought Mount Desert? I wouldn't mind living in Bar Harbor. I could spend all day in those shops."

"No kidding." Cam tipped her head. "Cooper, we'll have to come back here. Hike in Acadia National Park, maybe. Have a picnic."

Blaine looked at her in utter disbelief. "You? A picnic? A hike? In the outdoors?"

Cam frowned. "I hike. I picnic."

Blaine snorted. "When? Your experience in Girl Scouts? Family legend has it that you tried to reorganize the troop and got kicked out."

Cam bristled. "As I recall, Mom should've been the scout leader but you were still in diapers and needed her full attention." Remembering her last meeting as a Girl Scout, she felt a flush of old, rekindled embarrassment. Even as a girl, Cam had a hard time just being a part of something without finding a way to improve it. It's why she was good at her job, and why her boss loved her. But it didn't make her very popular with teachers or scout leaders. Or sisters. Or peers, for that matter. Her only true friend had been Libby, Cooper's birth mom.

CAM, AGE 10

Cam came home from the first Girl Scout meeting of the school year fit to be tied. "Mom! You have to be the Girl Scout leader or Libby and I quit."

Libby Cooper, Cam's best friend for as long as she could remember, stood beside her. "We'll quit, Mrs. Grayson," she said with a loyal nod. "We really will."

Mom was feeding baby Blaine in the highchair. Six-year-old Maddie colored with crayons at the table. "Tell me what happened."

"There's a new leader and she's awful. Terrible. And old. We call her Old Bag Watson—"

"That's Mrs. Watson to you, Cam," Mom said.

"—and she doesn't know what she's doing or how to do anything right. The troop is in chaos. A complete disaster."

"Utter chaos," Libby echoed.

Mom patiently continued to spoon mashed carrots into Blaine's mouth. "So you both want to quit—even though you were the top cookie sellers in the troop last year—all because Mrs. Watson has kindly volunteered her time to lead the troop."

"Mom, she doesn't know how to lead a troop. You should lead it. We'll help."

"I was your Girl Scout leader for two years, and Brownie leader before that. But since Blaine was born, I just can't do everything. We talked about this, Cam. Being a part of a family means we all give and take."

Cam gave Blaine a cross look. She had orange mush in her hair, on her cheeks. And she smelled just as bad as she looked. Why Mom had wanted another baby was a mystery to her. Maddie was barely getting tolerable.

Mom wiped Blaine's face, pulled her out of the high chair, and set her on the ground, where she crawled straight into Libby's open arms. "Mrs. Watson called me before you both arrived home. She said that Cam gave her a long list of ways to improve the troop. Some weren't so bad, she said, and she'd take them into consideration. But she wondered if you, Cam, might prefer another extra-curricular activity."

Cam's mouth dropped open. "Old Bag Watson is firing me? I've been fired as a Girl Scout?"

"Can she do that?" Libby said.

"Mrs. Watson thought you might enjoy something that didn't involve working in a group. Piano lessons, she suggested. Or maybe cross-country running. She feels you have leadership potential but that you use it to boss everyone around."

Cam slapped her palm against her flat chest. "Me? Bossy?"

"You boss me around," Maddie said, hunting through the box of crayons.

Cam ignored her and turned to Libby. "Tell Mom. Tell her how I never boss anyone around. At school."

"Ridiculous," Libby said, but she didn't look like she meant it.

"I'm going to quit Girl Scouts and take piano lessons. We both quit, right, Libby?"

Libby hesitated, then whispered, "But I can't take piano lessons. You know what my grandmother is like. Piano lessons cost money. Girl Scouts is free."

Mom intervened. "Libby, you stick with Girl Scouts. You two don't need to do everything together."

"Yes," Cam said. "We do."

"No, you don't," Mom said in a "subject closed" tone. "Camden, we'll discuss your role with Girl Scouts later. In the meantime, please change Blaine's diaper while I start dinner." She went over to the refrigerator and opened it, missing the horrified look on Cam's face. She hated changing her sister's diapers. Hated it!

"Never mind," Libby whispered. "I'll do it." She carried Blaine into the family room, where a changing station was set up.

Cam followed behind and flopped on the couch. "I'm definitely quitting Girl Scouts." If Old Bag Watson didn't appreciate her valuable input, why would she want to be a part of the troop? She was just about to say so out loud, but Libby was singing a song to Blaine as she changed the diaper. Her baby sister was giggling and kicking her chubby legs in a way she never did with Cam. On the other hand, Cam changed a diaper in ten seconds flat. Libby took her sweet time. "I hope you have a dozen kids someday."

Libby looked up, pleased. "Not a dozen. But definitely at least one. Maybe two. A boy and a girl." She snapped the buttons on Blaine's outfit and set her on the ground. "Don't you want kids?"

Cam watched Blaine pick up a toy and try to chew it. She didn't stink anymore, but she was drooling. Still pretty gross to look at. "No, I don't think so."

Libby sat cross-legged on the floor and leaned her back against the couch. Blaine lunged for her and she scooped her into her lap. "I'm going to quit Girl Scouts too."

Cam shot up to a sitting position. "Really?"

"Yeah. If you're not in it, I don't want to be in it. It wouldn't be any fun. But let's find something else that doesn't cost money."

Cam ran through some possibilities. "Today the PE teacher was passing out sign-up slips for an afterschool cross-country team."

"Free?"

"Free."

Libby put out her hand to high-five Cam. "Let's do it."

She slapped her palm. "You're a good friend, Libby Cooper."

"Friends forever."

Cam smiled. "And then some."

Four

HER DAD DROVE SLOWLY along a narrow road that ribboned its way north, up island. As she followed behind him, occasionally there was a break in the trees to her left and Maddie could see a splash of ocean. Mostly, it was a wall of thick trees, so tightly hugging the road that she felt claustrophobic. There were no houses out here, no telephone poles, no signs of civilization.

And then Maddie felt the start of an emotion so new she couldn't categorize it. Her heart was racing, her palms were sweating, and she felt like she couldn't get enough air into her lungs.

Too much. Too much change.

Oh my, oh no. She'd never had a panic attack, but she'd read a great deal about them in her graduate work. She must be having one, or a heart attack. One or the other. Both? She aimed for the next clearing and pulled the car over, hoping her father would notice she had stopped following him. She got out of the car and leaned over, her hands on her knees, taking in great drafts of air. Her father, oblivious, disappeared around the bend.

She tried to still her mind, tried to listen to the sounds around her, using all the techniques she'd learned in case studies on anxiety.

They weren't working.

What to do? What to do?

A bag. She needed a paper bag. Her breathing felt wrong. Her heart was going to explode. She dumped Peg's ginger scones out of the bag and into her purse. Then she breathed into the bag, in and out. Slowly, she felt her breathing settle. Mosquitoes nipped at her skin, drawing blood. Zika carriers, no doubt.

After a few minutes, Maddie's father's car came back down the road. He pulled up beside her.

"Enjoying the view?"

She pulled the paper bag away from her face. "Dad, this is a big mistake. That village is . . . no village at all. It's a crumbling ghost town. No way will I be able to get certified for licensing in a place like this." She put the bag back over her mouth and breathed in and out, in and out. "But I can't leave you here."

Her dad turned off his engine and got out of the car. He watched her breathe in and out of the paper bag a few times, then carried on as if this were an everyday occurrence. "Madison, you're only looking at the buildings. All that can be fixed."

Never one for picking up on cues, her dad's apparent dementia had only increased his obliviousness.

"This island just needs a little life in it. Once we get the camp up and going, it's going to bring in more people. And wherever there's people, then there's problems. People with problems need a counselor. In the meantime, consider the natural beauty of this place."

Okay. Okay, the nature thing, that Maddie could appreciate. Pine trees stacked up as far as she could see. The cove below was picturesque, with a small wooden dock jutting out. Far beyond the cove was the ocean, just far enough that the waves crested before they reached the cove but not so far that their crash and roar couldn't be heard. A piercing sound overhead caught her attention—an osprey soared above her.

He stood with his arms akimbo, like a captain at the helm of his ship. "Do you see it, Maddie? Are you catching my vision?"

Not in any way, shape, or form. But Dad looked so happy. So

very happy. The stress of the last few years peeled off and he seemed younger, lighthearted, the way he used to be. "Sort of, I guess."

"See? It grows on you, this big dream. That's the thing about dreams. They're contagious." He shielded his eyes and looked up the road. "We're nearly there. I saw a sign around the bend."

She followed him in her car. A few minutes passed before she saw a sign for Camp Kicking Moose that had fallen down and broken into two parts. Dad turned right and she followed onto a gravel road, stomach twisting into a tight knot. After that, the road got worse. Bumpier. A combination of rocks and mud puddles. Now they were really in the middle of nowhere. On either side, there was grass that grew wild and trees tall enough to block the view of anything else.

Up ahead, she saw her dad's brake lights come on. He jumped out of the car and slammed the door shut. "We're here!"

And there it was: the camp her father had come to claim.

Maddie felt a second panic attack start its warning signals. Her face grew warm, perspiration broke out on her forehead, and her heart started to *thump, thump, thump*. Two panic attacks in the space of a half hour! That was cause for alarm, right there. She had a theory that anxiety started like a fast-moving river in a person's brain, creating grooves of inlets and streams. Those grooves became the default as anxious reactions became easier and easier for the body to go to. Like a switch. She'd read about a woman whose mind and body reacted to any unexpected situation with crippling emotional responses, who lived with twenty-two cats and never left her house.

Maddie hung her head. Her future rolled out in her mind, looking eerily similar to that client's. She didn't even like cats. Doomed. She was doomed.

"Maddie, come on!" Her father was making his way through the trees toward a row of small cabins, each one built of age-blacked logs with moss-furred roofs. Over each cabin door was a bleached-white rack of antlers.

She sat in her car, not wanting to leave its safety. This decrepit camp looked like a salvage yard. There was junk everywhere, scattered all around: a big tangle of fishing poles, a metal canoe with its bottom rusted out, the skeletal remains of a car chassis, lobster buoys and traps, oil drums, coils of moldy rope. She felt her face heat up again and tried to take some deep, cleansing breaths. *Calm down, Maddie. Calm down. It's all going to be okay.*

She squeezed her eyes shut. If this was what it looked like in daylight, imagine it in a few hours, after the sunset, when those bears Peg had mentioned started hunting for dinner. How many bears? At least one. And a few bear cubs. Mother bears could be particularly violent if their babies were threatened. Fear vibrated through Maddie. Oh, the news stories she'd heard!

Dad stopped in front of the first cabin, hands on his hips, and gazed at the row of cabins like a king overlooking his kingdom. Then he inspected each one before he came back to the car, where Maddie remained tightly seatbelted.

Dad threw his arms wide, as if he wanted to embrace it all. "Isn't it amazing?"

Yes. Yes, it definitely amazed Maddie. But not in a good way.

Oh, this was so sad. It wasn't merely senile dementia that had a grip on Dad. Even worse. He was suffering from delusions of grandeur. She had gone to a seminar on it in grad school.

"We're not staying here. We'll be staying down the road a piece."

Oh, thank God! Maddie nearly swooned in relief.

Dad got back in his car and drove down the road, Maddie following behind, until he reached a narrow turnoff. She gripped the steering wheel as the car jiggled over the bumps and ruts in the gravel road, though it was in better condition than the road that led to the cabins. Past a thick stand of trees, they came to a large clearing. On the far edge was a pointy-roofed Victorian house, long past its prime, painted Pepto-Bismol pink with lavender trim. Half the windows were boarded up, those that remained were broken, and the roof was missing shingles here and there.

Someone had duct-taped a hand-lettered Office sign on the front door.

She rolled down her car window a mere inch when her father walked over to her. She'd already learned her lesson about the mosquitoes—so prevalent and persistent that she didn't want to give them a chance to get in the car again. "Wow."

"A beauty, isn't she?" He tilted his head to one side. "Though I don't recall that bright pink paint. Or the purple trim."

"Dad, that house . . . it . . ." It evoked a childhood memory of Barney the dinosaur. "It's . . ." Hideous. Atrocious. Should be knocked down, paved over. "It's . . . enormous."

"It was once a summer home for a lumber baron. That was in the pre–income tax days."

She got out of her car to get a better look, opening the door and shutting it fast. "You can't possibly . . . this can't be. No way. Do you mean to tell me this is Camp Kicking Moose? This is the rustic summer camp you've talked about?"

"Well, those cabins, they're pretty rustic. This building, we called it Moose Manor. It was the catch-all place. The dining room, the administration offices, the camp nurse. There's a big kitchen in the back. Then there's a front room big enough for the whole camp to fit into. Good for evening gatherings or rainy days."

Maddie stood there a moment, breathing deeply. The camp had been up for sale for years and it looked long abandoned. No wonder Dad was able to get that bargain-basement price. She slapped hard at her neck, looked at the smear of blood left behind on her hand. "Is this where the school is held? The one you mentioned."

"No, I'm pretty sure Seth was referring to the old carriage house." He shielded his eyes from the sun and turned in a half circle, then stopped. "Ah. Behold the schoolhouse."

There was a break in the trees to Maddie's left and she could see a wooden structure, with a beaten path that led to it. The carriage house was the same atrocious color as the house, the same pointy Victorian architecture. But it did look better cared for than the manor. The windows, at least, weren't broken.

Dad kicked at the hard ground with the toe of his shoe. "This was once a driveway that led horse and wagon to the carriage house." He made a sweeping gesture with his hand. "Soon, it will all be restored." He gave her an ear-to-ear smile. "Let's go check out our new home." And away he marched to the front door of Moose Manor. Maddie hurried to keep up.

The first thing she noticed about the house was the mothball smell. She pressed a hand over her mouth and nose, tentatively following her dad. The place was full of shadows, dark shapes and forms. Cobwebs hung in ropy skeins from the corners of the large meeting room Dad had talked about. Upholstered furniture was scattered here and there, and something made a crunching sound as she walked. "What is that sound?"

"Dead bugs," Dad said.

She tried a light switch but the light didn't come on, so she tugged a curtain to pull it back and sunlight poured in, thick with dust motes. Yup, those were dead bugs on the floor. Oh gross. Her stomach did a somersault. She turned to Dad. "Well. This isn't what I expected."

"Me, either." There was another long silence. Then, quietly, Dad said, "We'll make the best of it."

"Think so?" Maddie said, trying to sound certain instead of worried.

"I know so."

Maddie glanced longingly through the broken window out to her car.

The sound of a car driving up the bumpy gravel road made her squeal. She ran to the door to fling it wide open. "It's Cam and Cooper. Blaine's driving up behind them. Oh, thank God. The cavalry's come!"

Dad hadn't stopped smiling since Cam and Cooper and Blaine arrived. It lit up his whole face, made him look years younger.

But how long could Cam keep up this charade for her dad? In all good conscience, she couldn't support his craziness. Sooner or later her mouth would open and her opinion would explode, bomb-like: *Dad, you're losing it.*

While Dad and Cooper went to the cars to bring in luggage, the girls scrounged the boxes to put together a makeshift dinner: crackers, salami and cheese, apple slices, Cheerios, peanut butter on bread. "Tomorrow, we have to get to a grocery store," Blaine said.

"Good luck with that," Maddie said. "Apparently, it's only open when the grocer feels like it. There's a place called the Lunch Counter that was more inviting. In fact, I forgot about those ginger scones." She dug through her purse for the scones. "Here." She brushed off some lint. "Try one."

Blaine took a bite, chewed, made a face, and spit it out. "It tastes like soap!"

Cam made a grab for one. "Any port in a storm, Blaine." She broke off a piece and bit it. Then she, too, spit it out. "Scratch that."

For everything broken or run-down in Moose Manor, there was one surprise. The electricity, with a little persuasion, actually turned on. Dad was able to switch some breakers, and voilà, the overhead light in the main room went on. He knew just where the breaker box was. "It used to be my summer job to fix those breakers," he told them. "It was always a little exciting, wondering if today was the day I might electrocute myself."

"What does electrocute mean?" Cooper asked.

"Dad," Maddie said in her I-can't-believe-you-said-that-in-front-of-Cooper voice.

Cam stepped in. "Coop, it means that Grandpa would get a little shock. A tiny jolt. Like this." She pretended to pinch him and he giggled.

The heater, unfortunately, was not going to cooperate. The sun would set early behind that fringe of trees that ringed the old manor, and it was bone-cold inside the house.

"There is no way we can stay here overnight." Blaine's teeth chattered as she spoke. "Cooper's lips are blue."

"They are?" Cooper asked, hands on his cheeks. "Am I going to freeze to death?"

"Do not fear, Grandson. I anticipated this very problem. I'll be back soon."

Blaine reached for her coat. "Hold it! If you're collecting firewood, I'll come and help."

"Better than firewood. Stay put."

Cam watched him dash out to his truck and rifle through the cab. He carried two boxes inside. "Room heaters?"

"Yup. As long as we have electricity, we have heat."

"Dad, do you remember the electricity going off a lot?" Maddie said. "You know, like Peg described."

"Who's Peg?" Blaine said.

"Oh, she's a hoot. She runs the Lunch Counter in town. Part diner, part hardware store." Maddie looked to Dad. "So did it go off each day?"

"Every day?" Blaine said. "But . . . what about the internet?"

Maddie started to giggle. "What about it?"

Dad gave Maddie a not-now look that made Blaine look instantly suspicious. "Actually, I do remember losing power but not every day. And I didn't realize it was an island-wide occurrence. We stayed pretty removed out here. Seems like everything's gotten worse since I was here."

"You don't say," Blaine said.

Ignoring that dig, Dad opened the heater boxes and looked around the large room. "We need to pick a small room to heat." He pointed toward a door. "I think that was the nurse's office. Let's try that." He opened the door and something furry burst out, dashing through the front door.

Cooper screamed. Maddie, closest to him, grabbed him and held him against her. "What was that?"

"If memory serves me right"—all the sisters exchanged a dubious look as Dad peered out the front door—"I think . . . it was a coon cat."

"Oh great," Maddie said. "That's just great. More wild animals to be afraid of."

Cooper looked up at her. "Wild animals?"

"Coon cats are house cats, Cooper," Dad said. "They're bigger than your typical house cat. Deluxe-sized, you could say. Mostly tame."

"Not that one," Blaine added.

Dad went back to the room and disappeared into it. "All clear," he yelled out. "No more coon cats."

Cam closed the front door. "How did it get in there?"

"Broken window. I think we'll just stay put in the central room." Dad closed the office door behind him and looked for an outlet to plug the heater in to. He cocked his ear to listen to the heater's hum as it turned on, then straightened up with a smile. "Music to my ears. Cooper and I will go get firewood to light a fire in the fireplace. Between a fire roaring away and those heaters, this room'll warm up like a summer day in no time."

Hardly that.

Maddie unrolled a sleeping bag near the fireplace.

"Smart of you to bring it," Cam said.

"I keep one in the trunk of my car. Girl Scout training. You never know when you might need them."

Cam swallowed a snappy remark. Like most girls, Maddie had been a Brownie, then a Girl Scout. Unlike most girls, she kept on being a scout much, much longer than it was cool.

But then she started wondering how and where the rest of them were going to sleep. Fortunately, Dad had thought to bring blankets and pillows. Problem solved, he told Cam as he handed her a stack.

Not much later, as the fire grew from a flame to a steady blaze in

53

the fireplace, Cam watched Dad let out a sigh of relief. He seemed so happy here in this echoing, cavernous old manor. Shadows danced in the room as the fire flickered. She looked around the large room. This old house was a grand old dame, with remarkable old bones. The exterior pink paint color was offensive, but putting that aside, the house wasn't all bad. The interior was even bigger than it looked from the outside. The floors had been crafted of thick, wide planks, and the ceilings were tall. The walls were paneled in dark mahogany—happily no paint! Plus there were two staircases that met in the middle to lead upstairs. Tomorrow, she looked forward to exploring the house and its grounds.

For now, though, Cooper needed to get to bed. He needed a bath too, but that wasn't going to happen. She rubbed his small back as he nestled into the makeshift bed, watched his eyelids grow heavy. He thought he was on a great camping adventure, but in his hand was clutched his ball of string. That *string*. It drove Cam crazy, but he wouldn't go anywhere without it. Once that ball was used up, he would be adamant that he needed to buy a new one. After she returned from this business trip to London, she would need to deal with his string obsession once and for all.

She waited until she knew he was sound asleep, and then she whispered to her dad and sisters, "I have an announcement to make."

"Me too," Blaine said.

"Me too," Maddie said.

Cam pointed to Blaine. "You go first," but Blaine mouthed, "No way."

Dad had been feeding wood into the fireplace and stopped at that. He put the poker down and turned to face them. "What's going on?" He sat on the hearth.

Cam cleared her throat. "I've been asked to go on an international business trip. I know it's last minute, and that you've just barely arrived, but I was hoping you could watch Cooper during spring break while I'm away."

"So," Maddie said, disdain in her voice, "you're not here to check up on Dad's premature senility. You're here so we can babysit Cooper for you."

"Not senile, Maddie." Dad narrowed his eyes in Cam's direction. "Where, exactly, are you going?"

Cam licked her lips. "London. Just for a week."

Dad took that news in without expression. He glanced at Blaine. "And you? What's your news?"

"I've been kicked out of college. Not kicked, exactly. Told to leave."

Dad's brow furrowed. "Why?"

"They seem to think I can't make a decision."

Dad held on to his stoicism. "Maddie, what's your news?"

"My news?" She cleared her throat. "Tre . . . uh . . . um. He asked me to marry him."

Cam's heart dropped to her stomach. She glanced at Blaine and saw a look of dismay on her face. It wasn't that there was anything wrong about Tre, but there wasn't anything particularly right about him either.

Dad shifted around to gaze at the fire. He picked up the poker and nudged a log deeper into the fireplace. Sparks flew. He remained silent.

"Dad, can you say something?" Cam said. "Your silence makes us nervous."

"Tomorrow," he said, without turning around. "We'll talk more tomorrow. For now, the day has held enough surprises."

"Boy, ain't that the truth?" Blaine said as she climbed into Maddie's sleeping bag.

Five

CAM WOKE UP DISORIENTED, startled by a loud sound. Eyes open, she listened for the sound, but there was only silence. Utter and complete quiet. Where was she? Not Boston. No honking horns and sirens and the *beep-beep-beep* of trucks in reverse gear. Then she heard it again. A sound like someone was retching.

She sat straight up in bed—which was actually just a couple of blankets layered on the floor—and looked around the brightly lit room. No one else was in the large living room, but she heard voices coming from the kitchen. Everyone else was already up. She rubbed her eyes. She never slept late. Never.

Then came another sound of retching. She swiveled around under her blankets to see a cat—a huge cat—throwing up. She screamed, the cat bolted away, and everyone ran in to see what had happened. "A cat! More like a mountain lion. It was throwing up!" A fishy smell wafted through the room.

"Oh no," Dad said. "It's that coon cat."

"Cooper and I fed it a can of tuna this morning," Blaine said. "We found it in the back of a kitchen cupboard. Maybe . . . I should've checked the expiration date."

Cooper stood in front of Cam's big leather Gucci purse and peered into it. "Mom, it barfed in your bag."

Cam moaned and fell back on top of the makeshift bed, covering her face with her hands. "Coffee. I need coffee."

Dad's face scrunched up apologetically. "Ah. Unfortunately, there is none. But Cooper and I are on our way to town to pick up a few things. We'll bring back coffee."

"I'm coming with you," Blaine said, holding her nose. "The tuna smell in here is making me sick."

Dad drove straight to the Lunch Counter and strode inside, like the local he pretended to be. Blaine followed behind, crossed the threshold, and stopped abruptly. She blinked, taking it all in, surveying the room. It didn't make sense. What was this place supposed to be? To the left: a long counter, lined by red round stools. A big oven, stovetop, and sink. To the right: long narrow aisles, shelves filled with all kinds of junk. The walls were painted the color of flesh, all except one wall—a disgusting shade of green. The ceiling light was a lone hanging lightbulb. The entire environment offended her senses. Even the scent of burnt coffee offended her nose.

Dad didn't seem to be ruffled by any of it. "Good morning, Peg Legg. I need a little help."

A short, round woman had turned around from the stovetop when the bells over the door had tinkled their arrival. She was pretty in a merry sort of way, with bright red hair tucked neatly into two pigtails, covered by a yellow headband with a slightly off-center knot. Blaine hadn't seen a headband like that since she was a little girl.

"And a good morning to you, Paul Grayson." She handed him a cup of coffee. "And who are these beautiful children who are scrambling to keep up with you?"

"Sorry. Let me start again. Good morning, Peg. I'd like to introduce my youngest daughter, Blaine, and my one and only grandson, Cooper." He turned to Blaine and said, "This is Peg Legg."

Peg scowled at Dad. "Call me that one more time and you'll

find your truck tires slashed in the night." She turned to Blaine and her face burst into a bright smile. "Honey, pay no attention to your father's sense of humor and just call me Peg. You sure are a pretty little thing. Mighty young to have a child, but I'm not judging. No sirree! Goodness sakes, I graduated from high school and went into labor that very night."

"Oh whoa! Wait just a minute!" Blaine waved her hands in the air. "Cooper belongs to my oldest sister, Cam."

"So there's three of you? I met your sister Maddie. Or are there more?"

"Three."

"Ah ha!" Peg pointed a finger at Dad. "Three Sisters Island. I get it now." Dad grinned back like a schoolboy caught with his hand in the cookie jar. "So, honey, what are you doing with your life?"

"I'm in college. Sort of. Taking time off."

"What year are you?"

Dad coughed. "Excellent question."

Peg caught on fast. "Well, whatever year you are, I've never met a college student who didn't live on coffee." She poured another cup of coffee and handed it to Blaine. "Cooper, honey, I'm pleased to meet you." She held out her hand to high-five Cooper and Blaine cringed. Cooper was acutely shy around strangers and could act very awkward, turning rudely away to hide his face. To Blaine's shock, and her dad's, too, Cooper returned Peg's high-five. "You look like you could use some cookies."

"Thanks, but my sister Maddie said he's not allowed to eat sugar," Blaine said. Last evening, after learning about the chocolate ice cream cone in Bar Harbor, Maddie had given Blaine and Cam a long and boring lecture about the ills of sugar on children.

"I'm not," Cooper said. "No sugar. No wheat. No dairy. I might be lactose intolerant." He pushed the nosepiece of his glasses up. "Thank you anyway, Mrs. Peg Legg."

Peg looked blank. "No sugar? No sugar! But he's only a little tyke."

"I'm seven and a half years old," Cooper said earnestly, holding up two splayed hands. "I go to school. Third grade. I skipped kindergarten."

"What?" Peg's face took on a worried-mom look. "Oh honey, kindergarten's the best part of school. It's downhill from there."

No kidding. Blaine liked Peg Legg, despite her unfortunate surname. She appreciated her candor and wished Cam could hear it. Blaine thought Cam stressed Cooper out with her Type A-ness— she assumed everyone was Type A, or should be. Maddie stressed Cooper out with her diagnoses. She slapped all kinds of labels on Cooper and felt Cam was in denial that Cooper had serious issues. Dad stayed out of it. He said he'd had his turn at raising children and look how *that* turned out.

All three sisters weren't sure what he meant by that.

Blaine took a sip of coffee and gagged. It was tepid, terrible, with grounds floating in it. Fortunately, Peg had turned around to stir something in a blue bowl and didn't see her reaction. Her father had the same response. He set the coffee mug down, pushed it away, and sat on a stool. "Peg, how does a fellow go about gathering folks together for a meeting? Like, when is the next village meeting going to be held?"

Peg's attention was focused on stirring the contents of the blue bowl. Her face grew red as she beat the mixture like it was a rug on a clothesline. "Village meeting?" she said. "We don't have them much. I suppose when the council does meet, it's done in private. Everything runs through the mayor."

"That's encouraging news," Dad said. "So the island is big enough for a mayor?"

Peg chuckled. "Oh no. Only a village council, with elected selectmen. The mayor's been the longest councillor, so he calls himself the mayor and everyone else does too." She dropped spoonfuls of the mixture on a cookie sheet and pushed it into the oven.

Blaine had been watching Peg work. "What are you making?"

"Biscuits."

"But . . . they'll be so tough. You can't beat biscuits. Not like that. They'll end up like hockey pucks. You need to fold them."

Peg tipped her head. "You need to *what?*"

"As soon as you add the liquids into the dry mixture, you have to gently stir the dough." She pantomimed the motion. "The baking powder causes a chemical reaction that makes the dough harden. If you beat it too much, you end up with a rock-hard biscuit." Or scone, now that she thought of it. "Biscuits are supposed to be light and flaky."

"Well, I'll be." Peg looked at her thoughtfully. "That explains a lot." She peeked in the oven. "Think it's too hot?"

Blaine went over and put her hand close to the oven. "Not hot enough. If they bake too long, the interior ends up overcooked." She turned the oven temperature up. "Biscuits can be tricky, but once you get the hang of them, they're easy. And they're the foundation for lots of other baked goods. Shortcake, scones. It's kind of like making vanilla ice cream. If you get that right, it becomes the base for all ice cream."

"Ice cream?" Peg sounded shocked. She seized hold of Blaine's forearm. "Honey, can you make ice cream? Is it any good?"

"It's incredible," Dad said. "The world's best."

Blaine rolled her eyes. "I haven't made ice cream in years." It was something she and her mom used to do. They'd even attended a weekend of Ice Cream School at Penn State University. It was held every January, for obvious reasons, and all the greats had gone there: Ben and Jerry, Baskin and Robbins. It was the best weekend of Blaine's life. Time with her mom, time doing what she loved best. Blaine had come home from school one winter afternoon and Mom had their bags packed, ready to go. Several months later, her mom had died. Blaine hadn't made ice cream since.

"Blaine, honey, you like to cook?"

"I do. Baking, mostly. I love to bake."

"What's the difference between cooking and baking?"

"Oh, so so much!"

Peg smiled, an ear-to-ear grin that felt like the sun came out from behind a cloud. "Honey, get back here behind the counter and teach me how to make a biscuit that doesn't break a tooth."

"Now?"

"Now."

"Hold that thought, ladies," Dad said. "I've got a long to-do list today so we can survive another night at Moose Manor. First things first. Peg, what's this mayor's name?"

"The mayor?" Blaine said. "Dad, we need food! Good food—I can't eat another cracker and cheese. We need supplies. Cleaning products. More mosquito repellant. Glass for broken windows. Toilet paper. Cam needs coffee or she'll be a grizzly bear by noon."

"I can help with the coffee," Peg said, holding up the pot of luke-warm light brown coffee, swimming with grounds. Blaine nearly burst into laughter at the thought of bringing *that* to Cam.

"No! No, thank you," Dad said. "Cam is kind of fussy about coffee."

"About everything," Blaine said. "She's a princess."

Dad frowned at her. "Food is top on the list. First though, while I'm in town, I'd like to get some things rolling. Is there anyone who hauls away junk?"

"Haul away junk?" Peg repeated disbelievingly. "Why would you haul anything away?"

"Because it's . . . junk."

"Impossible. There's no such thing as junk on an island."

"Come on out to Camp Kicking Moose and you'll change your mind."

"Let me tell you something about island living." Peg leaned her forearms on the counter. "There's no point replacing something that still works, because you'd probably have to leave the island to find whatever it was you wanted."

Confused, Dad rubbed his chin.

"Better to find someone on the island who wants your old stuff." Peg pointed to an empty corner. "Like that. There used to be a

61

lobster tank right there." She shrugged. "But then our lobsters up and left the island, and it was just too hard to look at an empty tank. So I gave it to the Baggett and Taggett store. They use it to hold their bait for tourists who like to fish. They're not busy 'til November's deer hunting season. This time of year, folks just go there to swap hunting stories. 'Cept on Sunday mornings, of course."

If Dad seemed confused before, now he looked bewildered. "So is there anyone who'll haul j—uh, items away from Camp Kicking Moose and give them to someone who might find use for those said items?"

"Sure. Captain Ed. He should be down at the Boon Dock in a few minutes. Ferry's just about to come in."

Not two seconds later, the ferry horn blew. "How'd you know?" Blaine asked.

"Oh, honey, I can feel it in my bones. There's a rumble in the air right before the ferry comes in. That ferry, it's our lifeline."

"Hang on a second," Dad said. "What would happen to the Never Late Ferry if Captain Ed is hauling stuff away from Camp Kicking Moose?"

Peg shrugged. "It'll be later than usual." She stood up and crossed her arms across her ample chest. "Now listen up, Paul Grayson. The mayor has two sons. They'll offer to work for you and don't you believe it. You'll be lucky if they never show up. If they do, they'll sit around, drinking your beer the minute you turn your back, and charge you double for overtime. Worthless, those two."

"Noted. But since we're back on the topic of the mayor, I don't believe you told me his name. I'd like to meet him."

"Oh, that part is easy," Peg said. "The mayor's name is Baxtor Phinney. And he's already out looking for you."

"Me? Any idea why?"

"Sure do. He's the tax collector too. He was in here yesterday, telling everyone you're delinquent in paying taxes."

"Taxes?" Poor Dad. It came out like a croak. "I've only owned

Camp Kicking Moose for a couple weeks. How could I already be delinquent?"

Peg shrugged. "I'm sure the mayor will give you all the details." She leaned forward again on the counter. "But if I were you, Paul Grayson, I'd read through the fine print on your bill of sale."

Dad frowned. "Is there some kind of law enforcement on this island?"

"Sure there is. Baxtor Phinney. He's the police chief. Fire chief too. All volunteer. That's how we do things on this island. Have to make do and help each other out."

"What happens if someone has a heart attack?" Blaine said, casting a sideways glance at her dad.

He noticed. "My ticker's just fine, Blaine."

"Let's see," Peg said. "A few years back a lady named Betty Clark had a massive stroke. Her son called over to Mount Desert and they sent paramedics. Took a while, though. Betty died before they got here."

"That's terrible," Blaine said. Her friend Artie Lotosky had certified as an EMT during his freshman year and told her all kinds of gruesome stories. "If she'd had immediate care, her death could have been prevented."

"Not for long," Peg said in her matter-of-fact way. "Betty was ninety-six. Meaner than a snake too." She tucked a loose lock of hair behind her bright yellow headband. Suddenly, the lightbulb flickered, then the room went dark. "Shoot. There goes the power."

"Does that happen a lot?" Blaine said.

"Every day. Sometimes, twice a day."

"What about the internet?"

"What about it?" Peg started to pull open the oven door but stopped when Blaine screeched.

"Don't open it! Keep the heat in. They'll keep baking."

Peg tipped her head like a golden retriever. "Honey, I'm so glad you're here." She pointed to Dad. "Why don't you go do your important errands and let these two stay here with me 'til you're

63

done. I want to watch your girl make those light and flaky biscuits."
She pulled aprons off a hook, tossed one at Blaine, and wrapped
another around Cooper's tummy.

"Somehow I don't think that was a question, Peg Legg."

"Paul Grayson, you just might not be as dumb as you look."

Blaine looked up at Dad, shocked. He seemed shocked too.
Then a slow grin covered his face. It was a startling moment for
Blaine. Her dad had always intimidated people with that deep
voice of his. No one talked to him like that. No one! But then,
she'd never heard her dad tweak someone about a name before.

This island, it might be good for her dad. A ridiculous waste
of time and energy for the rest of the family, but it might just be
good for Dad.

Six

DAD RETURNED TO MOOSE MANOR with a bag of groceries, but no coffee, and no Cooper. No Blaine. He said that they wanted to stay at the Lunch Counter with a woman named Peg Legg. Maddie pointed out that while Peg seemed nice, she was a stranger to them. And was that wise to leave his grandson with a stranger?

No, it probably wasn't, Cam agreed. Also circling through her mind was Maddie's insistence that Dad was suffering from delusions of grandeur combined with senile dementia. Her overeducated sister tossed labels around like spaghetti, but she was right about one thing: something odd was going on with Dad. He was strangely happy, and from what she could gather about this camp, tucked away on a remote island, he'd been suckered. Poor Dad. His retirement package. Gone. And he was nearly sixty! So old.

Cam had just finished vigorously scrubbing all remains of coon cat vomit from her purse. Her *new*, expensive, glossy Gucci purse with calfskin handles—it made her want to cry. She picked up her car keys. "I think I'll drive into town and get some coffee," she said to Dad, trying to keep her voice cucumber calm. Inside, she fought a rising anxiety. What kind of woman was this Peg Legg? She sounded like she descended from pirates. And Blaine . . . what was Dad thinking? He left Blaine in charge of Cooper? Her little sister couldn't even remember to pack a hairbrush. She borrowed Cam's without asking this morning and left it full of blonde hair.

Cam drove slowly down the gravel road, trying to avoid the divots, until she reached the main road. Then, she pressed down on the gas pedal and sped toward town, weaving around the curves and bends, not slowing down until she reached Main Street . . . if you could call it that. Poor Cooper. He must be frantic by now, wondering where she was. He didn't do well with unexpected turns of events. Her father knew that. How could he have just left him?

By now her heart was pounding. She peered through the bug-splashed windshield to find this Lunch Counter joint. She thought she'd noticed it yesterday as she drove off the barge, only because it was one of the few storefronts that didn't have windows covered in butcher paper or boarded up with plywood. She wondered if this village ever really had its day in the sun, the way Mom had described it. If Cam had to guess, she thought it had probably always been sputtering to survive. This island, it was dying. Near death.

She pulled over in front of the Lunch Counter, grabbed her purse, and bolted toward the door. The entire scene inside threw Cam for a loop: a diner combined as a general store. A short woman in pigtails stood next to Blaine, and they were both bent over the cracked-open oven, peering into it. And there was a scruffy-looking lumberjack sitting on a counter stool, showing Cooper how to lather a biscuit with jam. Cooper had an apron wrapped nearly twice around his skinny body. He had smudges of flour in his hair, and he was giggling over something, but his mouth was full of food so that the giggles came out muffled.

But it was the familiar scent in this place that jolted Cam to the core. Biscuits. Her mother's biscuits.

Cam closed her eyes and inhaled deeply.

"You must be the third sister. I can sure see the family resemblance."

Cam's eyes popped open. The cheery-looking pigtailed woman stood in front of her, holding out a cup of coffee. She accepted it gratefully. "I'm Cam. The oldest." She took a sip of coffee, really good coffee, and felt her whole self unwind. She hadn't realized how tense she'd felt during these last couple of days.

"I'm Peg. Welcome to . . ." She turned to Blaine. "Honey, what's your dad calling this island? I keep forgetting."

"Three Sisters."

"That's right. Now that I've met all three of you, I'll be sure to remember it. Anyhow, welcome to Three Sisters Island."

Cam swallowed the coffee quickly and shook her hand. "Nice to meet you." She lifted the mug. "This is very good coffee."

"Folks been telling me that all morning. Don't give me the credit. Your sister made it."

"Blaine?" Her little sister? The one who oozed away like a barn cat whenever there was work to be done?

Blaine looked over her shoulder and gave her a smug smile.

Cooper heard Cam's voice and spun around on the stool. His mouth was covered in jam. He gave her a big grin and she cracked up. "Look at you!" And then her smile faded. "Blaine! Did you let him eat gluten?"

"What the Sam Hill is gluten?" Peg said.

"It's kind of like the glue in wheat," Blaine said before turning to Cam. "So now he's allergic to gluten? What happened to sugar?"

Cam sighed. "I don't know. Maddie wants to try some different diets and see if there might be any change."

The lumberjack swiveled on his stool to face Cam. "What change are you hoping for?"

Cam felt a little shock of electricity run through her. She hadn't expected the lumberjack to look like *that*. Slate-blue eyes, a chiseled chin, a roman nose.

"Seth's right, and heaven knows he's the one who understands kids," Peg said. "Cooper seems just about perfect to me. Right as rain."

Cam turned to Cooper, who was beaming. He did seem right as rain, as normal as a little boy could be. Jam was all over the front of his shirt, dripping down his cheeks, as he licked butter off his fingers.

"Honey, sit on down and have yourself one of your sister's biscuits."

Cam perched on the stool next to Cooper and sipped her coffee. Those biscuits did look pretty good. She hadn't had anything to eat—partly because there wasn't much food left at the house, partly because she felt nauseous from the lingering cat vomit smell that emitted from her purse. But as that memory faded, her stomach rumbled with hunger.

"Have you met Seth Walker? He's the schoolteacher on this island." Peg refilled Cam's coffee mug. "Seth, this one is Paul Grayson's eldest. Her name is . . ." She scrunched her face. "What's your name again, honey?"

"Cam. Camden Grayson." No, she definitely hadn't met him. Frankly, he wasn't the sort of person you would forget, appearancewise.

Seth Walker gave her a nod of a greeting. "Like the town?"

"Exactly." This teacher, he wasn't the kind of teacher Cam had when she was in school. "So, there's actually a school on this island?"

From the way his dark eyebrows angled together, she knew it was the wrong thing to say. Or maybe it was said in the wrong way?

He didn't answer her, he only sipped his coffee. He put down his mug and said, "I gather you don't share your father's optimism."

Swallowing a sip of coffee, Cam snorted. "Optimism?" She spilled a few drops on her cashmere sweater. She dabbed the spots with a paper napkin. "We're wondering if he might have dementia."

Wrong thing to say again. Peg Legg and the lumberjack stared at her.

The lumberjack finished his last swallow of coffee and slipped off the stool. He left a few dollars on the countertop, nodded to Peg, and tousled Cooper's hair. "One man's insanity is another man's genius."

Cam's mouth dropped to an O. "Joyce Carol Oates?"

Those dark eyebrows lifted in surprise. "Exactly."

He went to the door and stopped, sniffing the air and not in a good way. "Peg, are you serving tuna for lunch? If so, I think it's gone bad."

Shoot. Cam glanced down at her purse, wondering what he would say when she blamed the fish smell on a coon cat, but by the time she lifted her head to explain, the lumberjack was out the door and crossing the street. She spun around to see if Peg had heard him, but her focus was entirely on Blaine and the contents of a blue bowl. She relaxed and took a sip of coffee. Man, that coffee tasted good.

An hour later, Cam drove slowly back to Moose Manor, Cooper and Blaine beside her. She hadn't noticed how tall and green the trees were last evening, nor earlier this morning. Taller and more green than any place she'd ever seen. What were the words to describe them? Verdant, vibrant. Occasionally there was a break in the trees and Cam saw a splash of blue. When she came to a clearing, she saw the view and pulled the car over. "Wow," she said.

"Wow is right," Blaine said.

Below the road was a calm blue cove. At this late-morning hour, with the sun almost directly overhead, the water seemed to glow from within. Gentle waves lapping the rocky shoreline left a sparkling residue.

They got out of the car to get a closer look. Cam held on tightly to Cooper because there was no guardrail along the road. After a few more minutes, they got back in the car to head toward Moose Manor. The driveway unfurled in a lazy curl through strands of trees until it reached the clearing where the old house sat against a windbreak of pines. In front of the house were lilac bushes, with leaves just starting to bud out. Someone had planted those bushes long ago and spent years caring for them. This old house had the look of lost money and years gone by, but was full of stories it wanted to tell. Stories still to be told.

Suddenly, Cam had a vision: this shabby old house restored to its grandeur. The exterior painted a soothing charcoal gray—begone, hideous pink! She saw crisp white trim framing the wraparound porch, with hanging pots of red geraniums. She imagined a front door painted a cheerful cranberry color, with a wreath hanging on it. In the kitchen, copper and cast-iron pots and pans hanging from an iron rack above the stove. A hammered-copper farm sink, big enough to bathe a dog in. Dried lavender and rosemary and thyme hanging in bunches from the exposed timber beams of the ceiling. A living room with an eclectic mixture of shabby-chic upholstered furniture.

She saw people coming to Moose Manor from all over, returning every year. She envisioned families playing croquet on the grass lawn, and children swinging on the swings in a playground. Good meals served in the dining room. Breakfast served on the porch during summer. She saw it all, as vividly as if she were watching a movie unroll.

She shook the vision right out of her head. The lumberjack's quote floated through her mind: *One man's insanity is another man's genius.* No. No way. This was just plain insane.

Seven

A LOT OF PROGRESS HAD BEEN MADE on Moose Manor during Saturday afternoon. Maddie had divided up tasks and assigned duties. Dad and Cooper worked on resuscitating the heater while the three sisters attacked the kitchen with cleaning products. Cam took the refrigerator, which hadn't been plugged in for years. While empty, it was also moldy. She used an entire gallon of Clorox bleach to sanitize it. As she tossed the empty plastic bottle in a trash can, she said, "Hard to believe that Mom was the camp cook here."

Maddie and Blaine stopped their scrubbing of cupboards to turn to her. "You're kidding," Blaine said. "Mom was the camp cook?"

"That's how she and Dad first met," Cam said. "He was in here in the middle of the night, scrounging for something to eat, and she thought a raccoon had gotten into the pantry. She attacked him with a broom." She smiled. "Dad said it was love at first whack."

Maddie turned her attention back to scrubbing the stovetop, but she had a new vigor as she scrubbed a baked-on, fossilized piece of food. Very likely, her mother had scrubbed this same ancient stovetop. It gave her a good feeling to think so.

Cam emptied a bucket of filthy water into the sink and refilled it with hot water. "Blaine, what do you know about that guy in the diner who was teaching Cooper to eat spoonfuls of butter?"

"Seth Walker," Blaine said. "He's the schoolteacher on the island."

"That part I know. I mean . . . what's he like?"

"Rugged outdoorsy type. Cooper sure liked him." Blaine wiggled her eyebrows. "Eye candy."

Maddie stopped scrubbing. "No kidding. He's drop-dead gorgeous."

"If you're into the Paul Bunyan type, I guess."

Blaine gave her a puzzled look. "Maddie, when did you meet him?"

"Yesterday afternoon, as Dad and I came in on the Never Late Ferry."

"So, Maddie," Cam said in her big-sister-knows-best voice, "what's the deal with Tre? You told him no, right?"

Maddie braced herself. "What makes you say that?"

"You're here and he's not."

When Cam arrived last evening, Maddie knew it would just be a matter of time before she started in on advice giving. She was the last person Maddie would ask for advice about love and romance—the very last! Her love life was nonexistent. The only thing Cam loved, besides Cooper, was her work.

"The reason I'm here is to keep an eye on Dad," Maddie said. "One of us needs to be responsible for him. You're off to London. Blaine can barely take care of herself."

"Hey!"

"Sorry, Blaine," Maddie said.

"So you moved to this . . . forsaken island . . . because you think you're the only one who cares about Dad?" Cam rolled her eyes. "There you go again. Maddie the Martyr."

Humph. Maddie scrubbed so hard that she felt a bead of perspiration roll down her back. "Just go on and live your life, Cam. You always have. You do what you want to do, regardless of the fallout."

Cam narrowed her eyes. "What are you talking about?"

Blaine was all eyes and ears. "Yeah, which particular fallout are you talking about? Dumping Cooper on us so you can flit around the world?"

Blaine had hit her mark. "Dumping?" Now Cam was steamed, and she rolled off one rubber glove after another. "I'm not 'dumping' Cooper on anyone. What would either of you know about raising a child, day in and day out? You only have yourselves to think about."

This felt more familiar: one sister's insult set off a string of snarky digs. Maddie waved her hands in the air. "Let's not do this. It's counterproductive."

Cam and Blaine exchanged an eye roll. "Prepare thyself for psychobabble," Blaine said in a footman-announcing-the-coming-of-the-king voice.

"At least she's not diagnosing Cooper with some 'ism' or another."

Maddie glared at Cam. "Speaking of Cooper, you do know what's behind his obsessive behavior with string, don't you?"

Cam looked up at the ceiling, exasperated. "And here it comes."

Maddie let that remark pass. "D. W. Winnicott was a psychoanalyst who wrote about a child obsessed with string. Winnicott interpreted this behavior as a way of dealing with fears of abandonment. The boy's mother suffered from bouts of depression. The string was a kind of wordless communication for the boy, a symbolic means of joining. A way to hold on tight."

Cam scoffed. "Well, that's ridiculous. I'm not depressed and Cooper likes string. Big deal."

Denial. Cam was knee-deep in it. The very queen of denial. Maddie sighed. "Cam, all I'm trying to say is that Tre is my business. London is your business. Let's leave it at that."

"What about me?" Blaine said.

"What about you?"

"What's my business?"

Cam snorted. "Figuring out how to cram two years of college into five." She gazed around the kitchen. "Look, I have to leave early tomorrow morning to catch that flight." She pushed one hand into a rubber glove, then the other hand. "Let's finish this kitchen, or at least get it in working order. I don't want Cooper or Dad getting sick this week. Maddie's got me worried enough about the dust and mold in this old house."

She turned her attention back to scrubbing the refrigerator and missed Blaine's indignant look. "Notice it's not us she's worried about," Blaine whispered. "Only Cooper and Dad."

"I heard that," Cam said, scrubbing the interior of the refrigerator. She popped her head back out. "Blaine, you're nineteen years old. Cooper is little. Dad is old. You shouldn't need to have someone worry about you."

"If I did, I sure wouldn't expect it from you."

"Truce." Maddie waved her hand in the air. "Let's agree to a truce. Life is topsy-turvy for all of us right now. Each one of us. A little extra margin, please."

Cam and Blaine gave each other a frowning look. Then Cam softened. "I do appreciate the help with Cooper this week. I really do. I'm sorry that this London trip landed when it did. But it did, and I'm grateful for the care and attention I know you'll give Cooper."

"So," Blaine said, squeezing out a filthy sponge in the sink, "when are you going to get around to telling him you're leaving?"

"Tonight," Cam said.

"You can count on us," Maddie said. "The week will go fast. We'll make sure he's busy and happy. Right, Blaine?"

Blaine lifted her shoulders in a shrug. "Like Mom always said, it takes a village to raise a child, and we're Cooper's village."

"It was Maddie. She's the one who said that. Not Mom." Cam popped her head back into the fridge.

She was right about that, and it made Maddie happy to hear Cam talk about Mom. *That* didn't happen often. And all three of them were getting along fairly well. That didn't happen often, either.

CAM, AGE 25

It was a warm and humid spring afternoon, the kind that doubled Cam's hair in size. Today, she didn't care what she looked like. All she felt was a numbness. They'd just returned home from the lawyer's office for Libby Cooper and learned startling news. Libby, who had never thought past the next day, had actually made a legitimate, bona fide will. In it, Cam was declared the legal guardian for her child, with the request that she consider adopting him.

Dad, Cam, Blaine, and Maddie sat in the living room, all feeling sucker punched. "You had no idea she did this?" Dad asked.

"None," Cam said. "I mean, I do remember that once she told me if anything happened to her, she wanted our family to raise the baby. You know how she felt about us. She always wanted to be one of us."

"Well, she sorta was," Blaine said. "Libby ate more meals here than I did."

Maddie frowned. "She loved us. Mom treated her like a daughter."

"What happens if you say no?" Dad asked. "Who could take him if you say no?"

"I can't say no." Cam would never say no. Libby had been her closest, dearest friend, more of a sister to her than her own sisters.

"You have a choice," Blaine said. "Libby never even asked you to do this. She put you in an unfair position. You can say no."

Cam shook her head. "I don't know how I'll do this, but I'll manage."

"Why would Cam say no?" Maddie said.

Blaine, only sixteen, was skeptical. "Because Cam has a big, huge job. Her life is just beginning. There's probably another option for Cooper. Foster care, or maybe there's a long-lost relative out there."

Cam shook her head. "Libby had no relatives other than her grandmother. She wanted me to do this for her."

"What about the father?" Dad said. "Do you know where he is?"

"I don't even know who he is. Libby would never discuss him. Never even told me his name. She went to college, earned a spot sophomore year on the track team, came back pregnant, and boom. College for Libby ended. Track ended. Motherhood began."

"You were there, though," Dad said. "You've been with that little boy since his first breath."

Maddie had a thoughtful look on her face. "Mom always told us that life would surprise us with important choices, and our true character would emerge in how we responded." She pushed a lock of hair behind her ear. "I think this is a critical moment for Cam. The fate of a little boy has been put in her lap, and she has to decide if she's up to the challenge. Personally, I think she is. I think if she said no, she'd regret it for the rest of her life. But it is her decision, and hers alone to make."

"Thank you, Maddie. You should consider counseling as a career." Cam blew out a puff of air. "You're right. I would forever regret not taking care of him. This is the last thing I can do for Libby. Somehow, I will manage. I will figure it out." She slapped her hands on her knees. "In fact, I want to do more than be his legal guardian. I am going to adopt him. Legally. And I want to flip his name from Grayson Cooper to Cooper Grayson. For Libby's sake."

"I like that," Maddie said. "He's only four years old. You could use both names for a while and segue into calling him Cooper."

Dad gave a nod, crossing his arms against his chest. "Cam, you're not alone in this. We're here too. You can count on us."

"Dad's right," Maddie said. "It takes a village to raise a child, and we'll be Cooper's village."

A smile began in Cam and lifted her spirits ever so slightly, the first since that awful day.

Eight

PAUL STARED AT THE DISTANT SEA. He'd woken early and taken a walk down the path that led to the rocky beach below Moose Manor. He wanted to watch the morning light fill the horizon with that peachy glow he'd remembered. First break. It was one of his favorite things that he used to do as a college kid when he worked at Camp Kicking Moose. It was a sweet time in his life.

He had dreamed about Corinna last night. Coming here . . . it triggered all kinds of buried memories. It was what he had hoped for, to be able to think of her without his thoughts invariably ending on *that* day, to the frantic phone call from a hysterical Blaine that changed life forevermore.

Corinna's death had been so sudden. There'd been no time to prepare for it, and what happened to the mind after bereavement made no sense. You just coped, got through it, one day at a time. Until it was time to move on.

But to *this*?

He woke up this morning feeling overwhelmed, filled with uncertainty. It was one thing to buy Camp Kicking Moose from a distance, and an entirely different thing to be here, assessing its pitiful condition. Hundreds of hours of physical labor stretched out in front of him. And then what? He was no visionary. He had no experience in the hospitality business—running a camp or managing staff.

Oh, what had he done? What had he done?

Corinna had a favorite saying: life was full of simple miracles, if you just opened your eyes to them. His three daughters were here, under one roof. Cooper was here. That was a miracle and not a simple one.

Okay, he felt a little better. But what came next?

"Pray more, say less" was another maxim Corinna was fond of, especially so when Paul would get on a treadmill of worry. Like he was now.

"Okay, okay, I'm listening," he said, shouting to God in as loud a voice as he could muster. "Now what?"

No response.

She'd only be gone a few days. A week at most. Cam had brought along a map from the office to show Cooper where she'd be on her business trip. He had stayed with Dad or Maddie before when she'd had to travel for business, and she had developed a very specific strategy to provide reassurance for him. She even had a tracking device on her phone so Cooper could follow her every movement. It had been a successful method to relieve worries he had about her absence.

It irked Cam that Principal Voxer kept referring to Cooper's sensitivity as acute anxiety. Ridiculous. She was certain that highly intelligent people—Albert Einstein or Stephen Hawking came to mind—were very mindful of things as children, like their mother picking them up late from school, and attentive to the possibility of natural disasters, and had to be sheltered from the day's news because of the upset it caused.

To her shock, Cooper was not at all concerned when Cam told him about her business trip to London as she tucked him into bed that night. She should've been happy about his sense of comfort with her father and sisters. She should've felt a great relief that Cooper seemed more at home at this odd Camp Kicking Moose than he did in their city apartment, or at his expensive private school. She should've been grateful that her family was so willing to help her out when she needed it. After all, Cooper was her responsibility, not theirs, yet they never made her feel that way. Maddie had meant it when she said that raising a child took a village, and they were Cooper's village.

Super early the next morning, on her way to meet Captain Ed's car-toting barge—which, by the way, he charged a fortune to do—Cam drove past the Lunch Counter and noticed the light was on. On an impulse, she stopped in for a cup of coffee to go. Peg was standing near the oven with a baking sheet in her mitted hand, her brow furrowed. Her red hair was tied back in a royal blue polka-dotted headband.

Cam set her purse on the stool next to her, sat down, and leaned on her elbows to peer at Peg's latest creation. "What is it? Or . . . was it supposed to be?"

"Mornin', hon." Peg set down the baking sheet. "They're peanut butter cookies."

"Huh," Cam said. She wouldn't have even recognized them as cookies. If so, the batter had run together into a large blob. "Blaine used to make an incredible peanut butter cookie. I think she said the secret was in the brand of peanut butter." She hadn't thought about those cookies in years. Instantly, she craved one. But not Peg's. Those looked like something the coon cat had thrown up.

Peg pulled off the oven mitts. "How'd that girl learn to cook so well?" She picked up a coffee pitcher and held it up to Cam.

"In a to-go cup, please. I have to meet the ferry." She opened her purse to look for her wallet and got a whiff of tuna. Gross. "Blaine's always had a knack in the kitchen." She set a five-dollar bill on the countertop.

"But how? Someone must have taught her."

"Our mom. She and Blaine were constantly experimenting.

Our kitchen was a laboratory for cookies and pies and cakes. My friend Libby and I would race each other home after school to see what their latest concoction was." Wow, she hadn't thought about those days in a very long time.

Peg handed her a to-go cup of steaming hot coffee. "Honey, if you don't mind my asking, just where is that mother of yours? I would think she'd want to be part of this grand adventure."

Cam swirled the coffee, stalling. "She would've loved it. Apparently this whole cockamamie plan of Dad's was actually Mom's grand adventure. Dad's carrying it out." She set the coffee down. "Mom died a few years back. An accident."

"Oh honey," Peg said, her round face crumpled in sympathy. "Oh honey, I'm sorry. I didn't mean to sound so nosy. Mainers are known for their buttoned-up lips, and here I go, being a regular buttinski."

Cam smiled. "It's not a secret. Don't worry about it."

"You poor little gals," Peg said, her blueberry eyes getting shiny. "No matter how old a girl gets, she needs her mother." She rubbed her hands together. "One thing I know for sure, you either get bitter or better by what life throws at you."

Cam's breath caught. Her mother used to say that same thing. She could practically hear her mother's voice: *Life presents you with important choices. You can lash out, become bitter. Or draw closer to God, become better.* Cam added a packet of sugar to her coffee and stirred. She needed to give herself a moment to regroup, to shift the conversation to safer ground. "Peg, can I ask you a question?"

"One for one. Go for it."

"I need the down-low on that schoolteacher. Is he any good?"

Peg's eyes darted past Cam. "Any good?"

"As a teacher. He looked a little . . . scruffy. Disheveled. His appearance tells me that he's probably very disorganized." She shifted her perch on the stool and leaned forward. "You see, Cooper might be in need of a new school. He's a very bright boy and

81

I'm a little worried that the scruffy schoolteacher might do more harm than good."

Peg's eyes went wide. "Oh honey . . . Seth Walker is one in a million. A true renaissance man. He's a peach of a man. A real peach."

Cam snorted. "His cheeks sure are peach fuzz. Does he ever shave?" She stirred the coffee with her spoon. Why were so many coffee grounds floating on top? "Do you happen to know if he's taken any college classes? I'm hoping he's not just a local fisherman with time on his hands during the winter."

"Oh, I'm pretty sure he's got himself a college diploma. And in his spare time, he got himself a goshawk to train too." Peg leaned forward. "And just so's you know, he's standing right behind you."

Cam spun around slowly on her stool to face Seth Walker, holding his guitar case in one hand, a big yellow Labrador retriever by his side. "Oh." She cleared her throat. "Um, I suppose you heard that."

"Every word," Seth said, one dark eyebrow arched. "Every single word."

Shoot. "My Cooper . . . he's a special case."

"All children are special," Seth said. He set down his guitar. "Peg, may I trouble you for a cup of coffee?" He sat on the stool next to Cam. "You want my résumé? Fine. Undergrad—double majored in molecular biology and human development. Master's degree in educational administration. I'm here on this little island—"

"Three Sisters," Peg interjected. "Seth, we gotta start using it so others do too." She clapped her hands together. "Me, I'm growing fond of the sound of it."

Seth gave her a nod. "—on Three Sisters Island to teach so that my student loans can get paid off. They're rather sizable. Private universities, all." He took the cup of coffee from Peg and sipped it. "Anything else you need to know?"

Cam swallowed. In the distance, the blast of the barge horn

announced its arrival at the Boon Dock. "Uh, no. Thank you for the résumé. I'd better go meet Captain Ed. Long day ahead." She grabbed her coffee and her purse and hurried to the door, but turned back to wave at both Peg and Seth. "One question. What's a goshawk?"

"It's a large, short-winged hawk."

"And you train it?"

"In a way. With hopes of releasing it soon."

"I see." But she didn't. Now was not the time to ask more questions about training a hawk. She lifted a hand in a wave. Seth didn't return her wave. He stared at her as if she were an oddity from a circus. Even the dog stared at her with a baffled look.

After she drove her car onto the barge, she got out and walked toward its stern. She leaned against the railing to gaze at Three Sisters Island. The sun was cresting the trees that ridged the rim of the island, casting a red-gold eye over the harbor. A pair of seagulls squawked overhead, but the water lay quiet this morning. Mirror-like. Cam inhaled, touched by the island's natural beauty, grateful for it. Sunrises and sunsets, her mother had always said, were shows staged by God. Always new, always changing.

Mom. Why did this island bring up so much about her mom? Other than old stories, Cam had no association of her mother with this island. Maybe it was because Mom had always wanted to bring her daughters here.

Cam didn't let herself think of her mom very often. Doing so brought up sad, confused feelings; it was better, easier, to avoid thinking of Mom and stay busy with work and Cooper.

Just shifting her thoughts to work provided an immediate endorphin boost, a lift to her spirits. A week ago, if someone would've told her that she'd be leaving one island to fly to another, across the Atlantic Ocean, she wouldn't have believed it. Such opposite islands. The barge engine chugged, jerked to life, and eased away, reversing its path, wrinkling the reflections of boat masts in the water. Distance grew between Cam and Three Sisters Island.

She should've felt excited—she was on her way to London, for goodness' sake. A place she'd always wanted to go.

Instead, strangely, she felt like she was missing out on something.

The hum of an incoming lobster boat caught her attention. She cupped her hands around her mouth to shout, "Catch many bugs?" Bugs was lobster lingo for, well, lobsters. It was what she'd heard others say to each other in casual greeting, a Maine version of "How are you today?"

One of the fishermen looked up at her on the barge and shook his head sadly. "Not a one worth keeping."

Blaine heard a funny noise and went to the window to see what it was. An old green minivan rumbled through the break in the woods and stopped near the house. The door swung open and Peg jumped out, holding a plate covered in tin foil. Blaine hurried outside.

"Just the sister I needed to see," Peg said. "I had some messages to deliver and thought you might like some cookies to go along with them."

Blaine unfolded the foil on the plate of cookies. They did not resemble cookies.

"I know," Peg said in a woeful voice. "Didn't turn out the way I'd hoped. I know you're awful busy, but I was hoping you might come by the Lunch Counter and give me a few pointers. Your sister stopped by early this morning and said you had a good recipe for these."

Blaine broke off a piece and sniffed. "What are they?"

"You can't tell?" Peg sighed. "Peanut butter cookies."

Oh boy. Peanut butter cookies were supposed to be soft. These were brittle. "I think I might be able to help. I have a really good peanut butter cookie recipe." She covered the cookies back up with foil. Maybe the coon cat would eat them. "You had a message?"

"Three, actually. One for your dad. The mayor's looking for him. And then one for your sister. Some fellow with a very long name called to say he's trying to find your sister Maddie and she's not answering her phone."

"Ah. Bet that's her high-society boyfriend Tre." Or was he now a fiancé? Maddie had never answered Cam's question. Had she agreed to marry Tre? "And the last message?"

"For you. From a fellow named Artie who sounds like a gem. A real gem. He was smart enough to call the Lunch Counter first. He said he knew that a local restaurant was the hub of a town." Her face brightened in a big smile. "I think I might have a crush on that boy. Too bad he's too young for me. Anyhows, he wants you to call him just as soon as you can."

Dad walked out to join them. "Welcome to Moose Manor, Peg Legg."

"If he keeps calling me that," Peg said under her breath, "I might have to teach him a lesson."

"Go for it," Blaine whispered in return. "He thinks he's being funny. I try not to encourage his jokes."

"Morning, Paul. I made you some cookies." Peg took the plate from Blaine and handed it to Dad with a big friendly smile.

As her dad tried to take a bite of Peg's cookie—and it wouldn't break off—Blaine had to bite her lower lip to keep from laughing.

Whatever the task, Paul believed in doing the hard part first. A man could do any sort of job if he could break it down into parts and then deal with it, piece by piece, hard to easy. The first thing on his mind was finding painters for Moose Manor. That bright pink color made him nauseous, seasick-green, each time he drove into the driveway. Peg Legg had given him a list of names for men on the island who had spare time on their hands. He called the entire list and left messages. So far, no bites, but he remained hopeful. Cam had picked out house paint colors for him, so he acted on faith and ordered the paint from the closest hardware store in Mount Desert. Captain Ed told him he'd be bringing gallons of paint over on the ferry today, so he drove down to Boon Dock to pick them up.

As he carried the buckets of paint to his car, Cooper trailing behind him, he passed two long-bearded, heavyset young men sitting in a fishing boat, cleaning their day's catch. "Chout!"

Paul stopped. "Pardon me?"

"Chout! You're about to trip on a line."

Paul glanced down. Oh . . . he got it now. Chout. Watch out. "Say, you fellows interested in doing some painting when you're not fishing?"

"Might be. How much you paying?"

"Fair wage for a good job."

The one turned to the other, got the nod, then turned back. "Make it a little more than fair and we'll be there in the morning. Soon as we bring in the day's catch."

"Well, good, then. I'll write down the address. I'm Paul Grayson, by the way."

"We know. The one who stole Camp Kicking Moose."

Paul cleared his throat. "Paid full price for it." Everybody in this town knew everything about you. "Can I get your names?"

"I'm Peter and he's Porter." They pronounced it Peet-ah and Port-ah.

"Do you have a last name?"

"Phinney."

"As in, the mayor's sons?"

"That's right." Porter squinted at him. "Is that a problem?"

He recalled Peg's warning to stay clear of the Phinney brothers, but on the other hand, he had no other options. Besides, he felt it was always best to make up his own mind about people. "No, it's no problem at all. I'm headed to your father's house right now." He gave a slight nod. "See you in the morning."

"Hey!"

Paul turned around.

"Them girls of yours . . . they single? They's wicked cunnin'."

Paul read his T-shirt: *I'm Your Maine Squeeze*. "All spoken for. Each one." He headed down the rest of the dock, wondering if he had just made a colossal mistake by ignoring Peg's advice and hiring the Phinney boys.

Cooper trotted behind him. "Grandpa, what does that mean . . . all spoken for?"

"It means that those two need to stay far, far away from my daughters."

Paul drove to the address that Peg Legg had given him and stopped the car. "Cooper, this is the mayor's house. You coming or staying?"

"Coming." Cooper pushed his glasses up the bridge of his nose. "Aunt Maddie said to be careful of stranger danger."

Paul sighed. Maddie was a champion worrier, infecting others like a cold virus. "Come on, then."

It was an impressive classic Maine house for a ragtag island. A two-story saltbox, covered with silvered shingles. Paul let Cooper rap the heavy brass knocker in the center of the door. He knocked and knocked, and finally someone came to the door. A rather deluxe-sized woman, short and wide, answered and peered at them. You wouldn't call her a welcoming sort.

"Is this Mayor Phinney's house?"

"Ayup."

"Is he home?"

"No."

"Uh, by any chance are you Mrs. Mayor Phinney?"

"Ayup." She looked him up and down, lips pleated. "So you're Paul Grayson." She reached over to the table stand to pick up a letter. "Here you go. You saved the town a stamp." The door shut.

Paul opened the letter and skimmed it. It was an energy tax bill for $56,498.00. On top was stamped in bright red, Delinquent. He exhaled, as if he'd just been kicked in the gut. No wonder he'd gotten Camp Kicking Moose for a song.

Nine

LONDON WAS MORE THAN CAM could have imagined, modern and ancient, classic and quintessential. At least, it looked that way from the twenty-fifth floor of the office high-rise. She spent all day Monday talking to employees, in-depth, before she dove into reports. By Wednesday night, she hit paydirt. Something that made her want to do cartwheels up and down the office hallways. A simple accounting error had doubled promotion expenses and understated gross revenue; correcting it would increase sales by one million dollars. One. Million. Dollars. The company could have a sharp uptick in fourth-quarter profits—just what Evan Snowden, her boss, had sent her to do.

Early the next morning, she had a video conference with Evan and told him about her discovery. Oh, the joys of technology. She wouldn't have missed that stunned look on his face for anything.

When he recovered from being shocked speechless, he asked, "How much?"

"It will increase sales by one million."

"That means profitability is up by half a million." Evan shook his head in happy disbelief. "Could there be even more?"

"More of a sales increase? I don't think so."

"But there could be, right?"

"I went through everything with a fine-toothed comb, Evan."

He seemed unconvinced. "Cam, I need you to sit tight for a while."

"Sit tight? How long?"

"For a while. Weeks. Months. Maybe . . . indefinitely."

Somebody came into the Boston office conference room and Evan put her on pause, freezing him in an odd pose.

While Cam waited, she thought about staying on in London. She wanted to stay, so badly—she hadn't had a free moment to explore the city, not even one of those highly efficient Hop On, Hop Off bus tours—but she had Cooper to think of.

Cooper. She sighed. She'd seen two missed calls from Cooper's school. She meant to return the calls, but an eight-hour time difference made it a challenge. That phone call from Ada Voxer she didn't really want to get, anyway. She knew what it meant. She knew. Time to find a new school for Cooper. She'd made two inquiring calls over the last few days to potential London schools for Cooper. One international school sounded ideal for Cooper— small classes, high teacher-to-student ratio. But for one critical snag: a waiting list for his grade.

She had no idea how long Evan wanted her to remain in London, but she knew she couldn't say no. She didn't want to say no. But how would she handle Cooper and schooling? Maybe, if it was just for a few weeks, maybe just until summer vacation, she could pay a tutor to keep him up to grade level. Cooper was so bright, so exceptionally intelligent. A busy mind like his, it needed to be challenged. Maddie's warnings echoed in her head: What about Cooper's emotional needs? What about his sense of security?

But . . . wouldn't a stint of living in London help him? After all, life was full of change. Resiliency, flexibility, adjusting . . . these were important qualities. This experience might provide an opportunity for Cooper to develop them.

Argh . . . Cam's head was spinning. She needed time.

When Evan finally unpaused the video call, she had made a

decision. Before he could say another word, she told him that she had to get back to the States to take care of a few things, and then she would return to London to stay indefinitely. "Cooper will need to come back with me," she said. "That means some kind of schooling. And I'll need a short-term furnished apartment, not a hotel."

"Right, right. We can talk when you get back," Evan said, sounding vague and distracted. "Just get those verified sales figures faxed to me as soon as possible." He ended the call abruptly.

Strange. Something had grabbed Evan's attention in that brief minute or two while the video call had been paused. Normally, he ran things past her. She left the conference room feeling a little . . . let down.

Blaine dug through a few boxes marked "Kitchen" until she finally found her mother's recipe box. She sat down on the floor and sifted through the recipes, feeling a peculiar sting at the sight of her mother's neat handwriting. She hadn't touched this box since her mother had passed. But she hadn't stopped thinking about Peg Legg and her amazement at Blaine's skills and knowledge in the kitchen. Were they really that unusual? She'd never thought so. She had just followed her mother's instructions and done what Mom did.

It used to be their thing together, baking. Once she and her mom even did a three-tiered wedding cake for a neighbor's daughter. As they carefully walked it over to their neighbor's, an off-leash dog galloped up to them, barking, and they nearly dropped the cake. Blaine laughed, surprised by the memory. The cake made it across the street, and everyone oohed and aahed over it, and two people said they wanted to book them for upcoming parties.

But not one month later, her mother was gone and Blaine hadn't baked since. Not until Peg Legg's disastrous rock-hard biscuits jolted her out of her slumber. Peg seemed to need her, at least she said she did, and if her coffee was any indication of her kitchen sense, she definitely needed help.

Blaine found the recipe for peanut butter cookies and tucked it in her jeans pocket. On second thought, she took a few more recipes for cookies and scones and added them to her pocket. Dad and Cooper were pressure-hosing Moose Manor to get it ready for the painters—who, two days later, still hadn't shown up. Maddie was upstairs scrubbing the bathroom with Clorox bleach—it was the one cleaning supply she trusted to kill every germ that posed a danger—and would lasso Blaine into more scrubbing if she stuck around. Enough of that! She left a note on the kitchen table and drove into town.

The Lunch Counter was open but empty. Blaine sniffed an acrid smell—something was burning. She grabbed a mitt, opened the oven door, and pulled out a muffin tin filled with something that was oozing over the top. A minute later, Peg came through the back door with a big box in her arms. "Oh honey! I am so glad you're here. Thank you for saving those. I got a call from Nancy the grocer. She needed something to help her psoriasis and I completely forgot about those things."

Blaine looked down at the tray in her mitted hand. "What are these . . . things?"

"Blueberry muffins." Peg looked at them. "Leastways, they were." She let out an unhappy sigh. "Something went terribly wrong. What do you think happened?"

"Well, my mother used to say that problems happened in the oven when the cook left the kitchen."

Peg laughed. "That might be my number one problem right there. I'm trying to manage a general store and a lunch counter at the same time."

"Peg, have you thought of doing just one or the other?" Hopefully, keep the store and ax the lunch counter. Her eyes caught the little salt and pepper shakers shaped like lobster claws. So tacky they made her cringe.

"Can't. I need the income, hon. As you can see, this island isn't experiencing a robust economy." She grinned. "That's where you come in. You're going to help me get this lunch counter up to snuff before Memorial Day, when this place really gets hopping."

"That's in less than two months."

"I know, I know. So let's get started. Tell me what to do and I'll do it."

Blaine glanced up at the chalkboard menu. "Well, to start, what are your bestsellers?"

Peg looked up at it. "Well, bestsellers might be a generous way to phrase it, but I've had the least complaints about the peanut butter and jelly sandwich. I just slap on the Jif, toss on a big spoonful of grape jelly, and serve it up."

"The least complaints? You mean, you've gotten complaints for everything else on that menu?"

Peg looked up thoughtfully at the menu, then dropped her chin to look at Blaine in her matter-of-fact way. "Ayup." She put her hands on her hips. "Honey, how's about you do the cooking? Make some of that good macaroni and cheese you were telling me about the other day, the one with that stinky cheese—"

"Goat cheese."

"—and maybe some tomato soup that isn't out of a can. Heck, do whatever you want. Just get the customers in here and keep 'em coming back."

"Oh, I don't know, Peg." It seemed like a little too much, a little over the top. And a lot of responsibility. "With a little more work, I think you can be trusted to make some simple recipes."

"Hon, you're not catching my drift. I don't like to cook. Never have. But you do."

"The thing is, Peg, I'm not sure how long I'll be staying at Three Sisters Island. Dad wants me to head back to college. Well, first he wants me to pick a major, then he wants me to"—she deepened her voice to mimic her dad's low scratchy one—"get on back to college and finish up." She grinned. "He might have used more colorful language than that."

But Peg didn't appear to be listening anymore. "I'll handle your father. Look, sugar, for now, you're my angel, sent straight from Heaven."

Blaine liked college, but she'd never thought of it as Heaven. She let out a puff of air. Someone considered her to be an answer to a prayer. Amazing! Her heart started racing, and in a good way. This could be an exciting challenge, and her mind started spinning with ideas. "Peg, how would you feel if we revamped the menu, started from scratch? Create a new menu with dishes that I'll teach you how to make. Simple things, but really good food."

Peg let out a long hmm. "Honey, I was hoping you would do the cooking, but I'll take what I can get. I've just got to do something."

"First," Blaine said, wrapping an apron around her waist, "the coffee."

"What's wrong with my coffee?"

Oh, what's right with it? "Let's aim for a pot without grounds floating through it and work up from there."

By the end of the day, Blaine had taught Peg how to make a good enough pot of coffee and a scone that didn't chip a tooth. Blaine thought they'd have time to make a batch of cookies that didn't bleed into each other to form a giant glob, but the day ended too soon. The coffee-making took a ridiculous amount of the morning, five pots. And after all that, with Peg watching Blaine's every move, it was only good enough. Not great.

Peg did not have a natural instinct in the kitchen, something she admitted aloud, and a self-assessment that Blaine soon agreed with. It was astonishing to her. Peg was obviously intelligent, yet she could not seem to make a recipe turn out the way it was supposed to. Peg took copious notes on index cards for everything Blaine taught her. Every detail in the process. Cheat sheets, she called them. She thumbtacked the index cards on the wall. Above the coffeepot was the coffee-making card. Above the flour jar were tips on making scones. She treated Blaine as if she was a creative genius, as if she couldn't believe that the same ingredients in Blaine's hands turned into something amazing, while left to her own doing, turned into something barely edible. The strange thing, it was true. Side by side they sifted flour, added ingredients, gently worked the dough, and still, Peg's scones were truly horrible. Amazing.

"Honey," Peg said as she sampled Blaine's scone, "you have a gift. You just don't see it, but believe me, you've got a gift."

As Blaine drove back to Moose Manor, winding along the road that was starting to become familiar to her, she felt a queer feeling that had gone missing for a very long time. Happiness.

It was such a pretty day that Maddie brought Cooper along with her to town to buy more gallons of Clorox bleach. Afterward, they walked down to Boon Dock. She thought he might enjoy playing with the kittens that lounged on the dock in the sun, the ones that lived on the fish that escaped from fishermen's nets or bait dropped out of buckets. He refused and she didn't push him. Pushing Cooper got nowhere. She suggested that he make a sand castle or chase some waves, but he wouldn't take his socks and shoes off. He sat on a bench, watching sandpipers run along the shore. She walked closer to the dock to pick up the signal.

Peg had said the cell phone signal was coming from Mount Desert, just across the water. Like so many things Peg told them— things like warning Dad not to expect the Phinney brothers to show up and paint Moose Manor, and sure enough, they hadn't— she was right. The phone worked. Tre answered on the first ring.

"Mads! Are you all right? I thought something might have happened to you."

"I'm fine. Lots going on here and I have trouble getting phone service." Just as she started to tell him about the island, and the camp, he cut her off with bigger news.

"Mother booked the church."

"She . . . did what?"

"For us. Our wedding."

"When?"

"Saturday, September twenty-third."

"Hold it. Which year?"

"This year, silly."

That was crazy. Too fast. "Tre, I've always wanted a spring wedding."

"I think it's best to go with Mother's suggestion."

"Why? Why can't we decide on our own wedding date?"

"What does it matter?"

What does it matter? She sputtered, "It's *our* wedding!"

"Oh Mads, I don't know why you're surprised. I'm an only child. Mother's waited all my life for this. She doesn't do anything in a small way. She's got a wedding planner already booked. Someone impossible to get, she said, but she worked a miracle. She's got a magnificent wedding in store for us. The works. A formal church ceremony. Afterward, dinner and dancing."

Maddie felt like she was about to break down and bawl. "Tre, the thing is, I've always wanted to get married on the beach." Maybe even here, on Three Sisters Island.

Tre laughed. "On the beach?" He hooted. "Mother would never go for that."

"But . . . I can't ask your mother to plan our wedding."

"But you can! She's thrilled to do it." He paused. "She knows you don't have a mother. It's her way of trying to connect to you, Mads."

Oh, oh . . . well, that made it a little better. Sort of. Maddie and Mrs. Smith had a very tenuous relationship. No matter what Maddie said or did, even the clothes she wore . . . she seemed to evoke Mrs. Smith's disapproval, masked as disappointment. "Tre, come up and visit next weekend. I want you to see this island for yourself."

95

"I thought you'd be back in Boston next weekend."

"I can't. Cooper is here for the week while Cam is on a business trip. I don't want to leave him. Dad has a lot on his to-do list, and Blaine's here, but she's not much help. Anyway, I need to stay." It wasn't just for them. She didn't want to leave.

"Skippy's wedding. You're supposed to be my plus one."

Oof. She'd forgotten. Blocked it out, more likely. Skippy was Tre's fraternity friend, her least favorite of his friends. Her absolute *least* favorite. "I'm sorry, Tre."

"Wait. Just like that? You're not coming? You can't be serious."

Skippy would be too drunk to even notice her absence. "I'm sorry, Tre. I can't. I need to be here. Take someone else. Take your cousin Courtney. She loves weddings."

Silence. He was upset, and in a way, she didn't blame him. She would feel the same way if he bailed on her at the last moment. Going to events together was one of their top delights about being a couple. They were both shy introverts, socially awkward. But she would not, could not leave Cooper. Dad might forget him and Blaine would feed him sugar and flour. Maddie was Cooper's village.

A fishing boat returned to its slip on the dock, trailed by squawking seagulls. The engine and the seagulls drowned out her feeble attempts to make Tre understand her situation. "Tre, I really am sorry," she said, practically shouting.

"I gotta go, Madison."

Oh boy, oh boy. He must be really upset with her. He hardly ever called her Madison, only Mads, a pet name she didn't particularly care for. But on this, she wasn't budging. "Please try to come up soon."

"How long are you going to be up there? I thought you said just a few days."

She didn't know how to answer that, at least not in a way that would make any sense to him. A wisp of a dream had been sparked by Cam the other night—the notion of hanging her own shingle.

Opening a counseling office. She had never considered having a business of her own. "We'll talk about it when you come." Now she was shouting. "I'll call again soon!"

As soon as the phone call ended, the boat engine turned off and the air was silent-still, broken only by the lapping of waves on the shore. The natural beauty filled her in a way she couldn't find words to explain. Tre had to see this island for himself, then he'd understand.

Still, this phone call had ended on a sour note. Whenever there was friction in their relationship, Tre slipped into avoidance mode. Classic passive-aggressive behavior. It would be up to her to smooth things out.

The more she thought about it, the more it infuriated her that his mother had taken over their wedding, but Maddie knew she had to tread carefully on this topic. Tre and his mother had a very close connection, and he could be quite protective about her.

"Hello there."

She spun around to see Seth Walker and his dog walk toward them. Seth had one arm raised, elbow out, and it was covered in a large leather glove. Perched on his arm was a big . . . bird. "You're Seth, right? The schoolteacher?"

"I am. This is Lola, my goshawk. And the dog is Dory."

Lola the goshawk gave her a ferocious glare. Goodness, these island birds could be intimidating. "I'm Maddie. Maddie Grayson. One of Paul Grayson's daughters."

"I remember. You were on the barge with your dad. How's his sore throat?"

"Laryngitis, actually. He had a bad case a while ago and his voice hasn't recovered. Yet. It hasn't recovered yet. He's sure he'll get it back."

"Where did the other sister go?"

Maddie spun around and pointed to the Lunch Counter. "She's helping Peg with some baking."

"No, the other one."

"Cam? She's off to London for the week." She turned to the bench. Cooper had his eyes on the hawk on Seth's arm. "She should be back this weekend." Maddie hoped so, anyway. "We're watching Cooper while she's gone. We do that when she's on business trips."

"So Cooper's dad . . . he's not in the picture?"

Maddie took in a deep breath. "That . . . is a very long story. The short version is . . . there is no dad." The hawk swiveled its head toward Cooper, as if she knew she was being watched.

Seth frowned. "Guys like that—they chap my hide. But then God reminds me that it wasn't so long ago that I was that kind of a guy. But for his grace, you know?"

Maddie jerked her head up. "I do know." A surprisingly spiritually sensitive insight. She wouldn't have expected something like that from a guy with a hawk hanging off his arm.

Slowly, Seth turned to face the bench. "Cooper, want to come meet Lola?"

Eyes fixed on the hawk, Cooper slowly shook his head.

"You sure? She's tied down so she won't fly off. I won't let anything happen to you."

Cooper shook his head even more vigorously.

Maddie stepped in before Seth asked again. She could see Cooper's anxiety rising: his hands were fisted in balls, his knees were squeezed tightly together. "That's nice of you to ask. He's a little nervous around animals." Hawks, too. Frankly, so was Maddie. She kept a healthy distance from that mean-looking hawk.

Seth lowered his voice. "Is he okay?"

"He has some . . . social anxiety."

Seth watched Cooper and she wondered what he was thinking. From the look on his face, she could guess: Cooper clearly had some issues. "What I meant was . . . why is he dressed like that?"

"Like what?"

"Like a beekeeper."

Maddie turned to Cooper. She had insisted on the wide-brimmed hat and long-sleeved shirt and trousers. "To prevent sunburn." Of course.

"But it's very late in the day. And it's only March."

"Have you read the latest information about sun exposure? It's enough to make you want to stay indoors."

A look of alarm flitted through Seth's eyes. "Is Cooper's mom coming back soon?"

"Yes. Pretty sure." They hadn't heard from Cam, but hadn't expected to. If she was going to be delayed, she would have called the Lunch Counter.

"Good." He smiled, and turned to wave at Cooper. "That's good."

It was nice of Seth to show interest in Cooper. A sign of a good teacher, one who paid attention to children.

Whoa. Hold the train. Wait just a minute.

Seth kept circling the conversation back to Cam. If Maddie wasn't mistaken—and when it came to reading cues, she thought she had a talent for it—this lumberjack schoolteacher seemed more than a little interested in Cam.

Wow. Good luck with *that*, lumberjack Seth. Cam made no time for men in her life. Maddie couldn't even remember the last time she had a date.

Her phone rang and she lifted it to see who was calling, hoping it was Tre, but she didn't recognize the number. Seth excused himself with a nod and headed down to the water. Dory the dog trotted at his side.

Maddie's heart instantly sank when the caller identified herself as Ada Voxer, the principal at Cooper's school. "We've been trying to get hold of Cam," Mrs. Voxer said, "but she's not returning calls. You're listed as the emergency contact."

Maddie cringed. "Cam's in London for the week. Cooper's with me." She cleared her throat. "Is anything wrong?" *Please say no, please say no.*

"We had a staff meeting this week and came to the conclusion that our school can no longer accommodate Cooper's needs."

"Just . . . like that?" Maddie said, shocked. "You can't do that, can you?"

"We can."

"Does Cam have any idea?"

"Yes. Last week, before spring break, I told her this outcome would be likely."

"What did she say?"

The principal sighed.

Never mind. Maddie knew. Most likely, Cam didn't think they'd really do it. That was Cam, in a nutshell. If she believed something strongly enough, it would come true. A philosophy that worked until it didn't. "Mrs. Voxer, I'm a marriage and family therapist. There must be something that can be worked out. For Cooper's sake. He needs the stability of your school."

"You're a counselor?"

"Yes." Almost. Not yet certified, which meant she had not actually had experience with patients yet. But she was highly prepared for it.

"Well, then, it should be apparent to you that this little boy needs help. His anxiety problems are only getting worse, not better."

That much Maddie knew.

"He's a very bright boy. I don't think I've ever seen a child with his intellect. But it's getting buried, almost hobbled by his anxiety. I'm worried if there isn't some kind of concerted effort soon, he'll never reach his potential. And I do believe Cooper has tremendous potential."

Softening, Maddie said, "What do you suggest?"

"Off the record?"

"Yes."

"Another school isn't going to solve Cooper's basic problem. What he really needs is more of his mother's time and attention."

Maddie cringed. The two things Cam couldn't give him.

Ten

IT WAS DARK, nearly ten o'clock, but the porch lights of Moose Manor were lit as Cam finally pulled into the driveway on Friday night. The front door opened and out came Dad, striding down to greet her. A wash of gratitude overwhelmed Cam, and her eyes filled with tears.

"What's this?" Dad said when he opened her car door. He looked alarmed. He'd never been good with crying girls. He'd sent them to their mother for comfort. "Didn't the trip go well?"

"It went great." She wiped away tears. "Jet lag is catching up with me, that's all."

Relief washed over his face and he smiled. "In the morning, Cooper and I will give you a tour of all we've done this week with the cabins. Lots of clean-out, lots of junk hauled away. You'll be impressed." He pulled her suitcase out of the trunk of the car and started toward the house.

Cam stopped and stared up at the house. In the dark, when you couldn't see that hideous pink color, it looked lovely and welcoming. "Dad, I don't know why you're so determined to make this place a summer camp for kids. It could be so much more."

Her dad abruptly pivoted and set down the suitcase. "Like what?"

"The reason people come to this island only for day trips is because there's no place to stay. Those cabins—they could be used for families instead of kids and counselors. It wouldn't take much to make them cozy and inviting." Her gaze swept over the house. "And this old dinosaur . . . it could be an upscale hotel. A year-round destination."

Her dad stared up at the house. "What would bring people here in the winter?"

"Lots of things. Cross-country skiing, for one. Snowshoeing, for another. Hiking paths would be perfect for both of those sports, assuming Three Sisters gets enough snow."

"Seth Walker said it gets plenty of snow. He said the kids use snowmobiles to get around."

"See? There's another idea. Snowmobiling."

Dad turned around in a circle, peering out at the darkness as if he was trying to imagine what she'd described. "That's just winter though. What about fall and spring?"

"Hunting in the fall. There's plenty of deer. I nearly hit three on the road getting here just now."

"And spring?"

"Hmm, bird-watchers? After all, the island sits on the Atlantic flyway. Bet there's all kinds of migrating birds come springtime." She yawned. "Cooper's asleep?"

Dad jerked, as if jolted out of a daydream. "Sound asleep. He's been my chief assistant all week long. He's been a fine help. Didn't miss you at all."

Ouch. "Not at all?"

"Oh, well, I'm sure he did," Dad said. "But we kept him busy so he hardly had time to think about missing you."

It was a nice try, but Cam saw through her dad's pity-backpedaling.

As she followed behind him toward the house, she kept fighting the oddest feeling. Like she was being pulled apart, torn in half.

Cooper was asleep but still wearing his glasses, so she carefully took them off and set them next to his sleeping bag, right next to his ball of string. She sifted her fingers through his soft hair, and when he stirred, she scooped him into her arms, waking him gently. He hugged her in that way of his, all in, arms thrown around her neck as if he were clutching her for dear life.

She kissed each cheek and tucked the top of the sleeping bag up to his chin, then watched as he fell back to sleep. She loved him so much. He was growing up so fast. Too fast.

A few minutes later, she walked into the kitchen. Her dad and sisters sat around the big table, drinking decaf coffee made by Blaine. Cam inhaled the fragrance as she held the mug in her hands. "Cinnamon?"

"A dash in the grounds," Blaine said.

Cam sat down and said, "So, I have an announcement."

Blaine bolted from her chair. "I'm outta here."

"Sit down. You'll want to hear this." Cam ignored Blaine's dramatic slide back into her chair. "I had a great week in London. So great, in fact, that my boss wants me to return and spend more time in the London office." She took in a deep breath. "Of course I said yes."

"Why 'of course'?" Blaine asked. "Why can't you just say no?"

Cam frowned. "Because I don't *want* to say no. I work hard for opportunities like this."

"What about Cooper?" Maddie asked.

"I've got it all figured out," Cam said. "That's where you come in. Cooper's village, remember?" She explained about the waiting list for the school, and about hiring a tutor. "I'm thinking that I'll take Blaine along with me."

"As a tutor to Cooper?" Maddie said. "Blaine? You've got to be kidding."

"Seems like that could be pretty complicated," Dad said. "Getting a visa—"

"I think that could get ironed out. And it's just for a few weeks. Maybe a month or two. Or three. Maybe through the summer."

Blaine raised her hand. "You know, I might have an opinion about this."

Maddie was fixed on Cam. "This might be a good opportunity for you, but what about Cooper?"

"This *is* best for him. Living overseas will be an incredibly enriching experience for him. He can travel to other countries, learn a foreign language—"

"Pretty sure they speak English in England," Blaine said in a tetchy tone.

"He's only seven years old!" Maddie said.

Cam's jaw dropped. "As if you know how to raise a child . . . just because you've taken some online child development courses."

Maddie thrust a finger in the air. "One course was online. Just one."

"Yoohoo," Blaine said. "Does anyone wonder how I feel about this big idea?"

Dad waved a hand in the air. "Maddie's got a point, Cam. Cooper's needs should be considered as you make this decision."

"That's exactly what I'm trying to do!" Cam set down her mug a little too hard and the coffee sloshed out. "Dad, did you ever once consider our needs when you traveled the country? No. Work came first. Always, always, work came first."

"Hooboy," Blaine said. "You got *that* right."

"Even now," Maddie said. "You sold our childhood home without any warning and bought this . . . this old, decrepit camp on a forsaken island . . . and we're left to figure out what that means for the rest of us."

No one spoke for a very long minute.

Dad leaned back in his chair, the picture of surprise. "So do you all wish I hadn't sold the house?"

All three girls answered at once. "Yes!"

"Then why didn't you want anything from it? I asked, and you all said no. Not a single memento. Nothing."

Blaine spoke first. "You caught me by surprise. I couldn't process that fast."

Maddie agreed. "You gave us no time to think."

Dad sighed. "I suppose I should have or could have brought you all into the discussion. It was easier to just tell you than to ask you. But you're grown women now"—he glanced at Blaine—"nearly grown."

Blaine scowled.

"The truth about the house," Dad said, "is that I needed to sell it. I needed to move on."

"What about us?" Maddie said. "Maybe we're not ready to move on."

"I am," Cam said. "That's what this entire discussion is all about. I'm moving on. Dad's moving on. So maybe it's high time Maddie and Blaine move on too."

Maddie lifted her palms in exasperation. "Cam, you're not moving *on*. You've *never* moved on. You just keep moving. There's a difference."

Just as Cam opened her mouth to object, her dad stopped her. "Hold your fire. Look, girls, I admit I have regrets about how my career took me away from home so much. Maybe that's why I bought this island. I'd hoped it could bring us all together. Not to separate us. I can't stop you from going to London, but I hope you'll consider the cost. Every decision comes with a cost, you know."

Oh, now *that* was ironic. It was a phrase Mom used to say, not Dad. And she used to say it *to* him. "This is my life, Dad," Cam said, patting her hand against her chest. "Mine and Cooper's. You're the one who always pushed me to strive to be the best I could be. This opportunity—these kinds of things don't come along every day. I can't pass it up."

"Why not?" Maddie said. "What would be so terrible about recognizing your limits? About respecting Cooper's limits? Instead, you keep pressuring him to be a mini-you."

"Limits? Pressuring him?" Cam squeezed her fists. "Maddie, you analyze everybody except yourself."

"What does that mean?"

"What are you doing up here on this deserted island? Escaping from reality."

"Wait. What? How?"

Cam was on a roll. She knew she should probably stop, she was exhausted and irritable, but her mouth was moving faster than her caution. "You finally finished graduate school—"

"On time! Like everybody else. You're the only one who seems to think that every year of education should be condensed in half."

"—and you're supposed to be pounding the pavement to get an internship, so instead you run off to a remote island. You're as bad as Blaine. You can't finish anything."

"Hey!" Blaine said. "I can hear you, ya know. I'm right here." She jumped up from her chair. "Not that anyone is listening, but *I* have an announcement to make. I am *not* going to London. I know what that would look like. Cam, you're going to be traveling all the time. Home on weekends. Arriving late on Friday night, leaving early Sunday morning. Am I right?"

"Maybe." Probably. Slowly, Cam nodded. "You could travel with me."

"Oh great. Stuck in a hotel room."

"You wouldn't have to be stuck in a hotel room. You could take Cooper sightseeing."

"Cam, don't you get it? Cooper won't go anywhere. He's afraid of . . . everything!" Blaine crossed her arms. "I've been suckered into your big ideas before. I know this drill. Remember the summer I lived with you?" She shook her head. "As much as I love Cooper, I've got things *I* want to do."

"What?" Dad said, eyes fixed on Blaine. "What do you want to do? I'm all ears."

Blaine frowned. "I haven't decided on a major, if that's what you mean."

"Okay, then I assume you mean more short-term things you want to do."

"Yes. Short-term things. For now. This last week, I've started to see what Dad is trying to do. I like it here. I can see how this island needs help. People like Peg Legg, she needs help. I like teaching Peg how to bake, because she is truly terrible at it and she really wants to learn." Blaine slid back into her chair. "I'm staying right here. So no, thank you for considering me as your live-in help, but I am not going to London."

Cam sipped her coffee, now tepid. Her big plan was unraveling. It shocked her that her little sister wasn't willing to come to London. Blaine was usually up for anything. It was a tactical error on Cam's part to bring it up in front of Dad and Maddie. Maybe tomorrow she could talk to Blaine privately, add some perks like a trip to Paris.

But then another option popped into her head, an even better idea. "Maybe Maddie could come with me to London." Why hadn't she thought of that before? Maddie was much better with kids than Blaine. "You could put it on your résumé as Cooper's resident therapist."

"His nanny, you mean." Maddie shook her head. "I can't."

"Why not?"

"Lots of reasons."

"Such as . . ."

"I have a wedding to plan."

Cam stared at her. "So you did say yes."

Maddie gave a slow nod.

Dad looked at her, frowning. "What's happened to the tradition of a young man asking the father for his daughter's hand in marriage?"

"That's kinda old school, Dad. He did have his family at the restaurant to celebrate."

"Wait just a minute." Dad leaned forward and placed his palms on the table. "So Tre thought to include his family in a celebration . . . but not yours?"

His voice was barely above a whisper—the end-of-the-day rasp. But Cam was thrilled that he was the one to say it. Usually, it was her job to point out the obvious.

All eyes were on Maddie, who seemed preoccupied with swirling her coffee. In the waiting quiet, pitter-patter sounds floated in from the other room.

Dad looked at Cam. "Cooper's asleep, isn't he?"

"Yes. Sound asleep. I checked."

More muffled sounds. "I bet it's that coon cat," Blaine said.

Cam tiptoed into the big room and stopped short with a gasp. The full moon poured light through the tall windows. String had been strung all over the room, back and forth, from one side to another. Then she spotted Cooper. He was winding string tightly around the sleeping bag next to his.

CAM, AGE 14

It was a blistering hot July afternoon. Somehow Dad had talked Mom into getting a puppy for Blaine's fifth birthday, a golden retriever named Winslow. The deal was that Blaine had to walk Winslow every day, but he had grown so fast and so big that she couldn't handle him. That meant that Cam and Maddie had to take turns walking around the block with the dog. Today was Cam's turn, and her tendency was to make Winslow walks in half the time. Very fast.

She burst into the house with the puppy, found Blaine on the back porch, handed his leash to her, came back inside, and shouted to Mom that she was leaving.

"I'm upstairs packing," she heard Mom call back. They were finally going to this island in Maine where her parents had met. Mom had talked about it for years and years, and Dad always agreed that they should go. Next summer for sure, he'd say.

But baseball teams played all summer long. And Cam's dad was a good sports announcer. He was now an announcer for a major league baseball team, traveling around the country for his team's series. For the last two summers, Dad had canceled family vacations at the last minute.

At the bottom of the stairs, Cam repeated what she had shouted up to Mom. "Winslow and Blaine are in the backyard and I'm going out with Libby."

"Out where?"

"Just out." The phone rang and Cam picked it up, thinking it was Libby.

"Hey there, Cami." It was her dad calling, and the sound of his deep voice always made her smile. "Is Mom around?"

"She's upstairs packing for the vacation."

Her dad took in a deep breath.

Oh boy. "I'll go get her." Cam took the phone upstairs to her mom and handed it to her. "It's Dad." She waved, backing up. "And I'm going to meet up with Libby."

As she was heading back downstairs, she heard her mom's voice start out with a sweet hello, then instantly raise a decibel or two. "So what does that mean?" Pause. "What about our vacation? You promised that this year we'd go. You gave me your word." Pause. "Why can't you say no to the team? You have no trouble saying no to me and the girls." Another pause. "No, I'm not going to go by myself with three bickering daughters and a six-month-old puppy that's already the size of a bathtub." Pause. "Two more weeks on the road? Paul, you have got to be kidding! You've been gone three straight weeks." Another long pause. "You make it sound so insignificant, but every decision has a cost to it."

At the bottom of the stairs, Cam stopped, her stomach swirling. Lately, it seemed as if this was the only way her parents talked to each other. Somewhere on the road, Dad called in with news that he needed to delay his return home. Disappointed, Mom ended up quiet and sullen for the rest of the day.

She heard wailing coming from the direction of the backyard. She opened the door to Blaine, sobbing, her knees bleeding. The stupid puppy had jumped up and pushed her over. Cam helped Blaine to the kitchen, put Winslow in his crate, and considered whether she should go upstairs to get Mom. But it was very quiet upstairs, and Cam had a funny feeling about it. Blaine was still crying. Cam found her an old popsicle in the freezer—Mom's magic cure to stop Blaine's crying jags—and got out the first-aid box. By the time she'd cleaned up the scrape and put a bunch of Band-Aids on Blaine's knees, her mom had come downstairs. She'd washed her face and put on some fresh makeup, but Cam could see that she'd been crying.

"Oh Blainey, I'm so sorry."

"It's just a skinned knee," Cam said. "No need for stitches." She didn't want to ask, but she did. "Everything okay with Dad?"

Her mom looked away again, distracted. "The team is doing really well. A lot of the players have been picked for the All-Star Game." Her mom stepped to the sink and looked out the window. "Unfortunately, that means Dad's got to work. I'm afraid we're not going to be able to take that vacation."

Cam thought about that for a while. "What if we surprised Dad and go to the All-Star Game?"

Her mom turned to her, a surprised look on her face. "In Chicago?"

"There's lots to see and do. I can check out Northwestern for me and Libby." A city sounded much more exciting than camping on an island. "I bet Libby could watch Winslow."

Cam could see her mother's whole countenance change, from defeat to hope. "Let me work on this, Cam. You might have given me a very good idea." She kissed her on the top of her forehead. "When you grow up, you should run for the presidency. I think you could figure out most of the world's problems."

That Chicago trip was the best vacation they'd ever had. Dad was stunned when they showed up at the All-Star Game, surprised and overjoyed. He kept hugging Mom and kissing her, and she seemed so pleased. Every summer after that, they joined Dad on the road wherever he was, either for the All-Stars or the Home Run Derby if one of his team's players was included, because he had a little more time to spare during those events than during game series.

But they never did get to Maine for that island vacation.

Eleven

SLEEP WAS IMPOSSIBLE FOR PAUL THAT NIGHT. Worries about his daughters kept circling through his mind, just like the pesky mosquitoes that were part of Maine life. It had always been Corinna's job to worry about the girls. Even after she died, he carried on the way he knew best—busy at work, trusting the girls to manage their own lives. Then came that bout of laryngitis last Christmas. He had sat through the holidays without a voice, forced to be a full-time listener for the first time in his life. Ever since, he constantly worried about them.

Actually, he felt a little uptick in his spirits about Blaine. Of the three girls, she spoke of wanting to stay on the island for all the reasons he'd hoped. He had Peg Legg to thank for that—she seemed to spark a flame inside Blaine that he hadn't seen for quite a while.

But Maddie . . . marrying Tre? Maybe Paul was old school, but it rubbed him wrong that this kid hadn't even talked to him about proposing to his daughter. It bothered him even more that Maddie didn't seem to feel slighted that her family wasn't included in the engagement dinner. Did she feel that detached from her sisters? From him?

No. Not Maddie. Or did she? He didn't really know. Of all

three girls, Maddie was the one he had trouble understanding. She could be sensitive, intuitive, and insightful, but Corinna had always insisted Maddie was also shockingly insecure. One thing he did know, that girl needed to get her career going. Counseling was the right path and she had qualifications checked off, but she didn't seem to be able to get it off the ground. It still baffled him that she hadn't received a single offer for an internship. Not one. He wondered if she might be sabotaging herself in the interviews by sounding . . . underwhelming.

· Hmm. Kind of like how she sounded about being engaged to Tre. When Paul and Corinna got engaged, he wanted to shout it from the mountaintops. Why did Maddie seem so reluctant to talk about it? He shook his head. He just did not understand her.

Now Cam, that daughter he "got." This time in London—he might not have shown it, but he was right there with her. What an incredible résumé builder. For all Cam's shortcomings in the relationships department, she was brilliant in business. He'd seen that gift in her ever since she was a little girl. She could size up a situation and figure out the solution. It was a quality that didn't make her popular among peers—other than Libby, who'd been devoted to her—but once she hit the work world, watch out! She climbed the corporate ladder like it was a playground.

And yet, he was speaking from his own experience when he told her to consider the cost. When Blaine asked Cam why she couldn't say no to London, Paul felt a blow to his gut. How many times had Corinna asked the same question of him? So many times he had chosen work over family, always assuming there'd be plenty of time to catch up. Boy, was that a dumb idea. Time had no mercy.

He nearly said as much to Cam, but he knew his daughter well enough to know that she had to figure it all out for herself, like he did. No one could tell her. She'd just dig in her heels all the deeper. He knew because she was a female version of him.

But there was Cooper to think of. This last week, he was Paul's shadow, following him around the property as he did chores. Just this afternoon, he showed Cooper how to make a fire in the back behind the house. Into it they threw dead tree limbs and scrap wood, and Cooper seemed no different from any other boy; he could play with a fire for hours on end.

But tonight . . . the string, woven all around the living room, it shocked Paul, and he didn't shock easily. The poor little guy needed stability. He needed friends. He needed normal.

Paul's eyes popped open. An idea occurred to him. Something that might solve both Cam's and Maddie's problems. And Cooper's too. Most, anyway.

Cam made a list of must-do tasks for her dad. "Essentials, Dad. First on the list is to fix up the bedrooms in Moose Manor. Order mattresses. Cooper and I can't sleep on the floor anymore. You shouldn't be on the floor either. Too hard on elderly bones."

"Fifty-nine is not elderly, thank you very much." Dad stretched, grimacing. "But I don't disagree that it's time for a good mattress. A full day of cleaning out cabins, combined with sleeping on a wooden floor, and I'm starting to feel like Methuselah."

Blaine snorted. "Mom used to say that physical labor was a foreign concept to Dad."

"Not true!" He threw a dish towel at her. "I cleaned up the kitchen after the two of you made those enormous holiday meals. It was like a tornado had swept through."

"Woohoo. Twice a year." Blaine circled her finger in the air.

"This is good," Maddie said. "Talking about Mom. It's good for us."

Blaine clutched her forehead with her hands in exasperation. Cam stifled an eye roll. Once Maddie warmed to a theme, she could be a broken record.

"Let's stay focused on the Essentials List, please," Cam said.

Blaine dropped her hands. "Dad, remind me again why you gave all our furniture away?"

"You girls said you didn't want anything. The new owner bought the furniture as part of the house sale. End of story." Dad turned to Cam. "I have an idea that might hit two birds with one stone. Three, actually. You need to go to London for an indefinite period. Maddie needs to work. Cooper needs security. He should be in a school setting, among other kids. So . . . leave him here. Pay Maddie to be his aide."

Maddie's jaw dropped wide open. "An aide? I'm a therapist!"

"You know what I mean."

"No, I don't."

Cam shook her head. "He needs to be with me." Or maybe she needed him to be with her.

Blaine snorted. "You leave him to go on business trips all the time."

"Not all the time."

"I nannied for you last summer, remember? You were hardly home."

"That was . . . a very busy stretch for the company."

Blaine snorted again. "Like this wouldn't be?"

Dad held up his hand before Cam could respond. "Blaine has a point."

"I do?" Blaine looked stunned. "I mean, I know I do, I just didn't think any of you thought I did."

Everyone ignored that comment. "You don't really know how long Evan wants you there, Cam," Dad said. "From what you described, it sounds like he's not sure, either. But you do know it'll be busy. Why not give this a try for a few weeks, and see how it goes? By then, you'll have a better idea of what life needs to look like for Cooper."

Framed like that, Cam found her thoughts bending. "First I would have to check out the lumberjack's teaching skills. He seems kind of backwoodsy."

"I'll take care of convincing the teacher," Dad said. "I'm pretty sure once he knows that he's got a full-time aide—"

"Therapist." Maddie frowned at him.

"—pardon me, Madison, *therapist*, in the classroom, he'll be on board."

"Hmm. It might work, I suppose, if Paul Bunyan cooperates."

Blaine put her hands on her hips. "I still don't understand why Cam can't just say no to going? Who says more is always better?"

Cam tried to remain calm, even taking a minute to fill a teakettle with water and setting it on the stove to heat before she spoke. "Blaine, I'm the one who pays the bills for Cooper. Private schooling. Medical bills. Dental bills. Food and clothing. Please hold your judgment until you're actually self-supporting."

Before Blaine could sputter a response, Maddie pointed to the open package of oatmeal Cam held in her hands. "Is that for Cooper?"

Cam nodded.

"He won't touch it. That oatmeal has raisins in it. He hates raisins."

"He can just take the raisins out."

"You don't understand. He won't eat anything that touches the raisins."

"Raisins?" Her sister had a way of making Cam feel like she was missing out on Cooper's life by not knowing these kinds of details. "When did raisins get added to the list of Cooper's dislikes?"

"Two days ago. Raisins and grapes, both. He said the textures bother him."

Cam looked down at the dry oatmeal and shriveled-up raisins. A very uncomfortable feeling started to make her stomach twist like a pretzel. Cooper's list kept growing.

Late Saturday afternoon, Paul opened the door to his truck and discovered that coon cat curled up in the driver's seat. "So that's where you've been," he said, shooing it out of his truck. It leaped out and ran off to the bushes, switching its mangy tail at him. "Last time I leave a window open," he muttered to himself. He brushed his seat of cat hairs, drove into town, and went to the Lunch Counter.

Peg beamed when she saw him come through the door. "Paul Grayson! I've been reading up on home remedies for laryngitis. I wanted to try a few out on you."

Oh dear. He had nearly choked on her coffee. "Maybe some other time, Peg. I'm looking for the mayor. I need to discuss this energy tax bill with him." He held the notice in his hand. If he didn't pay by March 31, additional fines would be added.

"Ah, you just missed him. He was in here not ten minutes ago."

Strangely elusive, that man. "Why is the mayor so hard to find?"

"Busy, I guess. Lots going on. That's what he says, anyway." She lifted the coffeepot. "More coffee? It's improved some now that your Blaine is helping me. I missed her today."

"My eldest daughter returned last night. We've spent the day trying to get the camp organized. Cam's our resident organizer. I've been piddling around with projects this week, but she's the one who helps us figure out how to get from point A to point B."

"Well, I'm hoping Blaine'll be a regular. Summer's coming, you know."

Oh boy, did he ever. "She's planning on it. Thank you, Peg. It's good to see Blaine excited about something."

"Speaking of organizing, you know she's been doing a lot of that here."

"Blaine?"

"Ayup. She's a crackerjack organizer. Just look at that kitchen."

He looked past the counter to a wall as clean and orderly as a surgical operating room. He took a few steps closer to peer at it. Index cards with instructions in a tidy handwriting were taped against the wall in precise order. "My Blaine? She did all this?"

"Ayup. Remember how it used to look?"

Not really, he didn't. Only that it was a hodgepodge of mismatched items, much like the rest of the store. "Well, I'll be." He didn't know Blaine had the capacity to bring order out of chaos. There were times, like now, that he felt as if he hardly knew his youngest daughter. His career had started to skyrocket during her childhood, and he'd missed much of the everydayness of her upbringing.

The horn from the Never Late Ferry blasted and Peg clapped her hands together. "That reminds me. Seth Walker holds church services at the Baggett and Taggett every Sunday morning. Ten o'clock sharp."

"He mentioned something about a church. A church with no pastor, he said."

"Not yet. Seth's looking, though. We do a lot of singing, and Captain Ed gives a little Bible talk. It's real . . . soul filling. Like having a good meal."

She gazed at him so earnestly that he didn't want to disappoint her. "Then I'll come." Why not? He hadn't been to church in a long time. Wasn't this whole island venture about getting back to what was most important? "I'll try to get my girls to come too. Maddie will, for sure."

"So I can tell that Cam is most like you. Which girl is most like your wife?"

Most like Corinna? Hmm, interesting question. "Maddie, I suppose. Both try to keep the family connected." Tried. Corinna had tried.

"So, then, you married up?" Peg's blue eyes twinkled. So blue and round they reminded Paul of blueberries.

He grinned. "Definitely." He paused to gather his thoughts. "Do you sail much? Yes? Well, Corinna was like the rudder for me, for the girls too. She steered us all in the right direction. I traveled a lot for my work. I know it wasn't easy on her, but she kept things afloat. She reminded me of the most important things."

"Just what are those important things, Paul Grayson?"

"Family, for one. All too often, ambition led me." He pointed to his throat. "It worked, until it didn't work."

Peg laughed. "Ambition can be a poor bedfellow." She put her hands in her apron pockets. "But faith . . . now that is my anchor. The rudder in my boat. The mast. The sails. The whole kit and caboodle. Couldn't get through a day without it."

"Oh yeah? My wife was like that." It came out sounding rusty. His voice was about done for the day. It was worth it, though, to talk with Peg Legg. He left a few dollars on the counter for the coffee. "I'll try to get to church tomorrow. Won't be singing, though. Just listening."

"Must be a little funny to be raising three daughters without much of a voice. A father who's forced to listen."

Paul grinned. "It is. It just might've come a little too late." It came out in a scratch. His voice was fading.

"Oh, it's never too late to learn to listen." The overhead doorbell jingled. Peg looked at the customer in surprise. "Well, well, look what the cat just dragged in. Paul Grayson, meet the mayor."

Twelve

BAXTOR PHINNEY WAS NOTHING LIKE PAUL EXPECTED. Unlike his long-bearded, scraggly looking sons, who had yet to show up to paint Moose Manor, he was a small, bespectacled man with a jiggly Adam's apple. Unlike his terse wife, Baxtor spoke with a clipped, professorial air. But like his sons and his wife, he showed very little concern for Paul Grayson and Camp Kicking Moose.

"The energy tax bill is correct down to the penny," the mayor said. "Read the fine print of the deed."

Paul had read it, with a sinking heart. Whenever land ownership transferred to a new person, they were required to pay a hefty energy tax bill. "But it seems as if that particular tax is designed to discourage newcomers from buying land on the island."

"It does, doesn't it?" It wasn't really posed as a question.

Paul could tell this wasn't going to end well. Still, he thought he'd try. "This due date. That's a heap of cash due by week's end. Isn't there any way I can make quarterly payments on it?"

"Certainly, you can try, but expect your electricity to be shut off." The mayor steepled his fingers together.

Paul could see he would get nowhere with the mayor, and his voice was gone. He left the Lunch Counter with a heavy heart. That energy tax bill would create a sizable dent in the cash reserve he'd

120

planned to use to make improvements on Camp Kicking Moose. The sale of the Needham house had paid for Camp Kicking Moose. He still had retirement savings, but it was locked up in IRAs and 401(k)s and investments and he didn't want to tap into those. Not yet.

On the drive home, he felt sucker punched, broadsided, T-boned. With no one to blame but himself.

Cam. He hadn't had a chance to talk to her about the energy tax bill. She might have an idea about what to do. Cheered up, he stepped on the gas pedal.

There were times when Cam thought Libby should have made Maddie the legal guardian for Cooper. That was confirmed to Cam when Maddie started a conversation with her in the kitchen. "I want you to know I'll take care of him while you're in London, Cam. I'll protect him, even from himself."

She would too. While motherhood came naturally to Maddie, it was counterintuitive to Cam, a completely new paradigm of how she viewed life, one that she struggled with continually. She knew that much about herself. Then why did it bother her to lose control of her central role in Cooper's life?

Maddie patted her arm, misunderstanding her silence. "Cooper will be okay here, with us. It's you I'm worried about."

"Me? I'll be fine."

"Cam, being here, with Dad . . . it's been good for us. All of us—me, Blaine, Cooper. For you too. It's what Mom would have wanted. She wanted us all to be close."

Oh no. Not this again. Unlike Maddie, who seemed incapable of letting go, Cam understood and accepted that when their mother had died, their family had been irreparably broken. They would never be the family Mom had promised.

"How will you manage the loneliness in London?"

"I'm never lonely," Cam said stubbornly. "I'm not. I'm independent."

Maddie's face went all counselor-ish, full of pity and empathy. "Strong women face their fears. They talk about them."

Cam's fists clenched. Her sister could drive a person *crazy*.

In the living room, Blaine got Cooper involved in building a tall tower of LEGOs, and then sidled toward the kitchen door to eavesdrop on Maddie and Cam's conversation. She could tell Cam was uncertain about leaving Cooper at Camp Kicking Moose, and she could hear Maddie try to reassure her that he'd be fine without her.

Maddie kept going, circling back to Mom, and Cam sounded like she was about to blow a gasket. Maddie was convinced they had bottled up feelings about Mom that needed airing. All week long, whenever they were alone together, Maddie had kept bringing Mom up to Blaine—memories and stories—hoping to spark a conversation. Blaine didn't take the bait. No thank you.

Blaine knew it was strange that she didn't talk about Mom. She mentioned her in passing once in a while, but she never expressed all she had meant to her. She wasn't sure why.

Yes, she was.

Cam had left a message for Evan Snowden that she couldn't return to London until at least midweek, as soon as she could get Cooper settled in to the island school. She assumed Evan would react strongly to that, to coax, plead, beg, promise her anything. She knew he was particularly anxious about profitability and the third quarter was wrapping up by week's end. Surprisingly, when she checked her messages on Sunday morning down near Boon Dock, Evan hadn't returned her call at all. Surprising and strange.

Well . . . at least she had communicated her intentions.

And now, she was on a mission to get Cooper enrolled in this island school. Oh, she hoped, hoped, hoped this would work.

Blaine had told her that the schoolteacher boarded at Peg's and ate his meals at the Lunch Counter. She walked up from Boon Dock to the diner and found him at the counter, eating pancakes. He did a double take when he saw her, and his gaze grazed her. "So then, you're back."

She thought his eyes lit up for just a second . . . or maybe she imagined it? "I am." He had a semi-scruffy look, like he hadn't shaved in a day or two. Man. Somehow, he made stubble look good.

"Cooper must be glad."

"I think so." She hoped so. The string obsession thing was nettlesome. Was Maddie correct about it—could it be a subconscious response to feeling abandoned? Or maybe Cooper just liked string. Most little boys liked string, she was pretty sure.

"Coffee, hon?" Peg asked.

"Please." Cam perched on the stool next to Seth as Peg poured coffee into a mug for her. "I came by to ask how to contact the registrar so that I can get Cooper registered at school. I'd like him to start tomorrow."

"You're looking at the registrar." A slight smile began in Seth's blue eyes. "Have him show up at nine o'clock sharp. You know where school is held, I trust."

"What about his records? Where should I have them sent?"

Seth shrugged. "Peg, what's the address here?"

"Oh, hon, just have them address it to the Lunch Counter. It'll get here."

Seth spun on his stool to face Cam. "How old is Cooper?"

"Seven."

"Second grade?"

"Third grade." When his eyebrows lifted in surprise, she added, "I believe in living life at a full throttle."

His dark brows met in the middle. "Even for a little boy?"

"Absolutely." Actually, she'd never really thought about it.

"So he's reading well?"

"He's been reading chapter books since he was four. As I mentioned, he's extremely bright. Off-the-charts gifted." She seesawed her hand in the air. "Maybe a tiny bit quirky."

"Aren't we all?" Seth gulped down the rest of his coffee, picked up his guitar, and headed toward the door. "I'd better get to church."

"Church?"

She'd noticed a church at the top of Main Street. "That one?" She jerked a thumb in the church's direction.

"No. That's empty."

"Not entirely empty, Seth," Peg said. "There's a couple of old-timers who go in and sit there on Sunday mornings. What they're waiting for, that I don't know." She looked at Cam. "Didn't your dad tell you about it? He was in here yesterday and said he was planning to come." She put a hand to her chin. "But that was before the mayor showed up."

"No, he didn't mention it. He came home pretty focused on the tax bill." That was an understatement. He was positively rattled. Cam spent Saturday evening at the kitchen table, going over finances with Dad. She encouraged him to pay the tax bill as soon as possible, and then they created a plan to improve the camp in stages. Slower than Dad had originally planned, but better in the long run. Solvent, hopefully.

Seth smiled. "We meet in the Baggett and Taggett shop on Sunday mornings. I guess it's a stretch to call it a church, but a group of us meet regularly to worship. We meet at ten a.m. You're welcome to join us. Just come with an open mind. We aren't exactly . . . a formal church."

"Any religion in particular?" If it wasn't too out-there, too holy-rollerish, she was pretty sure Maddie, the faithful churchgoer in the family, would like it.

"Hmm . . . let's see. We study the Bible and we talk about it and we sing songs that praise God. You figure it out."

She startled. Oh my. She would not have expected that, all that, from a lumberjack.

"But"—and he lifted a hand in the air—"we are on the lookout for a pastor. If you know anyone who's willing to relocate to a distant island and live off table scraps, please let me know." Seth held the door open with his knee. "Cam, you should come."

Church? Me? The last time Cam had gone to church was for her mother's funeral. She had no interest in dredging up those feelings. "Thanks, but I have a few things to do."

Disappointment flickered through those blue eyes of his, at least Cam thought she saw it. Or wanted to? "Another time, then. We're there every Sunday morning. Ten o'clock. Bring Cooper."

Cam nearly cringed. She wouldn't be with Cooper next Sunday. Or the next. Or the one after that.

"Peg comes every week."

"Sure do. Wouldn't miss it."

"Seth, hold on." He was practically out the door but stopped abruptly when Cam called to him. "I'd like to sit in on school tomorrow."

Seth walked back inside, set down his guitar, and took a few steps toward Cam. "You want to shadow the class?"

"Yes."

He looked her over and she wondered about all that was running through his mind. *Good grief, Cam. You've been around good-looking men before. Get a grip.*

"If you want to tag along, be sure to wear your boots." He reached down to pick up the guitar. "Tell Cooper to wear boots too. And don't be late. Nature waits for no one." He swept out the door and it felt like the sun went behind a cloud.

Cam turned to Peg for an explanation, but none was forthcoming. Peg was watching Seth cross the street with an adoring look in her eyes. "Hmm, hmm," she hummed, one note up, then down. "If I were only twenty years younger." She sighed. "That man, he's the best thing that's happened to this state since Chester Greenwood invented earmuffs in 1873." She picked up his empty coffee mug with another sigh. "If we don't get a dozen children living on the island by August, Mount Desert will steal him away from us. They keep trying." Then her face brightened and she pointed to Cam. "Tell your dad. He's got to get us some island kids."

Right. Add it to the to-do list for Camp Kicking Moose, right under painting Moose Manor any shade other than that Pepto-Bismol pink. Like it was as easy as ordering a book from Amazon Prime.

Thirteen

CAM AND COOPER WERE THE FIRST ONES at the schoolhouse on Monday morning. It was early, breezy, and cold. Super early, because Cooper worried they'd be late, so they waited in the chilly morning air until Cam thought she must have the date wrong, the time wrong, everything wrong.

At nine o'clock on the dot, a small, beat-up yellow school bus rumbled up Moose Manor's gravel driveway and squeaked to a stop. The door opened, and out poured kids. A girl, about nine years old, with bright pink hair and a nose ring. Two boys who resembled each other strongly, though one was a foot taller than the other. Brothers, Cam decided. Two small girls who held hands as they walked. A couple of others who ran by her so fast she couldn't tell their ages, much less their gender. Everyone wore heavy rubber knee-high boots and thick parkas. Last off the bus was the driver, Seth Walker, followed by that huge yellow Labrador retriever. Cooper held Cam's hand in a death grip. Dogs terrified him.

Seth Walker strode to the carriage house, unlocked the door, and swung it open. "Everyone in." First in went the dog.

Cam watched Seth with a surprising little thrill in her stomach and waited for him to notice her. How often did she want that from a man? Not very often. What she really wanted, she informed herself, was for him to look at her in a particular way. But he didn't look at her like that. He didn't look at her at all.

"Yoohoo, I'm Cam Grayson. This is Cooper. Remember? Yesterday, at the Lunch Counter, I told you he'd be starting school today."

"I remember." Seth looked at her curiously. "I told you to wear rubber boots. Wellies are best."

Cam looked down at her riding boots, made of smooth black leather. She loved these boots. They cost her a fortune. "Rubber boots? You just said boots."

"You can't wade through tide pools in those."

"Tide pools?"

"Sure. That's what we do on Mondays. Collect specimens at low tide. And today's a spring tide." He glanced at his watch and frowned. "I'll give you five minutes to hurry back to the big house and get the right boots."

"We don't have them."

"You don't have Wellies?" Seth frowned. "Well, go get sneakers then. But bring an extra pair of socks and shoes to change in to. You'll have popsicle toes by the end of the morning."

Cooper's eyes went wide. "I don't want to get frostbit."

Cam bent down to Cooper's level. "He didn't mean that."

"Yeah, actually I did."

Cam ignored him. "Cooper, I'll be right back. You go on in the carriage house and find a seat." She unpried his hand from hers and looked up at Seth. "Can you help him find a buddy for the day?"

"Sure." Seth popped his head into the carriage house. "Quinn, come on out here." The girl with pink hair came to the door.

Cooper's eyes were fixed on her pink hair.

Quinn tugged on her pink spikes. "I was born with this hair, in case that's what you're wondering."

"Don't buy her nonsense, Cooper," Seth said nonchalantly. "Quinn, don't try to scam the new kid."

"Gotcha, preacher," Quinn said. "Okay, new kid. You got a name?"

Cooper turned his head away and hid behind Cam.

"Cooper Grayson," Cam said. "That's his name." She bent closer to Quinn to whisper, "Lots of change going on." She shouldn't accommodate Cooper's crippling shyness, but right now it was more important to help him feel comfortable. There was no way she could leave him with this pink-haired girl who lied to seven-year-olds, and a big dog waiting in the schoolhouse to pounce on him. She glanced at Seth, who was still holding the door open. "How about if Cooper and I both run up to the house to find better footwear? We'll be right back."

"Suit yourself," Seth said, eyes on Cam with a bemused look on his face.

As they walked back to the carriage house in better footwear, plus a backpack full of spare socks and shoes for Cooper (he had filled the backpack himself), she tried to reboot her attitude for the day. The chill would soon be gone, the sun would be out, and they would be at the ocean. Not a bad start to a new school.

But as they neared the carriage house, the big yellow lab blocked the doorway. Cooper took one look and made a break for the manor house.

Paul stood at the living room window and watched a curious interaction unfold in front of the carriage house. He thought he could write the script. Something had triggered a panic attack in Cooper. The boy was hightailing it to the house and Cam was gesticulating wildly to the schoolteacher, trying to explain away Cooper's odd behavior. As for the schoolteacher's response, that part Paul couldn't figure out. Calmly, Seth's head swiveled from Cam, to Cooper, and back to Cam, as if he was taking it all in.

Paul went to open the door as Cooper pounded up the porch

steps and burst through. "I'm never going back!" he yelled as he ran past. "That dog wants to kill me!"

It took another ten minutes to coax Cooper to give school a try, plus a promise to keep the dog away from him, and he was finally ready to join the other students for the field trip down to the cove below Moose Manor. Seth herded his chattering charges out of the classroom and along a tree-lined path that led down to a cove tucked along the shoreline.

Cam was sure Seth blamed her for the delay, though he didn't say anything other than they needed to hurry if they wanted to be there at the lowest point of the tide. Actually, he didn't say much of anything to her. To his students, though, he said plenty. He wore binoculars around his neck and stopped to point out birds in the trees. He asked them if they could identify the bird by its song. "Hear that clacking sound?" Seth said. "What do you remember I taught you about a bird that clacks?"

"Pileated woodpecker," one boy said.

Seth shook his head. "Clacking, not pecking."

One earnest little girl offered up a few suggestions. All wrong, but at least she tried.

"It's a crow," Cooper whispered to Cam. "They can make lots of sounds."

Seth jerked his head in Cooper's direction. "That's right! It's a crow. Part of the raven family."

"Good work, new kid," Quinn said, giving Cooper a gentle nudge with her elbow. "How'd you know that?"

Cooper shrugged, pleased. As the walk continued, the death grip loosened on Cam's hand.

Walking reverently along the path, Seth pointed out all kinds of interesting details: What did the formation of the clouds indicate about the day's weather?

"Cirrus," shouted a small girl. "My mom calls them mares' tails."

"She's wrong," Cooper whispered. "They're cirrocumulus."

Seth pivoted, glancing at Cooper. "Actually, you're both right. Who can tell me what the Latin word *cirrus* means?" He looked right at Cooper. "Do you know?"

Cooper looked down at the ground. "It means curl of hair."

"Excellent. Class, did you hear that? *Cirrus* is a Latin word for curl of hair."

Seth Walker didn't miss much, Cam had to admit. She also couldn't dismiss the way he connected with his kids. He joked with them and easily turned light conversations into more serious ones. Most of the kids called him Seth, all except Quinn, who called him "the preacher."

"Pretty smart, new kid," Quinn said. "Maybe you can help me do my math homework."

Cooper's death grip loosened another two levels. Feeling started to come back to Cam's hand, tingling like sharp little needles, and she was beginning to enjoy herself. She'd been to the beach plenty of times, but it was to have fun with her friends, to play volleyball or surf on a boogie board. She'd never explored tide pools, nor had she ever considered low tide to be particularly interesting.

After they hiked down a steep path to reach a rocky part of the shoreline, Seth led the kids up the beach, marching through heavy sand, stepping over huge pieces of driftwood. Finally they reached a cove and he stopped to gather the children in a group. "Tide pools at low tide give us a peek into what lives below the sea's surface. Good thing is, we don't need snorkels or scuba gear to see it. All kinds of treasures are waiting to be discovered today. So who's got an idea of the kinds of creatures we'll find living in tide pools?"

A blonde-haired girl raised her hand. "Seaweed."

Seth grinned. "That's a start, Chloe. Anything more unusual to look for?"

"Fish!"

"Worms!"

"Snails!"

Seth laughed. "Can anybody think of a creature that's a little harder to find?"

"Lobsters!" one boy said. "And crabs."

Seth pointed at the boy. "Billy, glad you brought that up. Crabs will probably be under rocks. Turning rocks over—gently—is a great way to find the really cool stuff. But watch out for pinchers. Anything else to look for?"

"Starfish!"

Seth nodded. "Yes, we should see lots of seastars today since it's a spring tide. They like to stay low in the tide pools."

"Anemone. Urchins."

Cooper tugged on Cam's coat sleeve. "What did he mean by a spring tide?"

Seth held up his hand. "Cooper asked a question. Who knows what a spring tide is?"

No one answered. Seth looked to Cam. "Care to take a guess?"

"Well, it is spring."

He shook his head, as if she were one of his students. "A spring tide occurs when the earth, moon, and sun are in alignment. It's called tidal amplitude. So what do you think happens at high tide?"

One of the boys shouted out, "Tsunami!"

"Not quite that dramatic. But it is a higher-than-normal tide. See the water line?" Seth walked to a huge rock and pointed to the water line. "If we were right here around three o'clock in the morning, we'd be under water. There's a lot of water moving in and out twice a day." His gaze swept over the group of children and landed on Cooper. "So if that's what happens during high tide, what do you think happens during low tide?"

"Super low," Cooper said in a regular voice, not a whisper. Cam noticed.

"That's right! Higher highs and lower lows." Seth put his hand up to high-five Cooper, and to Cam's surprise, he returned it.

"We're not at the lowest point of the tide quite yet. This is the best time of all to go exploring, as the tide is heading out. But a spring tide is the best of the best. This isn't just any old low tide. You'll see more exposed today than any other day. It's a living aquarium, just waiting for you."

As Seth started to number the kids off for the buddy system, Cam remembered Maddie's warnings to slather Cooper in sunscreen. "Hold up for a minute. Come here, honey," she said, pulling out an industrial-sized plastic tube. Within minutes, she'd covered Cooper in white lotion. Then she pulled out mosquito repellant and sprayed his arms and legs. Next she pulled out a big hat and covered Cooper's head. When she finished, she looked up to find Seth staring at her in that way he had, as if she were an eccentric. The other children had circled around them.

"What in the world are you doing to that poor boy?"

"This is what my sister said to do. You know . . . for bugs and sun."

"The sister who googles freak accidents?"

"Yes. No!" Yes. He had Maddie pegged.

Seth finished off numbering for the buddy system—one, two, one, two, one, two . . . it didn't take long—then had them fan out in different directions to find their own tide pools to explore. "Today's calm weather is perfect, but I don't want anyone getting close to the edge. Remember to always respect the ocean. Never turn your back on her. Don't trust her, because she will trick you." He handed out plastic buckets to the pairs. "What's the rule on picking things up?"

"Put them back where you found them."

"Exactly right, Quinn. Including rocks. But gently. Remember to handle everything with great care. You're more likely to hurt them than they are to hurt you. But some creatures do pinch."

With that, he clapped his hands. "Final word of advice. Take your time and truly look. Few observations worth making are quick ones. Spend several minutes on each pool. Just watch for incoming waves, and skedaddle when the ocean begins to surge into the pool. You are not as well adapted to tide pool life as the critters that live there." He smiled. "Have fun poking around, kids. Sing out if you see anything super bizarre. Share it with everyone."

Two by two, the children set out to claim a tide pool. Cam assumed that Cooper would want her to stay close to him, but his partner, Quinn, grabbed him and they took off. She started after them, but Seth stopped her.

"Let him go," he said quietly. "He needs to have time without anyone hovering over him, undermining his confidence."

What did Seth Walker know about Cooper? He'd hardly met him. Indignant, she started to protest but checked herself. For now, Cooper seemed quite content.

She spent her time walking from tide pool to tide pool, trying to keep an eye on Cooper without hovering.

Hovering! Humph. She did not hover. Her sister Maddie did.

The minutes turned into an hour, and Cam lost herself in the study of tide pools.

"Pretty amazing, isn't it?"

She looked up to see Seth standing a few feet away. "You really like living here, don't you?"

He gazed out at the sea. "This place gets into your soul. I kayaked into the harbor a few years ago and never left."

"Doesn't it ever seem confining? There's one restaurant, if you could call it that. There's one grocery store. If the ferry doesn't bring supplies in, you do without. No police. No doctor."

"If you need to have a lot of choices, I suppose you could say island living is confining. Personally, I think too many choices of salad dressing or cereal can get paralyzing. As for police and doctor, they're not far away—just over on Mount Desert." He looked back at her. "Most places, folks ask what your favorite TV show is, or your favorite football team. Here, they ask what your favorite view is. The beauty . . . it's just incredible."

All too soon, Seth gathered the group. "Who's hungry?" He grinned. "That's good, because it's way past lunchtime."

The kids whooped and cheered and dug into their backpacks.

They were mostly quiet on the walk back to the schoolhouse. Some spoke to each other in low voices. But then there was Cooper. He walked right next to Seth, chattering nonstop, asking questions about the types of seastars he'd found in a tide pool. Cam couldn't help smiling. Cooper's questions had that effect on her. He was curious about . . . everything. She wondered about his father, about the genetic imprint he'd left on him, because it wasn't a characteristic he'd gotten from Libby. Cam had to push Libby to open her mind to new things.

Apart from the annoying remark about hovering, Cam had to give kudos to Seth. It was impressive, the way he used the Socratic way to engage kids' interest. And boy, did they love him. Even Cooper. Normally, he took a long time to warm up to anyone new, especially teachers. Gone was the tight, troubled look in those blue eyes behind the thick glasses. He looked, he seemed . . . well, like a little boy whose only concern was an afternoon snack and not about a missile arriving from North Korea.

Cooper waved at the bus as it rumbled down the driveway. "Seth says I can ride on the bus with him back to town some afternoon. He wants me to meet Lola. He says I'll love her, if I just take the time to get to know her."

Lola? Oh. So, Seth Walker had a girlfriend. So what? Big deal. But a queer little feeling swirled in Cam's stomach.

As the school bus jiggled and jostled its way down the driveway, Paul saw Cam and Cooper cross the yard from the carriage house and hurried to open the door. "Good day?"

"Really good day, Grandpa," Cooper said as he hurried past him. "I can teach you all about tide pools. But first I have to eat."

Paul lifted his eyebrows appreciatively. He looked at Cam. "He seems happy."

"Seth Walker took them on a field trip down to the cove. Cooper loved it."

"Think this school is going to work out?" He tried to keep the smile off his face.

Cam shrugged her shoulders. "Hard to say in one day, but the kids were surprisingly welcoming to Cooper. And . . . Seth seems to like what he does."

"Peg says the island is lucky to have him."

"I suppose so," Cam said.

She seemed a little evasive about offering an opinion. Not typical of Cam. "So then, sounds like leaving Cooper in this school while you're in London will work out. Or are you still thinking of taking him with you?"

If he wasn't mistaken, he thought he saw Cam cringe.

"I'm going to shadow Cooper for a few days. Then make a final decision."

That seemed unlike Cam's normal decisiveness. "Your boss is okay with you holding off a few days?"

Cam lifted her hands helplessly. "Probably not, but no phone service, remember? I thought I'd go to town to check my voice mails. Do you mind watching Cooper if I go now?"

"No problem." He waited while she looked for her keys in her purse. "Before you go . . . uh . . . a few things to mention."

She glanced up, distracted. "What?"

"I took the check for the taxes to the mayor today. Let me tell you, that was a painful chunk of change to hand over."

Cam laughed. "No kidding."

"I asked the mayor about a village meeting, and"—he snapped his fingers—"he set one up for tonight. Just like that."

"Tonight? What about?"

"I want to share the vision for the village."

"What vision?"

"That's where you come in. I need a vision." He handed her a notebook and pencil. "I also need to rest my voice for tonight."

Cam's eyes went wide. "A vision? To present tonight?"

"You said something about the camp being year-round. That kind of thing." He cleared his throat. His voice was fading. "Something to inspire the locals."

"Dad!"

"Have at it. This is what you do best, Camigirl." He pointed to his throat and made a cut-off sign. It was true that he needed to rest his voice for tonight. This meeting—facing the locals head-on, explaining the vision of bringing new economic life to the island—it was going to be the make-or-break moment for Camp Kicking Moose. For Paul Grayson.

Fourteen

A FEW HOURS LATER, locals moseyed around the Baggett and Taggett store, waiting for the village meeting to get started. It was a pretty good turnout for a spontaneously called meeting, and Blaine recognized many as customers from the Lunch Counter. She'd discovered one consistent theme in their conversation: the coming of summer, which seemed to be getting later each year. Blaine had to wonder: if summer came late here, would it leave early? Because there was still a winter chill on this island, though the days were noticeably lengthening, even during the few weeks she'd been here. In the mornings, frost covered the grass, crunching as Blaine walked on it, and her breath puffed out in smoky circles.

Her dad stood by the store's entrance to shake hands with everyone who came in and help them find a seat on one of those gray metal folding chairs. At seven o'clock sharp, he stood in front of the room, his daughters seated behind him, and said, "Thank you all for coming today. I'm Paul Grayson, the new owner of Camp Kicking Moose."

"Speak up!" someone from the back row yelled.

"We can't hear you," an older man said.

"Louder!"

"I can't," Dad said, pointing to his throat.

An older woman stood up and held her purse in the air. Blaine's eyes were riveted to her hair. It was bluish, glued upward in the shape of a swirling soft-serve ice cream cone. "I've got some cough drops for that throat."

Dad waved her down. "Thank you, but it's just the way I sound."

A tall, hollow-cheeked man spoke up. "What's this foolishness about changing the island's name?"

"I'm glad you brought that up. I'm going to explain everything, if you'll give me a chance."

The hollow-cheeked man slowly eased back down in his chair. "Thank you. Now—"

"Paul, hold on a sec," Peg said, sitting near the front row. "You'd better wait 'til Baxtor shows up. He always arrives a little late."

"He loves the grand entrance," the blue-haired woman volunteered.

Dad tipped his head. "Peg, why should I wait?"

"Meetings don't start until the mayor shows up."

"Even if the meeting was supposed to start at seven o'clock?"

"Even then. We always wait for Baxtor."

Dad gave that some thought, then said, "As accommodating as that sounds, I'm used to the business world where leaders respect each other's time. So, let's get started."

Blaine saw many locals exchange eyebrow-lifting glances, but the room grew utterly silent.

Dad started out by explaining that he'd been on staff at Camp Kicking Moose while he was in college, and how he'd always loved this island. He quickly touched on why he chose to use the English translation of the island's name. "Tonight's meeting is all about revitalizing this island. I know there's been economic challenges and that most of the young people are moving away. That's all going to change."

The blue-haired woman interrupted him again. "When are you going to pave Main Street? I nearly fell into one of those potholes last week."

"That's the mayor's job, Nancy," Peg said.

A small man wearing old sneakers and a necktie that frayed at the knot stood up. "I thought you're the millionaire who was bailing us all out."

"Whoa!" Dad said. "I'm no millionaire."

Peg turned and frowned at the man. "Oliver, what kind of question is that?"

Oliver squinted at Dad. "Then what are you doing here?"

"I'm glad you asked. I'm here because I love this island and I want to help it prosper. I think this community can work together to find answers to this economic difficulty. I'm here to be part of the answer. Not the whole answer, but part."

Blue-haired Nancy clucked a tsk-tsk. "Oh, that's a shame."

The door opened and in walked Baxtor Phinney, followed by his two sons and his grim-looking wife. They were frequent customers at the Lunch Counter, especially his two sons, and Blaine didn't like them at all. The two brothers lingered around the diner long after they finished their meals, trying to get Blaine's attention with annoying lame jokes, until Peg shooed them away. And they never ever left tips. Not even the mayor.

"Carry on," Baxtor Phinney said in a patronizing tone. "Don't let me stop you from solving our island's economic woes. After all, Mr. Grayson, you've been here . . . what . . . a few days now?"

"A few weeks . . . and thank you for the warm welcome," Dad said in a good-natured tone. He turned his attention to the audience. "Now, as I was saying, there's a lot of good things that are part of this island."

"Like what?" Nancy asked.

"Like . . . there's a history of hardworking people."

"We sure are," Nancy said. "So what about the garbage collection?"

Dad looked confused. "What about it?"

"Haven't had it for the last year. We've had to burn our rubbish."

Peg spoke up. "Nancy, hon, that's another topic for the mayor."

The mayor stood up. "Basic services have been difficult to provide because we can't get enough taxes collected. Because there aren't enough people on this island making a year-round living who can pay their taxes. So, Mr. Grayson, how do you propose to fix that?"

"Excellent question, Mayor Phinney, especially since the town has just received a windfall. From me." Just as Dad tried to launch into his plan, another fellow stood up. Blaine couldn't remember his name but knew he was a fisherman. He came into the Lunch Counter each morning smelling fishy.

"We can't make a living here without lobsters. They're gone. They've been gone for a year now. Bring the lobsters back and then the island will fix itself."

Oh boy. Not those missing lobsters again. That was another theme Blaine heard locals complain about.

Dad scratched his head. Even he couldn't fix the lobsters-gone-missing problem. He regrouped and started again. "Mother Nature is out of my hands. But I might be able to help in other ways. New opportunities for industry."

An older man with a noteworthy overbite rose to his feet. "So you're bringing in a new business? Some kind of dot comb?"

Peg stood up and turned to the man. "Com," she said. "It's dot com, not comb, Euclid. And sit down so the man can finish what he's trying to say."

"Thank you, Peg," Dad said. "Bringing in an outside industry isn't my plan."

Euclid remained standing. "You're an outside industry."

"Actually, I'm not," Dad said. "I'm a local. So are my daughters."

The mayor scoffed, loudly. This meeting wasn't going well.

"What about Camp Kicking Moose?" Peg asked, trying to help.

"The camp on the north end of Three Sisters Island will be up and running by summer."

"What's he talking about?" Nancy asked. "Where's Three Sisters Island?"

Dad sighed. Blaine jumped from her chair to rescue him. "That's the name of this island, translated from the original language."

"No kidding?" Nancy said. "I never knew. Why don't we just call it what we've been calling it?"

Dad gave Blaine, still standing, the nod to answer that. "Because no two people pronounce it the same way," she said. "And nobody can spell it."

"That's true," Peg said. "Personally, I like using the English version. It's paying respect to the original Native Americans while moving our island forward. Besides, most of us just call it 'this island,' which doesn't differentiate it from any other island."

"That's exactly right," Dad said. "We want Three Sisters Island to stand out and be noticed, don't we?"

Silence. Blaine slid back onto her chair.

Dad carried on. "We need to examine all the things that are good about this island, and celebrate the things we have. Not what we don't have."

"Like lobsters," the fisherman scoffed.

"How're you going to change anything?" Oliver said.

"Through the development of small businesses."

Baxtor Phinney stood up, hands planted on his hips. "So who's paying for this scheme?" Money was obviously an important point with the mayor; his eyebrows were almost touching in the middle.

"There's all kinds of talent on this island. Fishermen, hunters, artisans, guides, furniture makers, decoy carvers. Imagine something like . . . a store that sells local products, like honey or maple syrup. Captain Ed, you used to make canoes."

Sitting to the right of Peg, Captain Ed jerked suddenly, as if he'd been nodding off.

"Canoes," Peg said loudly. "You used to make canoes."

Captain Ed lifted his bushy gray eyebrows. "That was a long, long time ago."

Dad grabbed it and ran with it. "Captain Ed, you told me once that your father had taught you, and his father taught him. Couldn't that be a side business for you? Apprentice someone young, teach them how you do it, pass on that knowledge. Canoe making could be a year-round business."

"Might be worth a try," Captain Ed said with a shrug. "Probably bring in more money than lobster trapping."

Dad beamed. "Excellent. What else is unique here?"

Nancy waved her hand high in the air. "I could take peepers on walks."

Dad's face went blank. "I do hope you mean peepers of autumn leaves."

"Yes. I know where there's a scarlet oak that takes your breath away in early September."

Dad nodded. "Well, I admire your can-do attitude, Nancy."

"Toothpicks," Oliver said. "Toothpicks were invented in Maine."

"Blueberries!" Nancy said. "Maine produces 95 percent of all the blueberries in the United States." She crossed her arms, pleased with herself. "I read that fact just today in the *Mt. Desert Reporter*."

"That's a fine fact," Dad said, "but I was hoping we could zoom in a little closer to this particular island. What's unique about *this* place?"

Silence.

The mayor stood up. "You come in here and think you've got the answer to fix us. Well, I've got news for you. We don't need fixing."

Peg jumped up. "We sure do need fixing, Baxtor Phinney. Another family moved out just last month. The school is shrinking. Under a dozen kids means that Seth Walker loses his job. If Seth Walker leaves, I lose my only tenant. And a good one at that. I'm not sure I can survive another winter."

The mayor waved her worry away like he was shooing a fly. "Summer is coming, Peg. Tourists will fix everything."

"Not anymore, it won't. Even the lobsters have packed up and

143

left. Baxtor, this island is in serious trouble and Paul Grayson is trying to do something about it. So sit down and listen to him."

The room fell silent.

Dad cleared his throat. "Well, the mayor is right about one thing. Summer is the glory time for the coast of Maine. I don't think we'll have any trouble drawing tourists to Three Sisters, once we get Main Street looking like it's open for business. The goal is to see every storefront filled for this summer—even if it's a pop-up."

"Say what?" Nancy said.

"A pop-up. It's meant for a short-term business, when a retailer uses a location to sell goods or services."

"The leases on this island are yearlong," the mayor said. "All of them. No exceptions."

"Maybe that's something that has to be reconsidered. What's the point of having empty stores? I'm sure the owners would rather have something come in than nothing."

"There's only one owner on Main Street, aside from the Lunch Counter." Peg pointed to the mayor. "He's the one we need to reconsider."

Baxtor Phinney crossed his arms over his chest. "I've done right by this town."

Peg snorted.

Blaine watched the exchange, then looked at her dad. He was watching them too, in that maddening hard-to-discern-what-he-was-thinking way.

"Go on, Paul," Peg said. "What other ideas do you have brewing? We want to hear."

Dad swallowed, cleared his throat, and Blaine could tell his voice was grinding down to a whisper. She jumped up. "Wi-Fi! He's going to bring in Wi-Fi!"

The entire room started to boo. "We don't want it," someone shouted.

Blaine was stunned. Were these people living in another century?

"Let's give that some more thought." Dad coughed, cleared his throat. His voice sounded racked. "Um, let's see. Where was I? Oh yes. Winter. Winter—that's the challenge for island living. How to draw people here in the winter. Those old carriage roads throughout Camp Kicking Moose could be used for sports like cross-country skiing, snowmobiling, snowshoeing."

Mayor Phinney let out a scoff. "And just where would these people stay?"

Dad smiled, ready to deliver what he called his pièce de résistance. "I'm planning to turn Moose Manor into a fine hotel."

The room erupted into laughter.

Dad had pushed his voice too far. It was nearly gone, sanded down to a whisper. Cam stood up beside him. "Let me take it from here, Dad."

He lifted his eyebrows in a look that asked, *You're sure?*

"I'm sure."

Dad went to sit down next to Maddie and Blaine and Cooper. Cam scanned the room to get her bearings, the way she did before a presentation, and it was then she noticed Seth Walker standing against the wall in the back of the room. For a quick second, she forgot what she was going to say, where she was, and why she was here. She felt her cheeks grow warm. *Pull it together, Cam,* she told herself. *Pull it together. You do this all the time.*

She took a deep breath. "Everyone, if you could stop laughing for a moment, I'd like to present an idea." As the room quieted, she kept her eyes away from Seth Walker. "My name is Camden Grayson, eldest daughter of Paul Grayson." She handed a stack of papers to Blaine and Maddie to pass out. "Here's how we can help. Anyone who wants to consider a business that benefits locals and encourages tourism can apply for a grant. We're going to offer five grants to the five best, most worthwhile business plans." Besides avoiding Seth's eyes, she also kept herself turned away from her dad's. She hadn't had time to go over this material with him before tonight's town meeting.

"Love it, hon," Peg said, looking over the papers. "You're giving Main Street a breath of fresh air."

"And that brings up another idea. A coat of paint can work wonders."

"Who's going to pay for that?" the mayor said.

Cam locked eyes with the mayor. "We'll pay half the cost of paint and supplies for those of you who want to paint your houses or businesses."

"I see," the mayor said, and Cam could tell from the frown he didn't see it at all. "What about labor costs?"

"We'll all help each other. We're neighbors." Peg stood up and turned around, sweeping a hand in an arc. "Around here, that's what neighbors do."

Cam gave her an appreciative glance before she said, "There's an even bigger problem on this island—getting a consistent supply of energy to everyone—and my father has a plan to fix it."

"I what?" Dad squeaked.

"This island is importing electricity. That's why your power goes out each day. The energy runs out and *poof!* Lights go off. But it doesn't have to be that way. You've got everything you need to make your own energy. Right here."

The room started buzzing with side conversations, loud ones, so much so that Peg stood up. Everyone immediately quieted down. "I'm a little lost, hon. Can you run that by us again?"

"You can create your own energy." Cam raised three fingers in the air. "Wind, water, sun."

"That we got plenty of!" someone yelled out and the room burst into laughter.

Peg waited until the wave of laughter settled down. "We're not laughing at you, hon," she said. "It's just that none of us have the know-how to turn wind and water and sun into power."

"But I do. That's what my work is all about. Creating renewable energy that is derived from a variety of sources."

Now the mayor rose to his feet. "That takes a heap of money."

"Sure, but there's ways to get it. Applying for government grants, for example."

The mayor turned around. "It seems to me that this Grayson family arrives here, out of the blue, with plenty of promises and no action."

"That should be your reelection slogan, Baxtor," Peg said, and Baxtor's feathers grew ruffled as chuckles rippled through the room. "I think we should give the Graysons a fair chance."

"I second that," Seth Walker said from the back of the room. His eyes were fixed right on Cam, and she felt her cheeks grow warm. Then she noticed a young brunette woman standing next to him. *So, that's Lola.*

Paul went into the kitchen to fix himself some tea before he went to bed. Cam was at the table, mindlessly stirring a cup of coffee.

"Coffee? At this hour?"

"It helps me think."

Paul filled the teakettle and set it to boil on the stovetop. A microwave, that was something else that should go on the Essentials list. He found a box of peppermint tea sachets and tucked one in the bottom of his mug, then poured the boiling water over it. "Cam," he said as he sat down beside her, "you did a fine job tonight." Better than fine. She had most of the locals transfixed with possibilities for the island. The meeting started with scorn and ended with optimism. Paul was astounded.

"Thanks. I see the potential here. I'm catching your vision." She stirred her coffee once, then twice.

"But something else is on your mind?"

"Cooper. He had such a good day at school today. Then tonight, I needed something in my suitcase. I hadn't had a chance to unpack, you see, and he must have thought I was leaving. I left the room for a minute, and when I got back, the suitcase was shut tight and wrapped up in string. It looked like it had been booby-trapped." She took a sip of coffee. "Dad, I get what Mrs. Voxer has pointed out all year. I see what Maddie has worried about. His quirky behaviors, they're troubling."

Paul nodded. Cooper's obsession with string—that was more than quirky.

"Sometimes, I wonder if he'll become Libby's grandmother. Genetically, I mean. Like, he's predisposed to her 'crazy.' She did weird things like he's doing. I remember she even nailed the windows shut, then duct-taped them so no fresh air could seep in." She cringed at the memory. Those windows. No one could get in . . . or get out.

"Too soon to make a call like that. There's plenty of time for Cooper to . . ."

"To what? Get better?" She sighed. "Time is what I don't have." She rubbed her finger over a dent on the tabletop. "I need to get back to work."

"I forgot to ask. Did you connect with Evan?"

"I checked my voice mail tonight and no, not a single one from him. I tried calling him, but he didn't pick up. It makes me nervous. I think he's probably upset with me for letting family take priority over work. He can be like that."

"So . . . Cooper stays here. You go to London." His voice scratched it out. "Problem solved."

She frowned at him. "Dad, aren't you listening to me? That is the problem."

CAM, AGE 13

Libby hardly ever let Cam come inside her grandmother's house. The two girls spent all their time together at the Graysons'. The few times Cam had gone to Libby's, she saw her grandmother sitting in front of an old television, watching soap operas and chain-smoking cigarettes. Libby said that was all she ever did. "She's depressed," Libby explained. "That's what you do when you're depressed."

"Watch TV all day? That sounds like fun."

"It's not. Not really."

"She's too mean to be depressed. I think she just inhaled too much hair spray." It was their running joke. When she wasn't watching TV, Libby's grandmother worked in a beauty salon. Not the cool kind, but the old-fashioned kind with antique hair dryers that fit over old ladies' heads.

Libby smirked. "If she's not watching TV, she does all kinds of weird OCD things."

"Like what?"

"Like, making lists and alphabetizing soup cans and washing her hands over and over and over again and keeping windows shut up tight because she's afraid of fresh air." She circled her finger around her ear. "She's cuckoo. If I ever get like my grandmother, take me out back and shoot me."

Cam laughed. "You're nothing like your grandmother."

Then Libby grew serious. "I might be more like her than you think. Grandma escapes real life through the TV. I escape by going to your house. Same thing."

"It's not the same, Lib. Not at all. You like to be with my family because you see another way of living. Better than that. It's what you want to have some day. What you will have one day."

Libby smiled, cheered up. "A house. A husband. Two kids, a boy and a girl—in that order. A picket fence. And no TV. No whirls of cigarette smoke floating through the room." She nudged Cam with her elbow. "And a guest room all ready for you. A place to stay when you're in town from jetting around as CEO of the world."

"Our perfect lives."

"Don't you ever want to get married?"

"No way. I see how much my mom has to handle while my dad is off doing the fun stuff. I want to be the one to do the fun stuff."

"Maybe your mom thinks her life is fun."

"Cooking? Cleaning? Running after Blaine? Listening to Maddie's what-if worries?" She made a face. "Boring."

"Not to me," Libby said. "That's all I want to do. Be a mom."

Libby would be a great mom. She was much more tolerant and patient with Blaine and Maddie than Cam was. "As my mom always says, first things first. Go to college, work a few years, then find someone wonderful and have those babies."

"I don't need to go to college to be a mother."

Cam practically sputtered her objections. "Yes, you do. Good grief, Libby! Look at my mom. She has to manage everything on her own while Dad's on the road. Pay bills, house repairs, why, she even buys and sells stocks. You are definitely, absolutely going to college."

"Maybe . . . then a beauty college."

Cam shrieked. "No way. Libby Cooper, you are going to a four-year college."

"Right." She gave a sideways glance at Cam. "How? There's no money for college."

"Scholarships. You run like the wind and you're plenty smart." And she was. Cam jumped up onto her knees. "You are going to be my project. Which college do you want to go to? Pick any one."

Libby rolled her eyes.

"Pick one. I mean it."

"Princeton."

"Done. You and I . . . we are going to Princeton in five years."

"Cam, you're crazy." But even as she said it, Cam saw a spark ignite in her eyes.

"Follow my program, and then we'll see who's crazy." Cam rubbed her hands together, like it was a done deal.

Fifteen

As glad as Maddie was to see Cooper excited about his new school, she had some serious concerns about Seth Walker's teaching. During the village meeting last night, she overheard some kids talk about school, and it sounded as if they went on a ridiculous amount of field trips. Maddie had plenty of college friends who were teachers, and that was certainly *not* how they managed their classroom. Field trips were a once-in-a-while thing, a special event, because they were disruptive to learning. Plus, there was always the fear of leaving a child behind in a museum or at a zoo. How awful that would be!

During breakfast, after Cooper went to brush his teeth, she casually broached the topic with Cam. You had to be careful with Cam when it came to Cooper. She could be tetchy. "I wonder how Seth Walker prepares his students for standardized tests."

"Tests?" Cam's face looked blank.

Just as Maddie suspected. Her sister had given no thought to the academic rigors of this one-room schoolhouse. "Standardized tests. Come spring, they're the focus of every school across America. Those tests are critically important."

"Why?"

"All kinds of reasons. To ensure the children are on track, for the state to determine where funding goes, to identify the teacher's strengths and weaknesses, on and on. Hugely important."

Cam went to the refrigerator to get some milk for her cereal. "I think Seth teaches them by using the outdoors."

Maddie shook her head. "Classic avoidance."

Cam closed the refrigerator door a little too hard. She swung around to face Maddie. "Of what?"

"Of actually teaching children. Preparing lesson plans. Correcting papers." Maddie lifted her palms in a helpless way. "Cam, if he's not preparing the children for those tests, well, I would question whether this is the right place for Cooper. I mean, Cooper is super bright. He needs to be challenged. Right?"

"Right. Of course." A preoccupied frown covered Cam's face.

Relieved, Maddie poured herself a cup of coffee. She always felt better when someone shared her concerns. It lightened her load.

The teaching style of Seth Walker was completely unorthodox—that, Cam could not deny. She spent a second day shadowing the class, fully expecting to be indoors. It was a foggy, cold day, and yet Seth had those children trooping to a marsh to hunt for migrating birds. "This is the best time of year to see the birds," he said when she asked why they were outside in this damp cold. "Birds are exhausted from their long flights, resting and recouping in the marshes, so we can get up close and personal to them. It's a wonderful opportunity for bird-watchers."

"But what about tests?"

"Tests?"

"It's nearly April," Cam said. "Standardized testing is just around the corner."

"Oh, those. Yeah, sure, they'll take the tests. Late May."

"But they need to prepare."

"They are. Nature is their classroom, their best teacher too. The natural world speaks loudest here. Think of what these children are learning, just by listening for the right sounds. The breathing of the tide across the rocks, the chatter of the gulls, the lap of water on the beach."

"But . . ."

"But what?"

"Lessons. Classroom."

"Well, if there's time left over, then we'll work on lessons in the classroom. But children's minds . . . they belong outdoors. There's much to learn that no book will ever teach you."

Hmm. So Seth Walker, Cam was learning, was a bit of an amateur philosopher.

Still, Maddie had a point about fundamentals. "I meant the basics of reading, writing, and arithmetic," she said. "Nature can't teach them those skills."

Oh, but it could, he said. "Watch and see." That day was all about studying decibels. He told the kids he wanted them to guess the birds' decibel levels. "Try to figure out what animals are communicating to each other by the pitch and urgency of their sounds." He led them along a narrow path, into knee-deep grass that ended by the marsh.

"Shhh," he said, pressing a finger to his lips.

They inched up to him to look. Far ahead of them were a mother sow and her two bear cubs, munching on the grass, pawing for fish in the stagnant water. The two cubs couldn't leave each other alone, they kept batting each other. The mother mostly ignored them and kept moving along in a shambling way. Now and then she stood up, let out a warning roar, and the cubs hurried to catch up.

Transfixed, Cam watched the furry beasts move through the grasses. Seth turned everyone around. "Bears win. Bird-watching will have to wait until tomorrow."

"Why?" Quinn asked.

"Listen," he said.

Just then Cam realized that there was no birdsong. There were no birds, no ducks. They were savvy to the dangers of a nearby predator. Seth was right. The natural world spoke loudest here.

After that she noticed every twig that broke beneath her and every whisper of the wind. Occasionally a plane sputtered overhead. She looked around. The beauty of this place, the majesty of it, overwhelmed her.

On the way down the path, Seth let the kids start and waited for Cam. "You seem surprisingly, hmm, what's the word? Relaxed . . . after a bear encounter in the wild."

She grinned. "Definitely not an everyday experience." She'd never seen a bear before, not even in a zoo. "I liked what you said about listening."

Now he got excited. "Nature has its own language. It's got a message to deliver. A forest is in a pine cone."

This guy, he was pretty remarkable. But was he able to provide enough of a challenge for Cooper?

It wasn't that she didn't find Seth's unorthodox teaching style to be quite compelling. If she were in the kids' shoes, she might have learned to enjoy nature in a way she never had. The closest encounters she'd had with nature had been on trips to the shore. She loved it, but what she loved was sunbathing and reading books and watching boys. Studying a tide pool was the farthest thing from her mind.

She had to admit, after Monday's tide pool excursion, she doubted she'd ever lie on a beach again without thinking of the life that was swarming all around her. Or after today, she would never walk through the woods without noticing birdsong—or the absence of it—and what it told a person. Or seeing how butterflies were attracted to certain flowers over others. Or knowing that rain might be coming if bees and birds were exceptionally active and the breeze ruffled the leaves of the trees so that they showed their undersides.

Those were fascinating things to learn, especially for a city girl like Cam, who avoided encounters with nature. Nevertheless, for all the practical knowledge the students were learning, statewide testing was on the horizon and those kids would be ill prepared for it. She worried about Cooper, mostly.

As the kids ate their lunch under a grove of balsam fir trees, Seth sat down beside her on a log and Cam picked up the conversation where they'd left off earlier. "It's just that . . . the children don't seem to do any paperwork."

He studied her for a full minute. "Paperwork," he said in a flat tone. "You think paperwork qualifies as an education. I call it busy work. Mind numbing, repetitive, soul crushing."

"Studies have found that repetition is key to learning." Ugh. Even to her own ears, that sounded like something Maddie would say.

"Did you know that children spend half as much time outdoors as they did when you and I were growing up?"

"No, I didn't know that."

"Seems like it might do Cooper some good to spend a little less time pushing pencils and a little more time outdoors, appreciating this natural beauty. This island has a lot to teach everyone, no matter how old you are. It's easy to forget to look up and notice all that's going on around you."

Beyond Seth, Cam noticed Cooper crouching down. He held out his hand to Dory to let her lick it. He giggled and did it again.

Seth turned to look at what had caught her attention. "I thought you said Cooper was afraid of dogs."

"He is. I mean . . . he has been."

"Yeah? Well, not anymore." He turned back to Cam. "Instead of ramping up his fears, maybe you should let him figure out a few things for himself."

Cam was nonplussed. Seth had a knack for turning the tables on her. "Hang on. Don't make this about me. This is about you. You're the teacher of this school. You're the one ultimately responsible for the education of these children."

"Exactly." He unfolded his wax-paper bundle and took out a neatly cut turkey-on-wheat sandwich, offering her half.

She accepted it, only because she'd forgotten to pack a lunch for herself, and watched him from the corners of her eyes. She couldn't figure him out. Seth Walker was an enigma, wrapped up in a mystery.

Midmorning, Paul went to town to see if those mattresses he'd ordered from a shop on Mount Desert had come in on the barge or the Never Late Ferry. That was one of the reasons. The real reason was he wanted to hear what the locals had to say about last night's meeting. He sat on a red stool at the counter to ask Blaine if she'd heard any scuttlebutt. She was focused on rolling out puff pastry and didn't want to be distracted. "Dad, this is a critical moment. I have to roll the butter in before it melts."

He watched her for a while, amazed at how absorbed she was by her task. He hadn't seen her like this, unless you counted the way she concentrated when texting a friend on her cell phone. He smiled, watching her pound the dough and turn it, over and over, all authority and confidence.

Peg swept in from the back room; she was everywhere at once. "Hello, Paul Grayson. I figured you'd be stopping by to find out what folks had to say about last night."

"Nonsense," he said. "Just happened to be in town and I thought I'd drop in to say hello to my daughter."

"Don't believe him," Blaine, the traitor, said without even looking up. "He wants the lowdown."

Peg set a stack of clean rags on the countertop. "Well, then, here it is. Most of them liked what Cam had to say."

"Not me?"

"Well, it's not that they didn't like what you had to say." She swapped the clean rags for the dirty ones. "They just couldn't hear you." And away she went to the back room.

At the end of the school day, Cam asked Seth if she could hitch a ride into town on the school bus to check her voice mails down by the dock. Dad asked Cooper to stay with him and help burn leaves—something he couldn't refuse. It was a nice offer by Dad. She knew that he was giving her time to talk to Evan without distraction.

Seth dropped her off on Main Street and then took the bus to the gas station to fill up. Gasoline, Cam quickly noticed, was very expensive on the island, and resupply came only on Fridays, so the entire family had already become more mindful about jumping in the car to run errands. Before going to Boon Dock, Cam stopped in at the Lunch Counter to tell Blaine she would need a ride home.

The Lunch Counter was empty but for Peg and Blaine, both in their pink-striped aprons. Blaine was in the midst of teaching Peg how to roll out a piecrust and barely looked up even when Cam came through the door with a big hello.

"Come on in, hon," Peg said, much friendlier than Blaine. "You can tell me what I'm doing wrong." Her pie dough was rolled to an oval shape, full of holes and cracks. Blaine's was a silky smooth circle.

"I have no idea," Cam said.

"Peg, roll from the center out, not back and forth." Blaine sounded like a drill sergeant.

"Is that what I'm doing wrong?" As Peg examined each piecrust curiously, her hair bow wiggled back and forth. Today's headband was the color of a grape lollipop. Cam had yet to see the same one on Peg. She envisioned a bathroom drawer filled with brightly colored headbands.

"I'm going down to the dock now to check my voice mail," Cam said, "and hoped to catch a ride home."

"I'm here until closing time," Blaine said, crimping the edges of her crust after sliding the dough into a pie plate. It looked like it could be in a magazine.

Cam glanced at her watch. Five o'clock was closing time, which meant she had about an hour and a half to kill. "Okay. I'll be back."

Boon Dock wasn't much more than a silvery wooden dock on toothpick piles, jutting out into the blue water, tilting from side to side in a gentle rocking motion. At its far end, two overturned canoes rested. She checked her voice mail and had two "Cam, call in ASAP" messages from Evan. She let out a puff of air. Her brief respite had come to an end.

Before she returned Evan's call, she looked around the small harbor. The weirdest image filled her mind: she had turned one of those canoes over and was paddling away in it.

It was so beautiful here, so peaceful and relaxed. Wind ruffled her hair. Gulls and shorebirds squawked overhead, wheeling and diving, floating on invisible tufts of wind.

There was something about this island that made her busy mind settle down. She was always moving on to the next thing, barely conscious of being present where she actually was.

Earlier today, watching Cooper hold his hand out to that big dog of his own volition—that was an enormous stride forward. It was the first sign she'd seen that he could conquer a fear instead of adding more to the list.

Did she really want to leave this and jump back on the hamster wheel? She wasn't sure. Before she could come to an answer, her phone rang. She glanced at her palm. It was Evan calling.

"Come with me."

She lifted her head to see Seth Walker standing ten feet in front of her, Dory at his side. "Come with me," he repeated. "It won't take long. Thirty minutes, forty-five, max. I want to show you something cool." He started walking toward the dock.

Her phone bleated again, then again, then again. Cam bit her lip, pressed decline, put it on silent, and hurried down the beach to catch up with Seth.

He helped her board a fishing boat, the flat-bottomed type, then unwound lines from the cleats and jumped into the boat. Dory sat at the bow like a sea captain.

"Where are we going?"

"I promised Captain Ed I'd check his lobster trap this afternoon. This is his boat. I'll bet you haven't been to the Atlantic side yet, have you? An entirely different world."

He motored out in the harbor and sped up, bumping across the waves, water splashing at their sides. He pointed out the cabins of Camp Kicking Moose, then the roof of Moose Manor. It was an entirely different view from the water. Buildings looked so small. So much more manageable.

He guided the boat up island and then slowed it down, idling the engine. "Look," he said. There was the sow and two cubs walking along an isolated shore.

Cam clapped her hands in delight. "That's her!"

Seth nodded. They watched for a while, and then he sped up the boat's engine. As he reached the northern tip of the island, she immediately saw the differences in the water. "The frantic Atlantic," Seth shouted. Cam squinted eastward. Out here, the sea was wild and white-tipped. Waves roiled and splashed the sides of the boat. It was beautiful, frightening, thrilling.

Minutes later, he steered the boat skillfully onto a small area of exposed beach of gray polished pebbles. He jumped over the side, grabbed a line, and pulled the boat as far onto the shore as he could get it. A rickety set of stairs built in the shape of a lightning bolt led from the shore to the bluff above. The wood had turned gray from age and was black from mildew; chicken wire covered each step. The stairs looked fragile, as if a battering storm could shatter them, but held up as Dory charged up them.

The tide had ebbed; mud coated everything, oozed along the shore, which was draped in seaweed and kelp. Clumps of shiny black mussels lay exposed on the rocks. Seth took her elbow protectively to lead her up the stairs. At the top, he dropped her elbow and waved his hand with a "Voilà."

There in front of them was a grassy meadow, punctuated by an old lighthouse. Cam gasped. "I didn't even notice it down below."

"Didn't I tell you? Folks forget to look up." He started toward it, then waited for her. "It's not in use any longer. But there's a certain poetic beauty it evokes."

They walked around the lighthouse, tried the door, but it was padlocked. Seth pointed out a sign attached to the side of the lighthouse.

Shipwreck Shelf Lighthouse Tower was constructed in the 1850s and discontinued in 1933.

"Amazing," Cam said, "to think of this little lighthouse, warning sailors off the rocks."

"Mighty but little."

"My mom used to say, 'Every island has a story.' Think of all the stories that lighthouse keeper could've told."

Seth shrugged. "Maybe there weren't enough stories. Maybe that's why it was discontinued."

"With a name like Shipwreck Shelf? Ah no, my friend. There's a reason it was put right here."

He laughed at that. They came around to the front again and walked across the yard to the stairs that led to the beach. At the top of the stairs, they stopped while Seth whistled for Dory. She came running toward him from behind the lighthouse.

Gazing at the lighthouse, Cam said, "It looks like everything else on this island. Neglected and abandoned." She turned to Seth and he looked away quickly, as if he'd been watching her.

"Yeah, your dad bit off a lot."

"He sure did."

"Why? Why would he bother? It's a huge risk."

"It's got something to do with our mother. She passed away a few years ago. They had met at the camp and fell in love. This was always Mom's dream, to come back here."

"Your family never came here during the summers?"

"Dad worked too hard. He was always, always working. And then the camp went belly up." She shrugged. "My sister Maddie's latest diagnosis of Dad is Acute Time Limited Mental Disorder."

"Is that another way of saying he's had a nervous breakdown?" Seth laughed. "Let's see. Is your dad sleeping?"

"Check. We're all sleeping on sleeping bags in the living room. For a man with a weak voice, he snores like a sailor."

"Eating?"

"Check."

"Carrying on with his daily tasks?"

"All good."

"Not having suicidal thoughts?"

"None that I know of."

"Then your sister is sorely mistaken."

"That's Maddie. Often wrong, but never in doubt."

"Frankly, I find it amazing to think what your dad is trying to do. To help bring new life to the island. Encouraging families to stay, to find a way to make a good living. I think it's pretty cool."

"Yeah, you know, so do I." She really did. A lot of hard work lay ahead of him, but she could see how invigorating this massive project was for her dad. "Having plans is a good thing."

"Plans *are* good. But they can also trip people up."

"I take it you're not a planner?" Now that she thought about it, he'd already told her as much. Hadn't he said he kayaked to the island and, on a whim, stayed?

"Short term is okay, but I'm not a big fan of long-term planning."

"Not a fan? Why, long-term planning is the key to success in . . . almost everything." It was a basic economic principle. Time + money = wealth.

"Maybe. I don't disagree with you. But the problem with focusing on long-term plans is that you can miss a lot of the short term. The here and now."

"Speaking of short-term plans, we'd better get back. I'm supposed to meet up with Blaine at five for a ride home."

Dory was already down the stairs and back at the bow, waiting for them. Seth took Cam's elbow and helped her down the steps and into the boat. The tide was just starting to come in. It would be beautiful at high tide, but she understood what it meant: this little beach would be inaccessible. "Do you come here often?"

"Now and then."

She shouldn't say it. *Don't say it, Cam. Don't say it.* "Do you bring Lola here?" Argh. She said it.

"No," Seth said, starting the outboard motor. "She wouldn't like the boat ride. And she's not much fun when she gets her feathers ruffled."

Interesting. Lola sounded rather high maintenance, which didn't seem like Seth's type at all. Cam cringed. Her sisters accused her of being high maintenance. A princess.

Seth steered the bow of the boat toward a yellow-striped buoy, then cut the engine. He leaned over the edge and removed a clip from the buoy, then attached it to a simple crank in the back of the boat. He wound and wound the crank until up came a lobster trap. "Look at that. A couple of crabs." He cleaned it out and baited it with slimy herring from a coffee can, then tossed it overboard. The crank spun and spun until the clip jerked. He reset it onto the buoy and turned back to her. "Captain Ed had some errands to run over on Mount Desert this afternoon and asked me to check his trap. He's a hobby lobsterman. The commercial license allows for eight hundred traps. Recreational licenses allow for only five traps. Captain Ed only has one." He shook his head, puzzled. "It's the strangest thing. Plenty of good-sized lobsters at Mount Desert. None of the right size over here. You have to throw them back if they're too big, too small, or a breeding female."

"I thought people were joking that the lobsters were leaving."

"It's no joke. It started last year and it's gotten worse this year." The engine roared to life and he steered the boat around the tip of the island. "I called the University of Maine's Lobster Project to report the concern, but they said we're too small."

"There's a Lobster Project?" She had to shout to be heard.

As soon as they cleared the top of the island and traveled south, the water settled somewhat and talking was easier. "Maine lobsters are big business here."

"Why do you think the lobsters' numbers have reduced? Climate change?"

"Not sure if it's climate change—that doesn't make sense for Mount Desert's fishermen. It could be a predator in the sea that's eating the eggs, or maybe a type of algae. Could be all kinds of reasons." He shrugged. "But it is a serious problem. Most locals depend on the seasonal lobster catch to survive. If something doesn't happen, the island's going to lose more of its population."

They were silent for a long while, until Cam thought of something. "Is there any benefit if the island loses its residents?"

"Benefit? How so?"

"Well, for example, has any corporation been nosing around, scooping up reduced properties?"

"Just your dad." He grinned. "Only benefit I know of would be to that mother bear and her cubs." He lifted his chin in the direction of the shore. The mother sow and cubs were curled up against a log, sleeping, with the afternoon sun shining down on them. "I'm sure she'd prefer the island to herself."

Cam watched the slumbering bears until they were nothing more than dots on the shore. Seth eased the boat into its slip, hopped onto the dock, and tied the mooring line to the metal cleats. Dory jumped out and sauntered down the dock. Then Seth reached down to help Cam onto the dock. They stood there for a while.

"Thank you for that . . . additional field trip. Three in two days."

Seth grinned. "The pleasure was mine."

They walked down the dock. "This little island, she has a lot of problems, doesn't she?"

"No kidding," Seth said. "Last night, you intrigued me when

you mentioned creating renewable energy. But it would take a lot to make that happen. Most of the locals, they resist change."

"Including the mayor."

"Especially the mayor. He's a third- or fourth-generation is-lander. He likes things just the way they are." He grinned and wiggled his eyebrows. "Which means there's not much chance of getting Wi-Fi for your little sister."

"Speaking of . . ." Down at the end of the dock was Blaine, rubbing Dory's head.

Blaine saw them approaching and cupped her hands around her mouth. "Seth! You'd better hustle. Lola's not happy to be kept waiting for supper. She's screeching."

"Oh shoot. I'd better go. See you in the morning, Cam." He started jogging down the dock and turned to say, "Wear Wellies tomorrow! We're heading back to the marsh to count birds for the Audubon Society. Tell Cooper."

Blaine walked up the dock to meet Cam. "Oh. My. Gosh." Her eyes were wide circles. "Did Seth Walker just take you out on a date?"

"No! Not a date. A boat ride. To check a lobster pot. Wipe that silly look off your face." She walked ahead toward Blaine's car.

Blaine got into the driver's seat and buckled her seat belt. As she turned the key in the ignition, she said, "I think Seth is dreamy." She drove up Main Street and turned onto the main artery that wove around the island. "Peg says he's the catch of the island."

"Well, tell Peg he's been caught. By Lola."

Blaine snorted. "Good one."

"What do you mean?"

"Lola's a bird. A goshawk. He keeps her in an enormous covered cage behind the Lunch Counter."

"Very funny. Lola stood next to Seth at the meeting last night."

"Next to Seth? Hmm, the brunette lady? She's a fisherman's wife. Peg said she's his fourth wife and they keep getting younger and she doesn't understand the appeal of that particular fisherman to these young women." Blaine gasped and turned to Cam. "WHOA. You have a crush on Seth Walker. I can't believe it!" She drummed the palm of her hands on the steering wheel. "Of all the men in all the world . . . you have fallen for a lumberjack. Wait'll I tell Maddie."

Cam shifted in her seat. "There's nothing to tell. I went on a boat ride with Cooper's schoolteacher. Big deal. Good grief, Blaine, sometimes you sound like you're still in seventh grade."

"Then why are you the one whose cheeks have turned cherry red? You always blush when you're embarrassed." Blaine gave her a smug look. "Oh . . . even better . . . to think you are jealous of a bird. I have to remember to tell Maddie that too." She started to giggle, then burst into laughter. "Danger, danger! Actual feelings might be emerging in Camden Grayson!"

Disgusted, Cam didn't speak to Blaine for the rest of the trip. How childish of Blaine. How immature. *Argh*. How . . . true. She did have a little crush on Seth Walker. He wasn't like anyone she'd ever met. Most men were intimidated by her, if not put off by Cooper's quirkiness. Not Seth.

It wasn't until much later that night that Cam remembered she'd completely forgotten to return her boss's phone calls.

Sixteen

WEDNESDAY MORNING. It was early yet, not even six o'clock, when Paul woke to the sound of Cam's car driving off. He got up, dressed, turned on the coffeepot, and sat on the porch steps with his cup of coffee, enjoying the peace and quiet of a new day before the onslaught of the long to-do list. The sun hadn't risen yet, but the sky to the east was filling with light. A miracle every morning, he could hear Corinna say.

Paul thought of all the things he had to do today: Scrape moss off the roofs of cabins 6 and 7, the shadiest of the lot. Recaulk the showers and bathroom windows in each cabin; bleach the bathroom in cabin 8 where the ceiling was mildewed; unplug the toilet in cabin 5; repair door locks. He made a mental note to ask Maddie to start the process of scrubbing out the canoes and kayaks in the boathouse.

But, he reminded himself, much had happened in the last two weeks. Bed frames and mattresses had been delivered yesterday, so the Grayson family all had their own new beds in their own bedrooms. He stretched, not feeling that creaky ache in his back that he'd had each morning after sleeping on a cold, hard wooden floor. That was a huge bonus. Cam said she would order furniture for the cabins today, to give each one a family friendly coziness. He wasn't quite sure what that meant, but he trusted Cam's judgment. And the coon cat seemed to have left for greener pastures. All good.

But the house still needed painting. Gallons of exterior house paint sat stacked at one end of the porch, but so far, he hadn't been able to get any painters to show up. He let out a heavy sigh. He wasn't sure how much longer he could stand looking at that bubble-gum-pink color.

Memorial Day was just eight weeks away, and with it came Opening Day, ready or not. Camp Kicking Moose had to be ready. He wished he had another couple of months—frankly, a year!— but postponing its grand opening wasn't an option. Income had to start coming in to offset the sizable expenses that were hemorrhaging his savings. He wondered how everything would get done in time.

Cam's organizational skills had been invaluable, but how long would she be here? Surely, she was expected to be in London soon, or back in the Boston office.

Maddie was a big help, though he felt a tweak of concern that she wasn't doing what she should be doing: job hunting. Or planning a wedding? He still hadn't warmed up to that notion. She didn't discuss it, so neither did he. By ignoring it, he hoped it would go away. A strategy that worked in many, many situations with his daughters.

Blaine was no help to him, but he didn't mind one bit. Peg kept her busy with baking at the Lunch Counter, and he felt he was watching his youngest daughter start to bloom. He had Peg to thank for that, though each time he tried, she flipped it around and said that Blaine was the one to thank for rescuing the Lunch Counter.

Strangely enough, for all the work still to do, as overwhelming as it was, he loved it here. Each day, rain or shine, he was outside, working on whatever needed to be done. When he finished a chore, he saw tangible proof of his labors. So unlike radio work that vanished into thin air.

Maybe it was the place that filled his soul with contentment. He still remembered the first time he'd come to the camp. The towering trees and rocky shoreline had seemed like paradise to a kid raised in a trailer on the poor side of town. A friend he'd met at college worked at the camp and said they were looking for a summer handyman, room and board provided. Was Paul interested? He'd grabbed the opportunity to avoid going home, if you could call living with his hard-drinking father in a cramped trailer a home. He returned for three more summers. It was during his last summer that he'd met Corinna.

This beautiful island . . . it had given him a great deal. It was still giving to him. His girls, to his shock and delight, hadn't mentioned their worry that he had early-onset Alzheimer's for at least two or three days now. At times, they even seemed glad to be here, at least for the time being. Cooper was settling in to the island. He talked nonstop about Seth the schoolteacher—quoting him, looking up bird facts for him—and, so far, he didn't object to going to school. That was a very big change. Best of all, Paul hadn't seen that blasted ball of string since Monday.

But there was much to do, and still so many decisions to be made. Grateful for Cam's suggestions to make Camp Kicking Moose a year-round destination, he intended to move forward with those plans. Last night, he had grabbed the opportunity to ask Cam some questions. She pulled out a yellow notepad, started scribbling, and within twenty minutes, she had whipped off a business plan for Camp Kicking Moose that included profit projections. She had in mind the kind of place where the same families would come back year after year to spend their precious vacation time. Families, not counselors and campers. The camp could provide activities and special events, but not be responsible for daily schedules. And the camp would open in stages, cabins first for this summer. Next year, hopefully, Moose Manor as a full-service hotel.

Boom. He was sold on the concept.

"Mom would've loved this, Dad."

He swiveled to see Maddie standing at the open door in her pajamas, a cup of coffee in her hand. "I think you're right." It came out in a scratch, so he cleared his throat to repeat himself.

She waved it away. "I know, I know." She grinned. "I went into town to call Tre yesterday. Afterward, I stopped by the Lunch Counter to say hi to Blaine. That lady with the blue hair—Nancy's her name, she runs the tiny grocery shop. She was at the town meeting and kept asking you when you were going to fill potholes in the street, remember? Anyway, she was having lunch. She was talking to Peg about your voice. I overheard Peg say she thinks your scratchy voice is sexy. She said it's unusual to find a man who spends more time listening than talking." She turned around and went back into the house.

Paul rubbed his throat. Sexy? Him?

Blaine woke up feeling lousy. Sad and out of sorts, embarrassed from her behavior last night. Cam had tried to talk to her about her future plans last night. About returning to college. The conversation started badly and ended horribly when Blaine stomped out of the kitchen like a child having a temper tantrum.

Blaine felt too fitful to hang around for breakfast and sidestep any more conversations with her family. After she dressed, she drove straight to the Lunch Counter. The morning sun hadn't risen yet, but the sky was lightening to a pink glow as she drove toward the village. She noticed, but just barely. Just enough for her prickliness to soften, ever so slightly. It was hard to hang on to a bad mood when you saw such brilliant colors fill the morning sky. It kind of jiggled your own petty fusses back into perspective.

She wasn't even through the diner's door when she smelled a weird, iron-like scent coming from a big pot simmering on the stove. "Peg! What in the world are you making?"

Peg turned around, holding a wooden spoon in the air. This

morning, a fluorescent lime green headband held her hair back, so bold and bright that Blaine thought it lit up the room. But maybe the room seemed brighter because of Peg's welcoming smile.

"Morning, hon. The Grayson folks sure are up early. I saw Cam down on the dock, holding her phone up in the air." She sniffed the air and frowned. "Lobster bisque is on the menu today. Captain Ed brought me a lobster over from Mount Desert last night. He asked me to make it for him for lunch. He said he's been missing it something fierce. It's just about done."

Blaine grabbed a rag to lift the lid of the soup pot. "The broth. It's so thin. Bisque is supposed to be thick. What did you use for the broth?"

"Water. And the lobster. He's in there."

Oh no. "Not lobster broth? No onions? No cream?" Just hot water and a big red lobster, still in its shell.

Peg peered over the rim of the pot. "Well, a thin broth might be good. Captain Ed is missing some key teeth."

"Mind if I help with the bisque?"

Peg handed her the wooden spoon. "Have at it."

Blaine turned off the burner and assessed the situation. She wasn't sure if it was salvageable, but lobster, even in Maine—and especially on Three Sisters Island—was a delicacy. She plucked the lobster out of the watery broth and set him on a platter. A thin watery broth was no way for a lobster's journey to end. "How about if I take it from here?"

"That bad?"

Blaine nodded solemnly. "That bad."

Peg sighed. "Oh, I forgot to tell you. Artie called again. Said he wants you to call him back by tonight or he's putting out a missing persons report."

Blaine grinned. "I'll call him. I promise."

"He seems like a good guy, that Artie."

"He's a great guy." She stopped and glanced at Peg. "Not *that* kind of a great guy. The kind of great guy you wish were your brother."

"Honey, let me give you a little bit of unasked-for advice. You know what it's like to walk inside a bookstore and get dazzled by all those fancy, pretty book covers? Don't get swept away by the outside package. Lots of books, they aren't worth reading. It's the inside of the book, that's what counts. Page by page. Down to the last word."

Blaine nodded thoughtfully. "I'll keep that in mind." As she stirred the sautéed onions, she pondered why she could easily accept Peg's advice but bristled with Cam's. Something about Peg made it seem more about Blaine's best interests than Cam did. That wasn't fair, Blaine knew. Cam cared about her. Maybe it was the delivery. Cam made Blaine feel like an inept employee. Peg had a way of making Blaine feel like she was fine, just the way she was.

After two cups of coffee and an hour in Peg's company, the world was cheery again.

Cam walked down along Boon Dock, examining her phone for bars. She had to get through to Evan this morning. She knew he'd be in his office, the man never slept. As soon as she found the spot with three bars, she froze. Pressed dial. She braced herself when Evan picked up on the first ring, expecting him to be angry that she'd gone MIA.

"Cam! At last. We need to talk." He didn't sound at all angry, just the opposite. He sounded relaxed, at ease, almost jovial. Very unlike Evan.

"I'm sorry I've been hard to reach. The reception is terrible on this island. I'm planning to head to London tomorrow and—"

"No need. Don't bother."

She felt a flare of worry, almost panic. "Evan, I'm genuinely sorry. My family, they've needed me—"

"Don't worry. It's all good."

Oh no. This was bad. Really bad.

"The news is hitting the *Wall Street Journal* today."

"What news?"

"I sold the company."

Stunned, absolutely floored, she didn't know how to respond. It took her a full minute to gather her thoughts. "You promised the team that you weren't going to sell. You said you wanted to take the company public. Two years from now. We had a plan."

"I know, I know. But an offer came in from an oil company that I just couldn't refuse."

"How do you know you couldn't refuse? You didn't let your team do due diligence."

"I did, actually. They did, I mean. And I would've brought you in the loop, but you weren't returning my calls." He blew out a puff of air. "It's done, Cam. Your work in London sealed the deal."

She felt her face grow warm and her heart start to pound. "Is that why you sent me there? To get those figures so you could bump up the purchase price?" She felt furious and tried to keep her voice level and even. "Evan, had you been in talks with this company without letting the board know?"

"The board knew."

"But not me. You didn't tell me."

Pause. "To be honest, yes." Another long pause. "Cam, you deserve a pat on the back. This oil company offered three times the sales price. Your discovery bumped up sales by one million dollars. It sold for thirty million dollars. Thirty. Million. Dollars." When she didn't respond, he said, "Are you still there? Can you hear me?"

She didn't respond because she was shocked by the price. "I heard. I'm . . . overwhelmed."

He laughed. "Well, one thing for sure, you'll have no trouble finding another job. Frankly, you'll have no need for another job."

Another kick to the gut. "Hold on. They don't want to keep us?"

"No, they just wanted the technology. We're done. We're all done. And richer for it!" Evan cleared his throat. "You can stay in Maine as long as you want. Take a vacation for once."

"I don't take vacations."

"I know. Neither do I. But it might be good for you to take some time off and think about what you want to do next. The world is your oyster. Cam . . . you're one of the first employees in the company. You, me . . . we're worth millions."

Cam's hand that was holding the cell phone started to shake. She saw a bench a few feet away, sat down, and listened to her boss describe the sequencing of the last week. Evan had no right to sell, she thought, but he did. He was the founder, the inventor of the technology that this oil company wanted. He could do anything he wanted. But she should have been a part of these discussions.

Now she knew why she'd been sent to London. True, those figures probably ramped up the purchase price, but he was also getting her out of the home office during negotiations. She would've steered him away from selling, poked holes in the offer, created doubt in the team's mind. But as she listened, she couldn't deny that it was a dream offer. Beyond anything they'd ever imagined at this stage of the business, anyway.

Evan finally ran out of things to say. "Cam, this is a good thing for us. For you, especially."

"How's that?" Her voice sounded flat.

"Well, besides the fact that you're not even thirty years old and you're fabulously wealthy, you can take some time off to be with Cooper. Work through his issues before they're set in stone. My mother used to say that children are wet cement."

Nice. Now she was getting parenting advice from Evan Snowden, a twice-divorced workaholic who never wanted children. "I'd better go."

He exhaled. "You could sound a little happier."

"If this is what you want, then I'm happy for you. For me, I just . . . need to get used to the idea. I'll be in touch." She clicked off her phone in a daze. She should go, wake Cooper up, make his breakfast, be sure he was ready for school.

She couldn't make herself budge. She leaned back on the bench and stared out at the water. Everything she had thought was predictable and reliable had turned upside down.

It was that last purple moment before the sun would crest the top of the hill behind her to announce the new day. In that silent, still moment, it seemed as if everything was holding its breath, waiting. As the sun's light broke and shone a few rays down on the harbor, a family of cormorants swam out, wrinkling the water's reflection of masts and boats. Sandpipers emerged from their hidden nests to run along the water after the wake receded. It wasn't long before exuberant gulls flew in, squawking their arrival. She heard the low voices of lobstermen as they walked down the dock to their boats. Everything looked so peaceful. By contrast, Cam's insides were churning with emotion.

She saw a man walking slowly along the water's edge, a dog trotting beside him, and a bird perched on the man's arm. She squinted, then realized the man was Seth. He recognized her at the same moment, and lifted his free arm in a wave. He came up the sand toward her but stopped about six feet away. "Morning."

She took in a deep breath and said hello.

"What are you doing here so early?"

She lifted her phone. "Only place that gets reception. What about you?"

"I bring Lola down here each morning before school."

"So this is the Lola who gets her feathers ruffled."

"Yes. She's very temperamental. I was hiking one day and found her on the path, barely alive. She was just a baby. I took her home and rehabilitated her."

"What do you think happened to her?"

"Not sure. She might have fallen from the nest. More likely, gotten pushed out by a sibling. I'm trying to help her gain skills to live in the wild." He sat down on the bench beside her, his left arm holding Lola still extended in an awkward position.

"Doesn't she get heavy?"

"Nope. Birds have hollow bones. Surprisingly light. And she's under the thumb. That means she's tightly tied to my glove this morning. She can't launch or fly off right now." Lola's head was turned to the sky above the water, where a seagull was circling. "But that doesn't mean she's stopped thinking about her next meal."

"How can you tell?"

"She's a predator. You know what they say: Eyes on the front, you hunt. Eyes on the side, you hide."

Cam had never heard that, but then, she knew nothing about birds. Any bird. "So you plan to release her?"

"Yup. As soon as she can survive on her own." He smiled. "After all, that's what parenting is all about, right?"

She gave him a sharp look. "If you're talking about Cooper, I've already received my morning dose of parenting advice."

"I wasn't, actually. I was talking about Lola. I've felt like her mother this last winter." Lola turned her head, following the seagull's path with her piercing eyes. "You seem a little out of sorts this morning. Is something wrong?"

Cam sighed, softening. "I just . . . I get a lot of suggestions about how to raise Cooper. It's like I've been wearing a sandwich board that says 'I don't know what I'm doing so please feel free to tell me.'"

"Well, you're doing something right. He's bright and sensitive and aware. Most kids aren't."

She glanced at him. "Sensitive and aware. Is that a politically correct way to say he's got some issues?"

"No. Not at all. It's my way of saying he's a great kid. A really great kid."

"Speaking of Cooper, I'd better get home and get him ready for school." She rose and looked at the bird, who eyed her with a murderous glare. "Nice to meet you, Lola."

Seth lifted his chin. "Are you shadowing at school again today? I've got something special planned."

Why not? She had nothing else to do. "I might send Cooper over at nine and come a little later. I received some news this morning that I need to tell my dad and sisters."

"I don't mind. Come when you can." He smiled at her, a genuine, not-mocking-you smile, and she felt a little dazzled by its warmth.

He walked Cam to her car, Lola possessively clutching his arm with her talons. Cam wondered how Seth's arm was able to stay up in that position, but then, maybe he was conditioned to it. She didn't think she could ever get used to that bird's hard glare—it unnerved her. As he opened the door for her, he said, "Cam, whatever's bothering you, you're not alone."

"I know, I know."

"I meant . . ." He pointed a finger upward. "You're not alone."

"Oh. You mean God?"

"Yup. There's a big picture going on, behind the scenes."

"Like a giant in the sky, holding marionette strings?"

Seth laughed. "Not quite. More like . . . a God who's paying attention. Working all things for good for those who love him. All things. Even the hard things. Even if it doesn't feel that way sometimes. Then again, feelings aren't facts, are they?" He closed the door with his right hand, stood back, and waved.

Expect the unexpected. That was another thing Cam was learning about Seth Walker. He had a way of weaving God into the conversation so naturally, so easily, like he was talking about a good friend. It must be nice to have that kind of faith.

Mom did.

And look what happened.

As Cam drove back down the road toward Moose Manor, she took her time. So much was happening, so fast. Facing her calendar each morning had always been better than a jolt of caffeine for her. For the first time in a very, very long time, the day was hers to plan. She wasn't sure if she liked the feeling or not.

Seventeen

WHEN COOPER HEARD THE SCHOOL BUS rumble up the gravel driveway, he grabbed his lunch off the kitchen table, yelled "Bye!" and bolted out the door to meet up with Quinn, the girl with pink hair. Maddie watched him go, a little mystified by this burst of independence, but pleased by it too. She couldn't remember Cooper ever having a friend before. She assumed Cam was going to follow behind him, but her sister remained in the kitchen. She had a fresh pot of coffee brewing and four cups waiting on the tabletop. Next to Cam was a yellow pad, topped with a pencil. Dad was absorbed in the newspaper. When Blaine appeared at the front door with a bag of day-old scones from the Lunch Counter, Cam said, "Good. Everyone's here. I've got an announcement to make."

Blaine crumpled like a rag doll. "Not again," she moaned. "I feel like you summon us to a board meeting. Besides, I just came home to pick up some recipes and get back to help Peg prepare for the lunch crowd."

"Crowd?" Maddie had to smile.

Blaine bristled. "Gets bigger every week."

"This won't take long." Cam poured coffee into each mug, passed them around, and settled into her chair.

It was interesting, Maddie thought, how they each had designated seats. Somehow it seemed a metaphor of their family roles—claimed and staked out. Unchanging.

Cam took in a deep breath, then exhaled. "I am not going to London after all. Apparently, Evan Snowden has sold the company. Thus, I am temporarily without employment. So, Cooper and I will be staying on for a while to help Dad get Camp Kicking Moose up and running."

Dad beamed. "That's great news. Great, great news."

"I'm glad you're pleased," Cam said, all business. "So I've got some ideas for the camp—"

"Hold the train, Cam," Maddie interrupted. "You just talked to Evan a few hours ago. In one phone call, you've discovered your company has been sold and you're no longer working."

"Correct."

"Cam, this is a very big deal. Your life has turned upside down and inside out. You can't just ignore the impact of this event. Let's talk about it. We can help process with you."

"Thank you, but no thank you. I'm processing just fine." Cam reached out to pick up the yellow pad of paper.

Maddie sighed. A classic denial moment. So Cam-like.

"I thought we would start in phases, of course. The cabins come first. They're rustic, but they have a certain appeal."

Dad lifted a hand. "I've overlooked a serious consideration. Where will these people eat?"

"Where did the campers used to eat?"

"Here, in Moose Manor. Simple fare back then, even with a kitchen staff. But we can't serve meals in Moose Manor."

"I agree," Cam said.

Blaine cocked her head. "Why not?"

Cam answered with a slight shrug of her shoulder. "We don't have trained staff. Better still, no qualified chef. I've wondered if guests could go into town to eat."

"That doesn't make sense," Blaine said. "It's too far to drive. They need to eat here."

"Good chefs cost a lot of money," Cam said. "We can't afford it. Not this year."

Blaine shook her head. "You've got to provide food here. Good food. Make it easy for them to stay. Otherwise, they won't come back next year."

Dad rubbed his chin. "Blaine has a point. Maybe we can provide a cold buffet breakfast, cereal plus coffee."

"We could do better than that," Blaine said. "I could do it. I'm the one who does the cooking at the Lunch Counter. Peg doesn't even set foot in the kitchen anymore."

"Here's an idea," Maddie said. "We could put microwaves in the cabins. Those hotel-style coffeemakers. Maybe provide a small fridge too."

"Hmm." Cam rose to pace around the kitchen. "Those are good ideas. In fact, we could even do both. Small kitchen set-ups in the cabins. And maybe a very simple breakfast on Moose Manor's porch. We could even set out lunch foods, right after breakfast, so they can make their own lunches. Maybe dinner is up to them. Encourage them to go into town to eat."

"EXCUSE ME."

They all turned to Blaine. "Why can't I be the cook at Moose Manor?"

"You're not qualified," Cam said.

"I've been cooking at the Lunch Counter!"

"For less than two weeks, Blaine. There's no pressure at the Lunch Counter. Peg lets you do whatever you want to do. It's going to be different at Moose Manor. Very structured. High end."

"How high?" Dad said, brow furrowed.

"Super high." Cam picked up her pen. "Blaine, decide on a major, go to college, graduate, then see if you still want to cook."

"My interests are different than yours, Cam, but I do have them." Blaine refilled her coffee cup. "Not everyone belongs in the Ivy League."

"Shoot for the moon. Even if you miss, you'll land among the stars."

Cam's patronizing tone only riled Blaine. "I happen to live on Earth." She glared at her, hands on her hips. "What's wrong with Planet Earth?"

Cam sighed. "Blaine, this is real life. Dad's entire retirement package is resting on the success of this venture. The energy tax wiped out his nest egg. He's ponying up a lot of money through those grants he's offered the townspeople."

"As I recall, you offered the grants," Dad said in his scratchy voice. "That was news to me."

Blaine was on a roll. "Well, that's another reason I shouldn't go to a fancy private ooh-la-la college like you and Maddie did. I don't want Dad to end up in the poorhouse."

"Whoa," Dad said. "My finances are just fine."

They weren't. Not really. Even Maddie knew that after over-hearing bits and pieces of Dad and Cam's conversations at the kitchen table late at night. He was just trying to be . . . the dad.

"Blaine, you're a home cook with a lot of potential, but you also have a history of starting something and losing interest. Just a few days ago, you overslept and ended up arriving late to the Lunch Counter." Cam's voice had turned corporate. "You can't do that here. Guests expect consistency. A sloppy work ethic isn't going to cut it. Camp Kicking Moose needs to remain simple and focused this summer. Expansion will come slowly and carefully. Too much too soon could spell disaster."

Maddie knew Cam's tactics. She was trying to force Blaine to back down and it was working. She felt sorry for her little sister. Blaine sat in the chair, arms across her chest, chin tucked. Shut down.

But Cam's attention had already shifted to Dad. "So it's de-cided. Cold breakfast buffet only. No hot food other than coffee and tea. Not this year. We need to start in a solid way that can be sustained. We can't overpromise and underdeliver."

Dad nodded. "I think you're right. Slow and steady."

Blaine stormed out of the room.

On the drive in to the Lunch Counter, Blaine's anger festered. Dad and Maddie treated Cam as if she had the Midas touch, turning everything she touched into gold. Her sister had a way of getting everything she wanted, all the time, for as long as Blaine could remember. Even a budding romance with the handsome schoolteacher—the only eligible bachelor on this island! Seth or Cam might not admit it, but it was obvious to everybody else. They were smitten.

Did Dad, Maddie, and Cam ever listen to Blaine's ideas? No. Did they ask her what she had in mind for a farm-to-table menu at Moose Manor? No. Did they ask her about the vegetable garden in the backyard that she had already marked off, with plans to grow food that could be incorporated into the day's menu? No.

They didn't listen. They *never* listened to her.

Cam's dig about Blaine's erratic interests was so unfair. You couldn't always know what would matter to you until you tried it. She was trying something new by working at the Lunch Counter, and she liked it. But did her family even notice what she'd been doing for Peg? The compliments from the customers? The new menu? The boost in foot traffic?

She pulled her car up to the Lunch Counter and turned it off. Out in front, a young man waited, leaning against the window to capture a ray of morning sun on his face. He stood up when she walked toward the door. "Are you Blaine Grayson?"

"Why?"

"I'd like to ask you some questions about your sister, Camden Grayson."

Blaine narrowed her eyes. Good grief. Was everyone in this world focused on Cam? "What do you want to know?"

"I'm a reporter for the *Mt. Desert Reporter*. Did you know

your sister just became one of the wealthiest women in the state of Maine?"

"What? No way." She shook her head. "You've got the wrong Camden Grayson."

"Her renewable energy company was just sold, wasn't it?"

Blaine stilled. Was that why Cam seemed all gung-ho this morning with plans for Camp Kicking Moose? Her mind started spinning with possibilities. It irked Blaine that Cam hadn't told the family that she'd made a lot of money on the sale of her company. It also irked her that she made it sound like Dad's venture was so risky. Why couldn't Cam just fund it? Why couldn't she just put up the money to pay for a chef at Moose Manor? *One like me?*

Blaine stood up her straightest, to her full height of five feet seven and a half inches. If she didn't take herself seriously, who would? "Come on in. We can talk over coffee. Good coffee. And how do you feel about brioche?"

Eighteen

STANDING IN FRONT OF THE CLASSROOM, Seth Walker wore a wily smile. "Perfect weather today, kids. That means one thing."

"Softball!"

"Softball." Seth grinned. "Great Cranberry Island School is on its way over for a game. Harrison, get the mitts. Quinn, you bring the bucket of balls. Timmy, don't forget the bases like last time. I'll carry the bats."

The kids popped from their seats like springs. Talking all at once, giggling, elbowing and pushing one another aside, running for the door.

All but Cooper. He sidled up to Cam, tucked into a corner of the schoolhouse, and looked up at her, chin quivering. "Mom, I don't want to play."

Cam never knew what to expect from Cooper. He was afraid of a lot of things. He overanalyzed most everything, convinced that something might go wrong and kill him. Some of his fears popped up so unexpectedly that it took a while to figure out just what they were, and why. Besides normal things that most kids were afraid of—snakes and spiders and shots from the doctor—he was scared of elevators and escalators, roosters but not chickens, helium balloons and anything orange, especially orange helium balloons.

And added to the list of fears were balls. For some strange reason that Cam could not understand, he was afraid of balls.

She smoothed the blond lock down on the back of his head. "I'll take care of it, Coop." After an uncertain nod, he went outside to join the other children while she waited for Seth to finish putting on his umpire gear.

"Seth, Cooper doesn't like to play ball games."

"He doesn't like ball games?" Seth buckled on his chest protector, doubling his chest size. If he had a cape on, and stood arms akimbo, he could be mistaken for a superhero. He glanced up at her before bending down to strap on his leg guards. "How long has he felt this way?"

Ouch. That question touched on a sore spot. She'd had her hands full with work, so it could be a long time before she noticed odd behaviors in Cooper. By the time she did notice, she had no idea how long they'd been there. "To be honest, I'm not really sure. It might have had something to do with a dodgeball game at school going awry. Ever since, he won't join in when kids play games that involve a ball. Any ball."

"Dodgeball can be kind of . . . aggressive. Team sports are my preference. Has he ever played on a team?"

Cam frowned.

"Any kind of team?"

"He's seven years old. Since when do seven-year-olds play on teams?"

Seth scoffed at that. "In this day and age, most seven-year-olds have been training for the Olympics since they turned three."

What? Why? Never mind. This was about Cooper. "Does he have to like everything?"

"No, but most kids do like to play ball games. Has he ever tried?" He squinted his eyes in doubt. "Or do you just excuse him?"

"No." Yes. It wasn't worth the hassle. Cooper had refused to go to school on Tuesdays and Thursdays unless he had a note from Cam that excused him from PE.

"Maybe he should be encouraged to try."

Maybe, but Seth had yet to see Cooper in full-blown anxiety mode. A total meltdown. And meltdowns caused setbacks.

"If it makes you feel better, we always beat Great Cranberry Island."

"I don't care about winning." She paused, her competitive spirit kicking in. She stopped a smile before it could form. "You always beat them?"

"Always." He grinned. "I have a hunch that if Cooper gets a glimpse of success, of possibility, his natural tenacity will take over." He pulled a strap on his chest protector to tighten it up. "He has a lot of tenacity, you know. Look how much he's learned about goshawks in the last week."

That was true. Cooper was becoming a seven-year-old expert in the rich history of falconry. Last night, he taught her about the mark falconry had made on common vocabulary. *Fed up*, for example, referred to a hawk fed to fullness. "Well, could you let him make a decision to give it a try? Not force him?"

"Of course I won't force him. As long as you don't get in the way if he wants to try." He jammed his ball cap on his head, then grabbed his face mask in one hand and hoisted a heavy bag of bats over his shoulder. "You sit under a tree and watch. No interference. No sideline coaching. Cheer for everybody, both teams. Got it?"

How rude. Cam lifted her chin. "Understood."

"Good." Seth gave her a nod as he headed to the door to join the children out on the lawn. "The GCI bus is here." A small minivan rumbled up the driveway and came to a squeaky stop. He grinned, looking like a kid at a carnival. "It's go-time."

Cam followed him out the door. Seth jogged over to greet the visiting team, and Cooper stood near a few kids huddled around home plate—a good sign—so she found a tree to sit under not far from the expanse of green lawn that was doubling today as a baseball field. The ground under the tree was hard-packed dirt, carpeted with a hundred years' worth of pine needles. She took off her jacket, turned it inside out to sit on it, and leaned against the tree to watch the game.

Seth was in his element. He organized his team and sent them to their positions while the teacher from GCI lined his team up to bat. She saw Seth ask Cooper if he'd like to play in the outfield, but he shook his head. Seth didn't push him.

Moments later, the game got underway. Seth umpired and the GCI teacher pitched. Sitting on the sidelines near the bat bag, Cooper watched the game with uncommon interest, though he didn't cheer. Not at first. After a while he started getting into the spirit of the thing.

When GCI had three outs and took its turn out in the field, and Three Sisters Island took a turn at bat, Cam realized something. Seth's students were good at softball. They must play a lot, she gathered, after watching Quinn hit a home run. By contrast, the GCI team was terrible. A tall girl swung at everything, even one pitch that rolled on the ground like a bowling ball.

Maddie's voice circled around Cam's head like a bird building a nest. If Seth's students played softball as much as it looked like they did, were they getting enough time on the fundamentals? They loved school and clearly adored Seth, but was that because he asked nothing of them academically? Were they all going to bomb the standardized tests?

And then Cam's worrisome thoughts abruptly shifted. She saw Seth crouch down to say something to Cooper. There were still no outs and the entire bench had batted. She knew what Seth was doing. He was asking Cooper to bat. Not fair! They had a deal. No pressure. No pushing. And from the look on her son's face, he was leery. But then something clicked and Cooper jumped to his feet, picked up a bat, and trudged over to home plate, dragging the bat.

Cam watched in stunned disbelief. Cooper was short for his age and when he bent into a very low crouch, almost ridiculously low, it made for a very small strike zone. The GCI teacher moved closer to him a few feet, then tossed an underhanded pitch.

"Ball one!" Seth shouted.

The next pitch was too high, another ball. Then came a strike. Same with the next one. Then a bad pitch. "Ball three!"

Cam's stomach clenched. The bases were loaded, the count was full. Cooper hadn't taken a single swing. This was just the kind of pressure she didn't want Cooper to have to deal with. She rose to her feet, fists clenched, ready for anything. Would Cooper strike out, start to cry? Would he run home? The game was being played on the expansive front lawn of Moose Manor. Home was only a few hundred yards away.

"Ball four! Take your base."

Suddenly Cooper dropped his bat and took off running toward first base like his life depended on it. Quinn, on third base, jogged toward home plate, and Three Sisters erupted in cheers, shouting Cooper's name over and over, chant-like. He stood on first base like he was king of the world. Victorious, confident, powerful.

Cam's eyes prickled with tears and she swallowed the lump of love in her throat. She was astonished by the things she'd seen in Seth's students. The kindness, the generosity, the inclusiveness. She'd never been around children much. She'd assumed, from Cooper's last three schools, that all children fell into two camps: those who bullied or those who got bullied. She was discovering there was quite a bit in between. Quite a bit.

Slowly, she eased back down to sit, leaning against the tree. After four more runs and no outs, Seth yelled for the teams to switch places again. This time, Cooper picked up a mitt and ran into center field. A few balls came his way and he missed them. He staggered, he floundered, but he never quit. He *never* quit. Cam's heart swelled to the point of bursting, and tears trailed down her cheeks.

Seth finally called the game over and announced it was time for lunch. The kids cleaned up the field and grabbed their lunches, forming huddles under the trees. She heard Quinn call for Cooper to join them and he hesitated, but she insisted, patting the ground next to her, and Cooper plunked down beside her. Like he was one of them. Now Cam's tears were coming down like a faucet. She couldn't stop them. She couldn't remember the last time she cried. She never cried. She didn't even cry at her mother's funeral, nor at Libby's. She just did not cry.

And here she was, dabbing at her eyes, willing herself to stop, but then she saw Quinn jab him with her elbow and Cooper jabbed her back and a flow of tears started all over again.

"Is something wrong?"

She pivoted around and saw Seth standing behind her, his face mask in his hand. He had a concerned look on his face.

"No," she said quietly. "Something is definitely not wrong." She wiped tears off her cheeks and took a deep breath. "I was pulling myself together until Quinn . . ." Her voice faded. If she said it aloud, said how kind Quinn was to include Cooper, that it was the first time a child had ever included him for lunch . . . first time . . . then the tears would start all over again.

"Did she say something to hurt Cooper's feelings?" he said, misunderstanding Cam's tears. "I'll talk to her. Quinn's a pistol. She leads the team in fistfights. But don't write her off quite yet. She's a pretty straightforward girl."

Cam shook her head. "It's her heart. She's got a straightforward heart." She pointed to where Quinn and Cooper sat under the tree. Quinn held out a bag of Cheetos to share with Cooper. He hesitated, peering into the bag, but then he took one out and ate it.

Cam opened her mouth and drew a breath, but she couldn't talk. She was choking up. Her eyes pooled.

"What is it? What's wrong?"

Cam wiped her eyes with her soaked tissue. She was surprised she had any tears left. Did a body have an endless supply? "He hates Cheetos. He's afraid of the color orange."

Now Seth understood. He smiled. "Falconers have a word for hawks in the mood to slay. They call the bird in 'yarak.' It comes from the Persian word *yaraki*, meaning power, strength, and boldness. When Lola is in yarak, she leans back, her shoulders drop, and her crest feathers rise. Her demeanor switches from 'Everything scares me' to 'I see it all. I own all this and more.'"

"That's it!" She laughed. "That's it exactly. That's how Cooper looked when he ran to first base. Like he owned it. Like he was in yarak." She sighed. "How did you manage to convince him to take a turn at bat?"

"I told him that the GCI pitcher was awful. If he crouched down low, he'd end up getting walked. A sure run."

"Well, I have to hand it to you. It worked. I was holding my breath the entire time he was up at bat. I was so afraid he would strike out."

"Striking out is part of the game. Even the pros strike out. I think it's one of the best things a kid can learn. That it's okay to fail. That you'll have another chance at bat."

Her dad used to say something like that. "Next time there's a softball game, ask my dad to umpire. He's a sports announcer. Was." She pointed to her throat. "Before."

"No kidding? I didn't know." They stood there for a moment, just looking at each other, until someone called to Seth. "I'd better go." He took a few steps, then turned around. "You'll be happy this afternoon. We're working on math." He grinned and wiggled his dark eyebrows. "Game stats."

She laughed. There were no stats. It was a shutout. Seth stopped keeping score after Three Sisters Island scored twenty-five runs. Great Cranberry Island never made a single run.

On Saturday, the *Mt. Desert Reporter* ran a front-page story about Cam and Camp Kicking Moose. The headline read "Billionaire Buys Bankrupt Island, Plans to Turn It into Maine's Atlantic City." Direct quotes were provided by Mayor Baxtor Phinney, Captain Ed of the Never Late Ferry, and Blaine Grayson.

Somehow, Cam got hold of a copy first. Blaine braced herself.

Cam read the headline aloud in a cold, flat tone and dropped the newspaper on the tabletop. "Blaine, what were you thinking?"

Blaine cringed. "I wasn't. The reporter was outside the Lunch Counter yesterday morning. He asked me some questions, and I answered, and then . . ." She looked at the paper. "And then *this* happened." She folded her arms across her chest. "You could've told us you made so much money. Don't you think she should have told us, Maddie?"

Maddie opened her mouth, then quickly shut it.

"Maddie, what is it?" Blaine came in closer, bearing down. "Oh, hold on. I get it. She did tell you. Just not me."

Cam was furious. "Wait just a minute, Blaine. This isn't about me—this is about you! Why did you tell . . . lies . . . to a reporter about me?"

"They aren't lies!"

"Blaine," Maddie said in her tell-the-truth voice.

Blaine shook her fists emphatically. "You're siding with her, aren't you? You're taking Cam's side."

"I'm not taking anyone's side."

"Blaine, I did tell you the business was sold. I don't know exactly what that will mean for me, but I know I'm not a billionaire." Cam pulled out a chair and plopped into it. "And look what you did! Why would you say that I'm going to fund a power station?"

"You are! You said so in that town meeting."

"I said that we could apply for government grants to fund it."

"That's pretty close."

Cam scoffed. "Now locals think I'm the sugar daddy to fix all of the island's problems. These people need to invest in themselves." She sighed. "And what is this about turning Three Sisters Island into another Atlantic City?"

"That came from the mayor," Blaine said quickly. "He doesn't like you. He thinks you're out to ruin the island."

Cam knocked her forehead against the tabletop three times. "The entire island has a skewed version of the facts."

"Well, that's what news is."

Cam's head shot up. "Don't make light of this, Blaine. This is serious. Every kook in Maine is going to be knocking on the door of Moose Manor, looking for handouts."

Blaine didn't buy that. Moose Manor was too hard to find, especially with the sign down.

"News comes and goes," Maddie said, trying to smooth the waters. "Maybe it'll be old news by tonight."

"Not the part about Three Sisters Island seceding from the United States."

Blaine lifted both hands in the air. "That wasn't me! That quote belongs to Captain Ed. Dad said he's been talking about seceding for as long as he's known him."

Cooper burst into the kitchen. "Guess what? Grandpa and I just got back from town. Peg had a ton of messages for us."

Cam groaned. "Oh, I don't even want to think what's going on with my phone."

Dad walked in with an ear-to-ear grin, holding up a handful of pink phone messages. "Good news. Lots of reservation requests for Camp Kicking Moose."

"What?" Maddie said. "Why?"

Dad jabbed a finger at the newspaper. "Because of that. It's gone viral. Picked up on national news." He sat at the table to silently read through the messages.

"See?" Blaine lifted her hands, open palms. "You should be thanking me for the publicity."

"It was all fictitious!" Cam said, throwing her hands in the air. Her voice rose with her gestures, big with righteous indignation. "Slanderous!"

"Ha! That's where you're wrong. Free publicity is good publicity. Any kind." That, Blaine knew from her Marketing 101 class. It took a lot to get Cam riled up, really upset, and it actually pleased her to see her so angry.

As Blaine walked out of the kitchen, she heard Dad say, "It

191

looks like the cabins of Camp Kicking Moose are booked solid from Memorial Day through Labor Day. Believe it or not, we have a waiting list."

Unbelievable, Blaine thought to herself. *Just unbelievable. How is it possible? Cam's Midas touch strikes again.*

Nineteen

MARCH GAVE WAY TO APRIL. There was so much to do, and time was running out. Opening Day was staring Paul in the face. He wiped his forehead with his sleeve and reached down for the weed whacker. He'd been working all day in the yard of Moose Manor, but it felt like a drop in the bucket, plus he kept noticing more things that needed to be done. The grass needed mowing, shingles needed to be replaced on the roof, the paint on the porch railing was chipped and needed sanding. And the house! Still bubble-gum pink.

If he couldn't find any painters soon, he'd just do it himself—something his daughters loudly objected to. They said it was too big a job for one "old" man (he took issue with that adjective) and he didn't know how to paint, and they were right on both counts.

But at least he could get the house ready for painters by clearing the foundation of weeds. He plugged in the extension cord of the weed whacker to the outlet, started trimming weeds, but either those weeds were tough or nothing seemed to be cut. Bent over, maybe, but certainly not trimmed. He turned it off, examined the spool, and found the plastic string had been used up. Blast. He would need to buy a new spool. He tossed the weed whacker into the back of his truck with a clanging thunk that rattled the bed.

Fifteen minutes later, he pulled open the door to the Lunch

Counter. "Afternoon, Peg." He gave her his brightest smile, forcing a cheerfulness he didn't have at the moment. Why did he feel the need to do that? Ever since Maddie had told him that Peg thought his grizzled voice was sexy, he felt as awkward around her as if he were back in junior high.

Peg barely looked up from going through receipts. "You," she said in a flat voice.

Uh-oh. "Did I do something wrong?"

"Yes."

He found the replacement spool for the weed whacker and set it on the counter. "Too many messages coming in? I'm working on getting a landline out to Moose Manor. The phone company promised we're in the queue."

Peg pointed to a pad of pink phone messages. "After I had a nice long talk with Artie Lotosky—"

"Who's that?"

"Blaine's fella."

"Oh! Not-the-boyfriend Artie."

"By the way, Artie says he wants to come up soon to visit me. Blaine, too, as long as he's here." She winked. "After Artie and I talked, I finally put the answering machine on. I can't get anything done with that phone ringing off the hook. You can listen to the rest of the messages yourself." She glowered at him. "But that's not why I'm mad."

Paul picked up the pad, filled to the end with messages. Holy Toledo. And there were more messages to listen to on Peg's "last-century answering machine"—Blaine's term for it. This was not going to be a short errand into town, like he'd planned. "Mind telling me why you're mad, then?"

"You took my cook." Now she did look up, frowning. "Yesterday, this place was packed. Today, it's empty." Peg lifted her hands in a helpless gesture. "Folks walk in, and if they don't see Blaine cooking behind that counter, they walk right out. You need to stop keeping her out there at the camp. I need her here."

Paul went to a stool and sat down. "How about a cup of coffee?" Peg stared him down, or tried to, then gave up and smiled. "Now you're talking." She poured him a mug and handed it to him.

"The thing is, Peg, I need all the help I can get out at the camp. Cam had everyone on a mission to clean out the cabins this week. Memorial Day doesn't feel very far off." He looked into his mug to see grounds floating on top of a pale brown color. "But maybe I can spare Blaine. She sure does seem happier when she's helping you."

Now Peg smiled. "Good. That's good, good news." She poured herself a cup of coffee, took a sip, and made a face. "Blaine tries to teach me how to do things, like make coffee, and I think I've got it. Side by side, I follow everything she does. But it never turns out the same. Never." She poured the coffee into the sink. She turned around and leaned against the stove, arms crossed. "So, Paul Grayson, how're you doing out there? Must seem a little lonely to be running an empty camp on an island."

"Lonely?"

"Compared to your big radio career. I read about it in that newspaper article. You never told me you were such a hotshot."

"Me? A hotshot?" Those were Blaine's words, not his. "In a way, my radio career was probably more lonely than this venture has been." He surprised himself, hearing regret in his voice. "I was on the road more months than I was home." He pointed to his throat. "And when it had to stop"—he swirled his coffee—"by then it was home that was lonely."

Peg's eyes grew soft. "Now, *that* I get."

"Get what?"

"The empty house. The loneliness. The solitude."

His eyebrows lifted in surprise. He hadn't let himself think much about loneliness. Oh, he noticed it now and then, ached sometimes for the loss of his wife, of someone to share his life. "I guess you get past being lonely. And you live for your kids."

"Ain't that the truth?"

He looked up. "Peg, does your son ever come visit you?"

"Now and then. More then than now." She scooped three heaping tablespoons of coffee into a filter, frowned, then added four more. "He suffers from depression sometimes," she said, filling the coffeepot to the top with water.

Paul hadn't expected that. He let it lie there for a minute, but then he couldn't help asking. "What has he got to be depressed about? He's got it made." Peg had told Paul once that her son had finished law school and was preparing to take the bar exam.

Peg clicked the coffeepot on and grabbed a cloth to start swabbing the spills on the counter. She was never still, always on the move. "I wish I could tell you. I know he's had his share of problems. His dad walking out, the divorce—it hit him hard. But sometimes, I just don't get it. I've done everything for that boy. I'm still doing everything. Where'd I go wrong?"

Paul shrugged. "Don't ask me. At the moment I'm pretty sure that two of my own daughters aren't speaking to each other."

"Let me take a wild guess. Cam's upset about that ridiculous news story and blames Blaine, who doesn't like being misunderstood. Maddie's running back and forth between the two."

Impressive. "Bull's-eye. You hit the target."

That drew a laugh out of Peg. Apparently it was what she needed, because she sighed with her whole body, and when she looked up, her cheerfulness had returned. She pointed to him with a grin. "That disappearing voice of yours . . . it ends up making a girl tell more than she planned to say." She planted her hands on her hips. "I must say, it's refreshing to be around a man who does more listening than talking. You're a rare bird, Paul Grayson."

Paul laughed—it came out in a rusty, gravelly sound because he'd already talked too much for the morning. Used up his allotment of words for the day, as Blaine would say. But then he saw something sitting on the stove. "Is that . . . ?"

"Ayup. Lime tart. Blaine's been baking them these last few days, trying to get them just right. She keeps sending Captain Ed off to

196

get more limes, and believe you me, that is no small errand in the month of April in Maine."

He could barely speak, and it wasn't because of his fading voice. "Could I have a piece?"

"Sure." She cut a slice and handed it to him on a plate with a fork. "Just don't tell Blaine. She says it's not perfect yet."

But it was. It tasted every bit as delicious as the lime tarts Corinna used to make to welcome him home. Somehow, even better. Peg set a brand-new pink answering pad by his coffee mug and went back to swabbing the countertops as he sat there enjoying the rest of the lime tart. He reached over to turn on Peg's answering machine and start transcribing, feeling pretty good, as if he'd turned a page. As if they all had.

Maddie and Blaine had been cleaning out cabin 6 together, until Blaine went back up to the manor house to get some more window cleaner and never returned. Maddie finished sweeping out the cabin and went up to the house. She called for Blaine but didn't hear an answer, couldn't find her anywhere, though she found the empty bottle of window cleaner left on the kitchen counter. Maddie followed a hunch and went upstairs to knock on her bedroom door. Without waiting for a response, she opened the door. The room was dark, Blaine lay curled on her side on the bed.

"What are you doing up here? Aren't you feeling well?" Maddie sat on Blaine's bed. "We've got a lot to do to get this place ready by Memorial Day. Come on back down to the cabins. We need you."

Blaine pulled the covers up to her chin. "I'm not needed here."

"Of course you are."

Blaine sat up in bed. "Why do you always have to take Cam's side over me?"

Oof. This whole newspaper fiasco had unleashed something ugly, had taken the family down a wrong turn. "Blaine, I don't."

"It's true!" Blaine was really crying now, and Maddie's heart melted for her. These weren't histrionic tears, but sad, uncontrollable ones. "You always do! You do. You always have. It's like she's the sister you really want. I'm just a spare. You always choose her over me."

That wasn't true, but that didn't mean that Blaine's feelings weren't real. In a way, Maddie understood them. All these years later, Maddie could still remember how it felt when Libby was around, and she was *always* around. Maddie had longed to be friends with Cam as well as sisters, but Cam had never wanted that. Libby had sufficed for her.

"Cam treats me the same way she treats you, Blaine. She treats everyone the same way. She's super smart, in that quick way. She wants everybody to be the best they can be, and she pushes everybody. You're no different than anybody else." She could tell she wasn't getting through to Blaine, and shifted to a more direct approach. "Look, you're the one who's picking sides."

"Me? How so?"

"You're so jealous of Cam that you can't see straight."

"Me? Jealous?"

"Yes, you. Why don't you try and see what's right about Cam instead of everything that's wrong about her?"

"Because everybody else is so busy doing that!" Blaine looked stricken, then closed her eyes. "Maybe I am jealous of her." She sighed. "I am. You're right. In fact, I'm having a very jealous stretch. I'm even jealous that you're going to marry Tre. That's how low I've sunk."

Oof. That smarted.

Blaine's eyes popped open. "Sorry. What I should have said was, I'm jealous you get to plan a wedding."

Maddie scoffed. "Tre's mother gets to plan a wedding." Mrs. Smith had interpreted her acceptance of help as a green light to take control over all aspects of the wedding. Every little part of it. Just yesterday, she returned a call to Tre's mother. Mrs. Smith told her that she'd found a bridal gown for Maddie, and was especially pleased because the bridal gown complemented the bridesmaids' dresses she'd already ordered. Maddie was nonplussed, absolutely speechless. She hadn't even decided on having bridesmaids yet! In her mind, a simple beach wedding didn't really need a stack of bridesmaids or groomsmen. Just the bride, the groom, and the preacher.

And the bridal gown? Maddie had in mind a simple white flowing dress, Bohemian style. Something she could wear again. She cringed at the thought of Mrs. Smith's formal, over-the-top taste. An image of Princess Diana's big poofy-sleeved bridal gown came to mind.

Before Blaine could ask another question, she quickly added, "Let's not get distracted by weddings. My point is that jealousy is insidious. Mom used to say that it's a slippery slope that takes you to a bottomless pit."

Blaine sat up. "You know . . . I can remember her saying that."

"You have no reason to be jealous of me or Cam or anyone else. Cam's life isn't all roses, you know. It can't be easy to be so"—she wiggled her hands around her head—"so smart. She intimidates everyone."

Blaine wiggled her eyebrows. "Not Seth Walker."

"So far, so good." Maddie smiled. "Let's hope Cam doesn't do anything to ruin it."

"Like set him on a rapid career path of one-room schoolhouses?"

"Exactly." Maddie laughed and climbed off the bed. "Come on. Let's finish up those cabins. I need to get downtown soon to mail a letter to Tre."

Blaine slid off the bed. "Maddie, I miss Mom here more than I did in Boston. Isn't that weird?"

There was a silence. A moment of shared loss. Maddie shook her head. "No. It's not weird. I've had the same feelings." She had thought about this quite a lot and decided it had to do with the fact that they had all left a whirring, fast city to live on a quiet, remote island. Everything had slowed down, including their thoughts. Doing so allowed the remembering to surface.

Later that afternoon, Maddie drove into town to pick up some groceries. She parked her car in front of the Lunch Counter, locked it, and spun around when she heard someone call her name. Tre was loping up from Boon Dock. She frowned, momentarily discommoded at the sight of him as he approached her. On its heels came a disloyal thought that she shook off as soon as it registered: he looked all wrong here, all preppy and buttoned up. He didn't fit.

"Tre! What are you doing here?"

He held his arms wide open to her, and she slipped right into his embrace. "You weren't coming to Boston, so I thought I'd come to you." He kissed her. "This place," he said, kissing her again, "is about as far from civilization as a man can get."

She laughed, relaxing. "Believe it or not, Maine is closer to Africa than any other state is."

"I believe it." He kissed her again, then released her.

"Goodness, for a man who makes his living as an actuary, you can be full of surprises! How long can you stay?"

"Until Thursday. Two nights." He sneezed. "They're recarpeting the office, so they gave everyone a few days off."

Oh, so that's why he'd come. Not because of missing her, but because of new carpet. Disappointed, she decided to make the best of the surprise visit. "Let me show you around. The tour starts by the water. Then we'll go to the Lunch Counter. You've got to meet Peg. After that, we'll head out to Moose Manor."

He took her hand in his as they walked across the street. "Before the tour starts, I want to explain something to you, in person. About those Instagram pictures from Skippy's wedding."

"Instagram? I didn't see any. Cell phone service is really spotty up here. Really, really spotty. As in, you have to stand in one certain spot to get it."

"Oh, I forgot." Relief filled his eyes. "Well, you told me to take someone else. Remember?"

"I suggested your cousin Courtney."

"I didn't take Courtney."

"Then who?"

"Do you remember that hostess at the restaurant . . . the night we got engaged? She was an old friend."

She stopped and released his hand. "She was an old girlfriend, I recall you saying."

"Oh Mads, don't look like that. Susan and I just happened to be texting after you told me you couldn't go to Skippy's wedding. She offered to step in for you. No big deal."

"Really? No big deal, huh? Then why are you worried about Instagram pictures?"

"I'm not. I just . . . wanted to explain the situation in person. I know how you get."

How *she* got? That was a bait-and-switch tactic if she'd ever heard one. "Tre, what was in those pictures that you felt needed explaining?"

"Nothing! Really. We were dancing, that's all. I just didn't want you to see them before I had a chance to tell you that she was my plus one." He reached out for her hands. "I would've had a much better time with you."

She weakened. "Really?"

He pulled her close to him. "Absolutely." Then suddenly, he released her and his body convulsed in a huge sneeze. Then another.

"Hey there, Maddie. Who's the stiff?"

She cringed, recognizing those voices. The mayor's sons had circled them. "Peter, Porter, this is my boyfriend, Tre."

"Your boyfriend?" Porter said, looking Tre over, and he obviously didn't like what he saw. "You never mentioned a boyfriend when we were making out the other night."

Maddie sighed. "That's Porter's idea of being funny." She'd been in the Lunch Counter a couple of times when they were there. For once Blaine hadn't been exaggerating when she described them as annoyingly immature.

Tre sneezed again, blew his nose on his handkerchief, then sniffed the air. "What gum are you chewing?"

Peter pulled out a yellow package of Juicy Fruit. "Want a stick to freshen your breath, lover boy?"

Tre shook his head and made a pinched face. "There's something in the smell of Juicy Fruit gum that makes me feel queasy."

Peter nudged Porter with his elbow. "It's called manhood." He winked at Maddie and the two trudged away toward Boon Dock.

"Sorry. It's unfortunate that those two are the first locals you've met."

Tre sneezed again. "I need to get indoors. I'm getting an allergic reaction." He looked up. "Pine trees. There's so many of them."

"Maine is the Pine Tree State."

He sneezed again. "I think I'm allergic to pine needles." He looked up and down at the cars parked along the street. "It's like every beat-up old car was sent from the mainland to this island." He pointed to one in front of the Lunch Counter. "Look at that dowdy old minivan! I didn't think they made those anymore."

"Boy, that's my car you're running down."

They whirled around to face Peg. She had just come out of the grocery store with a carton of eggs in her hand. "Peg, this is Tre. My . . ." Maddie fumbled on the word.

"Fiancé," Tre filled in. "Nice to meet you, Peg. And don't misunderstand. I'm a fan of old cars."

Peg couldn't be fobbed off that easily. "I didn't know you were engaged, Maddie. You never said a word about it."

Tre whipped his head around and pulled up Maddie's left hand, which had no ring on it. "Mads." His tone was filled with disappointment.

"I've been doing so much labor out at Moose Manor—I didn't want anything to happen to it." That was the truth. It was also true that the ring was not her style at all. It was huge, ridiculously big, with a thick gold band that made her small fingers look silly.

Tre seemed to accept her explanation. After Peg went inside the Lunch Counter, he whispered, "Well, she sure fits the stereotype for a BMW."

"What do you mean?"

"You must know the joke about BMWs."

"What joke?"

"Big Maine Women."

She stiffened, drew back. She didn't find it funny.

Cam sat through dinner with Tre, letting it all soak in, convinced that Maddie was making the biggest mistake of her life. Even Dad, who was pretty hands-off when it came to relationship stuff, pulled out his disappearing-voice card and excused himself early. He took Cooper up to bed for her so they could look through a book about falconry.

"So, Cams." (She hated that nickname.) "You're in the big leagues now." Tre winked at her. "How much did you rake in on the heist?"

"Tre!" Maddie said.

Cam kept a straight face. Tre had a knack for saying things all wrong. "I'm not sure what the final amount will be, Tre. And of course, taxes will swallow up 50 percent."

"What?" Blaine said. "Fifty percent? See?" She jabbed the tabletop. "That's why I can't support capitalism."

"Blaine," Cam said, "if we lived under a socialist system, like France, taxes would take more like 65 percent. Maybe more."

Her mouth dropped. "That's criminal!"

Cam turned to Tre. "Is there any particular reason you're interested in my income?"

"Just curious. It's big news down in Boston."

Cam waved her hand like she was shooing a fly. "News comes and goes."

Blaine gave her a look. "Well, that's what *I* said and you bit my head off."

Everything went downhill from there.

Later, Maddie gave up her room for Tre to use and came downstairs to fix him a cup of tea. Cam sat at the kitchen table, papers spread out. She spent a lot of time each evening to map out operational plans for Camp Kicking Moose. A lot of time. It made her feel better, as if she was in control of something. And the plans would help her dad, down the road, with execution. She sniffed the air. "What's that smell?"

Maddie looked up from the stovetop. "It's a special kind of tea for Tre. Helps his allergies."

Good grief. Tre and Maddie had already cooked some weird concoction made of horseradish for dinner, something that would help clear his sinuses, and the house still reeked. Her sister was engaged to a high-maintenance, needy young man firmly under his mother's thumb. Like Lola, tied to the glove. "How long is Tre staying?"

"A few days. Do you mind?" When the pause had gone on too long, Maddie said, "Can't you be happy for me?"

"I want to be," Cam said, and it was true. "It's just that you deserve the best." That was true too.

"This is the life I want, Cam. Tre and I are going to live in Boston, work, raise a family."

"You don't like city living. And you seem to love it here."

"Boston is where Tre's work is. And it's a better environment for him. You know, his allergies."

"Ah yes. He's allergic to everything."

"Not everything."

"Ocean air."

Maddie frowned. "So maybe most things." She put the spoon in the sink. "When you love someone, you make sacrifices."

Cam wanted to give advice so badly she had to curl her hands into fists.

CAM, AGE 20

Cam was curled up in a chair as Mom folded laundry. "I just don't think Libby's being realistic. She's talking about keeping the baby." She squeezed a pillow against her middle. "I keep telling her to give up the baby for adoption. It would solve everything. The baby would end up in a loving family, with two parents, and Libby could go back to college. Have a career." Get far away from her crazy grandmother. "It's the perfect solution."

Mom tucked one sock into another and tossed the ball on the coffee table. "It is *one* solution."

Cam sat up. "Don't tell me you think she should keep the baby?"

"No, I agree with you about adoption, Cam. It could be a wonderful solution for both Libby and her baby. I've even given Libby the name of a good adoption lawyer." Mom folded a pair of jeans and put it on top of Maddie's stack.

"Libby says she'd consider giving the baby up for adoption to our family."

Mom stilled and looked straight at her. "Cam, that's not an option."

"Yeah, I didn't think you'd go for it. Being older and all."

Mom frowned. "My age is not the reason. This baby is Libby's responsibility. You can't fix this for her, as much as you want to. You can't live other people's lives for them, even if you love them. Sometimes love means trusting people to make their own decisions."

"So I should just smile and hug her and tell her I think it's great if she keeps the baby?"

"Yes."

"Even though I think she's going to regret it?"

"I doubt she'll ever regret keeping her baby. But yes, it's going to be harder than she realizes. And that's where you come in."

"How so?"

"That's when she'll really need a friend. Someone who won't say 'I told you so.'"

Cam released her breath slowly. "In other words, I have to keep my mouth shut."

Her mom threw a folded ball of socks at her. "It's often the best solution of all."

Twenty

SETH ASKED CAM TO BRING the entire Grayson family to church on Sunday morning. She wanted to say no. Since the newspaper article ran, she didn't like going into the village. Before it ran, most locals were cool or indifferent to her, still undecided about the Grayson family. Now, the same people looked at her in a strange way, as if she were royalty or a movie star, and they all made a point to congratulate her. They didn't know how she really felt about losing her job, losing her identity: she was adrift in the world, standing outside the current and watching it go by. They didn't know because she hid her feelings well.

But Seth had persisted about church and so she had agreed to come this morning. It was held in the Baggett and Taggett shop, and only sixteen people were there—five of whom were Graysons. Seth led worship, Peg read Scripture, Captain Ed gave a long-winded talk on Psalm 23 that made no sense at all. Instead of it being about a shepherd and his sheep, he turned it into a story about a fisherman and a lobster.

Afterward, Seth sidled up to Cam. "Sorry about that. Captain Ed's preaching can be a little . . . inconsistent."

"Don't be. It was . . . charming. In a small-island sort of way."

"That's very kind. I thought it was terrible. I have to find a bona fide pastor, stat." He tipped his head. "Do you know of any aspiring seminary students?"

"Me? Uh, no." This whole faith thing, it was new for Cam. Not new, not exactly. Mom had dragged the girls to Sunday school whenever Dad was away, which was often, and Mom talked about the Bible as if it was real. But Cam didn't pay much attention. Her relationship with God—and she used that term loosely—was nothing like the way Seth talked about God.

But then, Seth still had his mother, and probably his best friend. He hadn't been to two back-to-back funerals.

Something at the end of the church service touched Cam. There was a moment to share prayer requests, and Peg stood up to say that the Grayson family's arrival was the answer to her prayers. "This island needed something and I didn't know what to ask for," she had said, "so's I just told God, 'Lord, you know. You know.' And sure enough, he did. He sent you here, no doubt about it, and you've been a blessing to us." She wiped her eyes with a red handkerchief and Cam felt herself tearing up too. Imagine that. Peg considered them an answer to her prayer.

But then Cam's skepticism kicked in. Did prayer really make a difference? She wondered. On the heels of her doubt came another surprising thought: hope that it did.

Seth interrupted her muse. "Do you like Thai food?"

"Here? There's a Thai restaurant on this island?" That's what Cam said out loud. What she was thinking was, *Are you asking me out on a date?*

Amused, he shook his head. "I'm inviting you to dinner at the Lunch Counter. Tonight. You and Cooper." He explained that he promised Cooper a visit with Lola, and Peg let him cook on Sunday nights when the restaurant was closed, as long as he left it spic-and-span.

So it wasn't really a date. Not really.

That evening, Cam perched on the stool at the Lunch Counter, waiting. She unbuttoned her blazer and smoothed the creases of her navy pencil skirt. Why hadn't she worn a more flattering outfit? All her clothes made her look like she was heading into a high-rise office. She could have rummaged through Maddie's closet to borrow something pink, sweet, loose, soft around the edges. Something feminine. But Maddie's clothes looked like hippy clothes. It took a few seconds before it struck her that her panic might not be about clothes at all. *Good grief. I am reverting back to seventh grade.*

She checked her lipstick again, waiting for Seth to return. Before he started cooking, Seth took Cooper out back to meet Lola in her big cage. Cam declined the invitation to go with them. Lola scared her.

About ten minutes later, Cooper came back into the restaurant. "Mom, Lola's wearing a hat. You should see it."

"It's called a hood," Seth said, following behind him. "It helps Lola stay calm when she's perched, so she doesn't hurt herself. As beautiful as goshawks are, they're not very smart. They have tiny little brains that get them in a tizzy whenever they get stressed."

"No kidding?" Cam said. "I thought Lola seemed unflappable."

"Some are. Not Lola. She gets stressed a lot. She's pretty high-strung. So the hood makes Lola think it's nighttime, and she takes a nice little nap."

"She likes it?" Cooper was intrigued.

"She was calm, wasn't she?"

Cooper nodded. He climbed up on the stool next to Cam and leaned on his elbows. "I'm going to be a falconer when I grow up."

Seth went behind the counter and picked up a knife. "You don't have to wait that long, Cooper. Keep reading about falconry. You can't learn enough. I'll take you along with me sometimes when I let Lola launch." He picked up a cabbage and then glanced at Cam. "As long as it's okay with your mom."

Cam lifted her hands. "Totally okay." One thousand percent okay. She couldn't believe that Cooper was initiating an interest in something like falconry. Of all things for an easily frightened, overly anxious seven-year-old to have an interest in. Wonders never ceased.

"Can we go see her again?"

"Oh, sorry, bud, but I need to get dinner started," Seth said.

Cooper looked at Cam. "Not me," she said. "I don't think she likes me much."

"Can't I go alone? I just want to watch her in the cage."

"Fine with me," Seth said, looking at Cam for approval. Slowly, she nodded.

She watched Cooper hurry down the aisle of the store to disappear out the back door. "Amazing," she said under her breath.

"What's amazing?"

She shook her head. "Cooper. He likes it here." It almost seemed as if he needed to be here on this island just as much as her dad did.

"Hoodwinked," Seth said, holding up a knife.

Cam squinted. "What? He's getting hoodwinked?"

"No, no." Seth laughed. "The hood that Lola is wearing. That's where the term *hoodwinked* got its origin."

"Interesting. Be sure to tell Cooper that little bit of trivia. He collects facts."

"I will." Across the counter, Seth handed Cam a glass of water. "Do you ever give in to a true sit? Or do you just perch?"

"Yes. No. Sometimes."

"Seems like you're always about to bolt. Shoot off in the sky like Lola."

"I'm not! I mean, I'm happy to be here."

He stopped chopping cabbage and looked right at her. "I'm glad you're here too."

She felt shy all of a sudden. She wanted to say something witty but nothing came forth. Her mind went blank. As a distraction, she grabbed the water glass to sip and ended up sloshing it all over her silk blouse. *Smooth, Cam.* She tried to shrug it off, but her face burned red.

What was wrong with her? She could address a boardroom and

not miss a beat. She could breeze through hard questions from major media outlets. Make a critical decision in the blink of an eye. But a romantic moment? Cam floundered. Sweated. Stuttered. Couldn't string two thoughts together. Romance, she avoided. She felt awkward and clumsy and stupid. Feelings she did not like to feel.

Worse still, Seth seemed to know. Mirth spread all over his handsome features. He was enjoying her awkward discomfort. She was glad to provide so much entertainment for him.

Cam's taste buds were her only sense unflustered by Seth, but it didn't take more than a few bites of his cooking to do the trick. He presented her with a dinner plate of butter lettuce cups filled with Thai chicken, spicy and savory, along with crispy coconut rice. "This is delicious," she said to Seth, her awe undisguised. "Restaurant quality. I'm shocked that you made this."

From the amused look on his face, she realized it hadn't come out as a compliment, the way it had started in her mind. "You probably don't have much time to cook, being a busy billionaire and all," he said with a smirk.

"Mom doesn't cook," Cooper said. "She microwaves."

"Thank you for that, Coop," she said, nudging him with her elbow. Silent shame covered her as she thought of all her microwaved meals for him.

And then she realized another astonishing discovery—Cooper had finished his entire plate. He liked Seth's exotic cooking. This was a boy who viewed anything new with suspicion.

After dinner, Cam helped Seth wash and dry dishes while Cooper went out to watch Lola again. "Lola has charmed him, it seems."

"My gut feeling tells me that he would be good at hawking. He's got the patience for it. Most kids lose interest in Lola because . . . well, she's not exactly the warm, fuzzy pet type."

Cam burst out with a laugh. "She's absolutely terrifying." She set a dry dish on the shelf. "Why would anyone train hawks?"

"Lots of reasons. For some, it's a sport. Others, a necessity. Farmers use hawks and falcons to keep mice and moles out of their fields. I have friends over on Mount Desert who keep hawks." He lifted a knife in the air. "Be careful with this, it's sharp." He gave it to her by its handle. "By the way, I want to take you and Cooper over to Cadillac Mountain for the sunrise."

"Sunrise?" She felt a little thrill at the suggestion.

"Most of the year, it's the first place on the continental United States to see the sunrise. We'll go, soon. Maybe next Saturday, if the weather looks good. We'd have to leave early. Really early. It's worth it, though."

She nodded, trying to act super cool, though she wanted to do a jig.

Unaware of her barely concealed excitement, he went back to the task of dishwashing. "Anyway, my hawking friends over on Mount Desert, they've given me a lot of help with Lola. They think I'm crazy to want to release her, but I think birds are meant to be free. Like the saying goes, 'A captive condor is a condor no more.'"

"But you have let her go, haven't you?"

"It's called 'carriage' when a hawk is released for a flight. And yes, she has had some flights."

"But she returns?"

"So far, but it's always Lola's choice to return." He handed her a dry dish towel. "At its heart is control. You pour your heart, your very soul into training a hawk, then relinquish control. Once the hawk leaves the fist, you can't control the outcome." He handed her a blue mixing bowl to dry. "Someday, when she's ready, I think she won't return to me."

"Isn't it hard to let her go? How can you love something, how can you work so hard to rehabilitate her, if all it means is loss?"

"But not allowing Lola the freedom to choose, isn't that worse?" He handed her a plate. "A little like parenting, right? You know all about raising a child on your own."

She pondered for a long, silent moment. "I adopted Cooper."

"Cooper's adopted?" He stopped washing dishes and pivoted toward her, staring at her. "Well, that explains why he doesn't resemble the Grayson clan."

"He was my best friend's son. She died in an accident and left me as his legal guardian."

"And you adopted him?" He tilted his head. "Cam, what a noble thing to do. I'm impressed."

"Don't be. She would've done the same for me. And Cooper has been a gift to me. Maybe more of a gift to me than I am to him."

Seth turned off the faucet to give her his full attention. Softly, he said, "Now why would you say that?"

She shrugged, avoiding his eyes. "Sometimes I think Maddie's the one who should've adopted him. She'd do a better job of raising him."

"How so?"

"She's the one who remembers Cooper's sunscreen. Gets his regular haircuts." She smirked. "She even takes him to the dentist and doctor for regular checkups. Would you believe that I didn't know kids needed regular vaccinations?"

"Maddie . . . the middle sister? Nope. I've watched her with him. She raises his anxiety by making more of everything. Over-empathizing makes anxiety worse. Even with animals—you don't want to bring more attention to a concern. I think you do better with Cooper by playing things down. He calms down around you. He feels secure when you're near. Then he feels safe to go out exploring."

Suddenly her hands fell still. She swallowed and looked down, shocked. It was the first time someone had ever complimented her as a mother. Ever.

"What? Did I say something wrong?"

"No." She lifted her eyes. "You said something very right."

They stared at each other, wide-eyed, for some seconds. Then a smile started in his eyes—those beautiful blue eyes—and she smiled in return. He reached out a soapy hand to brush her hair out of her eyes, and she wondered if this was why everyone made such a big deal about romance. She was always so in control, moving forward on the path she saw for herself, she never let herself slow down long enough to feel anything. To listen to what her heart had to tell her. But it sure was trying to tell her something now.

Twenty-One

AFTER A WEEK OF DAMP, COLD FOG, the sun shone bright on a day in mid-April to remind everyone that spring was here. It was a gorgeous day, with a flawless blue sky and warm sun; one of those days you threw open the windows and packed away your wool sweaters.

That evening, just after sunset, Seth rode his moped out to Moose Manor. "I bring tidings," he told Cam when she opened the door to him. "A message for Blaine from that fellow Artie. He wants her to call him ASAP." He leaned a little closer to Cam. "My keen nose for romance tells me that he is trying very hard to court your sister and she is unaware of his ardor."

Cam folded her arms against the open door. "So you have a keen nose for romance?"

"I do." His eyes smiled. "So take a walk down to the beach with me."

Her heart skipped a beat. Maybe two. "But it's dark."

"Night brings out the best in the ocean."

She thought about it for less than a half second. "Let me just tell Cooper. Blaine's reading him a good-night story. You want to come in?"

"No, I'll wait for you on the porch. Uh, Cam, you might want to change your shoes."

She glanced down at her pink fluffy knitted slippers. Libby had made them for her, years ago, when the two of them had been on a knitting craze. "On it." She took the stairs two at a time, kissed Cooper good night, grabbed a sweater, exchanged sneakers for pink slippers, and stopped at the bathroom mirror. She frowned, painted a thin black line over each eyelid. Mascara. Blush. A smear of lipstick. Ran a comb through her hair. Okay, that was the best she could do.

She hurried back downstairs to join Seth. Her heart did a little stutter step when she saw him, and she suddenly felt girlish. He was sitting on the porch steps, leaning against the pole, looking up at the evening sky. He was wearing a gray long-sleeved T-shirt with a hole in it, and long khaki shorts. His lean legs stretched to the bottom step.

She found herself staring at his calves. Very muscular. She shook off that silly thought. So he had nice legs. So what? Legs didn't mean anything. They just held you up.

"Lilacs," he said.

"What?"

"The scent of lilacs is in the air tonight."

She took in a deep breath. He was right. The lilacs near the house were starting to bloom and they did smell heavenly. She'd been walking past them all week and hadn't noticed. Not once.

He was on his way down the porch steps and she hurried to catch up. They walked single file along the narrow path that led to the beach. "Do you go to the beach at night very often?"

Over his shoulder he said, "Whenever conditions are right."

"Such as?"

"No fog. Clear skies. New moon. A pleasant evening without much wind. And, of course, the tide."

"What about the tide?"

"It's on its way out. You never go to the beach on this island without knowing the tide tables."

"Why?"

"These outer islands . . . the shelf drops off abruptly, which makes for more intense tidal action. High tide can be a dangerous time to be near the water."

She admired how much knowledge he had of the natural world. She knew next to nothing.

As they reached the rocky beach, he stopped and took it all in. "I never fail to be mesmerized by this view."

She looked out at the black water that consumed the earth. This wasn't much of a view.

"Look up, Cam. Look at those stars."

She lifted her eyes and nearly gasped. They were like sparkling diamonds against the crush of black velvet. Okay, now she got it. She saw the view through his eyes. She wondered how the world could be so beautiful and yet so heartbreaking.

"'Lift up your eyes on high and see: who created these? He who brings out their host by number, calling them all by name, by the greatness of his might, and because he is strong in power not one is missing.'"

"Shakespeare?"

"The prophet Isaiah. Old Testament dude."

"Do you believe all that?"

"What, you mean the Bible?" He sat down on a rock and edged over to make room for her. "I do. My dad is a pastor. I was practically raised at church. But the minute I hit college, I checked out and put it all on the shelf. Became kind of a prodigal. I made a lot of impulsive decisions. Bad ones. My poor mom. She had more than her share of sleepless nights over me. But I finally figured things out. Got back on track." He scooted back on the rock. "I say that with a touch of irony because I was on the track team in college." He gave her a nudge with his elbow. "What about you?"

"Me?" She remained quiet for a long moment, thinking about what she thought of God. "I . . . I don't know what to believe. There's Someone up there, I suppose, but . . . is he down here? That's the part I'm not so sure about."

"So you don't think God is involved in your life?" Seth asked in a way that made her think he was genuinely interested in what she believed. Strangely enough, he didn't seem at all bothered that she wasn't on the same page as him.

Could she risk being candid with him? "Not really."

"So what would you say if I asked you why you're here?"

"Here . . . on earth at this point in history? Or on this island, right now?"

"Both."

She took some time to mull that question over. "I'm not sure I have an answer. I don't think there's a grand designer, weaving things together. Like that verse you quoted—not one star is missing." She shrugged. "That just seems hard to believe. Personally, I think we're kind of on our own to muddle through."

"Sounds kind of sad."

"Life *can* be sad." She lifted her face to the sky, to those twinkling stars. It looked like someone had scattered a handful of glitter dust.

"Why do I get the feeling that all the Graysons are working very hard to pretend that they're not dragging a heavy suitcase behind them? And that one sister, the one who's always worried . . . her suitcase has a bum wheel, to boot."

Cam bristled. "Maddie's more sensitive than most people." She was allowed to complain about her sisters all she wanted, but she never let anyone else do it, not even Libby. She knew she was probably deflecting Seth's insightful question, but she didn't want to go into more. Not now. Tonight she wanted to soak up the moment. The sea was calm, silky smooth, and a low-hanging crescent moon silvered the tops of lazy little waves that hit the rocky beach.

"So how're you doing without a job? I would think it's not easy for you."

She snapped her head around, again surprised by his intuitiveness. "What makes you say that?"

"You talk about plans a lot. I would think that suddenly not having them would make you feel a little . . . off-kilter."

Softly, she admitted, "I am . . . struggling." She turned to stare unseeingly at the water. Somehow, it was easier to say hard things without making eye contact. Her mother had taught her that. Whenever she was upset or in a foul mood, her mom would suggest they go for a car ride, and out would spew the reason for all of Cam's angst.

"I don't know what to do or where to go or how to take the next step. I've always known. Always." She slapped the back of her hand onto her other palm, a drumbeat. "College." *Slap*. "Business school." *Slap*. "Intense job." *Slap*. "But for the first time in years, I don't have a to-do list that's longer than my arm. Actually, each evening, I prepare long lists to manage Camp Kicking Moose and leave them on the kitchen table for everyone to find along with their favorite breakfast cereal. Even Cooper gets a list. Micromanaging is my coping strategy, Maddie declared this very day."

She worked her palms together nervously. "I should be so . . . grateful. I mean . . . I really don't have to work anymore. Cooper will be able to go to college, to graduate school. I'm in a situation most people only dream about. And yet . . . I feel like I have no purpose without my work. Like a boat with its mooring line cut. I feel like I'm just . . . adrift. Like I'm nothing anymore." As soon as the words spilled out of her, she wished them back. She braced herself, waiting for him to offer words of pity that would only annoy her.

Seth's head and body tipped slightly to one side to face her. "I don't think that's God's point of view, Cam. You don't 'earn' purpose."

Her eyes lingered on his. "I don't get it."

"We all have to let go of the need to prove ourselves. Our souls aren't a matter of commerce, we're a matter of faith."

She turned her gaze out to the sea, to the incessant waves pounding the rocks. "Faith isn't that easy."

"It's not," he said, almost laughing. "It most definitely is not. But everyone starts somewhere. And it's okay to start with a small faith. We've got a big God."

Again, she didn't know how to respond, so she said nothing, and he didn't seem to mind. They sat there for a while, listening to the gentle surf, gazing at the stars. It was nice, being here with him, getting to know him, talking about deep matters. She liked that they could talk about God and faith, but she didn't feel that he was trying to make her believe what he believed. He shared his thinking with candor, but not pressure. They met on equal terms. It was more than nice. It was wonderful.

She wondered if he had the same thoughts about her, but when she glanced at him, she realized he was studying something far out on the horizon. "Strange."

"What?"

"A fishing boat trolling without any lights on."

"Think they need help?"

"No, the engine's working just fine. They're heading north at a good clip. It just seems . . . odd."

After the fishing boat disappeared from view, they took off their shoes and walked along the edge of the ocean, letting the waves crawl over their feet. A piece of driftwood blocked their path and Seth took her hand to help her jump over it, then didn't let go. They held hands for the rest of the walk, all the way back to Moose Manor.

On Saturday morning, Maddie drove into town for her regular appointed time to call Tre—something he had suggested if she insisted on remaining on the island, which she did.

As she walked down toward the water, her head was down, staring at her phone to look for bars. She stopped, noticed the tops of two pairs of black rubber boots, looked up to find the Phinney brothers sneering at her. "Calling lover boy?" Porter said.

Maddie sighed.

Peter leaned closer, snapping his gum in her ear. "What does that dweeb have that we don't?" His greasy hair hung in her face, he smelled of fish and Juicy Fruit gum, an altogether sickening mélange. Blaine had warned her: "You don't want to get downwind of those Phinney boys."

She glanced at Peter's chest. *Blink If You Want Me* was today's T-shirt slogan that stretched over his big belly. When she and Blaine were little, they used to have staring contests. Those years of practice worked, because Maddie took Peter on in a staredown. A full minute passed, then another. Eyes watering, Peter caved and blinked. Triumphant, she said, "Excuse me, gentlemen, but I'm expecting a phone call."

Porter and Peter elbowed each other, amused at the term "gentlemen," and Maddie wished she had some of Blaine's moxie right now. Her bold little sister would have told them off; she saw them regularly at the Lunch Counter and considered them shifty, sketchy, and lazy. Day after day they kept insisting that, come tomorrow, they'd be at Moose Manor to paint, but they never showed up. The hot pink color remained.

Peter made a little gesture with his bait bucket and moved off, but Porter lingered. "How's 'bout you and me, we go out on the town to Bah Hahbah tonight? I know a place . . ." He wiggled his eyebrows in a leering way.

Oh gag me. "Can't," Maddie said, pointing to her ringing phone. She turned away to answer Tre's call and walked closer to the water, far away from portly Porter.

Tre chatted about work for a few minutes, and he gave her updates on the wedding. (Her wedding! She was the bride! Yet what could she do? She was the one who had exited stage left right after they got engaged.) Then there was a pause. He'd run out of the week's news. Timing, she knew, was everything with Tre. Carefully, Maddie cast out the idea she'd been mulling over since his visit to

Three Sisters Island. "Tre, I've been thinking that we could live here. After we get married."

"Good one." He thought she was kidding.

"I could have my own counseling office."

"Wait, you're serious?" He laughed. "Mads, that's ridiculous. There's no work to be done there."

"Wherever there are people, there's need."

"I meant me."

"Maybe you could open an office for your firm up here."

"I work as an actuary. I try to reduce risk for insurance companies. My entire day is spent asking the question, 'Does this make sense?' No, living on that island does not make sense."

"But . . . what kind of risk would it be, to live here?"

He scoffed again. "Setting aside the allergen count that creates an enormous risk to my health and well-being?"

She was glad he couldn't see her eye roll. "Besides that particular risk." She had read up on allergies this week and came to the conclusion that his body could build up immunities to allergies if he just gave it a chance, the way his hay fever was lessened when he ate local honey.

"Mads, sweetheart, think about it realistically. It takes most of the day to drive there, then a ferry ride, which has no set schedule. And that's when the weather is accommodating, which is about mid-June to mid-August in the state of Maine." He scoffed. "Consider Main Street. It's the headline of the town as you come in off the Never Late Ferry, and it's a beat-up, worn-down welcome. Maybe a painter could make a living on that island. It sure could use a facelift."

She turned around toward Main Street, tented her eyes from the sun, and squinted.

"That island is on the fast track to nowhere."

Actually, a couple of storefronts had taken her dad up on his offer to split the paint costs and had given them a fresh coat. Paint was a wonderful resource. Already, Main Street's appearance was improving. "There's so much potential here. Don't you think so?"

"None."

"Dad sees the island's potential. So does Cam. The natural beauty here, you can't deny it. Dad and Cam are confident they can create tourism here."

"It's pretty, sure it is. But there's plenty of other little islands in Maine to go to first, ones that are much easier to get to than hoping the Never Late Ferry shows up. You'd need some big, compelling reason for folks to go all the way out there to see the things people go to Maine for—lobsters and lighthouses and a rocky coastline." He sighed. "There is no reason to go to Three Sisters Island. Nada. Nyet. Much easier to stay in Bar Harbor on Mount Desert."

"Some people think Bar Harbor's gotten too crowded."

"Because they have to wait ten minutes in high season for a dinner reservation." Again, he scoffed.

Those dismissive scoffs! Very annoying.

"Mads, let me be very honest with you. This isn't about helping the island's recovery. This is about you and your family dynamics."

"What's that supposed to mean?"

"Whenever you're around your family, you slip into that I'll-fix-everything-for-everybody role. Your dad, Cam and Cooper, Blaine—you're the Mother Hen of the Graysons. You can't take care of them anymore. You've got your own life to live. It's time you start thinking of taking care of me. Just me."

The subject swung back to wedding details, and the topic of making a life on Three Sisters Island was closed. *For now*, Maddie thought.

Twenty-Two

AFTER CHURCH ON SUNDAY, Seth invited the Graysons, all of them, to take a ride out to the lighthouse with him on Captain Ed's fishing boat. "I promised Captain Ed I'd check on his lobster trap. Camp Kicking Moose has so much furniture and boxes arriving, he says he can't do anything but ferry back and forth with boxes."

"Oh, thanks for the invite, Seth," Dad said. "But we need to shuttle those boxes out to the camp and unload them."

With that, Blaine's eyebrows shot up. "Count me in, Seth!"

"Me too!" Cooper said.

"I don't know, Cooper," Maddie said. "It's awfully rough water."

"I think it's fine," Cam said.

"He doesn't know how to swim."

Cooper's head whipped back and forth between the two sisters.

"Got it covered," Seth said. "There's a child's life vest someplace around the dock."

"I've read those aren't reliable," Maddie said. "What if he panics when he goes overboard?"

"Wait. I'm going overboard?" Cooper asked, pressing the nosepiece of his eyeglasses.

"No." Cam's eyes flashed briefly to Seth's, then back to Cooper. She knew exactly what he was thinking. Maddie started this.

"Then why do I need a life vest?"

"Just in case."

"So that means there *is* a chance that I'm going overboard."

"Yes. No. Maybe. I mean . . ." Cam gave Maddie a look of annoyance. "It's just a safety measure, Cooper. Just like a seat belt in a car. I'll be with you. I won't let anything happen to you."

Sensing tragedy, Cooper balked. "I don't know."

Seth stepped in. "I could sure use your help hauling in that lobster trap, Cooper. It takes two men to do it right."

That did the trick. Cooper's worried look slipped away. "I guess I could go."

"I'll find a life vest for him," Maddie said. "But I think I'll stay behind to help Dad."

"Go ahead and go with them, Maddie," Dad said. "As long as my entire work crew is on strike, you might as well go too." He winked. "It'll give me a chance to take an afternoon nap." Peg called to him to meet someone and he walked away to join her.

"Come with us, Maddie. It's such a pretty day. How many chances do you get to go out on the ocean?" Cam saw Peg and Dad cross the street to the Lunch Counter. "Let's get some picnic supplies and enjoy the afternoon."

Cooper swayed her. "You should come, Aunt Maddie. It's good for you to practice being brave."

"I am brave."

Cam and Blaine, even Seth, burst out with a laugh.

Maddie's eyes went wide. "I am! There's lots of different ways to be brave."

"True words," Seth said. "We'd better get a move on while the tide is going out. We don't want to get caught at high tide."

"Uh-oh," Cooper said.

"Not a problem," Seth said reassuringly. He patted his shirt pocket. "I've got the tide table right here."

Not twenty minutes later, they were settled into Captain Ed's aluminum fishing boat, with a hastily thrown together picnic lunch bought at the Lunch Counter: sandwiches, apples, a bag of Blaine's day-old cookies, water bottles. As Seth steered the boat toward the northern tip of the island, Dory the dog seated next to him, Cam pointed out the little shore where she'd seen the mother sow and her cubs. "Where do you suppose they are now, Cooper?"

Cooper squinted his eyes and scanned the beach. "Do you think they went to Moose Manor? Grandpa is there alone, taking a nap. They might attack him in his sleep."

"No, no," Cam said forcefully. "Bears don't like people any more than people like bears. They're probably climbing a tree, looking for honey."

Cooper peered at her solemnly, then noticed a bird fly past them. He pointed to it. "That looks like Lola!"

"It's an osprey," Seth said. "Some old-timers call it a fish hawk." As he neared the open ocean, the water grew choppy. "Grab on to something, everyone. I'm going to speed up."

Cooper grabbed for Seth, nearly toppling him. "Hold it, pal. I haven't sped up yet." He straightened up and patted the seat between his legs. "Cooper, how about if you sit here with me? You can help me and Dory steer the boat."

In the blink of an eye, Cooper was the bravest boy in the world. He scrambled up on Seth's lap and put his hand on the handle of the stern drive. Seth's hand covered his. "Okay, now I'm going to make the boat go faster so it'll be more stable." Seth looked over his shoulder at Cam. "Hold on, ladies!" The boat lurched forward, then settled into a smooth ride—at least, as smooth as a flat-hulled boat could be on the open sea. Seth took it around the tip of the island, into the frantic Atlantic, and pointed out the lighthouse. "There's a good view of it."

"Is it still in use?" Blaine said.

"No," Cam said. "Not any longer. It's locked up tight."

Seth slowed the boat near the lobster trap buoy, then idled the engine. He leaned over the boat's edge to grab the buoy clamp and start pulling in the trapline, then stopped abruptly, turned, and said to Cooper, "I sure could use your help with this."

Maddie gasped, then rose to her feet as Cooper leaned over the side of the boat. Cam wasted no time. She pointed a finger to Maddie to insist she sit down and pressed a finger to her lips to silence her. Seth turned the crank, and Cooper, looking like he'd caught the moon, let the line slip between his hands to curl on the bottom of the boat. When the trap came up, it was empty of lobsters, filled only with crabs and sea kelp.

"I don't get it," Seth mumbled, peering at the trap. "I just don't get it."

"What?" Cooper said.

"Yeah, don't get what?" Blaine asked. She examined the trap.

"There should be lobsters in this trap." He baited the trap with herring, then had Cooper help him toss it over as Maddie cringed and squeezed her eyes shut. Seth brushed off his hands, and Cooper copied him, brush for brush. Cam felt her heart grow two sizes.

Seth docked the flat-bottom boat up on the gray-pebbled beach and helped everyone off. Cam led the way up the steep staircase on the bluff. "Look at it up close!" She pointed to the lighthouse, standing tall in the wind.

"It's huge!" Cooper said. "It looked smaller from the boat."

"Wow," Maddie said, and even Blaine looked impressed. She wasn't easy to impress.

"Can we go inside?" Cooper said.

"Last time we checked, it was locked up tighter than a drum," Seth said, carrying Dory up the stairs. "It's been abandoned for years."

"Let's have our picnic, first. Then we can walk around it."

They sat under a tree for the picnic, protected from the sea winds. Maddie passed out sandwiches and apples to each person. "Cooper, yours doesn't have blueberry jam on it. Only honey."

Cam tipped her head. Since when did blueberry jam go on

Cooper's do-not-eat list? And why didn't she know that? Her sister seemed to know things about Cooper that she didn't.

Blaine peppered Seth with questions about the lighthouse. "Why was it abandoned?"

Seth shrugged, swallowing his bite of sandwich. "It was decommissioned. A lot of lighthouses are no longer used. GPS has made them unnecessary."

Dory sniffed around everyone's food until Seth pushed her away. She went a few yards away, sat down, and actually looked hurt, so Cooper got up and tossed pieces of his sandwich to her.

"Thanks, Cooper," Seth said.

"No problem. I hate honey."

"Oh no," Maddie whispered. "Another one for the list."

Hold on, Cam thought. *Hold on. Cooper has always hated honey.*

Blaine peppered Seth with more questions about lighthouses. "Who makes those decisions . . . to turn off the lights?"

"The Park Service."

"So does the government own the lighthouse?"

"No. If I'm not mistaken, when it was decommissioned, the land was sold."

Maddie tossed an apple to Blaine. "To whom?"

"To Camp Kicking Moose."

"Wait a minute," Cam said. "That means . . ."

"Dad owns it," Blaine finished. "Woohoo! Now that is cool. We own a lighthouse!"

Cam's imagination lit up. "Can't you see it as an overnight destination?"

"Oh, how awesome would that be," Blaine said. "Honeymooners' delight." She looked at Seth.

Suddenly Maddie gasped. "Where's Cooper?"

Cam's head whipped around as her stomach did a somersault. "Cooper?"

Maddie's face reflected disaster, her eyes were wide with fear.

She jumped up and flew like a windjammer before a gale to the edge of the bluff to see if Cooper had fallen over the edge. Blaine followed behind Maddie. Seth stood, cupped his mouth, called Cooper's name over and over, turning in a circle as he shouted.

"Oh no." The words came out of Cam in a puff of air, a whispered lament. Reactions tumbled through her in swift succession: *He's got to be here . . . he couldn't have been gone that long . . . he knows not to wander near the edge of the bluff . . . he doesn't know how to swim . . . where could he be?*

She clutched her arms as tremors ran through her. She felt utterly helpless, unable to move, besieged by memories of receiving the news of the fire that took the lives of her mother and Libby. *No. Not again. Please God, please. Let Cooper be found. Let him be all right.* It felt strange to her that her automatic response was to pray, though she hadn't prayed in years. Did it matter? Was God listening? She had no idea. All she knew for sure was that, in this moment, she had nowhere else to turn but up. *Oh God, please let us find him.*

Seth shielded his eyes, turned in another circle, then whistled for Dory. A bark came in response. He swung around to pinpoint where the sound came from, and whistled again. Another bark. "The lighthouse!" He bolted over to the lighthouse and tried the door, but it didn't open. He banged on the door with the palms of his hands. "Cooper! Are you in there?"

"Yes! I'm here!"

By now Cam had rushed over to the lighthouse. "Coop! I'm here. Are you okay? Can you open the door?"

"I'm trying! I can't. The wind blew it shut."

Seth tried shoving against it, but it wouldn't budge.

Cam called out to Maddie and Blaine. "He's here!"

Maddie ran back from the bluff, Blaine trailing on her heels. "Cooper, we're going to get you out of there soon," Maddie yelled, her breath coming in heaves after her headlong run. "Don't worry!"

"I'm not worried," Cooper shouted back. "Dory's here." Some odd sounds floated under the door. "Plus there's cool stuff in here."

"Could he run out of oxygen?" Maddie said.

Seth stopped fiddling with the door handle to look up at her. "Not a chance of that." He turned the handle again. "Cooper, what does the lock look like inside?"

"Um, there's a latch up high."

"Can you reach it?"

"No."

"Is there anything in there that you can push against the door so you can reach up and undo the latch?"

"No. There's only a bunch of small metal things. Lights and stuff."

"What's the problem?" Cam whispered.

Seth groaned. "The problem isn't the actual door handle. There's a latch. It must have dropped when the door slammed shut." He leaned against the door, thinking. "Cooper, do you have a shoelace on your sneakers?"

"Nope. I wear Velcro sneakers."

Maddie gave Cam the Look. "I told you to buy him shoelaces. He needs the practice with fine motor skills. I told you that very thing."

Cam lifted her shoulder in a shrug. "Velcro is faster when you're late for school."

"I have my ball of string," Cooper shouted.

Seth's eyebrows lifted. "Perfect! Now, remember those knots I was showing you on the boat, while we waited for Maddie to find a life jacket? I'm going to go over that slipknot again with you, just like you're one of the crew on my ship. Listen carefully, Coop." Seth gave him very clear blow-by-blow instructions to make a loop on one end of the string, tighten the loop, then try to hook the latch. After ten minutes of trying to lasso the latch, it was clear it wasn't working.

Seth let out a puff of air.

"Seth," Maddie said, "I'm concerned that the tide is coming in."

That, Cooper heard. "The tide is coming in?"

Seth glanced at his watch. "Not for a long, long time, Cooper." He motioned to everyone to step away from the door, then spoke in a low voice. "Maddie and Blaine, go down to the boat and sit inside, one on each end. Wait there. Your body weight will keep it anchored in place on the beach. We'll join you in a few minutes with Cooper."

Maddie's eyes went wide. "What if the boat starts heading out to sea? We don't know how to drive a boat."

Seth remained calm, though Cam was sure he wanted to muzzle her. "If that starts to happen, then one of you needs to get the line out. Maddie, you get on the beach and hold the standing end while Blaine sits on the boat's steps. Whatever you do, don't let that boat go. If you do, we'll be stuck here until Captain Ed notices his boat is gone."

As soon as they left, Cam turned to Seth. "But we'll get him out, won't we? And the tide isn't imminent, is it?" A wave of panic mounted and broke. "I mean, all the things Maddie said—the lack of oxygen, the high tide—those are all Maddie-worries, right? He'll be okay, won't he?" The words sounded strange, for her throat was tight with a rising hysteria.

They looked at each other wordlessly, then Seth wrapped his arms around her and pulled her close to him. "It's going to be fine. I just needed to give your sister something to do. She was starting to drive me crazy. Just like she's starting to make you crazy now. Don't go down the crazy path, okay? I need someone here with a clear head." He released her and went back to the door. "Cooper, you said there's some metal stuff? Can you move a piece or two against the door—just enough for you to stand on it? You might have a better chance of getting a loop around the latch."

They heard dragging and scraping and huffing as Cooper tugged something against the floor. Again and again, he tried to toss the string loop around the latch. Patiently, Seth talked him through one more try. Then another, and another. Until . . . it worked! Cooper lassoed the loop around the latch. "Careful now, Coop.

This time, you're going to need to lift it up. Remember how I had you keep two long ends of the string? This time, you're going to pull on only one side. Let the other side go slack."

Cam watched Seth in wonder. His patience, his ingenuity, his unruffled composure—he was heroic. This next step took another few minutes, but the latch finally lifted and the door opened a few inches. Seth stuck his shoe in to keep it open, then leaned against the door to move all of the pieces of metal equipment that Cooper had shoved against it. He slid inside, reached for Cooper, and lifted him in an enormous bear hug. "I'm so proud of you!" Dory scooted around them and out the door to find the nearest tree.

Cam squeezed inside the lighthouse and Seth scooped her into the hug. "Cooper, you were so brave." It was dark inside, spooky. And the floor was filled with all kinds of paraphernalia. "Why didn't you tell me where you were going?"

Cooper wiggled out of their hug and Cam was a little disappointed. "Dory ran to the lighthouse and I followed her. I tried the door and it opened, so we went in." He went to the door and turned back. "Where's Aunt Maddie and Aunt Blaine?"

"They're down at the boat."

"Can I go?"

"Okay. Be careful as you go down those steps. Tell Maddie we'll clean up the picnic and be right there."

Cooper ran across the yard and waved from the top of the bluff, then disappeared down the steps.

Seth picked up a few things, then flicked on the flashlight app on his phone and beamed a light around the small round room. "Oh wow. Oh man. I can't believe what I'm seeing."

"What is all this stuff?"

"It's night vision equipment." He walked carefully around the small chamber, shining his flashlight over the floor. "Cooper and Dory stumbled on something quite unexpected."

"What?"

"The lobsters. They haven't left at all."

232

"What do you mean?"

"Those infrared lights . . . night vision equipment. Someone's been coming through at night to empty the lobster traps." He tipped his head. "Remember that night on the beach when we saw the fishing boat trolling without lights?"

She did remember that night, but for an entirely different reason. "Who? Who could it be?"

"That, I don't know." Seth walked around the small room, then his flashlight caught something on the ground. He bent down and picked it up, then sniffed it. "Or maybe I do." In his fingers was a bright yellow Juicy Fruit gum wrapper. "Still fresh."

Seth cautioned Cam not to say anything about their discovery on the boat ride back to the harbor. He was quiet on the ride, as was Cam, but Cooper talked nonstop, retelling the story to Maddie and Blaine. To him, getting locked inside the lighthouse was a great adventure. Cam smiled, watching him.

As the boat neared Boon Dock, Seth slowed it down, drifted sideways into the dock. He jumped off and looped a line around a metal cleat. He helped each one of them off the boat, Cam last. He held her hand and didn't let go. He pulled her close to him to whisper, "I'm heading over to Mount Desert to notify the police. Don't say anything yet. Not to anyone. I'll let you know what happens as soon as there's something to tell." He brushed her cheek with the back of his hand before he tossed the line on the boat and jumped back in.

She waved as he eased the boat out of the slip.

"A bold move," Blaine said, nudging her gently with her elbow. "Giving you a little love right in front of us."

Cam didn't respond. She didn't need to pretend there wasn't something going on between them. That was undeniable. But what it meant, to either of them, that she didn't know.

Twenty-Three

JUSTICE CAME SWIFTLY FOR LOBSTERS. Late on Sunday evening, Seth drove his moped out to Moose Manor to fill Cam in on what was going on. Around ten o'clock, she heard the puttering of his moped and hurried outside to meet him in the driveway.

Seth turned off the moped, took off his helmet, and looped it over the handlebars. When he turned to greet her, she immediately saw the broad smile spread across his face. "You can't believe how quickly the Mount Desert police responded. They took me out in a police boat to the lighthouse. They were all over it, gathering evidence."

"Think they'll have enough evidence to make an arrest?"

"Two." He held up two fingers. "Two arrests tomorrow. The detective was getting warrants tonight." He glanced at the house. "Don't say anything to your family. Blaine, especially. She's the one in town every day." He took a step closer to her. "Didn't I tell you? Maine takes their lobsters very seriously."

"I remember. You did good work."

"Cooper's the hero. I'll let you figure out how and what to tell him, and when, but he should know he was a key figure in solving an island crime." He reached out to tuck a lock of loose hair behind her ear. "Your hair looks pretty, let down like that." He then caressed her jawline with his fingertips, sending shivers down her spine. He picked up his helmet and held it in his hands. "On the ride out here, I was thinking that Cooper was locked inside a dark lighthouse, with a big dog, for at least, what—half an hour? Maybe longer? Did you notice how brave he was? In some ways, his calm, clear-headed reaction was even more impressive than solving the mystery of the missing lobsters."

Oh, she had noticed. She'd thought of little else.

By evening of the next day, the island was buzzing with the news of the arrest of the mayor's sons. Blaine brought home the first wave of information and shared it over Maddie's mushy macaroni and cheese casserole.

Blaine had been working at the Lunch Counter when the police arrived with warrants to arrest Porter and Peter Phinney for the thieving of lobsters in their traps. "It was surreal . . . like a movie! One minute, those two were sitting on the stools, eating grilled cheese and trying to flirt with me. Ugh, their jokes. So bad." She rolled her eyes. "The next minute, in walk the cops. They hand-cuffed Porter and Peter and marched them out to the police boat. And then . . ." Her eyes went big and her voice rose in excitement. "Locals came out of nowhere to watch. The grocery store, the Baggett and Taggett, the gas station near Boon Dock. The side-walks filled up! Someone yelled out to ask what in the world had happened and a policeman yelled back, 'Ask your lobsters.' And then a fisherman cheered . . . and so did everyone else!"

It got even better. "The mayor and his wife were in the grocery store and saw the commotion. They hurried down to Boon Dock to try to stop the police from taking their sons away." She lowered her voice to add a nasal twang and strong Maine accent, like the mayor's. "'Halt! Halt and desist! I'm Bax-tah Phinney! May-ah of this town. You have no jurisdiction here!' But they did. And then Porter started wailing for his mommy, like a little boy."

Standing outside the Lunch Counter, Blaine had watched the whole thing. Peg had come up to stand beside her, arms crossed. "You don't mess with another man's bugs."

As Blaine recounted the story to her family, she couldn't hold back her delight. "Work at the Lunch Counter is looking better already. Those two creeped me out . . . winking at me while I cooked. Chomping and snapping their gum." She made a face. "Never again will I see Juicy Fruit gum without thinking of them."

"No kidding," Maddie said. "Those stupid T-shirts they wore." She waved a hand across her chest. "Ask Me What's Honkin'."

"Be My Maine Crittah," Blaine said, cringing.

Dad frowned. "Thus ends my last hope that the Phinney boys might show up to paint."

"That's sweet, Dad," Cam said. "Naïve but sweet." She turned to Cooper. "If you hadn't wandered off into that lighthouse with Seth's dog, no one would've ever known that the Phinney boys were the reason that the lobsters had gone missing."

"You know, you're right," Blaine said. "Coop! You're the town hero."

Until now, Cooper hadn't been listening. He was absorbed in dissecting his macaroni and cheese. "I am?"

Blaine held her palm up to high-five him. "Totally."

Pleased, Cooper high-fived her back. His attention returned to his plate. He pushed a noodle to the side. "It doesn't look the same as Aunt Blaine's."

Blaine looked down at her plate. The macaroni noodles were mushy from overboiling, the cheese sauce had broken, turning it greasy and unappetizing. Lumpy too. She pushed it away. "I can't eat this."

Maddie peered down at her plate. "I followed your recipe exactly."

"To borrow a line from Peg Legg, something has gone terribly wrong."

Blaine dumped her plate in the sink and went to the fridge to see what she could muster. "Who wants a bacon, green onion, and cheddar cheese omelet?"

Everyone.

Long after Cooper had been tucked into bed, Seth arrived at Moose Manor on his moped to fill the Graysons in on more specific details. Blaine went upstairs to take a shower, and Maddie was writing Tre a letter, so it was only Cam and Dad who sat around the kitchen table, riveted to Seth's unfolding story. "The Mount Desert police confiscated the night vision equipment and made two arrests based on fingerprints found all over the equipment. Baxtor Phinney is over at Mount Desert now, trying to arrange bail for his boys."

"Not the brightest lobster thieves, are they?" Dad said. "Stealing out of traps from their own neighbors."

Cam found it hard to believe those two had come up with this scheme without any help. "Seth, do you think the mayor was involved?"

"He claims innocence." Seth grinned. "He also claims his sons are innocent. His wife insists her boys were framed."

"Do you believe the mayor? After all, he seems to know everything that's going on."

Seth shrugged his shoulders. "Innocent until proven guilty, you know? But he's sure getting a lot of heat from the locals. In fact, that's the reason I couldn't get out here earlier tonight."

"What do you mean?"

"The village council held an emergency meeting tonight and impeached the mayor. He's off the council."

"Whoa," Dad said. "For a town that moves pretty slowly, that was fast."

Seth lifted up his palms. "Lobsters, you know."

Two months ago, Cam hadn't known, but she was getting a good idea of how important lobsters were to this island's economy.

Dad yawned once, then twice, which Seth took as a cue to leave. She grabbed a sweater and walked him outside. The sun had set, but there was still a faint glow in the west, enough to provide a pale light that made everything seem so perfect. Against the gradually darkening sky, the pine trees looked like tall soldiers standing guard around the camp.

Seth stopped on the bottom porch step and turned to look at Cam. She was one step above, so they were at eye level, inches apart. He had shaved tonight, and a little bit of shaving cream remained under his ear. "You got your wish. The locals have something else to talk about than your billionaire status."

She smiled. "I'm delighted to no longer be the focus of interest on this island. Each time I go into town, someone stops me to ask if I'd like to give a donation to their favorite charity. Which, when asked, turns out to be . . . that very someone."

Seth laughed. "Actually, you're not off center stage yet. The council wants you to run for office to replace the mayor."

"What?" Cam thumped her chest with the palm of her hand. "Me?"

"They think you could do a good job for the town. They like your ideas."

"No. No, they like my money." Which she had yet to receive. Evan Snowden said it was in the works, but it could take months before she'd receive her share of the company's sale.

"That, too. The locals want you to stick around for the long haul and put your money where your mouth is." He tipped his head. "So . . . *are* you planning to stick around for the long haul?"

Was she? She hadn't quite decided on what she was going to do. It was a very strange place for Cam to be . . . unsure of the future. "I didn't think you were a proponent of long-term planning."

"Some things are worth it." He leaned closer, so close she could smell a hint of shaving cream. "I hope you'll say yes."

Cam couldn't say yes if she wasn't convinced yet. "How 'bout I'll think about it?"

"That's all a man can ask," Seth said. His eyes found hers and for a moment she thought he meant to kiss her. Just as suddenly, the moment was gone. He nodded formally and clambered aboard the moped. Cam swung around to look at the house and saw Blaine and Maddie peering out the sidelights of the front door. She frowned at them and they vanished. She turned at the sound of Seth's sputtering engine, and he was gone.

The following Saturday, Cam drove into town at three o'clock in the morning to meet Seth. He'd arranged the whole thing with Cam on Friday afternoon, after checking weather reports. No fog, clear skies. The perfect weather for watching a sunrise, he told Cam. Cooper was invited too, but when he heard that Grandpa was cutting down dead tree limbs and burning them in a bonfire, he opted to stay at Moose Manor.

Seth wanted to show off the sunrise at Cadillac Mountain to Cam. It was low tide, and they crossed the bar on his moped— her first time crossing it. "You'll never forget it. It's one of those bone-deep moments."

She was glad of that reassurance, because while she was an early riser by nature, there weren't many reasons she felt the need to get up *this* early. Only for Seth.

To her surprise, they weren't alone. There were plenty of cars on the Park Loop in Acadia National Park, with the same goal of a sunrise in mind. At the top, Seth parked the moped, helped her off, and pulled a backpack out of the basket. They climbed over the large granite rocks and found a high open spot apart from the crowd and away from photographers with tripods. Seth pulled a rolled-up blanket from his pack and spread it on a large rock. "It won't be long before the horizon starts lighting up." For a guy who said he didn't put much stock in plans, he'd outdone himself. He'd even had Blaine pack a picnic breakfast for them: croissants, blueberries and yogurt, homemade granola, freshly squeezed orange juice.

Cam sat down, shivering. Her one contribution to the picnic was a thermos of Blaine's hot coffee. She poured two cups and gave one to Seth. "Cheers."

He took a sip. "Ah." He took another blanket and wrapped it around the two of them, resting his arm around Cam's shoulder to snuggle her close to him. "It won't be long now until first break. That's the first changing of the light."

She didn't mind the wait, not at all. Not like this.

Soon, too soon, the sky started to lighten up. They sat there in a library hush, watching a peach glow appear at one point on the horizon.

"Let there be light," Seth said. "First spoken words of God in the Bible."

As if on cue, the peach glow rose on the horizon as the sun crested, and the sea took on its color. The entire horizon was bathed in an apricot orange. As the top of a red ball started to emerge on the horizon, someone, somewhere, let out a cheer. She turned to Seth at the same moment he turned to her. Their eyes met, and she was scarcely able to breathe. He leaned in to kiss her lips, their first kiss, given as the sun rose on Cadillac Mountain. He was absolutely right—it was a moment she'd never forget as long as she lived. Bone-deep.

By the time the sun was fully visible, most of the viewers had returned to their cars to head down the mountain. "Show's over until tomorrow," Cam heard someone say.

They stayed, though, and had a leisurely breakfast on a cold, hard rock, until the wind came up. Back at the Boon Dock, they held hands as they walked to her car, and Seth told her a story about Cooper at school. Her favorite kind of stories. "Yesterday, Cooper and Quinn were neck and neck in the spelling bee and she threatened to punch him in the nose if he beat her, but he didn't back down." They stopped at her car. "Cooper's getting increasingly—what's the word?—sturdy. That's it. He's becoming sturdy. When he first arrived, he reminded me of a birch sapling.

Frost tender, easily windblown. But now, he's, well, maybe not a tree but certainly no longer a sapling."

This was music to Cam's ears. She'd shadowed Cooper that first week of school, but after that, he hadn't insisted that she come, so she stayed at Moose Manor to help Dad with the mountain of work they faced. She appreciated Seth's interest in Cooper, a characteristic that endeared him to her all the more. Not that she needed much encouragement. Her feelings for Seth, they shocked her. She hadn't felt such an overwhelming attraction for a man in a long, long time, if ever. There were moments throughout the days when she wondered if she could be falling in love with him. Could this be love? Thinking about a person from the moment you woke up until the moment you fell asleep? Counting the hours until you saw him again? Reliving every moment you spent together? If this was love . . . then it was consuming and thrilling and wonderful . . . but also frightening and unsettling.

Sure, she wanted a partner *someday*, but that day was far, far away, after everything else was checked off. She had plans, so many things to do.

Like what? An inner voice, sounding oddly similar to her sister Maddie's, poked her. Like what? What is more important than love? Than having a family? A home? You've already gotten a taste of how dispensable you truly are at work. How does that feel compared to being with Seth?

Darn it, Maddie! Stop making me . . . you.

She shrugged those pokes off and looked at Seth, and she felt her insides settle. He had that calming effect on her, like a whirling top that was spinning off-kilter and suddenly righted, finding its proper pull of gravity. "Being here on the island, I feel as if Cooper is thriving. Like he's turning into the boy his mom had always imagined him to be."

"You've never told me about Cooper's birth mom."

She unlocked the car door and put the empty thermos on her seat, along with her purse. The sun was shining bright; the day would be as crystal clear as a perfect diamond. A perfect day. She turned to him, leaning her back against the car. "Cooper's mom was my lifelong best friend. We grew up across the street from each other." She smiled. "Mostly, she lived at our house. Her grandmother raised her, if you could call it that. Libby didn't think she was the type to go to college. She thought she wasn't smart enough, that she'd end up as a hairdresser like her crazy grandmother. But I knew how smart she was, how gifted she was as a runner. So I made a plan for her, pushed her, studied SATs with her, went to all of her track meets. We were going to go to the same Ivy League college and be roommates all four years. It was all mapped out from the time we were in junior high. Then, she got into our dream college"—she put a hand against her chest—"and I got rejected!" She let out a laugh. "Even still, I was so proud of her. And when Cooper was born, the way he was born, well, that created a permanent bond."

"What do you mean . . . the way he was born?"

"Sophomore year, Libby had to drop out of college because she was pregnant. Her grandmother was furious with her and wouldn't help, barely acknowledged that she was having a baby at all, so my mom and I, we were Libby's birth coaches. I even cut his umbilical cord. She named the baby Grayson, after our family. We'd become her family. After she died, I adopted him and flipped his name. I gave him her surname as his first name."

"No father in the picture?"

"Nope. He told Libby to get rid of it. That's why she left Princeton despite a full-ride scholarship and a spot on the track team."

"Princeton?" Seth's smile faded. "Libby?" He fell silent for several long, long seconds. "So . . . if you flipped his name, does that mean her name was . . . Libby Cooper?"

"Yup."

Cam could see the color in Seth's face drain, as if someone pulled out a stopper.

CAM, AGE 20

The sky was perfectly blue. Not a cloud to be seen. It took Cam less than five minutes after arriving home from college for summer break to drop her suitcases in her room, grab some cookies—Mom's special twist on chocolate chip cookies—and hurry across the street to see Libby. It had been a busy semester—Cam had taken more classes than normal so she could double major—and she'd hardly connected with Libby. When she had, Libby seemed kind of distant, distracted. She knocked on the door once, twice, waited, heard the television blaring, so she walked right in. Libby's grandmother turned away from her soap opera and pointed to the stairs. "You can try, but she won't see you."

Cam froze. "Why not?"

Her grandmother looked as if she just chewed on a cactus. "Go on up. Find out for yourself." She turned back to the TV.

On her best days, Libby's grandmother was eccentric. On her worst days, she could be downright mean. Cam wasn't sure where she fell on the scale today. She hurried up the stairs to Libby's room. She knocked on the door. "Libby, I'm home from school." She tried the door. Locked. "Libs, it's me. Come on, open the door." She knocked again, harder this time. She wasn't going to leave without having a real face-to-face conversation. "Open up, Libby. We need to talk."

Finally, Libby opened the door, head down. One hand rested on her abdomen.

Cam gasped, astounded by her appearance. She put her hand over her mouth to hide her shock and stared at her friend for one agonizing moment. "Oh Libby," she said in a sigh, for now she understood. "What happened? I mean, I can guess. But what happened? Tell me everything."

Libby fumbled around for something to say before she turned

around and went back to her bed to lie down. It was as close as Cam could get to an invitation to stay. She sat on the floor, Indian style, facing Libby. "What does your grandmother say about it?"

Libby stared at the ceiling. "Grandma?"

"Yeah."

"We don't really discuss it."

"You don't really discuss it," Cam echoed in a flat tone. "But . . . she took you to see a doctor, didn't she? You've been to a doctor, haven't you?" From the pinched reaction on Libby's face, Cam knew she was talking a little too quickly, a little too loudly.

"No. Like I said, we don't discuss it."

How could her grandmother have such a noticeable lack of sympathy when her only grandchild was facing the biggest crisis of her life? Cam had never thought much of Libby's grandmother, but now she thought even less of her.

Libby's eyes would not engage. Finally, Cam jumped up, sat down beside her on the bed, and tried to grab hold of her gaze. "So, big surprise. Your grandmother is not leading the parade to cheer you on."

The tiniest lift on the corners of Libby's lips revealed that she was listening, that Cam was reaching her. "But I'm cheering you on, Lib. My mom will. You know that you can count on us. We'll help you get through this."

Finally, Libby sat up and looked at her. "I don't know what to do."

Cam felt her own throat constricting as she watched her friend's beautiful face slowly collapse into pure sorrow. And then the tears came, one rolling down her cheek after the other, until she put her face in her hands and her shoulders shuddered with sobs. Cam held her in her arms and patted her back until she cried herself out.

They sat on the bed and talked all afternoon. The only thing Libby revealed about the father of her baby was that he told her to get rid of it. "I couldn't, Cam. I couldn't do it. Instead I left college and came home."

"Does he know you're about to give birth to his child?"

"No. I haven't heard from him since I left Princeton."

"Don't you think he should be told?"

Her eyes flashed, the first sign of a spark of life. "No, I don't," Libby said firmly. "And that's why I'm not telling you his name, either. Ever. So don't badger me to find out. He made his choice. I made mine. Some things are best left behind." She looked at Cam. "Promise? You'll leave it alone."

"I promise." Cam didn't want to make that promise, but the baby's father was the least of her worries. "Libby . . . he didn't take advantage of you, did he?" She'd heard all kinds of stories about naive college girls at fraternity parties. Her own college had banned the Greek system.

"No. He didn't take advantage of me. Not at all. I was a willing accomplice. More than willing."

"So . . . did you love him?"

"I thought so. I thought he loved me. I thought he was the one for me."

How had Cam never heard about this guy? It didn't completely surprise her, though. Libby could be private about her feelings. Cam could too. In high school, they both liked the same boy and never told each other. They only found out because they were both mad at him when he asked a girl from another school to the prom.

Libby brushed away some tears. "Stupid, stupid, stupid."

"You're not stupid. He is." Cam hated this nameless guy. Hated him.

Libby took in a deep breath, let it out. "I'll figure it out."

"You're going to give the baby up for adoption, right?"

"Maybe." She shrugged. "I suppose so. Sometimes, I think about keeping the baby. Like maybe this baby is meant to be, that he or she . . . has an important purpose in life. And I'm part of it."

Keep the baby? Be a single mom. *How?* Cam wondered. *How are you possibly going to be able to raise a baby on your own? You're nineteen. You only have a year and a half of college under your belt. Your work experience consists of sweeping hair at your grandmother's beauty salon. Your crazy grandmother is no help at all.* But what she said was, "Then I'll help. I'll help you figure out what to do. So will Mom." She draped an arm around Libby's shoulder. "After all, we're family."

"Better than family," Libby said, and for the first time, she relaxed, smiled. For the first time, she seemed like the old Libby.

Cam looked around at the mess of the room, at the empty soda cans, wrinkled bags of chips, candy bars. Did Libby ever leave this room? She seemed to be rotting away here.

"First things first, I'm going to go home and tell Mom. We're going to get you to a baby doctor right away. And you're going to eat your meals at our house." Vegetables and fruits and chicken and hamburgers and air without cigarette smoke. "We'll help you get back on your feet, Lib."

As Cam went down the stairs, Libby's grandmother was still in her chair watching TV, cigarette between her teeth. In the ashtray was another lit cigarette. Two fisted! The afternoon light seemed suddenly flat and dull. "You need to stop smoking inside. For the baby's sake."

As she pointed at Cam, her cigarette dropped ashes on the carpet. "I blame you for this."

Cam slapped her palm against her chest. "Me?" It came out in a high-pitched squeak.

"You're the one who filled Libby's head with big ideas." She made a scornful tongue-clicking sound. "Going to college."

"What's wrong with that?"

She looked at her, considering the question. "Because she slept with the first college boy who walked by with unzipped trousers. Just like her mother did."

All at once Cam was furious. "If you believe that, then you don't know your own granddaughter." She waved away the puff of cigarette smoke. "Libby is brave to have this baby. She'll figure out how to manage this."

"Oh? Are you going to quit college and stay home to watch a screaming baby all day? Change its dirty nappies?"

No. No way. "How 'bout if right now we focus on helping her through this pregnancy?"

Libby's grandmother snorted.

There was something so frustrating about this woman, a deliberate mulishness that went beyond the resentment of a woman caught in the position of raising her granddaughter to keep her out of foster care. "Why can't you support Libby? Even when she went to college, to an Ivy League college on a full scholarship, you belittled her. Why don't you want her to succeed?"

"And have her think she's better than me?"

That remark nudged something out in the open, something Cam had considered many times before. It jumped out of her mouth against her better judgment. "Libby's always been better than you."

Her eyes moved as she puffed on her cigarette, a glare of contempt, suddenly replaced by a look of blankness as she turned around to go back to her TV show.

Twenty-Four

ARTIE LOTOSKY HAD TOLD Blaine he wanted to come up to see the island, but she didn't really believe him. Until the second Wednesday in May, just an ordinary day, and there he was when she arrived for work, sitting on a stool at the Lunch Counter just like a local. Peg clapped her hands with glee when she saw the surprise on Blaine's face. "We've been hatching up this plan for two weeks, Artie and me. Hon, you've earned a day off. It's a gorgeous day. Go have fun with your beau."

Artie wasn't her beau, not at all, but he was a good pal. She took him to Camp Kicking Moose to introduce him to Dad and her sisters, showed him the house and the cabins, and then they packed a picnic lunch and hiked to the lighthouse. Seth had shown her how to get there, via land, by sketching a map on a napkin at the Lunch Counter.

An hour later, Blaine and Artie reached the northern peninsula that held the lighthouse. From where they stood, they could see waves crashing against the rocks far below. Two ospreys glided overhead. Artie shielded his eyes from the sun and looked over the expanse. "Blaine, this is incredible. Your dad owns all this?"

"Yeah. But it's sure not easy to get to." Even on a cool spring day, she was sweating from the hike. They walked across the bluff to the lighthouse and sat down for a picnic under the same tree where she'd picnicked before. She took off her backpack and Artie joined her. They ate crackers and cheese and apples, and she caught him up on the latest island scoop—the recent arrests of the Phinney brothers, the impeachment of the mayor that had left him still stuttering in disbelief and excuses.

Artie took an apple and polished it against his shirt. "For such a little island, there sure is a lot of drama. I feel like you're in the middle of a soap opera."

Blaine laughed at that. How true. There wasn't much of a population on this island, but more than enough quirky characters. She pointed to the lighthouse. "Cam has a notion to turn that lighthouse into a bed-and-breakfast." It amazed her that Cam could almost see a place the way it could be, and not the way it was. She remembered the hours Cam spent poring over design magazines when they were kids, dog-earing pages of scenes and settings she liked. Maybe that's where her vision-capacity got started. She could see what wasn't yet there, and bring out its best. It was a unique skill, quite astonishing.

But then, Peg had said the same thing about Blaine as they set out to make cakes or cookies. She couldn't believe that Blaine had something in mind that the end result matched. It seemed so easy to Blaine, as natural as breathing. Maybe everyone had her own way of seeing.

Artie bit into the apple and chewed, then swallowed. "Other than the shocking pink color of Moose Manor, the camp is looking pretty good."

"Cam deserves a lot of that credit. Dad and Maddie didn't quite know where to start until she arrived. She got us all organized, created spreadsheets to tackle the projects, complete with timelines. Storyboards, too. Each cabin has one."

"What's a storyboard?"

"A unique theme for each cabin. Furniture, accessories, plus coordinating fabrics for the bedspreads, quilts, draperies, rugs.

You saw those first few cabins, all dolled up, complete with quarterboards. 'Never Enough Thyme' is the one in soft green fabrics. 'Sea La Vie' was the blue and white one, all beachy, with that big jar of seashells on the mantel. That's all Cam. You should've seen them a few weeks ago." She shuddered. "Spiders and mice and rusty cots and moldy mattresses."

"Think the camp will be ready to open in a few weeks? Memorial Day weekend, right?"

"Ready or not, it'll be open. The camp is fully booked for the summer." *Thanks to me*, she thought, *though no one gives me any credit for that gift.*

Artie stretched out his legs, one ankle over the other. "So, last week I got the email."

"What email?"

"From one of the universities I applied to. I've been accepted into the pre-med program. I start in late August."

She'd been taking a swig of water from a bottle and nearly choked on it. "Artie, that's great! Why didn't you tell me as soon as you got here? That's big news!"

"It's in Portland."

"Nice. Not far at all."

He brushed a buzzing bee away. "The other Portland. The one in Oregon. I got a full academic scholarship. Tuition is covered."

"Oh." Oh, wow. Far, far away. She felt a tinge of disappointment. "I read that Portland, Oregon, owes its name to a coin toss. Two New Englanders went west. One from Boston, one from Portland, Maine. They tossed a coin for naming privileges and the man from Maine won."

"The man from Maine. I like that. That's how I'll introduce myself."

She tipped her head. "You don't seem very excited. I would think you'd be ecstatic. Getting into a good pre-med program has been your plan as long as I've known you." She folded her arms around her knees. "I can't imagine being so sure about anything."

"You seem pretty excited about helping Peg at the Lunch Counter. I could see you as a famous pastry chef one day."

She knew he was just teasing her, but his words struck her in the heart. "I'm a pastry chef, huh?" Not just a cook or a baker. A real, bona fide pastry chef. She liked the sound of that.

They sat there for a long while, enjoying the peaceful surroundings. "Blaine, I've been thinking that I might come up here for the summer. To help your dad with projects. Be, like, a handyman."

Her head snapped up. "What about working for your dad?" His dad was a potato farmer in a little northern Maine town. Artie was one of the only kids from his high school to go to college.

"I think he'll understand."

She let out a laugh. "No he won't. Plus, you need to earn money for college expenses." She knew he was putting himself through school. "I'm sure Dad could pay you this summer, but you'd make more working for your dad."

"Maybe, maybe not. Hard to say."

"Last summer you made a bundle."

"That was last year. A good potato crop. The summer before was a bust." He stood up and stretched. "I thought I'd talk to your dad about it before I leave. Assuming that you don't mind."

She shrugged. "Suit yourself. Be prepared for a chilly reception from the locals. Most of them think the Grayson family is out to fleece them. The others think Cam is their golden ticket. And all of them resist change of any kind."

"Not Peg Legg."

Blaine laughed. "Nope. She's one of a kind."

"Think Cam's staying here? I read about her company getting sold. Won't she want to find another start-up? Make another billion before she's thirty?"

Blaine grinned, then shrugged. "I don't know. She doesn't tell me much about what she's thinking." She leaned back to look at him. "Artie, what would it take to become a pastry chef?"

He thought for a moment as he sat back down. "Culinary

251

school, I think." He lifted a chocolate chip cookie out of the bag. It was a recipe of her mom's that she'd been tinkering with. (Mom used to make it by adding cornflakes, but she tried Rice Krispies and thought it made them melt in your mouth.) He took a bite, then another and another, until he finished the cookie and reached for another. And then he sounded convinced. "Yes. Culinary school."

Opening Day was just weeks away, and things were ramping up at Moose Manor. Furniture, rugs, bedding, lamps, and accessories for the cabins were trickling in, so Cam and Maddie spent most of their days unpacking boxes and setting the cabins up to look welcoming and homey. Polished, too, with rustic charm. They were having fun, and by Thursday, five cabins were ready for guests. They looked good. Really good. Dad was astounded when they gave him a tour. They looked nothing like the kids' housing of the past, with rusty, squeaky cots lining the walls, army style. The newly decorated cabins were as inviting and comfortable as upscale hotel rooms.

But there were five empty cabins left to be furnished. And still to be dealt with was that dreadful pink paint that covered Moose Manor.

Late Friday afternoon, Cam drove into town with Dad and Cooper to pick up supplies and check to see if Captain Ed had brought any more furniture in on the ferry. She hoped to run into Seth too. Other than a brief wave when the school bus chugged up the driveway in the mornings, Cam hadn't seen him since the night he arrived to let her know about the Phinney boys' arrest. She was almost too busy to notice. Almost.

Was it the kiss on Cadillac Mountain? Was she that bad at kissing? So bad it made him change his mind about her?

No. Seth wasn't shallow like that.

But then again, she was shockingly inexperienced with romance.

No. He had asked her to run for the council job and stay at Three Sisters Island. But wait . . . did he ask her before or after the kiss?

She gasped. *Before*. She cringed. Maybe she *was* that bad a kisser.

Dad and Cooper went to the Lunch Counter to see Peg while Cam went to the post office to drop off some mail. No sooner had she left the post office than she saw Seth stride across the street toward her, Dory following. Without any kind of greeting, he said, "Do you have time to talk?"

"Sure. I was going down to Boon Dock to wait for the ferry to come in. Captain Ed's been bringing boxes over from Mount Desert for us."

"Good. We'll have some privacy there." He was looking at her in a different way, and she could sense herself becoming stiff and businesslike, her reaction to stress of any kind.

He didn't talk on the way down to the dock but led her to the bench where Cooper liked to sit. They sat facing the water, and Seth leaned forward, his elbows on his knees. He took a deep breath, and then sat up. "Cam, you mentioned your friend Libby the other day, after we got back from Cadillac Mountain. You said she had gone to Princeton."

She remembered. He had left abruptly, saying Lola needed breakfast, so she didn't think much about it. Other than her perseveration over the kiss.

"Cam, I knew a Libby Cooper at Princeton."

Her mind started to spin. "Hold it. You went to Princeton? How did I not know?"

"I suppose it never came up."

"And Libby? You *knew* her? My Libby?" Her chest eased, and a smile began.

"I met Libby sophomore year. She'd been on the track team and she encouraged me to try out. We conditioned together. She was very motivated, and I wasn't. I think I told you, I was a spoiled kid back then. A true jerk."

Cam found it hard to believe that Seth was ever a jerk.

"Libby Cooper, she was . . . unspoiled. Very refreshing to be around. She cared about being there, about getting an education. But I do remember her saying that she wouldn't have been at Princeton without this friend who kicked her butt." He glanced at her. "It occurred to me that she was talking about you, Cam."

Cam's smile grew bigger. A burst of emotion flooded through her. How incredible! To think that Seth had known Libby, that she had talked about her to him. Absolutely incredible. *Maybe there is something to this notion of God having a hand in a person's life. I mean . . . what are the odds of a coincidence like this? Crazy!*

"Cam, there's something else I need to tell you."

She noticed that his hands were shaking, and a touch of nervousness returned.

"It's a confession, really. To a very terrible thing." He said it slowly and with some deliberation, sounding genuinely unhappy. "I'm hoping it might help to say it out loud."

"Go on." The joy that filled her only seconds ago slipped away as she turned a quizzical expression to him.

"It's very probable . . ." he began slowly, his speech punctuated by consideration and a few uneasy breaths.

Her heart started a weird ticking in her chest.

"I am fairly confident that . . . I am the father of . . . Cooper."

She heard what he said, but none of the words made sense, like pieces of a jigsaw puzzle that couldn't fit together. The ticking from her heart accelerated into a wild knocking. Panic tore through Cam. Her mouth went dry, her palms felt damp. She kept her eyes closed for what seemed like a full minute. She had to get out of here, get away from him. She stood, but he jumped up to stop her.

"Please, Cam, don't go."

His fingers had curled around her arm, but she pulled away and moved out of his reach while her eyes flew to his. "Don't! Don't touch me."

His hand hung in midair for a tense moment, then fell to his side. "Sit down. Please." His voice cracked as he spoke. "Telling you is the hardest thing I've ever had to do. Please, please sit down."

She wouldn't sit down.

She felt the tears in her throat and behind her eyes, but she wouldn't cry. She refused to cry. "You knew about Libby's baby."

"I knew she was pregnant. She told me before she left for Christmas break." He swallowed hard. "We talked about what to do. She said she was going to handle it."

"She said you told her to get rid of it."

He didn't deny it. "Something like that."

"She loved you. Did you love her?"

He sighed thickly, dropping his chin to stare at the sand. "No, I didn't love Libby." He looked regretful. "I wish I could say that I was a better man at nineteen, but I wasn't. Libby was cute and fun and helped me get a spot on the track team. But that's all she meant to me. When she didn't return to college after Christmas, I'm ashamed to say, all I felt was relief."

He sickened Cam. She had to get away from him, far away. She caught sight of Dad and Cooper walking out of the Lunch Counter and down toward Boon Dock. Cooper had Peg's enormous long-lens binoculars looped around his neck. He stopped to peer through them up at an osprey, squealing a high-pitched screech as it soared around the dock. She pointed to him. "See that?"

Seth had been staring up at Cam intently, a pleading look in his eyes. Reluctantly, he pulled his eyes away to see where she was pointing. An expression of longing crossed his face as he watched Cooper peer at the osprey.

Again his blue eyes sought hers. When they did, she said, "There's the *it* you told Libby to get rid of."

Twenty-Five

A SMART PERSON IS AFRAID OF MARRIAGE. Maddie had written a graduate school paper with research supporting that one sentence and received an A+. The professor, divorced four times, had told her that he wanted to make it the MFT department logo, to emblazon it on T-shirts and coffee cups and pens.

She'd been thinking quite a bit about that paper lately. As she had worked on the paper, it was with the assumption that being afraid of marriage was a logical thing. After all, it was a daunting commitment. But as September drew closer, the fear she felt was less about logic and more like a feeling of slowly suffocating.

Tre was moving awfully fast. In their last phone call, he told her he'd found a new apartment for them and his mother had—get this!—"generously" offered to decorate it for them. At first Maddie objected, but then she came around, reminding herself that she didn't have strong opinions about those kinds of things, not like Cam or Blaine did. So maybe it was all right for his mother to decorate their first home. But why did it make her feel so diminished?

This was her pattern. She talked herself up. She panicked. She talked herself down.

Maddie needed to process with someone but made the mistake of confiding in Cam. She should have realized the timing was all wrong. Her sister seemed preoccupied with something today, really bothered and out of sorts. She'd hardly said a word all morning while they worked on "Mainestay," Cabin 6, and "Fantasea," Cabin 7. Normally, they chattered as they worked. They had fun. Today, Cam was stone silent. Still, stupidly, Maddie plowed ahead and told her about Tre's mother furnishing their new apartment.

Cam put down the box cutter. "Did she at least ask you what colors you might like? Does she have any idea what your taste is like?"

"No." Not about the apartment. Not about the wedding. But then again, she wasn't sure she would know how to answer if Mrs. Smith did bother to ask. Maddie slumped into the plump oversized chair and put her feet up. "What if his mother . . . what if the wedding isn't anything like I wanted it to be?"

"I remember once when Mom told me that a wedding doesn't make a marriage."

"But what if it's a sign of the marriage? What if . . ." She stopped and started again. "Cam, do you think it'll always be like this? With his mother?"

"Yes." Her voice was suddenly soft. "I do, Maddie. It's a two-for-one deal. Marry Tre and you get his mother thrown in for free."

Maddie coughed a laugh. "I knew you'd put it in perspective."

"Sometimes what we need most is a little perspective."

"Cam, I'm scared. What if this marriage to Tre . . . doesn't work out?" There it was. The clay beneath it all.

Cam crouched down beside the chair and put her hand over Maddie's. "I can't believe I'm saying this to you, I really can't. But I think you need to pay attention to your worries." She squeezed her hand and released it. Straightening up, she glanced around the room. "I forgot to bring down the box of pillows. Be back in a second."

In the silence that followed, doubt crept into the cabin and settled into Maddie's head. Her eyes popped open. "Darn it, Cam."

Why had she asked her anything? Cam was not the person to ask about love and marriage and happily ever after.

But Maddie knew the doubts had been there all along.

There was so much more that Cam had wanted to tell Maddie about her engagement to Tre: How can you be an overeducated therapist and miss so many red flags? What could possibly make you think that his mother will respect your boundaries after the wedding if she doesn't now? And then there's Tre. Can't you see how tied he is to his mother's apron strings? Why, each time Blaine asks, do you always make a lame excuse about not wearing the engagement ring? And most importantly, if you really loved Tre, why are you here and not there, with him?

She held back. She had bitten her tongue and left the cabin as quickly as she could make a graceful exit. She had to get out before she said things to her sister that she had no business saying. What did she know about love? Absolutely nothing.

CAM, AGE 13

It was Mom and Dad's wedding anniversary. Mom was getting dressed to go out to dinner with Dad that night. She'd bought a new dress, and even had her hair highlighted that afternoon. While Mom was putting on her makeup, she gave Cam instructions for babysitting Maddie and Blaine. Draped over the bed, Cam was only half listening. She'd noticed a small picture in a frame on the bedside table and reached out to examine it. It was Mom and Dad on their wedding day, looking so young, so happy. "Tell me about your wedding."

Mom was putting mascara on her eyelashes. She stopped, mid-stroke, and turned to Cam. "Let's see, the florist canceled due to illness on the morning of our wedding, so I had to walk down the aisle with an awful weird plastic thing that I carried instead of my gorgeous planned bouquet. The photographer went bankrupt after shooting the wedding and we never got any photos. Just a few random snapshots on 110 film. That one you're holding there, it's one of the only pictures of our wedding day."

She turned back to the mirror to finish applying mascara, then stopped again. "The pastor! The one we had wanted was stuck at the airport, so we had to get a stand-in. He had a thick Cuban accent and I'm not really sure what vows I actually agreed to."

"It sounds awful!"

Mom smiled and sat down on the bed. "It was the best wedding ever, simply because of the people who were there, the God who blessed us, and the man who stood by my side and promised to live life with me."

"Still. All that planning and look what happened."

"Planning doesn't make the wedding. And the wedding doesn't make the marriage. The marriage is what we live with, day in and day out."

Cam set the frame back on the nightstand. "I'm not sure I want to ever get married. There's too many things I want to do."

"Oh, someday I think you'll meet a guy who's worth giving a few things up for. Wait for *that* guy, Cam."

"How will I know who he is?"

"You'll know." Mom bent down to kiss Cam on the top of her head. "He'll be the one who helps you to be your best self."

Twenty-Six

CAM TURNED A CORNER IN THE ROAD and saw Seth driving toward her in the yellow school bus. He lifted his hand in a wave, but she didn't wave back.

Could this island get any smaller? One tiny main road served for the entire island. Just one.

She was still trying to absorb the information Seth had given her last Friday. It was hard to get her head around it, all that it meant, how it changed things between them. How it changed everything about Three Sisters Island for her. For Cooper. *Do I hate Seth?* she wondered. *Did I ever really care for him?* It surprised her how much she was thinking of him, how often she thought she saw him.

Late in the afternoon, Dad sought her out to say that the village council wanted an answer from her. Would she run for the open position? He wanted her to say yes. Everyone wanted her to say yes. She hadn't given any thought to it.

That night, as Cam was trying to fall asleep and her thoughts felt like Cooper's ball of string all undone, she did think about it. She mainly thought of why she would not do it. She couldn't stay here and see Seth Walker every day without thinking of how he had wounded Libby, had left her alone when she needed him the most.

Okay, then. She'd made her decision. Cam was going to take Cooper and leave Three Sisters Island.

⁓

The next morning, Blaine saw Cam lug a suitcase out of the top shelf of her bedroom closet. "What are you doing?"

"Getting ready. I'm going to head back to Boston soon."

"You're leaving?"

"Soon. The cabins are nearly done. Maddie can finish up the last two."

"You're letting Dad handle the summer without your help?" She was shocked. Disappointed too. "Why? How could you just . . . leave him?"

"Dad will be fine. He has you and Maddie. Peg too. And Dad told me your friend Artie is coming to work here for the summer. There's a lot of people rooting for Camp Kicking Moose's success."

"What about those grants for a new power plant?"

"I can work on grants from Boston."

"Dad counts on you." Blaine heard a tiny flare of bitterness in her voice and tried to rein it in. "How could you be so selfish?" There was the bitterness, full flame.

"Selfish?" Cam's mouth dropped open. "I've been here for weeks. I've cleaned and scrubbed and decorated. I've set up all kinds of programs and systems for Camp Kicking Moose. All that needs to happen is implementation." She picked up the suitcase and set it on the bed to open it. "Like I said, Dad'll be fine."

"I thought we were doing this together, as a family," Blaine said in that crisp you-don't-care voice. Even to her own ears, she knew she sounded childish. But it wasn't fair! They were just starting to hum as a family, finally, the way Mom had always promised they would, and Cam was leaving. Moving on without them. Like she always did.

"I'll be back now and then to check on things." Cam paused,

drew in a breath. "I'm sorry if you feel like I'm ditching the camp. I'm not. I wouldn't leave if I didn't think everything would be okay. I just have some things I need to take care of."

"You won't tell me what's really going on, will you?"

Cam rolled her eyes. "Blaine, not everything is about you."

"I didn't say it was. I said that you won't tell me anything. You treat me like a child."

"That's because you often act like a child."

"Oh, here we go. So I didn't finish college. Therefore, I will forever be a child in your eyes."

"I've never said that. I have said I want you to finish college. I want you to make something of yourself, Blaine."

"Maybe this *is* me!"

"Working for minimum wage in a diner. That's enough for you?" Cam sighed. "You have so much potential."

"Why can't you just accept me for me?"

Cam looked weary. "Fine. I've done all I can to try to persuade you to go back to school. If you don't appreciate what college can do for you, then . . . well, it's your life to mess up."

"'To mess up,'" Blaine repeated flatly. "You think I don't know why you're always putting me down? Making me feel insignificant?"

"What are you talking about?"

Blaine felt a dam burst within her. "You blame me. For Mom's death."

"Blame you?" Cam sounded stunned. "Why would I blame you? It was an accident. If anyone is to blame, it would be Libby's grandmother, who left those stupid cigarettes burning too close to the drapes. And how can I blame her? She died too. How could I blame anyone?"

"Because I'm the one who should have stopped Mom from going back in the house to get Libby." Saying it aloud made it real, and Blaine felt sobs start laddering up inside her chest. She covered her face with her hands. "I should have! I should have stopped her."

Blaine and Mom had been in the kitchen on that late spring afternoon, baking a lime tart to surprise Dad. Lime tarts were Dad's favorite, and he was coming home tomorrow after being with his team on a long road trip. Blaine had just piped the meringue on top of the pie and put it in the oven to brown. Winslow, their old dog, was barking relentlessly, so Mom watched the broiler while Blaine went to see what had upset him. Across the street at Libby's house, she saw smoke curling off the roof. "Mom, come quick!"

But Mom told her to hold on, that she needed one more minute to get the meringue just right. An ordinary response. But this was no ordinary moment.

"Mom! Call the fire department! Libby's house is on fire." The front door of Libby's house opened and Blaine saw her run outside with a screaming Cooper in her arms. Without thinking, Blaine burst into action. She ran across the street and held her arms out for Cooper. Libby dropped him in Blaine's arms, kissed him on the forehead, and started back into the house. By now, Mom had seen what was going on and ran to join them. "No, Libby, no! Wait! I called the fire department. They're on their way!"

Libby turned at the door. Smoke was pouring out around her. "She's in the living room. I've got to get her." And she disappeared into the house.

Mom looked down at Cooper, who was hysterical, then at Blaine. "I'll get her. I'll get them both. Stay here. Do not follow. Keep him safe, Blaine."

Blaine felt as if she were frozen, in a dream, yelling without any sound. Cooper screamed for his mother, the dog barked, and Blaine couldn't get any words out. She watched her mother disappear into the house, watched and watched and watched. But no one came back out. It felt like an hour was passing, though it was only minutes. Flames broke through the roof to lick the shingles, and then windows started shattering, one after the other. More flames erupted through the windows at the burst of oxygen that fed the fire. The approaching whine of the fire engine's siren reached some part of Blaine's mind, and she felt a sweep of relief.

"In there!" She pointed to the house as the truck arrived. "Three people! In there! In the living room."

As soon as the words left her mouth, a thunderous crack sounded, and the center of the house collapsed. Even the firefighters stopped, retreated.

"Go in!" Blaine yelled. "Go save them!"

One of the firefighters pulled her and Cooper farther away from the burning house, now engulfed in flames.

Blaine yanked her arm out of his hold and screeched at him. "Go get them!"

He responded stoically. "We'll do all we can, but you have to take the boy and get off the property. We need to get this house contained before other houses catch fire."

Blaine kept screaming, over and over. "You can't let them die! You can't let them stay in there!" But even she knew the answer to that.

Neighbors arrived, and the firefighter pushed Blaine and Cooper into their care. Cooper had stopped crying and had buried his face into Blaine's neck. Something shut down in him. Even now, just thinking of that awful day made Blaine shudder.

Cam put her hands on Blaine's shoulders and made her look at her. "That day . . ." Her voice cracked. "It was not your fault. Mom did what she had to do. You couldn't have stopped her if you tried." Tears filled her eyes. "You couldn't have, Blaine. You know Mom."

Blaine's face crumpled. "I should have! I should have told her no. I should have grabbed her, held her back. But I didn't say anything. I just stood there, watching."

Cam wrapped her arms around Blaine as she sobbed. Maddie appeared at the doorjamb and stopped abruptly when she realized Blaine was crying. "What's going on? I could hear yelling all the way down in the kitchen. What did you do to Blaine to make her cry?"

"I guess," Cam said, patting Blaine's back, "we're finally having that talk you keep wanting us to have about Mom."

Maddie crossed the room and sat on the edge of the bed, facing them. "Get me up to speed."

"Blaine thinks she should have stopped Mom from going into the house to rescue Libby and her grandmother."

Maddie chimed in. "You were fifteen years old, caught in a crisis, holding on to an absolutely terrified four-year-old boy. You did nothing wrong, Blaine."

Cam released Blaine and gave her shoulders a tight squeeze. "I do not blame you. Do you hear me? I do not blame you. No one blames you. And you need to stop blaming yourself."

"We were supposed to have time," Blaine whispered, feeling tears choke her throat again. Time to laugh and talk and be a real family. Mom had always promised that there'd be a time when the girls wouldn't define each other as oldest, middle, youngest. They'd be true friends. "Mom knew I was always trying to catch up with you and Maddie. But when she died, I knew I'd never catch up." Tears streamed down her face. "We'll never be the family Mom promised."

Cam pulled her back into her arms and stroked her hair. Maddie rose to put her arms around both of them. "We are a family," Maddie said. "We love each other, we tell each other the truth, and we keep working on things. That's what families are all about."

Blaine wiggled out of her sisters' embrace to reach for a tissue from the box near her bed. She wiped her eyes, blew her nose, and turned around. "Do we tell each other the truth? I don't think so."

"The truth?" Cam sat down on the bed where Maddie had been. "Here's a truth. I've always been envious of the two of you."

"Us?" Blaine and Maddie exchanged a confused look. "Why?"

"Lots of reasons." Cam wiped tears off her cheeks. "Maddie, it's like you can see into the heart of people. I might be smart in a business sense, but I am so dumb people-wise. When you ever do get around to being a bona fide counselor, you'll be wonderful at it." She looked to Blaine. "And you. You were Mom's favorite. The two of you had a special connection. You had the most time with her."

Blaine scoffed. "No way. Remember the summer that you and Mom were always gone, doing stuff together? Maddie was away at Girl Scout camp and I was practically abandoned. You and Mom were out shopping for college and having fun while I was stuck home alone."

"Having fun? Shopping?" Cam let out a laugh. "That summer was all about Libby—her doctor appointments, Lamaze classes. We were her coaches. Mom was, really. Don't you remember? It was the summer Cooper was born."

Shocked, Blaine sat on a gray metal folding chair, which doubled for the bed's nightstand. "Why didn't you or Mom ever tell me? I used to wake up in the morning and the house was empty. It made me so angry."

"Libby didn't want anyone to know she was pregnant. Her grandmother was campaigning hard to give the baby up for adoption . . . and Mom and I thought that was Libby's plan too. Right before Cooper was born, she'd even contacted an adoption agency. But then Libby gave birth, and she refused to give him up." Cam looked genuinely apologetic. "I'm sorry, Blaine. Helping Libby was a full-time job that summer. You were only eleven or twelve, and Mom and I didn't think about it from your perspective."

"Blaine, they didn't tell me anything, either," Maddie said. "I came back from Girl Scout camp in August and there was a baby across the street."

A corner of Cam's mouth lifted. "But that doesn't change the fact that you were Mom's favorite, hands down."

"I agree," Maddie said, nodding. "It's like you both spoke the same language, something Cam and I couldn't understand. I have so many memories of the two of you, working in the kitchen on a new recipe, chatting and laughing."

Blaine tucked her chin, unable to look at Maddie. These words from her sisters, they were a gift. They meant more to her than she would ever be able to convey. Like she had a hole inside that was finally getting filled. "Here's a truth," Blaine said. "I'm stuck. Frozen. I can't make any decision past the day's immediate demands. It's been that way since Mom died. I don't know why I'm like that ... and I don't know how to get unstuck."

A long moment passed before Maddie said gently, "Do you think it's possible that you feel if you move forward, you're moving away from Mom?"

"That day she died," Cam said, "that terrible day. You took the brunt of it, Blaine."

She had. Dad was away with the team. Cam and Maddie were at university. Blaine and Mom were home alone when they saw the fire break out across the street at Libby's house.

Cam slipped an arm around her. "I'm sorry I've been pushing you so hard. You'll know when you're ready to move forward."

Blaine ducked her chin, feeling tears prick her eyes. "I hope so."

"I know so."

"Okay. My turn to tell the truth." Maddie took in a deep breath. "I can't marry Tre."

Blaine's head shot up. She and Cam exchanged a look of shocked delight, then they squealed with joy.

After a few hours of cleaning out the boathouse, battling mosquitoes and humidity, Paul came into Moose Manor to get a glass of iced tea. As he opened the door, he heard Blaine yelling and sobbing upstairs—he thought he heard Cam's voice raised too— and then he saw Maddie bolt up the stairs.

He froze. Upstairs, things got quiet. Very quiet, for a very long time. And then came happy shrieks.

It was always like this. Just when he thought he had a handle on this daughter-rearing thing, the next monster reared its head.

He skipped the iced tea and hurried back outside to finish cleaning the boathouse.

⁓

As Cam and Blaine discussed options with Maddie about how to gently disengage an engagement to Tre, Cam realized that Blaine was right. The Graysons weren't truth tellers. It's not that they were liars—they weren't. But they didn't tell each other important things. Dad, either. He sold the house without telling anyone. Maddie got engaged without telling anyone. And Cam . . . she didn't reveal much to her sisters, either. She had held herself apart from them for as long as she could remember. As the eldest, as the one who blazed the trail, as the one most responsible . . . and then came Cooper. Suddenly, Cam was thrust into the unexpected role of motherhood—a role that separated her even more from her sisters.

Maybe it was time to change that. Her sisters were growing up. These last few weeks, Cam had seen them in a new light. They were special, gifted in unique ways. Mom had always said that one day, the years between the sisters would disappear and they'd all be close friends. Maybe that day was now.

Cam took a deep breath. "So I have one more truth to tell." Blaine and Maddie turned to her, all ears. "I'm pretty sure I know who Cooper's father is."

Twenty-Seven

ONLY MADDIE AND BLAINE KNEW Cam planned to leave for Boston, but they begged her to wait until after Opening Day weekend. Plus, they insisted she not tell Dad until then. "Let him have that first weekend with all of us together," Maddie said. "Let him have that much."

Reluctantly, Cam agreed. But that was all she would promise, and only after Maddie and Blaine had sworn to her that they would not reveal they knew Seth Walker was Cooper's biological father.

Cam didn't know what to do about that. Should she insist on a DNA test? Would that trigger Seth to sue for joint custody? He hadn't said anything of the sort, but that could change. Seth was fond of Cooper long before he knew he was his father. How did he feel about him now?

Maddie kept pressing Cam to give Seth a chance to prove himself. "Trust your instincts, Cam. Trust what you know about him."

That made no sense to Cam. She thought she did know him, but it turned out she didn't. And right now, her instincts were telling her to leave, to go to Boston, to get back to the life that suited her best. Work. She needed work. It was much easier than a failed relationship.

She had no desire to go to church on Sunday, but Cooper insisted on going. She sat on the far side of the room and avoided Seth's eyes. She hadn't seen him in days, because she'd taken pains to avoid him. When she did steal a glance at him, she saw that he had his eyes fixed on Cooper; sorrow was evident on his face.

Good. Good, Cam thought. There should be sorrow. He blew it. He missed the most wonderful blessing a man could be given. He treated Libby, dear Libby, shabbily. He said so himself—that he was relieved she hadn't returned to college after Christmas break. His problem was over. Libby's had just begun.

"Can I go see Seth?" Cooper whispered.

"No," she said, a little too sharply. Then, softer, "Maybe . . . afterwards. He needs to concentrate on leading the music." Boy, did he ever. She thought of all the times Seth had talked about God to her, as if he were such a man of faith. Why, he had even influenced her to start believing, to start praying! Cam felt a sharp swirl of anger toward Seth fill her to the point of overflowing. *Such* a hypocrite.

Seth waited until ten o'clock sharp, then picked up his guitar and stood in front of the group. "I have a new song to teach you today," he said, tuning the strings on his guitar. "It's by Crowder, called 'I'm Forgiven.' The band leader of Crowder said he can't get through it without crying. It's a song about a prodigal, who finally understood how much God loved him, just as he was. Not after he got his life together, but right where he was."

He never met Cam's eyes as he spoke, other than once when his eyes flicked up, then quickly down again, but she felt he was trying to send her a message. *It's not that easy*, she thought. *Poof. I'm forgiven. All is well. It shouldn't be that easy.*

But she couldn't deny what a beautiful voice Seth had, and a talent for the guitar, and the sincere way he led worship, as if his whole focus was on God. She tried to keep her eyes on anything except him, but time and again as the song went on, Cam's gaze got tangled up with Seth's.

After the song was over, Peg rose to read a section of Scripture.

"This is from the book of 1 Kings, chapter 19. Elijah the prophet is running for his life from that awful Queen Jezebel—and doesn't she sound like a holy terror? How'd you like to meet up with that little gal in a dark alley?"

Cam smiled. Peg always did that, interrupted herself to put her own unique spin on the reading.

"So the poor boy is hiding and he's hungry and he's plumb worn out." Someone came in and the air from the door blew the pages in her Bible. She frowned and turned a few pages, hunting for the passage. "Oliver Moore, look what you did. Why can't you just show up on time like everyone else?"

"I'm sorry, Peg," Oliver said. "I went to the wrong place."

"Good grief, Oliver, we meet here every blessed Sunday morning." Peg shook her head and her pigtails bounced. "Never mind. Okay, where was I? Ah, here it is. Now listen up. Elijah's getting his comeuppance." She smoothed out the pages. "And the word of the Lord came to him: 'What are you doing here, Elijah?' He replied, 'I have been very zealous for the Lord God Almighty. The Israelites have rejected your covenant, torn down your altars, and put your prophets to death with the sword. I am the only one left, and now they are trying to kill me too.'" She paused, looked up. "Oh my heavens. That poor boy. Coming at him every which way." She looked back down at the Bible. "The Lord said, 'Go out and stand on the mountain in the presence of the Lord, for the Lord is about to pass by.' Then a great and powerful wind tore the mountains apart and shattered the rocks before the Lord, but the Lord was not in the wind. After the wind there was an earthquake, but the Lord was not in the earthquake. After the earthquake came a fire, but the Lord was not in the fire. And after the fire came a gentle whisper. When Elijah heard it, he pulled his cloak over his face and went out and stood at the mouth of the cave. Then a voice said to him, 'What are you doing here, Elijah?'"

Peg gently closed her Bible with a pleased sigh. "Don't that just beat all? Imagine that, all that noise going on"—she clasped her hands over her heart—"and it's a whisper that God uses to get that poor boy's attention." She smiled, satisfied, as her eyes swept the small group. Then her smile faded. In a flat voice she said, "Where's Captain Ed?"

"He's running the ferry this morning," Oliver Moore yelled out. "I just saw him. He sends his apologies. High season's starting with a bang, he says to tell you."

"Shoot. Who's going to preach?" Peg turned to Seth, looking a little panicky.

At that moment, Cam realized something. People on this island instinctively looked to Seth to lead them, to bring them all together.

Seth's gaze took in each person before resting on Dad. "Paul, would you like to say a few words?"

"Me?" It came out like a rusty nail.

"Please?" Seth said.

"About what?"

"Anything . . . spiritual . . . that comes to mind," Seth said. "As long as it's biblical."

Blue-haired Nancy sat next to Dad and elbowed him. "Just talk 'til your voice goes out." She snorted. "At least it'll be short."

Dad bent over for a moment, hands folded tightly over his knees, and Cam realized he was praying. Dad was praying. She'd never seen him pray before. Mom prayed a lot, but not Dad. Not that Cam knew, anyway.

Dad rose to his feet and took the open Bible from Peg's hands. She gave him a reassuring smile before she sat down. He looked out over the small group. "Peg just read about God using a whisper to get the prophet Elijah's attention."

"Speak louder!" Oliver Moore said.

"He can't!" Nancy shouted over her shoulder. "Just listen louder." Two people in the back row rose and walked up to sit in two empty front-row seats. "Okay, start again," she said.

Dad cleared his throat and began again. "Life can be pretty distracting. It's easy to mix up what's truly important with what turns out to be much less important . . . in the big picture. So God has to get our attention. Sometimes he uses a burning bush, sometimes a whisper. Sometimes an unexpected death, sometimes"— he glanced at Cam—"an unexpected success." He stood a little straighter. "For me, it was losing my voice. I had to finally stop talking, stop rushing through life with my foot stuck on the gas pedal, and start paying attention. When I did, I realized God had been trying to get my attention for a very long time."

Dad paused, and Cam thought his eyes were glassy. Hold on . . . was he tearing up? Dad?!

"Here's what I've discovered these last few months. I'd rather lose my voice and start listening to God than have kept my voice and continued to ignore him. Because walking with God is, well, it's just the best thing we've got going for us." He gazed out at each person, each daughter, before resting his eyes on Cooper. "I hope God doesn't need a two-by-four to get your attention, like he did me." He looked to Peg, who was mopping up tears running down her cheeks, then to Seth. "That's it," he said, shrugging. "That's all I got." He returned to his seat.

Seth rose, picked up his guitar, and started strumming, and they all sang a final song.

Afterward, Cam stayed in her chair for a long moment. Cooper asked if he could go talk to Seth now and she nodded. She watched Seth's face brighten as Cooper approached him, and he reached out to ruffle his hair and smooth down his rooster's tail, which immediately popped up again. He held out his guitar for Cooper and showed him how to strum the strings. She watched them for a while and experienced a sick feeling of dread in the pit of her stomach. Cooper seemed to be growing before her eyes like a tree, spreading branches wide, becoming strong. She felt suddenly sad for him, for herself.

Then Peg appeared, blocking her view of Cooper and Seth.

"Peg Legg, what're you crying for?" Dad said. "Trust me, I'm not that good a preacher."

"Don't you know, Paul Grayson?" She wiped her eyes again with her handkerchief. "Your voice. It held up. Finished strong. It didn't fizzle out like it usually does."

～⬦～

Maddie walked outside of the Baggett and Taggett and blinked from the bright sunlight. Then she rubbed her eyes. Could it be? She squinted and moved forward with uncertain steps. There was Tre, walking up the hill from Boon Dock. She met him halfway and he kissed her cheeks, one after the other, like a Frenchman. "Tre! I had no idea you were coming. How long are you staying?"

"Not long, Mads. I left my car at Mount Desert."

She reached for his hand and noticed he was quivering. "Tre, is something wrong?" Had something happened to his mother?

The silence stretched long, until a seagull shrieked overhead. "Mads, let's talk."

"Okay. Let's . . . let's go down to that bench." As they walked down toward the water, she saw a few beads of perspiration trickle down his forehead, though it wasn't a very warm morning. She sat down, then he sat down and faced forward. "Okay, Tre. What's going on?"

She saw him swallow. When he finally spoke, his voice cracked with emotion. "Do you remember the night we got engaged? The restaurant. Actually, the hostess."

"The blonde. A girl you once dated at boarding school. The one you took to Skippy's wedding." She recalled that Tre had seemed worried about Instagram photos that were posted of the two of them.

"Right. Yes, that's her. Susan is her name. Anyway . . ." He paused, avoiding her eyes.

"Go on." Whoa. Hold the phone. Was Tre breaking off their engagement? Was that why she hadn't heard from him these last few weeks? He had a new girlfriend? She was supposed to be breaking up with him! Her sisters had helped her craft a plan for a gentle letdown.

"Well, this was all very unexpected . . ."

Wow. He was. *He* was breaking up with *her*.

"Mads, I don't know how to tell you this, but I've fallen head over heels in love with Susan. Actually, I think I never stopped loving her. And . . . well . . . yesterday, we eloped."

Words failed her. Conflicted feelings ping-ponged through her. Was she happy? Was she sad? She didn't know! Slowly, she pulled a few thoughts together. "Tre, I am stunned."

"I know. I'm so sorry to spring this on you like this. I feel like a heel. And yet this . . . our love . . . Susan and me . . . it's bigger than both of us. I'm crazy in love with Susan, Mads. In a way you and I never felt for each other."

"So you eloped," she said in a flat tone. It occurred to Maddie why Tre had greeted her the way he did, with a kiss on both cheeks like a Frenchman. Not like a lover.

She had to remind herself that she was planning to break off the engagement. She should be happy, and in a way she was, but she also felt outraged. Betrayed. Diminished.

"Susan had a concern that Mother might try to manage our lives. So she thought we should just do it. Give her a message, right from the start."

Maddie had to bite her lip to keep from bursting out with a nervous, hysterical laugh. That girl, she'd do just fine with Mrs. Smith as a mother-in-law.

But Tre mistook her lip biting for near tears. "I hope you can forgive me someday."

She took her time answering. "I hope so too."

Tre reached out to hug Maddie. "Thank you. You have no idea what your forgiveness means to me."

"Oh, I think I do." She pulled away from him. "Tell me, what did your mother have to say about your elopement?"

"We haven't told her yet." Then he pulled away to ask, "So . . .

Mads, I hope this doesn't seem audacious, all things considered, but could I have the engagement ring back? I'd like Susan to have it."

It *was* an audacious request, delivered after shocking news that he had eloped, but it snapped something into perspective for her. She hated that ring. She didn't want to be married to Tre, or spend a life dominated by his mother. As they walked up the hill toward her car, she realized that the only thing wrong with this scenario was that she wanted to be the one to break things off. That, she knew, was nothing but pride. That, she could let go of.

As the reality of this unexpected turn of events settled in, relief flooded through Maddie, as sweet and welcome as a warm summer breeze, and she felt as if she could take a deep breath again. Fill her lungs with sea air. Suddenly, the sky seemed bluer, the sun seemed brighter, and all was well with the world.

Twenty-Eight

IT WAS A DREARY GRAY DAY, foggy, cold, windy. Cam hoped the bleak weather would improve for Memorial Day weekend—just ten days away.

Late on Wednesday afternoon, Cam picked up the mail and stopped in the Lunch Counter to tell Peg that they finally had land-line phone service out to Moose Manor. "Just in time for Opening Day. So you won't need to be our answering service any longer."

Peg didn't give Cam her usual warm welcome. "So, you're really leaving here."

Cam was surprised that Peg had figured that out, but upon reflection, she shouldn't have been. Peg had taken messages from some private schools in Boston that Cam had contacted to see about enrolling Cooper. "Yes, soon. I haven't . . . shared that news with others yet. Not even Dad." Or Seth.

"Honey, Seth told me what's gone on between the two of you."

Cam took in a quick breath. "He had no right to tell you. No right at all." She could be a bit blunt when cornered. Who else might he have told? And why? Maybe he *was* going to try to sue her for joint custody of Cooper. Her mind started spinning. Did she know of a good family lawyer? No. Evan Snowden might. He'd been divorced twice.

Peg leaned her palms on the counter. "Honey, I'm going to give you a piece of unasked-for advice."

Cam braced herself.

"How'd you like to be defined by your nineteen-year-old self for the rest of your life? That's a pretty heavy suitcase to keep lugging around your whole life. A suitcase full of regrets. Even you, I would think, at nineteen, probably had some growing up to do." She started swabbing the counter with her rag. "That's it. That's all I wanted to say."

That might have been all Peg wanted to say, but it carried impact.

Cam felt stricken, sucker punched, the wind knocked out of her. She perched herself on a stool, needing to think for a minute. She kept her eyes down, glued to the counter. Libby had been nineteen when she got pregnant with Cooper. Naïve, insecure, immature. Cam at nineteen was thoroughly selfish, convinced the world revolved around her. Blaine was nineteen now. Lost and clueless and trying to figure out life.

Being nineteen . . . it was all about making mistakes. Mistakes . . . and learning from them.

Cam's head lifted. In a quiet voice she said, "Peg, where is Seth?"

"He's taking Lola for a walk on the beach."

Cam hopped off the stool, went to the door, and stopped, then turned back. "Ask Blaine to make you vanilla ice cream."

"I've tried. She won't."

"Insist on it. Don't take no for an answer. For you, she'll do it." For Peg, Blaine would do anything. "And Peg, you should be on the town council. You should run for the mayor's spot."

Peg's eyebrows shot up to her lime-green knotted headband. "Me?"

"Yes. You. You're the best candidate for the job. The very best one." She smiled and walked down the hill to the dock area.

Fog coiled along the waterline of the harbor. There were only a few fishermen out in this weather. She buttoned her sweater and folded her arms across herself. Then she saw him.

Seth was approaching along the beach, his gloved arm raised up as Lola's perch. He glanced up and saw her and his step faltered, but he continued in her direction until they met. Two seagulls soared overhead and suddenly Lola shot off, flapping her wings until she was circling up and out in what Cooper had told her was called a widening gyre. "There she goes," he said, watching them until all three disappeared behind a fringe of trees. "She's after the pigeons of the ocean." He managed a shaky smile.

"Lola . . . will she come back?"

"I don't know. It's her choice. It's always been her choice. Only she knows when she's ready for the life she was meant to live." He took a step closer to Cam. "Can we talk? Please?" He had a slightly desperate look. "I'd like to explain a few things. At least hear me out."

She nodded. She felt such a messy ache in her heart.

"Cam, I was a different guy in college. Think stupid frat guy and you've got me pegged. A true prodigal, who caused my mother all kinds of sleepless nights. Barely squeaked through my classes, wasted on most every weekend. I even got kicked off the track team during junior year." He dropped his left arm, as if he just now realized Lola was not perched on it.

"The summer after graduation, my mom talked me into doing a half marathon with her. She wanted to get into shape, and she thought I needed some kind of goal. It ended up being good for both of us. By the end of summer, after hours and hours of training, we were ready to run it. I was proud of my mom. She'd worked hard for this. On the day of the run, we were making pretty good time. I remember we were on mile 7, about halfway through. We were on a narrow section of a trail, and some guy came along in a big hurry and shoved my mom out of his way—literally elbowed her. She fell, twisted her ankle. The guy never looked back."

His eyes lifted to meet Cam's, and he looked sincere. "A year

279

before, that guy could've been me. But this time, I had a different view. I'd seen how hard my mom had worked, and I knew what this half marathon meant to her and how sidelined she was after she hurt her ankle. That moment, seeing the other side of something . . . it changed me. I started going to church again, talking to God again. Listening to God again. I was changing."

"Did you ever tell this to Libby?"

"I tried. She shut me down. She told me not to contact her again, and she hung up on me."

That sounded like Libby. She could be loyal to a fault, but once she had made up her mind about a person, nothing could change her mind. Libby had written Seth Walker off as worthless and there was no turning back.

"Cam . . . I didn't know about Cooper. If I did . . ." His voice started to crack. "If I did, I would've stepped up. I hope you can believe that."

Did she believe that? From deep inside her, she knew she did.

"By the end of that summer, I was baptized. I was ready to give my life to Something More."

"More . . . what?"

"More of everything. Purpose. There's purpose to our lives, even if we don't acknowledge it. There's something bigger going on. It's no accident that you're here, that your dad bought *this* island, that Cooper's in *my* classroom. This smacks of God's doing. Bringing the two of us together these last few months. Full circle. Wrapping up loose ends."

"You really believe that?"

"Heart and soul."

"My mom, she believed that kind of thing." *I want to believe it. So badly.*

"I gathered your mom was that kind of person when you told me she died trying to rescue people. That's a woman who knew there's Something More. My mother's like that too. In fact, you remind me a little of her."

Cam looked up, surprised. "Me? I would never run a half marathon. Not even a quarter marathon."

He smiled. "In other ways. Outspoken. Bossy. A know-it-all."

"I love your mother. She sounds wonderful."

A short laugh burst out of him, then he grew sober again. "I made a terrible, grievous mistake. I can't take it back, I can't undo it, but I do accept responsibility—and blame—and I apologize. Whatever my failings, I intend to be a good man." He looked down at the sand, then up at Cam again. "I want to be part of Cooper's life. He's my son. I hope you'll give me a chance to be a father to him."

They looked at each other for long seconds, as long as a full minute. Softly she said, "A boy needs his father."

"A father needs his boy."

She felt her chin tremble, and suddenly Seth's image grew wavery while she tried her hardest to keep the tears from showing. But Seth saw the glisten, and suddenly he took a few steps to close the gap between them. "Cam, I want to be in your life too, if you can ever forgive me."

She looked at him with wonder. He was so much better at this relationship stuff than she was.

"Stay here. Give us a chance. Don't leave Three Sisters Island."

The surprising part was that she didn't want to leave, not really. She wanted to stay and make a life for herself and Cooper on Three Sisters Island. She could see it, just like she was watching a movie. In her mind's eye was a tidy little gray-shingled house overlooking the sea, with pink roses—Cam's favorite—climbing over a picket fence. Cooper was in the yard, playing with a dog. And there was Seth.

"I'm falling in love with you," he said quietly. "I think it started the day I first laid eyes on you and it hasn't stopped since."

He was close to her, just a kiss away. All she had to do was give him the slightest encouragement—a nod, a smile, some movement—and

281

he would close the gap between them. But she also knew he would wait for a sign from her.

She stared at him, realizing now, all at once in a sweep of goose bumps, that she loved him. It stunned her, to realize that she had it in her to love a man like this. It was like she woke from a long sleep, opened her eyes, and discovered she was in another country, someplace she'd never expected to be. "Me too, you. I mean, I think I love you too."

That was what he'd been waiting for. Head bending, arms reaching, he embraced her for a kiss, his wide, warm lips finding hers, and she felt her senses career off-kilter. It was like she'd never been kissed before, like these were the first lips she'd ever touched. Suddenly, Lola rocketed past them. Startled, they broke apart, the spell broken. The goshawk made a sharp turn at Boon Dock and circled back, soaring overhead.

Seth smiled at Cam. "Looks like Lola's found her way home." He caressed her cheek with his ungloved hand as if it were a precious treasure and gazed down in her eyes as he whispered, "Hold that kiss for later." Smiling, he walked down toward the water, gloved arm held out at a right angle for Lola's return to it.

Cam had thought nothing could top that sunrise at Cadillac Mountain. This day, this very moment of clarification and definition and a *major* life course correction—infused with love—this topped even that.

Early Saturday morning, Paul woke up with a sense of dread. House painting day. He had put this off long enough. The weekend weather was clear, he was an able-bodied man. Opening Day was a week away. He could do this. The girls said they would help with the trim. His goal was to get the front of Moose Manor painted. If that was all he could manage before Opening Day, then so be it. He had no idea how he was going to get that third-story section painted. Could he hang off the roof and paint upside down? No, he'd probably end up killing himself.

Paul heard the sound of a loud engine rumble up the driveway. He pulled himself out of bed. Who would be coming here at this hour? He looked out the window to see the tiny yellow school bus come to a stop. Hold on, what day was it? What time was it? Was he losing it, like his daughters so often accused?

The school bus doors opened and out poured everyone from the church at the Baggett and Taggett. Seth, Peg, Captain Ed, Nancy, Oliver Moore. A small girl with pink hair. Another fellow he didn't recognize stepped off. He opened the window sash and leaned on his hands. Why, that was Artie, Blaine's not-the-boyfriend friend. They were all dressed in old clothes and carried paintbrushes and buckets. Strapped to the top of the school bus was a fireman's ladder, the kind that unfolded. Big enough for a three-story house.

Paul's throat felt tight. He was surprised at how deep his gratitude ran. He had come here to this island to honor Corinna's memory, to fulfill a neglected promise to her. He hadn't realized until just this moment how deep his own love for Three Sisters Island ran. He loved this place. Even more than the camp and the island, he loved these people. They were his people now.

Twenty-Nine

MEMORIAL DAY WAS JUST A FEW DAYS AWAY. Blaine couldn't believe that more than two months had passed since she'd first set foot on Three Sisters Island, that before then, she'd never even heard of it. She felt she belonged here more than anywhere else.

She hadn't been able to stop musing over that comment Artie had made at the lighthouse, about seeing her as a pastry chef. What was it she wanted to do with her life? Did she love to bake as much as she thought she did?

Peg kept after Blaine to make this vanilla ice cream she'd heard so much talk about. Apparently, even Cam had told her about it. "I can't stop thinking about that ice cream," Peg told Blaine while they were painting the porch last weekend. "Let's give it a go. Will you? Please? I'll beg if you want me to."

"You don't have to beg." Blaine would make it for her. But she would make it at home, when she was alone. She stopped at the grocery store to buy the ingredients and told the family she needed the kitchen that night. No questions allowed. After they cleared out, she found her mother's recipe card and carefully made the custard, adding the vanilla beans at just the right moment to let them steep and infuse the flavor. She let it set in the freezer, then scooped it into airtight containers to harden.

The next morning, she took the ice cream to Peg at the Lunch Counter. "Here," she said, setting the containers on the counter.

Peg gasped, as if she'd given her the Holy Grail. She grabbed two bowls and two spoons and started to scoop. She took a spoonful and froze, her eyes went up as if she'd had a taste of heaven. "Oh, honey. This is the best ice cream I have ever tasted. Ever, ever, ever." Peg and Blaine had finished off their first bowls and were polishing off their second one. "We have to get this on the menu."

"About the menu." Blaine glanced around the store. "Peg, is this store for dry goods? Or for eating?"

"Both. I need both to make my mortgage." Peg looked at Blaine. "Go on. Say what you want to say."

"I don't mean to sound critical of your restaurant or your general store."

"It seems as if you're doing both in a halfhearted way."

Blaine walked a few steps and swept a finger along a dusty shelf full of first-aid kits. "I wonder if you shouldn't bother with these kinds of products. Instead, stay focused on food."

"Make it a full restaurant, you mean? There just isn't enough business in the town for that. I'm the only one even trying."

"I don't mean a full restaurant. Instead, a lunch counter plus food items."

"There already is a grocery store. Nancy would be furious with me if I took her business away."

"Not a grocery store like Nancy's. Though, I gotta say, that store sure could use a facelift. I think you should sell products she doesn't sell."

"Like what?"

"Like . . . picnic supplies. Fresh bread. Good wine."

"That sounds good for the summer. What about the rest of the year?"

"Well, maybe we start with summer and go from there."

"I don't know. The markup is big on those dry goods."

"Oh Peg, Peg, Peg." She sighed. "They're just not selling."

Peg's gaze swept around the store. "I'll make you a deal, honey." She lifted her empty bowl. "You sell this ice cream here this summer, and I'll give it a try your way."

"You mean it? I can make ice cream every day? Different flavors?"

"Ayup. If it tastes as good as this, you can make any flavor you want."

"It's a deal." Blaine clapped her hands together. "Can't you just see it, Peg? I do! People lined up outside, waiting to make an order for sandwiches, all the way down to Boon Dock."

Peg squinted, peering out the storefront. "I don't see it. But your vision is better than mine."

"Oh . . . an idea is coming to me!" Blaine jumped off the stool and turned in a slow circle. "Peg, what would you think if I rearranged the store? Made more room for customers. And moved some of the shelving, so people might have impulse buys. We could get a refrigerated counter, glass front, filled with incredible deli salads."

"Huh?"

"You know . . . coleslaw and pickles and pasta and potato salads. And there . . ." She pointed to where the lobster tank used to be. "There could be a baker's rack with baked goods, ready to go."

"Who's baking those baked goods?"

"Us. Me." Blaine glanced up at the walls. Oh, that awful flesh color. It had to go. "Maybe, give everything a fresh coat of paint." Soon. Immediately. Before Friday.

"Honey, you planning to change everything?"

Blaine bit her lip. Yes. Everything. "Not the name. I like the name."

Peg smiled. "Just run everything by me first."

"I will. I promise." And they shook hands on it.

When Blaine's dad dropped by for a cup of coffee, they told him all about their plans. He didn't say much—they didn't give him much of a chance—but he listened, and had a grin on his face like a Cheshire cat.

It was Friday morning, the kickoff to Memorial Day weekend, the jump start of the entire summer season, and Paul woke before dawn to hurry down to the beach. He wanted to take a moment there to reflect, to pray, to give thanks to the Almighty, before opening day at Camp Kicking Moose officially began. Things were changing so fast . . . it made his head spin.

Even the weather had begun to change. Summer was sweeping in with blue skies and puffy white clouds. It was nearly June, a glorious time of year. So much was in bloom. Color was everywhere, bordered by glossy green bushes and a thicket of pine trees.

He stared out at the water, so deceptively calm and gentle during low tide, and thought of that moment when he stood right here and shouted to God, "Now what?"

God answered. Boy, did he answer.

As Paul walked back to the house, he took a few minutes to look over the property. He couldn't believe his eyes. Camp Kicking Moose, the very place where he'd spent so much of his young adult years, where he'd fallen in love and proposed to Corinna, had been transformed.

Moose Manor, front and back and sides, had been painted from bubble-gum pink to an elegant charcoal gray with crisp white trim, teal shutters, and a cheery cranberry front door. The once-wild yard had been tamed, trimmed, and mowed. Hanging pots of red geraniums and trailing periwinkle lobelia lined the wraparound porch. Underneath it all, as a backdrop, was the sound of the ocean. As for those picture-postcard views—those hadn't changed at all. Mother Nature always got it right.

As Paul walked along the side of the carriage house—also painted charcoal gray with white trim—he noticed Cam and Cooper swinging in the porch swing (Cam! Sitting, relaxed. It was a wonder.) with Dory dozing nearby. Maddie was watering a pot of zinnias. As he came closer, he realized Seth was there too. And not-the-boyfriend Artie. They were engrossed in screwing a loose strap hinge onto the window shutter. Blaine came through the front door, her hands in oven mitts, holding a tray of blueberry muffins. "Who wants to try one? It's a new recipe. I added ginger and peaches. If you like them, I'll add them to the morning rotation of breakfast goods."

They all gravitated to the warm muffins, oohing and aahing over them, and Paul lost himself in the moment. This was it. This moment. A dream fulfilled. This was exactly what he had hoped for, what he had envisioned by purchasing this worn-out property. His girls, enjoying each other. Cooper, growing strong and sturdy. The family, knit together. It amazed him. Corinna had been right. The world was full of simple miracles. He lifted his eyes to the blue sky and sent a thank-you upward.

Not two moments later, a minivan appeared through the bend in the driveway. Paul swallowed down the last bite of muffin. "That would be our first guests. The Kline family, I believe, from Kalamazoo."

"Put them in cabin 2," Maddie said with a professional air. "They requested a crib for a baby. I've ordered more, but so far, Captain Ed has only brought one over from Mount Desert."

Paul looked at his daughters, each one, and then at Cooper. Happy tears pricked his eyes. "Ready or not, Grayson family, Camp Kicking Moose is now open for the season." And down the porch steps he walked to greet the first guests.

∽ *Blaine's twist on her mother's* ∽
"Can't Have Just One" Chocolate Chip Cookies

Pre-heat oven to 350 degrees.
In a large bowl, cream butter and sugar:

2 sticks	butter, room temperature
1 cup	brown sugar
1 cup	white sugar

Add and beat well:

1	egg
1	tablespoon milk
2	teaspoons vanilla

In a separate bowl, sift dry ingredients:

3½	cups flour
3	teaspoons baking soda
1	teaspoon salt

Stir flour mixture, alternating with oil, into wet ingredients:

1 cup	vegetable or canola oil

Add remaining ingredients until blended:

1 cup	oats
1 cup	Rice Krispies
1 package	semi-sweet chocolate chips (12 oz.)
optional:	2 cups chopped walnuts or pecans

Spoon out one tablespoon of cookie dough, roll into a ball, and drop onto ungreased cookie sheet. Bake 12–15 minutes. Let cool on a wire rack. The more they cool, the crisper they will become. Then . . . eat.

Freezes well, if you are a person of enormous self-control.

Read On for an Excerpt of
Suzanne's Stunning Story

One

A YEAR HAD PASSED since Luke Schrock's exile from Stoney Ridge began. A very long year. He'd been in and out of rehab twice. Wait. Hold on. Make that three times. He'd forgotten the three-day holiday weekend he'd checked himself out and went on a bender.

The bus swerved and bumped on the country roads, stirring his stomach and ratcheting up his anxiety. The bus was stuffy and hot; it made him long for fresh air and cold, all at once. He was on his way back home.

Home. Luke had a feeling he couldn't name exactly, but one he'd never had in relation to home before. It used to mean security, belonging, unconditional acceptance. What he felt now contained that, all that, but to today was added a hint of desperation.

This was a bad idea. A terrible idea. He'd never intended to return to Stoney Ridge. The counselor had strongly recommended that Luke find sober, supportive living arrangements. What could be more sober than an Amish farm? he asked Luke.

Uh, well, that depends. Luke had been living among the Amish as he developed a dependency on alcohol.

But then David Stoltzfus, his bishop, agreed with the counselor. He had told him to stop running away from his problems, that coming home again was the only road to manhood.

He recognized the fork in the road that would lead the bus straight into Stoney Ridge. Pulling the cord to hop off the bus seemed like a very appealing option. He could head right toward Lancaster, rather than left to Stoney Ridge. He could do it. He should do it.

But he didn't. The bus zoomed left.

David had promised he'd be waiting at the bus stop. Luke held out a sliver of hope that his mother might be there too, and maybe his younger brother Sammy. There was no chance that Galen King, his mother's husband, would be there. No chance. Not after what had happened to Galen's prized horse. Nope. No chance.

When Luke had asked David what he would do with himself once he was back in town, the bishop was vague. "One thing at a time, Luke. Let's get you home first."

Luke had wanted to ask him if home meant the Inn at Eagle Hill, where his mother and brother and stepfather lived, or if he was using "home" as a metaphor. But something inside held him back from asking, partly because he had a feeling David didn't know the answer.

David Stoltzfus had gone above and beyond the call of duty for Luke this last year. He'd come to visit him regularly, even when Luke told him not to bother. But David did bother, over and over again. He brought books to read, for he knew Luke loved to read. He read them too, and then they would discuss them. Conversation grew easier between them. Those visits, they meant a lot to Luke, and he hoped David had some idea how much. The reason David had never given up on Luke was, he said, because God never gave up on people.

The bus hit a pothole and jolted Luke against the window. He recognized the passing farm as Windmill Farm, belonging to Amos and Fern Lapp, and took note of the new mailbox. Not so long ago, he'd put a cherry bomb in their old one and blown it to smithereens.

Why had he done that? It was a circling discussion in group

therapy—what were triggers that caused destructive behavior? The counselor encouraged everyone to identify those triggers, so they'd know to recognize them. And then, to redirect thoughts and feelings and behaviors toward something beneficial.

Luke had tried to identify his triggers, tried and failed. Why had he hurt people, like the Lapps, who had been so good to him? He couldn't find an answer.

For a short while, before blowing up the Lapps' mailbox, he'd even apprenticed for Jesse Stoltzfus's buggy shop at Windmill Farm. Like so many opportunities Luke had been given, it hadn't gone well. The counselor suggested that if anyone got too close to Luke, he would do something to push them away. Translation: self-sabotage. If anything went too well, he would find a way to ruin it. He saw that in himself. What he didn't know was *why*.

That was another reason the counselor had consistently encouraged Luke to return to Stoney Ridge. "Find out *why*," he'd told Luke. "You'll never move forward until you find out why."

"Moving forward." Translation for counseling code: *aftercare*. Luke had grown savvy to counselor code. The first time he was released from rehab, he was adamant that he would not return to Stoney Ridge. Moving forward, he was convinced, meant moving on. Make a fresh start.

He tried. He failed. Back he went to rehab.

This time, rehab lasted a little longer. Instead of sixty days, it was ninety days. "Better chance for long-term success," the counselor said. Not so for Luke. As soon as he was released, he went on that three-day bender. David bailed him out of jail and took him back to the clinic. This time, it lasted more than six months. Now *that* should give him a much, much better chance not to relapse. Added to that was the warning from David that this was the last rescue. If he relapsed, if he ended up in jail, he'd stay there. Three strikes was the limit, even for David, the most tolerant man in the world.

Luke had to agree with the counselor on one thing: he didn't seem to be able to move forward. "Why not go back and face your past?" the counselor said. "What do you have to lose?"

Nothing. Absolutely nothing. Absolutely no one. Grudgingly, Luke agreed to return to Stoney Ridge. It was one thing to say no to your counselor, but nearly impossible to say no to your bishop, especially one like David.

After making that decision, he'd had the first good night's sleep in . . . well, maybe in the entire last year. But that didn't mean he wasn't anxious about his homecoming. He was. These Amish, they had long, long memories.

At the turnoff to Windmill Farm, he noticed a woman standing behind a beat-up farm stand. Amos had fine orchards, old trees that had been lovingly tended. Luke remembered that very farm stand, topped with baskets of tree ripened fruit, jugs of cider, and an honest jar. He also thought of how often he used to dip into that jar when he was low on cash.

Ouch. Another stinging memory.

David called those stinging memories one of the greatest gifts given by the Holy Spirit. Convicting memories, David called them. Conviction was meant to turn us to confession. And confession brought us back to God.

Luke doubted David ever had much of anything to confess. If he did, he would know the sick feeling that came along with the stinging memories. The disgust and self-loathing.

The bus jolted again. He squinted, wondering if Fern Lapp was the woman at the farm stand, but quickly dismissed that thought. Fern was thin, wiry—small but mighty. A force to be reckoned with.

This woman looked young. She was tall and held herself erect, like a queen. She wore a Plain lavender dress with a black apron. A blue kerchief kept the hair out of her eyes. Luke leaned closer to the window to peer at the woman as the bus passed by. Who was she? Just then, she looked up and waved at the passing bus, and Luke felt a shock run through him. *Izzy Miller.* She'd been a patient at the rehab center during his first attempt to get clean and sober. He'd been in a group session with her once or twice. She hadn't talked much, but he did notice her. Oh yeah, he noticed her all right. She wasn't the sort of person you'd easily forget. He remembered thinking she was the prettiest girl he'd ever seen. High, wide cheekbones; snapping dark brown eyes; luxurious brunette hair. He also remembered her as being frustratingly aloof; he had tried, without success, to get her attention a few times. Why in the world was she at Windmill Farm, of all places? And why was she dressed Plain?

Well, well. Luke's grim spirits lifted considerably. Stoney Ridge was looking better already.

Izzy Miller rearranged the freshly picked red cherries in the bowl so they'd look irresistible, which they were. Plump to the touch, bright red in color, juicy in taste. Too luscious, she thought, to end up in jam or pies. Not these cherries. They were meant to be eaten the way nature intended. Freshly picked, still warmed from the sun, bursting with juice.

She took pride in how her displays looked, improving their appearance from Fern's practical, no-nonsense style. Even the weathered old farm stand was small and rickety, easy to overlook. She couldn't do anything about its condition, but she could definitely present Amos's orchard fruits in an eye-catching way.

Amos harvested bushels of fruit from his orchards—old trees that produced bumper crops of delicious fruits. Wie der aum, so die Frucht, he had taught her. *Such as the tree is, such is the fruit.* He treasured his old varieties. Heirlooms or antiquities, they were now considered. Amos said they were just the varieties his wise grandfather knew to grow.

The season started with early flowering cherries in late May and early June, peaches and plums in July, pears in August, and ended with apples in the fall. Fern had a huge garden—bigger than most anyone's backyard, at least the yards Izzy'd seen—and harvested a wide variety of vegetables and flowers. Thanks to her greenhouse, Fern was the first in Stoney Ridge to bring a vine-ripened tomato to the dinner table. Amos said that Fern didn't just have a green thumb, she could grow anything out of nothing.

Growing fruits and vegetables, even flowers, was Amos and Fern's expertise. Izzy was the one who'd arranged the displays with an artistic flair, so much so that they drew attention and became a feast to the eyes as well as the stomach. Like the bus driver who just passed by—he used to zoom past the farm stand without any acknowledgment. Last year, Izzy had set up bouquets of flowers in galvanized buckets, and the driver stopped the bus and jumped out. It was his wife's birthday, he told Izzy, and he hadn't remembered until he saw those bright, bold peonies in the buckets. His wife's favorite flower. Last year, he'd forgotten her birthday and he didn't want to face her wrath again, so he bought two bundles. One for this year and one to make up for last year. He thanked Izzy profusely and told her she might have saved his marriage.

Since then, that bus driver would stop the bus to let everyone out to buy produce. He must have told others too, because Amos and Fern's farm stand had been included on the route of summertime tourist buses swirling through Amish country from Lancaster. By last October, as they were closing up for the year, Amos announced that Izzy had quadrupled the profits from the farm stand. Four times! Fern joked they could soon retire and let Izzy manage the farm.

It was astounding to Izzy. It really was. She'd never been told she had any natural talent, had never thought she could be good at anything. She knew Fern was just teasing, but her words sparked a deep yearning in her, struck a chord in her heart. What Izzy hoped Fern had meant was that she could remain on indefinitely at Windmill Farm. *Ein Platz am Tisch*. It was a Plain expression that meant a person had a place at the table. That they had a family they belonged to. Izzy loved repeating the phrase to herself, trying hard as she was to master the Penn Dutch language. For the first time in her life, she was wanted. First time.

Look at me, she thought. *I'm living the life I've wanted for as long as I can remember.* She had a roof over her head, she had a true friend—Jenny Yoder—and she had Amos and Fern Lapp. She had everything she'd ever dreamed for. Almost everything. There was still one more piece of her dream—to find her mother. To bring her to Windmill Farm.

The counselor at the rehab clinic had warned her about holding on to such a dream. "I'm all for tying up loose ends," he said, "but I'm worried you're setting yourself up for disappointment. You can't control other people, Izzy. You can only control yourself. A dream like that—it's closer to a miracle."

But, oh my soul, "miracles do happen," Izzy had told her counselor. "Just look at me."

As promised, David Stoltzfus was waiting for Luke at the bus stop on Main Street in the heart of Stoney Ridge. He thrust his hand out to shake Luke's and clasped him warmly on the shoulder. "Welcome home," he said, and Luke felt tears sting his eyes. No one else was here but David. No mother, no brother. And yet . . . David was here.

Luke followed him to the buggy, tossed his backpack in, and climbed up. David handed him the reins, but he shook his head. "I'm a little rusty." There was truth to that, but more important, he felt disoriented, as if he'd never been in a buggy before.

David slapped the reins and clucked to the horse to set it trotting; it lurched forward before settling into a steady walk. "Luke, there's been a few changes in Stoney Ridge."

"Like what?"

"Well, for one, Amos Lapp is now the deacon. Abraham moved to Florida to be with his daughter."

"And the ministers? Have they changed?"

"Just one. Gideon Smucker."

"Sadie's husband?" Luke squinted. "I always thought he was afraid of his own shadow."

David glanced at Luke. "He's a fine minister. Wise and humble." He handed Luke a sealed envelope.

It was from Luke's mother, Rose. He made no effort to open it. "Let me guess. She wishes she could've been here today, she really, really does. But Galen isn't quite ready to welcome me home."

"Maybe you should just read it."

Luke sighed and broke the seal.

Dearest Luke,

I'm sorry, so very sorry, that I'm not in Stoney Ridge to welcome you home. I'll let David explain our circumstances. Please believe me when I say that the timing of this opportunity had nothing to do with your homecoming. I am so proud of you, Luke. You've fought a great battle, as I knew you could. And I believe that a bright and wonderful future is ahead for you.

Love,
Mom

Luke wasn't surprised. He looked up. "So what are these oh-so-special and ill-timed circumstances?"

"Galen was needed in Kentucky. His cousin breeds Thoroughbred horses down there and had some kind of accident. Broke his leg in two places, needed surgery and pins." David shuddered. "Anyway, he asked Galen to help him get through the next few months. Busy months for horse breeding. Galen's stable was empty—he hadn't purchased any horses to train for the summer, so he said yes to his cousin. It's just short-term. They left ten days ago."

Luke ran through the scenario in his mind. He knew of that particular cousin. Each spring, Galen would travel to Kentucky to buy two-year-old Thoroughbreds, retired right from the races, to train them for buggy work. He always stayed with that cousin of his. They loved horses more than people, Luke always thought. "She didn't even say goodbye." He cringed. Had he said that out loud?

"Your mother wanted to. She did. But your counselor advised against it."

Luke snorted. "Because I might decide not to return to Stoney Ridge, had I known?"

"Because you need to make your own decisions, based on what's best for you. Your mother wants you to come visit in Kentucky, as soon as you're ready."

Ready. What did that mean?

As they reached the turnoff to the Inn at Eagle Hill, David drove the buggy right on by. "Uh, David, I'd like to go home."

"Well, that's another one of the changes. The Inn is being run by someone else."

"Who?"

"Ruthie." He glanced at Luke. "Patrick's helping her."

Ah, the second blow to Luke's gut. Ruthie, David's daughter, had been Luke's childhood sweetheart, the one person who understood him, whom he counted on, up until that messy time when everything fell apart. Ruthie met Patrick and Luke ended up in rehab.

"So where are you taking me?"

"Windmill Farm."

Luke let out an indignant huff. "Oh, David, come on. Your own son used to call it Fern's Home for Wayward Boys. I think I've gotten past that stage."

"Amos needs help with his orchards this summer, and . . ."

"And *what*?" What was it that David didn't want to say? That Amos was a kind man, and probably the only one who would be willing to host Luke.

"Amos is willing to provide room and board for you, in exchange for working his orchards." The horse had slowed to a crawl, so David flicked the reins to urge it back into a trot. "Birdy and I would have welcomed you into our home, but there's not an inch of space to be spared, not with the babies. And there's no work to be done. I'm no farmer."

"I could work at Bent N' Dent. I could sleep in the back room. I could stock shelves. Make deliveries."

David was quiet for so long that Luke wondered what was running through his mind. Probably . . . that Luke might be bad for business. But then David surprised him. "Let's try this first. If it doesn't work out, then you can work at the store. But I think you might enjoy working for Amos. He's a wealth of knowledge about farming. About all kinds of things. And he truly needs help this summer."

Luke was silent for the rest of the trip, eyes fixed on the rhythmic clip-clops of the horse's shoes on the pavement. So, all these changes told him a great deal. His family had left town, he wasn't trusted to run the Inn, or to work at the store, and no one in Stoney Ridge seemed to want him here. Why had he even come home at all? He had no home, no one to welcome him back. Where did that leave him? Without his old life and not quite coming up with a new one. In between, floating, nowhere.

He still couldn't answer why he'd come back to Stoney Ridge, even when the counselor had tried to get him to put feelings into words. For some inexplicable reason, Luke knew that David was right. The only path to manhood was to be here, to face his past and make amends. After that, he could leave.

He would leave.

Discussion Questions

1. Much of this story is about how family roles and events shape a person. Of the three sisters, Cam, Maddie, and Blaine, which one did you most relate to and why?

2. Those girls were hard on each other! They seemed reluctant to allow their childhood perceptions of each other to change. Why does that seem to be a common dynamic among families? How do you relate to your adult siblings?

3. Did your impressions of the three sisters change throughout the story and if so, how and why?

4. Cam had a gift. She was able to envision how something could be better than it was. Can you describe someone in your life with an ability to see potential? How has that person affected you?

5. Seth tells Cam, "Everyone begins somewhere. It's okay to start with a small faith. We have a very big God." Cam appreciates that Seth doesn't put any pressure on her to have a faith that mirrors his. Why do you think Seth felt comfortable with Cam's spiritual dormancy?

6. Seth invited the Grayson family to church, and continued to invite them. Consider the previous question. Why do you think Seth persisted?

7. How much of the sisters' character and personality was impacted by the tragic circumstances that took the lives of their mother and Libby?

8. Maddie drummed on one theme: she wanted her family to talk about their mother's death and not just keep it bottled up or stuffed down. Why is it better to talk about painful issues than to ignore them? What happens when light breaks through to a closed subject?

9. Blaine and Maddie noticed that they missed their mother on Three Sisters Island more than they did in Boston. Maddie decided it had to do with the fact that they had all left a whirring, fast city to live on a quiet remote island. Everything had slowed down, including their thoughts. Doing so allowed the remembering to resurface. What happens to your thoughts when you step away from your busy life? Why is setting time apart so necessary for healing, for perspective, for revitalization?

10. Did the full circle of Cooper's biological parents take you by surprise? What did it reveal about how God was guiding or protecting Cooper, and Cam, even though she couldn't see it?

11. Maddie tells Cam to trust what she does know about Seth. Was that good advice? Why or why not?

12. In a pivotal moment, Peg told Cam, "How would you like to be defined by your nineteen-year-old self for the rest of your life?" Do you have some perceptions of people in your life that you need to "recalibrate" and allow for the whole story?

13. Can you look back on your own life and see ways that God was resolving a situation in a very unlikely, unexpected way? What does that reveal about God? "For nothing is impossible for God" (see Mark 10:27).

Acknowledgments

Thank you to Andrea Doering, my editor, for reading this story when it was about 80 percent finished, and pointing me toward helpful improvements. Andrea, you are so wise. I am truly blessed to work with you.

Thank you to my agent, Joyce Hart, for being so loyal and encouraging. To my sister, Wendy, for being a crackerjack travel assistant. To my daughter, Lindsey, for being an insightful first draft reader. To my very wonderful husband, Steve, who helped me figure out the mechanics of the sale of Cam's business. To Frances and Lynn, for sharing their insiders' view of Maine.

Thanks to everyone at Revell for their enthusiasm and hard work, book after book. To my faithful readers, who have come along with me into new genres. To God, for providing opportunities and refreshing my imagination. A famous author once said that a part of him emptied out each time he wrote a book, like his imagination was a well with a finite supply of water. I feel the opposite. Asking for God's blessing on my imagination is like tapping into a well of living water.

Suzanne Woods Fisher is an award-winning, bestselling author of more than thirty novels, including the Nantucket Legacy, the Amish Beginnings, The Bishop's Family, and The Inn at Eagle Hill series. She is also the author of several nonfiction books about the Amish, including *Amish Peace* and *Amish Proverbs*. She lives in California. Learn more at www.suzannewoodsfisher.com and follow Suzanne on Facebook @SuzanneWoodsFisherAuthor and Twitter @suzannewfisher.

Suzanne Woods Fisher invites you back to Three Sisters Island where *family, forgiveness, and a second chance at love await.*

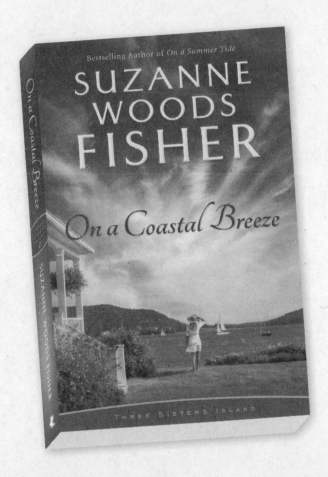

Everything happens for a reason, Maddie Grayson believes. But her motto gets sorely tested when the new minister parachutes into town and offers her a chance to change what happens next.

Continue Reading the
Three Sisters Island Series

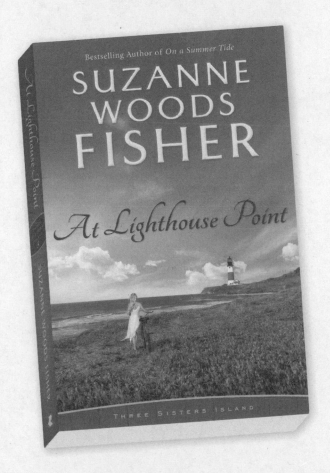

Fresh out of culinary school, Blaine Grayson returns to
Three Sisters Island with big plans for work, family, and love.
But the island and her not-my-boyfriend best friend Artie have
changed, leaving her to wonder if her plans might need to factor
in more than just her own desires.

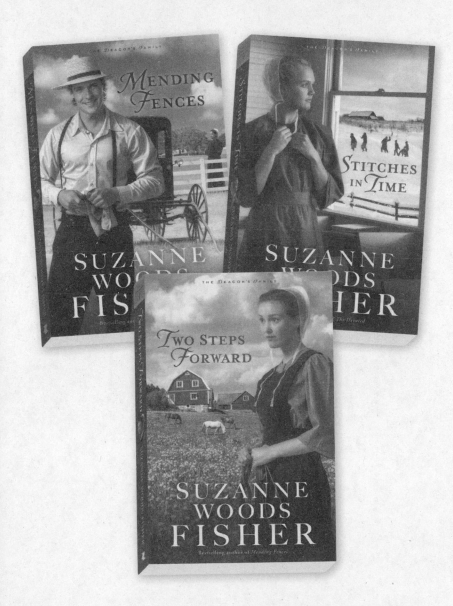

MEET SUZANNE

www.SuzanneWoodsFisher.com

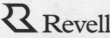